Cynthia Harrod-Eagles was born and educated in Shepherd's Bush, and had a variety of jobs in the commercial world, starting as a junior cashier at Woolworth's and working her way down to Pensions Officer at the BBC. She won the Young Writers' Award in 1973, and became a full-time writer in 1978. She is the author of over fifty successful novels to date, including twenty-three volumes of the *Morland Dynasty* series.

Also by Cynthia Harrod-Eagles

The Bill Slider Mysteries

ORCHESTRATED DEATH
DEATH WATCH
NECROCHIP
DEAD END
BLOOD LINES
KILLING TIME
SHALLOW GRAVE

The Dynasty Series

THE FOUNDING
THE DARK ROSE
THE PRINCELING
THE OAK APPLE
THE BLACK PEARL
THE LONG SHADOW
THE CHEVALIER
THE MAIDEN
THE FLOOD-TIDE
THE TANGLED THREAD
THE EMPEROR
THE VICTORY
THE REGENCY
THE CAMPAIGNERS
THE RECKONING
THE DEVIL'S HORSE
THE POISON TREE
THE ABYSS
THE HIDDEN SHORE
THE WINTER JOURNEY
THE OUTCAST
THE MIRAGE
THE CAUSE

Blood Sinister

CYNTHIA HARROD-EAGLES

A *Warner* Book

First published in Great Britain in 1999
by Little, Brown and Company

This edition published by Warner Books in 2000

A CIP catalogue record for this book
is available from the British Library.

ISBN 0 7515 2907 9

Typeset in Amasis by
Palimpsest Book Production Limited,
Polmont, Stirlingshire
Printed and bound in Great Britain by
Mackays of Chatham plc, Chatham, Kent

Warner Books
A Division of
Little, Brown and Company (UK)
Brettenham House
Lancaster Place
London WC2E 7EN

For Bill's good friends, Marcia and Geoff,
and Sharon and Chris;
and of course, as always,
for my indispensible Tony, with love.

If the red slayer think he slays,
Or if the slain think he is slain,
They know not well the subtle ways
I keep, and pass, and turn again.

Ralph Waldo Emerson: *Brahma*

CHAPTER ONE

Big horse, God made you mine

'Have you noticed,' Joanna said as they sped along the M4 towards London, 'how the self-drive hire business has been completely taken over by that Dutch firm?'

'What Dutch firm?' Slider asked unwarily.

'Van Rentals.'

'How long have you been thinking that one out?'

'I resent the implication that my wit isn't spontaneous.'

'I resent your having been away,' he countered. 'It was daft going to Switzerland when it's cold enough here to freeze the balls off a brass tennis court.'

'Do you think I wanted to go?' Joanna said. 'Beethoven Eight six times in one week – and in a country where they still think fondue is cuisine.'

Despite the best efforts of that husband-and-wife circus act May Gurney and Cones Hotline, he had got to the airport in time to meet her. Though it was the umpteenth time he'd done it, there was still that thrill when she came out of the customs hall doors with her fiddle case in one hand and her battered old fits-under-the-seat-in-front travel bag over her shoulder. It had bothered him when she came through with the trumpet section, Peter White and Simon Angel. Put those two horny young bloods – only one of them married (and it was a well-known fact that blowing the trumpet had a direct effect on the production of testosterone) – together with a curvaceous love goddess like Joanna Marshall, and it spelled trouble with a capital Trub. But she had kissed him and pressed herself against him with an avidity that had had the lads whooping, so his pride was assuaged, and he led her off like a prize of war to find the car.

The Orchestra of the Age of the Renaissance, despite the handicap of a name that wouldn't fit across a poster unless it was in characters too small to read, had come in as a life-saver. Its fixer had called Joanna as a last-minute replacement for the pregnant deputy principal, whose blood pressure had gone over into the red zone. Post-Christmas was always a drought period for musicians, but this year was particularly bad. Her own orchestra had nothing for two months and freelance work was as rare as elephants' eggs.

Joanna's thoughts were evidently on the same track as she watched the chill, bare fields of Middlesex reel past the windows. 'Do you know what's in my diary between now and March?'

'Yes,' he said, but she told him again anyway.

'Two Milton Keynes dates and one Pro Arte of Oxford – and I'm lucky to get those.'

'Why are things so bad?' he ventured.

'They're just getting worse every year,' she said. 'Fewer people going to concerts or buying records, and more and more musicians pouring out of the colleges. And then,' she made a face, 'we all have to do this blasted "outreach" crapola, going into schools and encouraging more of the little beasts to take up music. If we had any sense we'd be breaking their arms, not telling them what a fulfilling life it is, ha ha.'

'Have you just come home to complain at me?' he asked, trying for a lighter note.

She didn't bite. 'Seriously, Bill, it's getting to be a hell of a problem. The Phil's in financial trouble and there's more amalgamation talk. That old chestnut, "Can London sustain four orchestras?" The Government's threatening to withdraw the grant from one of us, and everybody knows we're the likeliest.'

'But all this has been said before, and it never happens,' Slider comforted her.

'Even if it doesn't,' she said, sounding very low, 'we aren't getting enough dates to live on.'

'We'll manage somehow,' he said. 'Tighten our belts. We'll get through.'

'Hah!' she said. She didn't elaborate, for which he was grateful, but she meant, of course, how much belt-tightening can you do when your salary already has to go round an almost ex-wife and two school-age children?

But she wasn't a whiner, and a moment later she said, 'Peter and Simon were telling me on the plane about this wonderful scam for parking in the short-term car park while you're on tour. All you have to do is borrow a tuba.'

'A tuba?'

'Well, of course it only works if you're touring with a big orchestra. Anyway, apparently a tuba is a big enough mass of metal for the automatic barrier to mistake it for a car. So, when you get back from tour, you walk up to the entrance barrier holding the tuba in front of you, and it issues a ticket, which you then use to get out, throwing away the original one. You pay for ten minutes instead of two weeks. *Voilà*.'

'Should you be telling me this? I am a policeman.'

'That's what makes you so sexy.' Her warm hand crept gratefully over his upper thigh. 'I'm glad to be back,' she said. 'Have you missed me?'

'Does a one-legged duck swim in circles?'

'Nice hot bath and an early night tonight,' she said.

He'd just got to the bit where the motorway narrows to two lanes and his attention was distracted. 'I suppose you must be tired,' he said absently, keeping his eye on a BMW that didn't want to move in.

Her hand slid further up. 'Who said anything about sleeping?'

* * *

The office was its usual hive of activity when he got in. DS Jim Atherton, his bagman and friend, was sitting on a desk reading – of all things – *The Racing Post*.

'What do you reckon for the first race at Plumpton, Maurice?' he said.

'Shy Smile,' DC McLaren answered, without looking up from the sausage sandwich and *Daily Mail* that were occupying him. Atherton opined that McLaren read the tabloids only because the broadsheets needed two hands, which meant he couldn't eat and read at the same time.

'Are you sure?' Atherton probed. 'Everyone else gives Ballydoyle.'

'Not after that frost last night. Ballydoyle likes a bit of give in the ground.'

'Shy Smile?' Atherton pressed.

'She'll walk it,' said McLaren.

'How d'you know about horses anyway?' Anderson asked, clipping his nails into the waste-paper basket. 'I thought you grew up in Kennington.'

'Y'don't have to have a baby to be a gynaecologist,' McLaren answered mysteriously, sucking grease and newsprint off his fingers.

Slider, at the door, said, 'It would be nice if you could at least *pretend* to be usefully occupied when I come in. Give me an illusion of authority.'

'Didn't know you were there, guv,' McLaren said imperturbably, rolling a black tongue over his lips.

'That much is obvious.' Slider turned to Atherton. 'And why are you reading the racing pages? Since when did you have the slightest interest in the Sport of Kings?'

'Ah, it's a new investment ploy,' Atherton said, unhitching his behind from the desk. 'I'm thinking of buying a part share in a racehorse. I saw this ad in the paper and sent off for the details. I'm going to put my savings into it.'

'Have you been standing around under the power lines without your lead hat again?' Slider said mildly.

'Well, there's no point in leaving cash in deposit accounts, with interest rates at rock bottom,' Atherton said. 'And anyway, it's not a gamble, it's a scientific investment. Serious businessmen put big money into it. This Furlong Stud is a proper company: they've been putting together consortia for years. It's all in the information pack. It's no more risky than the stock market, really.'

'What's the name of the poor wreck of a horse they're trying to flog you?' Slider enquired.

'The one I'm looking at is called Two Left Feet,' Atherton announced, and when Slider groaned he said, 'No, it's a really cute name, don't you see? All horses have two left feet.'

'Mug punter,' said McLaren pityingly, turning a page. 'It's sad, really. Bet on the name, every time. Here,' he recalled suddenly, looking up, 'talk about names, did you see that story in the paper a bit since, about those two Irish owners who tried to register a colt, and Tattersalls wouldn't allow it? They wanted to call it Norfolk and Chance.'

'I'm worried about you,' Slider said, as Atherton followed him into his office. 'You didn't used to be irrational.'

'How do you know?' Atherton said cheerfully. 'Anyway, I need a bit of excitement in my life. I used to get it chasing women, but now I'm settled down in cosy domesticity, I have to look elsewhere for that thrill of danger.'

'I wish I thought you were joking,' Slider said, going round his desk. He shoved fretfully at the piles of files that burdened it. They bred during the night, he was sure of it. 'What's this steaming pile of Tottenham?'

'Case files. Ongoing. Mr Carver's firm passed them over, Mr Porson's orders. They're down four men again, with the 'flu.'

'Carver's firm are always catching things,' Slider complained. 'What do they do, sleep together?'

'I wouldn't be a bit surprised,' Atherton said. 'It's worse than it looks, anyway. Most of it's to do with that suspected fags-and-booze smuggling ring.'

'Take 'em away,' Slider decreed. 'I'm too frail for gang warfare at this stage of the week.'

WDC Swilley, who had answered the phone out in the office, came to the door now, her posture suddenly galvanised, which, since Swilley was built like a young lad's secret dream, was hardly fair on the two within. 'We've got a murder, boss!' she announced happily.

'Gordon Bennett, what next?' Slider said. 'It shouldn't be allowed on a Friday.'

'Phoebe Agnew!' Atherton enthused as he drove, with an air of doing it one-handed, through the end of the rush-hour traffic. How come so many people went to work so late? 'I mean, I know she's a bit of a thorn in the copper's side—'

'In spades,' Slider agreed.

'Yeah, but what a journalist! Took the Palgabria Prize in 1990, and winner of the John Perkins Award for '97 and '98 – the only person ever to win it two years running, incidentally. And she really can write, guv. Awesomely chilling prose.'

'Well, don't get so excited. You're not going to have a conversation with her,' Slider pointed out.

Atherton's face fell a fraction. 'No, you're right. What a wicked waste!'

As they turned off the main road they found their way blocked by a dustcart. It had a selection of grubby teddy bears and dolls tied to the radiator grille. Why did scaffies do that, Slider wondered. With their arms outstretched and their hopeless eyes staring ahead, they looked depressingly like a human shield.

Atherton backed fluidly, turned, and roared down another side street. 'Anyway, AMIP's bound to take the case from us,' he said.

The Area Major Incident Pool took all the serious or high-profile crimes and, these days, virtually all murders, unless they were straightforward domestics. Judson, the present head of 6 AMIP, was an empire-builder. He was that most hated of creatures, the career uniform man who had transferred to CID purely in pursuit of promotion.

'Judson's welcome to it,' Slider said. 'He'll probably enjoy being crawled over by the press.'

'You are in a doldrum,' Atherton said, turning into Eltham Road, which was parked right up both sides, like everywhere else in London these days.

'You can't have a single doldrum,' said Slider. 'They always hunt in packs. This is it. You'll have to double park.'

'It's the reason I became a policeman,' said Atherton.

The house was one of a terrace, built in the late nineteenth century, of two storeys, plus the semi-basement – which Londoners call 'the area' – over which a flight of wide, shallow steps led up to the front door. Eltham Road was in one of the borderline areas between the old, working-class Shepherd's Bush and the new yuppiedom, and a few years ago Slider would have said it might go either way. But rising incomes and outward pressure from the centre of London were making his familiar ground more and more desirable in real-estate terms, and there was no doubt in his mind now that the 'unimproved' properties in this street soon wouldn't recognise themselves. Anyone who had bought here ten years ago would be sitting on a handsome profit.

The house in question was divided into three flats, and it was the middle one which had been occupied by Phoebe Agnew, a freelance journalist whose name was enough to make any policeman shudder. An ex-*Guardian* hack with impeccable left-wing credentials, she had made a name for herself for investigating corruption, and had concentrated in late years on the establishment and the legal system, exposing bad apples, and sniffing out miscarriages of justice with the zeal of perfect hindsight.

Slider was all for rooting out bent coppers; that was in everyone's interest. His biggest beef with Agnew was that she had been instrumental in the release of the Portland Two, attacking the evidence that had got a pair of exceedingly nasty child-murderers put away. Well, the law was the law, and you had to play by the rules: he accepted that. Still, it galled coppers who remembered the case to hear Heaton and Donaldson described as 'innocent', just because some harried DC at the time had got his paperwork in a muddle. And who was the better for it? The Two had been quietly doing their porridge, and would have been up for parole in a couple of years. Getting them out on a technicality had simply banged another nail into the coffin of public confidence. According to eager *Guardian* polls, half the population now believed the police went round picking up innocent people at random for the sheer joy of fitting them up.

Well, now Phoebe Agnew was dead. The biter bit, perhaps – and theirs to identify the guilty dentition.

At the front door PC Renker was keeping guard and the SOC record. With his helmet on and his big blond moustache, he looked like exotic grass growing under a cloche.

'Doc Cameron's inside, sir,' he reported, 'and the photographer, and forensic's on the way. Asher's upstairs with the female that found the body – lives in the top flat. Bottom tenant's a Peter Medmenham, but he's not in, apparently.'

'Probably at work,' Slider said. The front door let into a vestibule, which contained two further Yale-locked doors. They were built across what was obviously the original hall of the house, to judge by the black-and-white diamond floor tiles. One gave access to the stairs to the top flat; the other was standing open onto the rest of the hall and Phoebe Agnew's flat. It had been the main part of the original family house, and had the advantage of the fine cornices and ceiling roses, elaborate architraves and panelled doors; but it had been converted long enough ago to have had the fireplaces ripped out and plastered over.

There was a small kitchen at the front of the house, a tiny windowless bathroom next to it, and two other rooms. The smaller was furnished as an office, with a desk, filing cabinets, cupboards, bookshelves, personal computer and fax machine, and on every surface a mountain range of papers and files that made Slider's fade into foothills.

'Oh, what fun we'll have sorting through that lot!' Atherton enthused, clasping his hands.

'We?' Slider said cruelly.

The other room, which stretched right across the back of the house, was furnished as a bedsitting room.

'Odd decision,' said Atherton. 'Why not have the separate bedroom and the office in here?'

'Maybe she liked to get away from work once in a while,' Slider said.

'I suppose it saves time on seduction techniques,' Atherton said, always willing to learn something new. 'Shorter step from sofa to bed. I wonder what she spent all her money on? It wasn't home comforts, that's for sure.'

The furnishings were evidently old and didn't look as if they'd ever been expensive. There was a large and shabby high-backed sofa covered with cushions and a fringed crimson plush throw, which looked like an old-fashioned chenille tablecloth. In front of it was a massive coffee table, of dark wood with a glass inset top, on the other side of which were two elderly and unmatching armchairs. One had a dented cushion, and a bottle of White Horse and a glass stood on the floor by its right foreleg. The other was a real museum piece with metal hoop arms and 1950s 'contemp'ry' patterned fabric. There was a folded blanket concealing something on its seat. Slider lifted the edge and saw that it was a heap of papers, correspondence and files, topped off with some clean but unironed laundry. The quickest way to tidy up, perhaps.

Along one wall was a low 'unit' of imitation light oak veneer, early MFI by the look of it, on top of which stood a television and video, a hi-fi stack, a fruit bowl containing some rather wrinkled apples and two black bananas, a litre bottle of Courvoisier and a two-litre bottle of Gordon's, part empty, some used coffee cups and glasses, and a derelict spider plant in a white plastic pot. The hi-fi was still switched on, and several CDs were lying about – Vivaldi, Mozart and Bach – while the open case of the CD presumably still in the machine was lying on the top of the stack: Schubert, Quintet in C.

Along another wall were bookshelves with cupboards below, the shelves tightly packed, mostly with paperbacks, but with a fair sprinkling of hardback political biographies. 'Review copies,' Atherton said. 'The great journalistic freebie.' Slider looked at a title or two. Hattersley, Enoch Powell, Dennis Healey. But Woodrow Wyatt? Wasn't he a builder?

The window was large and looked over the small, sooty garden, to which there was no access from up here. It was the original sash with the lever-lock, which was, he noted, in the locked position. Of course, someone breaking in that way could have locked it before departing by the door.

'But then, why should they?' said Atherton. 'The Yale on that door's so old and loose a child could slip it. You'd have thought someone in her position would have been a bit more security-minded.'

Slider shook his head. 'Obviously she was unworldly.'

'Other-worldly now, if you want to be precise.'

The right-hand end of the room was furnished with a wardrobe, a tallboy, a low chest of drawers doubling as bedside table, and a double bed, pushed up into the back corner and covered with a black cotton counterpane. The wardrobe was decorated with a variety of old stickers: CND;

Nuclear Power – No Thanks; Stop the Bloody Whaling; Troops Out of Vietnam; and, fondly familiar to Slider, the round, yellow Keep Music Live sticker. Instead of pictures there were posters stuck up on the magnolia-painted walls, amongst them a very old one of Che, a couple of vintage film posters, some political flyers and rally leaflets, and some cartoon originals which were probably pretty valuable. The room, though tidy, was scruffy and full of statements, like a student bedsit from the early 1970s. Given the age and status of the occupant, it seemed a deliberate two fingers raised at conventional, middle-class expectations.

The body was on the bed.

Freddie Cameron, the forensic pathologist, straightened and looked up as Slider approached. He was as dapper as a sea lion, a smallish, quick-moving man in a neat grey suit, with a dark waistcoat and, today, a very cheery tartan bow-tie – the sort only a very self-confident man or an expensive teddy bear could have got away with. It was the kind of bow-tie that had to be sported, rather than merely worn, and Cameron sported it, jaunty as a good deed in a naughty world.

'Bill! Hello, old chum,' he warbled. 'Good way to end the week. How's tricks?'

'Trix? She's fine, but I've told you not to mention her in front of the boy,' Slider replied sternly.

Freddie blinked. 'Ha! I see they haven't knocked the cheek out of you, anyway. You know who we've got here?'

'I do indeed.'

'There won't be many tears shed for her in the Job, I suppose. Sad loss to journalism, all the same.'

Slider raised his eyebrows. 'I didn't think you read the *Grauniad*.'

'*Indy* man, me,' Cameron admitted. 'But she wrote for that occasionally, and the *Staggers*, which I read sometimes. Got to keep an open mind. I always liked her pieces, even when I didn't agree with her.'

'*Someone* didn't agree with her,' Slider said, and – there being no more excuse for ignoring it – for the first time looked directly at the corpse.

What had been Phoebe Agnew was sprawled on her back, one leg slipping off the edge of the bed, toes touching the carpet. Her arms were flung back above her head, and her wrists were tied together and to the bedhead with a pair of tights. Her auburn hair, long and thick and loosely curling, was spread out around her like a sunburst, vivid against the black cloth, seeming to draw all the life and colour out of the room. It was amazing hair in any circumstance, but if, as Atherton had told him, she was around fifty, it was doubly so, because the colour looked entirely natural.

She was wearing a large, loose, oatmeal-coloured knitted sweater and was naked from the waist down; a pair of grey wool trousers and scarlet bikini briefs lay on the floor at the foot of the bed. Slider flinched inwardly, and felt a stab of pity for the woman, so exposed in this helpless indignity. It was always the worst bit, the first moment of acknowledging the person whose life had been taken from them without their will. There she lay, mutely reproachful, beseeching justice. A body is just a body, of course, but still it wears the face of a person who lived, and was self-aware, and who didn't want to die.

The nakedness seemed worse because she was not young: there is an arrogance to the nakedness of youth which defies ridicule. In life she must have been good-looking, perhaps even beautiful, Slider thought, noting the classical nose, the wide mouth, the strong chin; but no-one looks their best after being strangled. The face was swollen and suffused, the open eyes horribly bloodshot; her lips were bluish, and there was blood on them, and in her left ear; and round her neck was the livid mark of the ligature. The ligature, however, had been removed.

After all these years, the first sight of a corpse still raised Slider's pulse and made him feel hot and prickly for a moment – almost like a kind of violent teenage embarrassment. He took a couple of deep breaths until it subsided.

Atherton looked away, shoving his hands into his pockets. Tall and elegant, gracefully drooping, he looked as out of place in this room as a borzoi in a scrapyard. 'Wonder why they took one ligature and left the other,' he said.

'Maybe the one round her neck was traceable in some way,' Slider said. 'Time of death, Freddie?'

'Well, she's cold and stiff, so that puts it between eight and thirty-six hours, according to the jolly old textbook. It's not over-warm in here, and though she looks reasonably fit she's no spring chicken, so I'd put it in the middle range, say twelve to twenty-four. Not less than twelve, anyway.'

'So we're looking at sometime yesterday, probably evening or afternoon,' Slider said. 'And I suppose the cause of death was strangulation?'

'I wouldn't like to commit myself until I've got her on the table. There are no other apparent injuries, but I'm not blessed with infra-red vision, and it's getting dark as Newgate Knocker in here. These hypoxia cases are notoriously tricky, anyway. But she certainly has been strangled.'

'There doesn't seem to have been a struggle,' Slider said. 'No furniture overturned or anything.'

'She may have been drugged, of course,' Cameron said. 'Which is why I reserve judgement on the cause of death. Have you seen enough? Well, let's get the photos done, then, and we can get her out of here.'

Slider left him to it and went to look at the kitchen. It must have been fitted in about 1982, with cheap units whose doors had slumped out of alignment, and daisy-patterned tiles, all in shades of brown: pure eighties chic. The electric cooker was old and flecked with encrusted spillings that hasty cleaning had missed. The fridge was also old, with leaking seals, and filled with a clutter of bowls containing leftovers: bits of food on plates, ends of cheese in crumpled wrappings, an expiring lettuce, and tomatoes that had gone wrinkly. A bottle of skimmed milk was past its sell-by date and there was a platoon of yoghurts, one of which had a crack down the side of its carton and was dribbling messily. The comparative tidiness of the bedsitting room was evidently only skin deep.

The sink, with draining boards and a washing machine under it, had been fitted into the bay window. There was a plastic washing-up bowl in the sink. In it, and on the draining boards, was a collection of dirty utensils: plates and bowls, knives, forks and spoons, saucepans and various serving vessels. It looked as though there had been a dinner, featuring some kind of casserole, vegetables and potatoes followed by tiramisu. The last wasn't hard to guess as the remaining half of it was still in its glass dish sitting on top of the grill hood of the gas stove. There were several empty bottles standing at the back of the work surface – three wine and one brandy – though there was no knowing how long they'd been there. They might not all appertain to the same meal.

The meal surprised him a little. Knowing Phoebe Agnew's politics, he would have bet on her being a vegetarian. And actually, given the state of the flat and the fridge, he would have expected her to be above cooking, just as she was apparently above home-making. The cookery books lying open amid the clutter of the work surface suggested a certain lack of practice in the art. *Casserole Cookery*, with the unconvincing, orange-toned food photographs of the seventies by way of illustration, was obviously old but had not, to judge from the lack of food splashes, been heavily used in its life. It was open at Italian-Style Chicken With Olives and had a fresh smear of tomato paste on one edge. The other book, *New Italian Cooking*, was brand new – so much so that the page had had to be weighted to stay open at Tiramisu.

So she had entertained someone to a home-cooked meal yesterday and gone to some trouble about it: in his experience women never got out the cookery books for a man they were sure of. But was it the murderer she had cooked for? Or had she been dozing off the effects of the grub and booze when someone else called to cancel her ticket?

'Guv, come and look at this,' Atherton called.

He was in the bathroom. Being windowless it had one of those fans that come on with the light. It was as ineffective as they usually are: the room had that sour smell of rancid water you get in towels that have been put away damp. It needed redecoration: the Crystal tiles staggered crazily over the uneven walls, the grouting on its last legs, and the paint on the woodwork was lumpy and peeling. There was a calcium crust around the taps, and the bath and basin were mottled white where the hard water had marked them, which looked particularly nasty since the suite was brown.

'My whole life just flashed before me,' Slider said. A brown bath had been the *dernier cri* when he first married.

There was a washing line strung over the bath, on which hung more undies from a well-known high street store. Naturally she would shop at Marks and Engels, Slider thought. He counted six used towels – on the rail, over the edge of the bath, stretched over the radiator, and 'hung up on the floor', as his mother used to say.

'And the plug hole's clogged with soapy hair,' he commented, looking, though not too closely, into the sink.

'Never mind that, see here,' Atherton said, and drew back for Slider to look into the lavatory bowl. The sad little rubber 'o' of a condom looked back at them.

'She definitely had company,' Atherton said.

'We already knew that,' said Slider. 'Better fish it out.'

'*Me*?'

'Don't whine. You've got gloves on.'

'It's the principle of the thing,' Atherton grumbled. 'I was fashioned for love, not labour.' As he reached fastidiously into the bowl, he was reminded of an anecdote. 'The plumber I use now and then told me about how this woman called him out one time because she wanted a new lav fitted. He asked her if she wanted a P-trap or an S-trap, and she went bright red with embarrassment and said, "Oh – well – it's for both, really."'

'Get on with it,' Slider said. Outside there was the sound of reinforcements arriving, and a voice he hadn't expected. 'Is that the Super? What the chuck's he doing here?'

'The voice of the turtle was heard in our land,' said Atherton. He secured the floating evidence and followed Slider out.

It seemed to have got even colder, and the sky was now featureless, low and grey, like the underside of a submarine. Detective Superintendent Fred 'The Syrup' Porson was on the doorstep, draped in a wonderful old Douglas Hurd coat of military green, voluminous and floor-length. What you might call army surplice, Slider thought. Behind Porson stood three of his DCs, presumably brought in the same car – the Department was short of wheels, as always.

'Ah, Bill,' Porson said. The cold air had given his skin a greyish tinge. With his big-nosed, granite face he looked remarkably like one of the Easter Island heads; the preposterous toupee was like a crop of vegetation growing on the top. 'What's the current situation, *vis-à-vis* deceased? Let's have a stasis report.'

Porson used language with the delicate touch of a man in boxing gloves playing the harpsichord. It was one of the endearing things about him – as long as you didn't suffer from perfect literary pitch.

'It looks as though it wasn't suicide, sir,' Slider said. He recapped briefly, while Porson tramped restlessly on the spot like a horse, using his hands thrust into his pockets to wrap the strange coat about him.

'Hm. Yes. Well. I see,' he said. He seemed in travail of a decision. 'You are aware, of course,' he said at last, 'that this 'flu epidemic has precipitated a crisis situation, Area-wide, with regard to personnel? It's a problem right across the broad, and as such, AMIP has asked if we'd be prepared to keep the case.'

Slider raised his eyebrows. 'It'll be high profile, sir.'

'The highest of the high, to coin a phrase,' Porson agreed. A few tiny pinpoints of snow were drifting down, settling on the eponymous rug. It looked as though it was developing dandruff. Slider dragged his eyes away – Porson didn't like the wig to be noticed. 'The papers will be full of it,' Porson went on. 'Our every movement will be scrutinised with a tooth-comb. I'm well aware it'll be no picnic, believe you me. But the fly in the argument *is*', he explained, 'that AMIP's even worse hit, absentee-wise, than we are. Half their manpower's been decimated, *plus* they've got three other major investigations on the go as well. So the upshoot is, they've asked if we'll do the premilinary work, at least to begin with.'

Slider shrugged. Upshoot or offshot, his was not to reason why. 'I hope the budget will stand it, sir,' he said.

'Don't you worry about that.' Porson seemed relieved at his docility. 'I'll sort all that out with AMIP. Well, now I'm here you'd better show me round, recapitate what you've got so far.'

Slider obliged. Only as Porson was leaving did he think to ask, 'By the way, sir, how did AMIP hear about it so soon?'

Porson gave a grim smile. 'They heard it from Commander Wetherspoon. Some reporter rang him at ten this morning, asking who was heading the investigation.'

'Good God,' said Slider.

'So you see the problem.'

He tramped off down the steps to the car, his coat brushing regally behind him. Atherton, at Slider's shoulder, said, 'Given who she was, I suppose there was never a cat in hell's chance of keeping the press out of it.'

'Not a toupee's chance in a wind tunnel,' Slider agreed.

'That's not an original toupee, you know, it's an elaborate postiche,' Atherton said. Another car pulling up further down the road caught his attention. Two men got out and headed towards them with an air of restraining themselves from running. 'I hope the Super's sending us some more uniform – the vultures are beginning to gather,' he said.

'If you stand around there you'll get your picture taken,' Slider warned. 'Time to go and talk to the female that found the body, I think.'

CHAPTER TWO

Many are cold, but few are frozen

In contrast to Phoebe Agnew's unreconstructed seventies pit, the upstairs flat had been through the sort of make-over that wouldn't have disgraced a *Changing Rooms* designer. Its tiny fragment of hall was made almost unbearably elegant by a bamboo plant stand bearing a vase of artificial roses, a large mirror in an elaborate gold plastic frame and, dangling from the ceiling, a Chinese lantern with tassels.

The Chinese theme continued up the stairs with red and gold wallpaper, vaguely willow-patterned. The carpet was crimson, and at the top was a small landing and a glimpse through an open door of a dark and sultry boudoir, with red flock wallpaper and velvet curtains, a double bed covered in a purple and gold brocade counterpane, a velvet chair stuffed with tasselled silk cushions, pierced-work incense burners, and a surprising number of mirrors, including a full-length cheval standing at the foot of the bed.

The sitting room, by contrast, was furnished in cheap, bright Ikea pine and jolly primary colours, chiefly yellow and lime. There was a window-seat occupied by a row of stuffed toys; the mantelpiece and various tables bore a collection of china animals, mostly pigs, frogs and mice; and on the walls were pictures of winsome puppies and kittens and other adorable fluffy baby animals in agonisingly lovable poses. There were enough moist eyes in that room, Slider reckoned, to have supplied an entire sultan's banquet.

'The occupant of this flat', Atherton concluded, 'is either seriously schizophrenic, or a working girl.'

'Oh dear, how will we ever tell which?' Slider wondered.

The occupant was sitting on the sofa before a gas fire, sniffling into a Kleenex. WPC Asher stood at hand with the box, and made an enigmatic face over her head as the two appeared in the doorway.

'Miss Jekyll, I presume?' Slider enquired.

She looked up. 'Eh?'

'What's your name, love?'

'Candi,' she said. 'With an "i". Candi Du Cane.'

'Real name?'

She looked a trifle sulky. 'Lorraine, if you must know. Lorraine Peabody.'

She had a chubby, snubbily pretty face which gave her an air of extreme youth, though closer examination suggested she was in her middle twenties. Her hair was straight and dyed blonde, pulled back carelessly in a wispy tail; her juicily plump figure was outlined by a black body, over which she wore a tracksuit bottom, and a vast knitted cardigan which looked as if it came from the same needles as Phoebe Agnew's sweater. It was so much too big for her that she'd had to roll the sleeves into thick sausage cuffs just to get her hands free. Her eyes and nose were red with weeping, and there was a black smudge under her eyes where the mascara had washed off with her tears.

'Lorraine's a nice name too,' Slider said, taking Asher's place on the sofa. Candi/Lorraine looked at him with the automatic alarm of the born victim. 'I want to ask you some questions – nothing to worry about,' Slider said. 'I'm Detective Inspector Slider. You're the one who found the body, aren't you?'

She shivered in automatic reaction, and then excused herself by saying, 'It's bleedin' taters in here. The central 'eating never works prop'ly, but old Sborski – the landlord – he won't never do nothing about it.'

'You don't own the flat, then?'

'No, s'only rented. I did talk to Phoebe once about buying a place, but she said for girls like us what was the point? She said you might as well spend your money on yourself an' enjoy it as tie it up in bricks an' mortar. But it's just you can never get nothing done.' She was talking rapidly, and her voice was tight and too high. 'I mean, Sborski's a real old bastard. Last year there was water coming through the roof right over my bed, and he wouldn't do nothing about it until Phoebe got on to him. She was brilliant. She jus' stood up to people, you know? If it wasn't for her—'

She shivered again and hunched further into her vast jumper, her eyes wide and strained.

'Shall I turn the fire up a bit?' Slider asked, eyeing it doubtfully. It was a vintage piece with brown and wonky ceramic panels and four flames of uneven height, one of which was yellow and popped rhythmically.

'Nah, it don't work on the other setting,' Lorraine said. 'I'll be all right. I jus' can't get it out me mind – you know, what I seen down there.' Her arms wrapped around herself, she began to rock a little.

Slider saw hysteria not too far off. 'Don't think about it for the moment,' he said in his cosiest voice. 'Tell me about you. You're – what? – a model?'

'Well, I've done modelling,' she allowed. 'I do escort work mostly. Hostessing. Promotional. That sort o' thing.' She met his eye and, as though goaded by an irresistible honesty, blurted, 'Well, *you* know.'

Slider nodded. He did indeed. 'Lived here long?'

'Two years, nearly.'

'You've done it up really nicely,' Slider said with his fatherly smile, the one that melted the golden hearts of tarts.

'Ju like it? My mum always said I got a flair for it – colour an' that. Said I shoulda gone in for it, for a living.'

'I bet you could have. And all these animals – quite a collection you've got.'

A little more of this and she had stopped shivering and staring and was beginning to unwrap her arms. Slider led her gently up to the fence again. 'So Phoebe only rented the flat below, then, like you?'

'Yeah. I don't think she cared much about stuff like that. Possessions an' stuff. She was always on about causes an' everything.'

'You knew her well?'

'Yeah. Well, she was always really nice to me, done things for me, like making old Sborski mend the roof an' that. I used to go down for a chat an' we used to sit an' have a drink an' a laugh an' everything. She was great. She always had time for you.'

'You obviously liked her.'

'Yeah, she was a great laugh. You'd never've fought she was as old as she was. I mean, I could never talk to my mum, but Phoebe was like as if she was the same age as me. Ever so modern and young in her attitudes an' everyfing. Except for abortion. Funny, she was really down on that. The only time she ever went for me was when I got up the duff an' said I was gettin' rid of it. She tried to talk me out of it – I mean,' she said in amazement, 'what'd I do wiv a kid? She wouldn't talk to me for ages after that. But it blew over. She was a real mate.'

'She lived there alone, did she? She wasn't married?'

'Nah, she never had time for all that. She said she had enough of dealing with men all day, without having to come home and look after one. She had *'ad* boyfriends – she was quite normal in that respect,' she assured him earnestly, her blue eyes wide. 'But she said, "You and me, L'raine," she said, "we know the trouble men cause in the world," she said, an' she said, "You and me know marriage ain't the answer to every problem." Not like some o' them daft girls you see on the telly, think gettin' a man's the most important thing in life.'

'Did Phoebe have men friends come to visit her?' Slider asked casually.

'She had friends all right,' Lorraine said cautiously. 'I've see people go in and out, but I couldn't tell you pacificly, not names or anythink. Up here, I wouldn't know if someone come unless I was looking out the window. But she did have someone in yesterday.' She looked at him hopefully, wanting to please.

'How do you know that?'

'Well, I went down to the hall about twelve o'clock time to see if there was any letters. I'd just got up. And as I open me door, Phoebe comes in wiv her arms full of shopping.'

'She came in from the street?'

'Yeah, wiv all bags of food an' that. So I says, how about a cup a coffee an' that, because we hadn't had a good old chat for ages, not since before Christmas, really. But she says no, she can't stop because she's got someone coming to dinner and she's got to get the place tidied up.'

'Did she say who was coming?'

'No, but she seemed sort of excited, so I reckoned it was a man. I mean, she wouldn't tidy up for a girlfriend, would she? I made a joke about it, because she never normally tidied anything. Me, I like things nice, but her place was always a tip. Tell the trufe, I couldn't see her cooking for a girlfriend either. I mean, she mostly eats out, or buys a Marks an' Sparks thing, from what I've seen.'

'Did she say what time this person was coming?'

'Nah, but when I was going back up I asked if she fancied coming down the pub later, an' she said no, she couldn't, because of this person coming, and she said she didn't want to be disturbed and not to knock on her door or ring her up for any reason whatever. So I just said pardon me for living, an' I went. And that was the last time I see her.' She sniffed. 'If I'd of knew it was the last time, I'd of never of said that. But she got up my nose.'

'Why did she? Was she bad-tempered about it?'

'Oh no, not really. Like I said, she seemed kind of pleased an' excited when she said about someone coming; but then when she said that – about not disturbing her – she went all strict and teachery, an' I just thought, well, I thought, excuse *me*! I know when I'm not wanted.'

Slider was accustomed to the habit of the ignorant of taking offence for no reason. She must have been a trying neighbour for the intellectual Agnew – probably forever 'popping down for a coffee'. A person who worked from home was always vulnerable to the dropper-in with an empty schedule and a vacant mind.

'I suppose you didn't see the visitor arrive?' he asked without hope.

'Not as such,' she admitted reluctantly, 'but I think I heard music playing down there later, so I reckon he must of come all right.'

'What time would that have been?'

'I dunno, really.' She thought for a moment. 'It must a' been about hapass six, summink like that, 'cos I had the radio on before that, but I turned it off when I went to have me bath, and then I heard the music downstairs, that classical shite she likes.' She made a face. No votes here for Vivaldi and Bach, then.

'What about during the evening? Did you hear any other noises from downstairs?'

'Well I wasn't in, was I? I went out about seven, down the club.'

'Which club?'

'The Shangri-la,' she said. 'D'you know it?'

He did indeed. It was a well-known pick-up place for prostitutes, and he had always wondered whether it was by design or accident that the illuminated sign over the door had lost its 'n'.

He was about to ask the next question when she evidently thought of something. 'Oh, wait! I dunno if it matters, but I did hear the door downstairs bang. That'd be about sevenish. I was just pulling the curtains in here, 'cos I was going out. So that could of been him going. And now I come to think of it, when I went past her door just after, there was no music playing inside, in her flat. So he must of went.'

'Didn't you look down and see, when you heard the door bang? You were standing at the window.'

'Well, no, 'cos I'd just pulled the curtains closed. And I wasn't that interested, tell you the trufe.'

Slider sighed inwardly. 'And what time did you come back from the club?'

'It was about – I dunno, going on ten o'clock.'

'Alone?'

She looked away. 'Maybe, maybe not. What's it matter?'

'Of course it matters. Look, Lorraine,' he explained carefully to her stubbornly averted profile, 'we're going to have to ask everyone if they saw anyone entering or leaving this house yesterday evening. We'll get hundreds of reports, and we'll have to go through them all. Now if we can cross out the ones we know came to see you, it'll help us find the right one. Do you see?' She didn't answer. 'Don't you want to help find out who killed Phoebe?'

She wavered, but said, 'I ain't gettin' meself into trouble. I ain't getting no-one into trouble.'

'There's no trouble in it, not for you or your visitors. I just want to eliminate them.'

She looked sidelong at him. 'What if I don't remember their names?'

'A description and the time they came and left will do, if that's all you've got. You'll have to write it all out for me.' She still looked far from convinced, and he left the subject for now and went on, 'Tell me what happened this morning.'

'Well,' she said cautiously, 'I just come down this morning to bum a bit of coffee off of her, 'cos I'd run out. I rung her bell and, like, shouted out through the door, "It's only me, Feeb," but there was no answer.'

'What time was that?'

''Bout quart' to ten, ten to ten maybe.'

'Go on.'

'Well,' she said, and paused. 'The thing is,' she went on, and paused again.

He thought he saw her difficulty. 'If the door was closed, how did you get in? Have you got a key?'

'Well, not *as such*,' she said reluctantly, 'although she has give me a key from time to time, when she wanted someone letting in, a workman or something, you know?'

'But you didn't, in fact, have a key this morning?' Slider pressed.

Now she looked defiant. 'All right, if you must know, I slipped the lock. Well, I knew Feeb wouldn't mind. She never minded me lending a bit o' coffee or whatever. And it was me what pointed it out to her in the first place, how rotten that lock was and how anybody could get in. I told her she ought to make Sborski get a new one fixed, but she never got round to it. I don't think she was that bothered. She trusted people too much, that was her problem.'

Slider nodded patiently. 'So you went in?'

'I called out, "Are you there, Feeb?", 'cos the front room door was open and I could see the curtains was still shut, so I thought she might be sleeping in.'

By 'the front room' she meant, of course, the living room. Slider was accustomed to this Londonism and was not confused. 'Was the light on or off?' he asked.

'Off. That's what I mean, it was dark in there, so she might have been still in bed. Well, so I went up to the door and just stuck me head round, and I see her laying there. I could see right away something was wrong, the way she was laying. So I went and pulled the curtains back.' Another pause. The chubby face was very pale now, and the hands gripping the handkerchief were shaking as she relived it. 'Then I see her face and everything.'

Slider prompted her gently. 'So what did you do?'

'I jus' dialled 999.'

'You used her phone? The one in the room?'

She nodded. So that ruled out last number redial, which might have been useful.

'It was awful, with her laying there, you know the way she was – and her eyes open an' everything. After I phoned they said to wait there but I couldn't stay in the room with her like that. So I went out in the hall and pulled the door to. It felt like hours, waiting. I thought they'd never come. And', the thought struck her, 'I've never even had me cup a coffee yet.'

'Well, I shall want you to come down to the station and make a statement,' Slider said, 'so we can give you a cup of coffee there.'

'What, I've got to say all this again?' she asked indignantly.

'For the record,' he said. 'And you've got to list all your visitors for me. But it's nice and warm there, and the coffee's not bad. You can have a bun as well. They do a nice Danish.' She shrugged and sighed, but had plainly resigned herself to her fate. 'By the way, did Phoebe ever mention to you anyone that she was afraid of,' he went on, 'or anyone that might want to do her harm?'

She shook her head slowly. 'No, I don't know about that. There was this bloke I seen hanging about sometimes – Wolsey, Woolley, some name like that. She got him off this charge. He was s'pose to've blagged some building society, but he reckoned he was fitted up, an' she found some evidence to get him off.'

'Michael Wordley?' Atherton suggested.

'Yeah, Wordley, that's him,' Lorraine said.

Slider nodded, remembering the case. It had been a sore

point at the time: Miss Agnew hadn't hesitated to generalise from the particular. 'But why would he want to harm her? He'd be grateful to her, wouldn't he?'

'You haven't seen him. He's a right tasty bastard, built like a brick khasi, face like a bagful o' spanners. He's a nutter, and you never know what them sort'll do next. I tell you, I never liked having him come round here, I don't care what Phoebe said. I mean, you've only got to say one wrong word, or look at 'em a bit funny, and you've had it. If anyone coulda done – what they done to her,' she said with a shudder, 'it was him.'

Ungrammatical, but emphatic. 'When did you last see him round here?'

'I can't remember exactly. It would be – I dunno, maybe last week or the week before.'

'Well, we'll certainly look into him,' Slider said. 'Anyone else you can think of?'

'No, but she had been worried lately,' Lorraine said. 'She never said what about, but for weeks now she's been a bit—'

'Preoccupied?'

'Yeah. Yesterday was the first time I seen her smiling an' happy for, like, a couple o' months. Well, since Christmas, really. An' then some bastard goes an' does that to her! It's not fair,' she mourned. 'I bet it was that nutter.'

'One more thing,' Slider said, 'do you know who her next of kin was? Are her parents still alive?'

'I dunno. She never said.'

'Any brothers or sisters?'

'She never mentioned any to me,' Lorraine said slowly. 'We didn't talk about that sort o' thing much. Maybe Peter'd know – him what lives down the area. He's lived here longer'n me. He was always in there, chatting away. Real bunny merchant. Bored the pants off Phoebe, if you want my opinion, but she was too polite to say. Always too nice to everyone, that was her trouble.'

'He doesn't seem to be in at the moment. I expect he's at work, isn't he?'

'I 'spec' so. He's a reporter, works for the *Ham and Ful,*' said Lorraine.

The *Hammersmith and Fulham Chronicle* was a local paper, but with ambitions to be the next *Manchester Guardian* and go national. It took itself seriously, reported hard news, uncovered local council scandals, campaigned for the homeless and refugees, and hardly ever mentioned jumble sales or 'amdram' pantomimes.

'So,' said Atherton as they went downstairs again, 'another newshound. Maybe that accounts for the rapid response.'

'What, you think he was the reporter who rang the Commander? But how could he have known about it?'

'Maybe he did it.'

'Down, boy,' said Slider.

Back in the Agnew flat, the body had been taken away. The room was strangely lifeless, all colour gone with her. The tattiness was now merely depressing rather than defiant.

'There's a mess of stuff to be sorted through,' Atherton said gloomily. 'Why did she live in a place like this, anyway? I'd have thought she earned plenty.'

'You heard from L'raine what a saint she was. Maybe she gave it all away to charity.'

'And leapt tall buildings in a single bound,' Atherton said. 'No, I see her as one of those pathetic pseudo-intellectuals who leech on dimwits to give themselves a sense of superiority. Better to reign in hell, etcetera, etcetera.'

'I don't know,' Slider said. 'With Candi up-atop and Peter the Bunny down under, I'd have thought Phoebe Agnew was the one being leeched on.'

'Precisely my point,' Atherton groused. 'Why didn't she stop slumming it and move somewhere else?'

'Did you get a package of hostility through the post this morning? I thought you thought she was a brilliant writer.'

'She was obviously a slob,' Atherton said, watching the forensic team opening cupboards and drawers. The tidying had evidently been done student-style, by bundling up everything visible and stuffing it into hiding. 'Why can't we ever investigate someone with a minimalist lifestyle?'

Slider had left his side and was talking to Bob Lamont, who had come in person to lift the fingerprints. 'What's it look like?'

'Dabs everywhere. A real mess. She wasn't houseproud,' said Lamont. 'I've done all the usual places – door, light switch and so on.'

'Do the cutlery, wineglasses and bottles in the kitchen, will you,' Slider said. 'Working on the assumption it was the killer she cooked for—'

'You don't want much, do you?' Lamont complained.

'Have you done the CD covers?'

'Just about to.'

'Good. Maybe he put music on to kill by. Oh,' he added, 'and what about the flush-handle on the loo – that's one they often forget.'

'Shall be done.'

Slider's own troops were already starting to sort and bag papers from the areas that had been finished with. Atherton turned as he came back to him. 'I suppose we've got to sort through all this lot to find the next of kin.'

'No, you can ring one of the papers,' Slider said. 'They're bound to have a morgue piece on her.'

'Brilliant, boss.'

'That's me. Try the *Independent* first. Better not start off by suggesting to the *Grauniad* that they know more about the case than you do. And when you've done that, ring the *Ham and Ful* and find out where the downstairs tenant is.'

'He's probably somewhere giving himself an interview,' Atherton said.

Just as Slider was leaving, Lamont came back to him. 'I think we may have something,' he said. 'The cutlery and glasses and so on in the kitchen, and the coffee cups and brandy glasses over there,' he nodded towards the unit, 'have all been wiped clean on the outside. *But* the whisky glasses have both got lip and finger marks on them. Now, assuming one set belongs to deceased—'

'Nice,' Slider said, brightening. 'They always make one mistake.'

CHAPTER THREE

Three corns on a Fonteyn

WDC Swilley burst into Slider's office. 'Boss?'

'Don't you believe in knocking?' he said sternly.

'No, only constructive criticism,' she said.

'Don't you start. One smartarse in the firm's enough,' he warned. 'I hope you've come to bring me a cup of tea?'

She shook her head. 'Sorry. There's a bloke here from the local paper.'

He frowned. 'Why are you telling me? You know I don't talk to the press.'

'No, boss, but he says he's got information about Phoebe Agnew. His name's Peter Medmenham.'

'That's the man who lives in the basement of her house,' Slider said. 'Concentrate, Norma!'

'Oh, yes. Sorry.' She'd been distracted lately. Her long-standing engagement to the mysterious Tony was at last nearing fruition: at the Christmas party (which, typically, Tony did not attend) she had announced the date for the wedding.

The announcement had set the department seething, because nobody had ever met Tony, and the uncharitable had claimed he didn't exist. Norma was tall, leggy, blonde and glamorous, so the idea that she was a saddo who had to invent a love-interest ought to have been ludicrous; but policewomen who reject the advances of their colleagues have to take what gets dished out. Those she had scorned most cruelly had labelled her a lesbian (and probably fantasised about her in studded leather wielding a whip). Now the same thickheads were saying she was getting married because she was in pod: spite and wounded pride took no account of logic, of course. But even Slider had to admit to a curiosity about what sort of magnificent demigod Tony must be to have captured his firm's own warrior princess.

'So, d'you want to see him?' Norma asked. 'He's downstairs, in interview room one.'

'Eh?' Slider said, startled.

'This Meddlingham bloke.'

'Oh! Yes, I suppose I'd better. Is he alone? He hasn't got a photographer with him?'

She grinned. 'You're safe. He's not even sporting a notepad.'

Peter Medmenham was not at all what Slider had expected. A reporter for a local paper he would have expected to be young and poor; and the name somehow suggested tall and handsome, in the manner of a model in a men's knitwear catalogue. But what he found in the interview room was a short, plump person of indeterminate age, wearing cord trousers in a silvery-olive shade with a lovat-green lambswool sweater. A tweed overcoat, of the venerable wonderfulness that put it in the loved-family-retainer class, hung from his shoulders. His soft face sported a tan which, in the unforgiving fluorescent light, looked fake, and his pale blue eyes were rimmed with lashes so dark they must surely have been helped, especially as the sparse, carefully tended hair was white – or, to be absolutely frank, pale blue. As Slider paused in the doorway, Medmenham opened his eyes wide and made a little theatrical movement of his hands, first out and then to his chest.

'Oh, don't!' he cried in a surprisingly deep, cigarette-husky voice. 'I know! You're looking at *this*!' He touched his head. 'It's a *disaster*! Just *enhance* the white, I said – because when all you've got is a few poor little bits and pieces like mine, you've got to make the most of them – and, lo and behold, out I come, looking like the Blue Fairy in *Pinocchio*! Believe me, this is nothing to what it was like when she first did it. Kylie – that's the girl's name, don't ask me why – said it would wash out, and it *is* doing but, my God! Serves me right for going to a unisex salon, I suppose. *That's* a bad joke, and so was the salon.'

'Mr Medmenham?' Slider asked mildly.

'Yes, and listen to me running on! It's nerves, that's all. Do you mind if I sit down? My poor feet are killing me. What I suffer with them is nobody's business! Of course, these shoes don't help – but you can't argue with vanity, can you?' He had a refined accent, and behind the mascara, his eyes were alert and intelligent. 'You're Inspector Slider, are you?'

'Yes, that's right. And this is Detective Constable Swilley.'

Medmenham sat gracefully, slipping the coat off over the back of the chair in the same movement, and flashed a very white smile at Norma. 'How d'you do? My goodness, you look much too glamorous to be a policewoman! Did you ever think of going on the boards, dear? You really should, you've got the legs for it. Mind you, your feet wouldn't thank me. I used to dance, as well, though you wouldn't think it to look at me now. No Fred Astaire, but I was a decent hoofer in my time. It's all I can do to take three steps now. My trouble always was, my feet were too small for my weight. Put too much strain on them. If I were to show you, it would make you weep, I give you my word.'

Slider sat opposite him and tried to fix his attention. 'I understand you've got something to tell me about Phoebe Agnew.'

'Well, not exactly, but I thought you'd be sure to want to speak to me, as we were so close, so I came straight here as soon as I heard about it.' The blue eyes wavered swimmingly. 'I suppose it *is* true? There's no mistake?'

'I'm afraid not. How did you hear about it?' Slider asked.

'I picked up a *Standard* at the station, and there it was – just a paragraph at the bottom of the front page. It didn't give her name, just said a well-known journalist had been found dead in a flat in West London, but, call me Mystic Meg, I just had an awful *premonition* about it. So I went straight to the nearest telephone and called the *Ham and Ful* news desk, and of course they knew all about it. One of our own had been first on the scene. My God, what a way to find out! I thought I was going to faint, right there in the railway station. I'm still not feeling quite myself.'

'It must have been a shock,' Slider said kindly. The unnatural-looking tan, he had discovered, was make-up after all. Medmenham might well be pale under it: he certainly had a look of strain.

'It was,' he said. 'To tell you the truth, that's another reason I came straight here. I didn't want to go home. Is that silly of me?' He gave a little nervous laugh.

'Understandable,' Slider said.

'I'm not sure if I'll ever want to go back there again. She – she isn't *still there*, is she?'

'No. The body's been removed.'

'The body! Oh dear!' His lips began to tremble and his face threatened to collapse, but he said, 'No, I must stay calm. Can't blub in front of the police.' He drew out a handkerchief from his trouser pocket and carefully applied it to his eyes and lips. 'And I want to *help*,' he added, emerging. 'Poor, darling Phoebe! Who could have done such a thing?'

'Your editor said you weren't at work today,' Slider said.

'My editor? You mean Martin? He doesn't edit *me*, love,' Medmenham said with sudden vigour. 'Barely literate, like most of the staff, but then that's the progressive education system for you. Gender awareness and finger-painting, oh yes, but reading and writing – *oubliez le*! And as for grammar—'

'But I understood you were a reporter for the *Ham and Ful*?'

He looked shocked. 'Oh, not a *reporter*! I do the reviews. Books, theatre, TV. And the interviews and articles – everything on the arts side. Not the music scene – that's *very* different. Very cliquey. I don't have the in. But I'm virtually the arts editor, otherwise. I used to be on the stage, of course, so I've got the contacts. I come from a long line of theatricals. My parents were in variety. I first went on as a Babe in the Wood at the age of six. Golden curls I had then, if you'll believe me! I've done a bit of everything. From panto to musicals, Shakespeare to Whitehall farce. But I went over to the writing side when my feet let me down. It's not only that I can't dance any more, I just couldn't stand on stage for three hours every night. You wouldn't believe how it takes it out on the feet, acting. It's not a thing anyone talks about, really.'

'Tell me how you first met Phoebe Agnew,' Slider said.

'Ooh, that would be – let me think – thirteen, fourteen years ago. Nineteen eighty-five, was it? Back when dinosaurs ruled the earth! My lord, doesn't the *tempus* fuge when you take your eye off it? Time flies like an arrow – but fruit flies like a banana, as they say! Anyway, I met Phoebe at a Labour fund-raiser. Well, there's always been a lot of interplay between politics and the theatre. The luvvie connection. I think a lot of politicians are actors *manqué*, don't you? Especially our present lords and masters – but never mind, that's another story. I could tell you some things but I won't. And the other way round, of course – a lot of actors fancy themselves politicians. I could name names, but nobody loves a gossip.' He pursed his lips and turned an imaginary key over them.

'So how did you come to live in the same house?' Slider pursued.

'Well, when I met her at this do, she was looking for somewhere, and the flat upstairs happened to be empty.

She and I took to each other first minute, we were like brother and sister, so I jumped at the chance of having a soul mate upstairs and she jumped at the chance of a nice let that was cheap *and* central.' He sighed. 'If we'd known then what property prices were going to do! We had the chance to buy, and at a price that would make you laugh if I told you it now, but the rent was so reasonable, and neither of us had any dependents, so it hardly seemed worth it. We were quite happy to go on renting. But we were sitting on a gold-mine, if we had but known it. Of course, Sborski would love to get us out now, he could get a fortune selling the flats, but I've been there so long I'm a protected tenant, and it wasn't worth selling the top flat alone. I suppose,' he added starkly, his verve dissipating for a moment, 'now Phoebe's gone, he might sell the rest of the house and just leave me all alone in my basement. Oh, poor me!'

'You're not married?'

'No, I always look like this! Jokette,' he explained, looking round with a pleased smile. 'No, seriously, I should have thought it was obvious I'm not the marrying kind.'

'I don't like to assume anything,' Slider said solemnly. 'So you and Phoebe were close, were you?'

'She was my best, best friend. She was a wonderful person. She *lived* her principles, and there's not many you can say that about. Most people just talk about issues, but she got up and *did* something about it. Mind you, we didn't always agree. I mean, there is such a thing as being *too* liberal. Everything's so upfront and in-your-face these days. I've never made any secret about what I am – where'd be the point? You've only got to look at me – but my generation didn't make a song and dance about it. We kept ourselves to ourselves – and the Brigade of Guards. No, naughty! I didn't say that!' He twinkled. 'But nowadays everybody seems to want to tell everybody everything, whether they want to know it or not. And then, some of Phoebe's lame ducks weren't as lame as they made out, if you ask me. I know a thing or two about persecution, believe you me, and if they were victims I'm the Queen of Sheba's left tittie! Those two awful men she got let off, who murdered those kiddies. Oh, there might have been some doubt about the evidence, but they did it all right, and as far as I was concerned they were in the right place. Well, we argued about that a few times, I can tell you. But you couldn't fault her in the intentions department. She was all heart, Phoebe. When they made her they broke the mould.' His eyes swam again, and he reapplied the handkerchief, sniffing delicately.

Slider nodded sympathetically. 'Have you any idea who might have wanted to hurt her?'

He shook his head gravely. 'No, not at all. She didn't have any personal enemies. She was too good and kind. I suppose some people in authority mightn't have liked her – she did rather stir up things that *some* might have preferred unstirred – but you don't murder someone for that, do you? Well, not in this country. No, I can only think it was one of those random attacks. I mean, there are so many drug addicts and nutters on the loose nowadays, aren't there? Why they ever shut the bins and threw the poor things out on the street I'll never know! Call me an old softie, but they were much better off locked up inside, being looked after.'

Slider thought Medmenham had got into his stride and was playing to his audience, hearing himself and enjoying the flow of words. It was time to bring him down a bit.

'So, tell me, why weren't you at work today?'

'Oh,' he said, almost as if he'd been slapped. 'Well, that's a straight question if ever I heard one! I had the day off, as it happens. I went to see my mother. She's not been very well recently.'

'And where does she live?'

'In Danbury. It's near Chelmsford.'

'Yes, I know where it is,' Slider said.

'You do?' Peter Medmenham seemed very interested in that.

Slider said merely, 'I'm an Essex boy myself. You went down this morning?'

There was a very slight hesitation. 'No, last night.'

'By car? You drove down?'

'No, I don't drive, actually. Never got round to learning – well, I've always lived in London, so there didn't seem much point. I took the train. Stayed overnight. Took the Aged Mum out to lunch today, bless her – she loves eating out – and got the train back straight afterwards. I had to hurry to catch it, so I didn't see a paper until I got to Liverpool Street. That's when I saw the bit about Phoebe, and I came straight here.'

'What time did you go out last night?' Slider asked.

He seemed put out by the question. 'Me? Last night? Why do you want to know?'

'Have you some reason not to tell me?' Slider countered pleasantly.

'No, of course not. Why should I? Well, if it's important to you, I left at eight. I wanted to catch the 9.02 from Liverpool Street, and I always leave myself plenty of time to catch trains. With my blessed feet, I can't afford to have to run for one.' He looked enquiringly at Slider as if for a quid pro quo.

Slider said, 'It seems that Phoebe Agnew had a visitor yesterday. I don't suppose you saw them arrive or leave, did you?'

Medmenham chose to take that as the reason for the previous question, and his face cleared. 'Oh, I see! Well, I didn't see him, but I know who it was. It was Josh Prentiss.'

He said the name as though it ought to mean something, and when Slider continued to look politely enquiring, he went on, 'Goodness, you must have heard of him! He's the set designer who won the BAFTA award for *Bess and Robin*. Wonderful sets – very dark and moody – and then the Coronation scenes, very sheesh! *Please* don't tell me you've never heard of *Bess and Robin* because, frankly, dear, I shan't believe you!'

'I've heard of the film,' Slider acknowledged. Everyone said it was going to sweep the Oscars board this year, and it was being heralded as the harbinger of a new Hollywood love affair with the British film – something that seemed to be harbinged every couple of years with hopeful regularity but never arrived. And these days everyone was supposed to be so interested in the cinema that they not only knew the names of actors, but everyone else involved as well – smart people could discuss the merits of different directors, scriptwriters, producers, even cameramen. Slider felt like a caveman. 'I hardly ever get to the cinema. No time.'

'Poor you!' said Medmenham kindly. 'Well, Josh is an architect by training and has his own company – very successful, makes oodles of money – but he's *famous* for his sets. Hollywood's *mad* to get hold of him, he could name his price, but he doesn't need the money, so of course he can pick and choose, happy man!'

'Was he a friend, or did he visit Phoebe on business?'

'Oh, he and Phoebe are old friends. They go way back. And his wife Noni, too. She was Anona Regan – have you heard of her?' Slider shook his head. 'She was an actress, but she never really made it big time. She was in that sitcom a couple of years ago, *Des Res* – you know, about the estate agents?'

'I don't think I ever saw it. I don't get to see much television, either.' Unless he could bring the conversation round to real ale or the Police and Criminal Evidence Act, Slider feared he was going to end up with *nul points*.

'Oh, my dear, you didn't miss anything! It was a spectacular disaster. Flopperissimo! Poor Noni was the best thing in it, and it was a complete kiss of death to her, poor lamb. She was just trying to revive her career, and after that no-one would touch her *avec le* bargepole. Well, she'd never really made a name for herself, but she was a real trouper, and one can't help feeling sorry for her. Not that she needs the money, of course – Josh has loads – but that's never why one does it. One lives for one's art – well, most of the time!' He smiled again and almost batted his eyelashes.

Slider grabbed the tail of the straying subject. 'So, if you didn't see Josh Prentiss, how did you know it was him visiting yesterday?'

'I saw his car. You see, I knew she had a visitor, because I went and knocked on her door at about a quarter to seven, to see if she was coming down later to watch the serial. You know, *Red Slayer*? The past couple of weeks we've been watching it together over a bite of supper in my place. But when she answered the door she said she had someone with her and she couldn't come.'

'Did you see him?'

'No, she didn't open the door right up, and she stood in the gap so I couldn't see past her. So I said, all right, I'd tape it and we could watch it some other time.'

'And what time was the programme on?'

'Eight till nine.'

'But you were leaving at eight to catch your train,' Slider pointed out.

He turned just a little pink, for some reason. 'Well, that's when I decided to go up yesterday instead of today. If I was going to tape the serial there was no point in staying in, so I thought I might as well go to Chelmsford. And it was when I left for the station', he hurried on, 'that I saw Josh's car. It was parked further down, and I passed it on my way to the tube.'

'You know his car?'

'I've seen him arrive in it enough times. It's a Jaguar – one of those sleek, sporty-looking ones.'

'An XJS?'

Medmenham smiled charmingly. 'If you say so. I wouldn't know. It's dark blue, and the registration letters are FRN, which I remember because they always make me think of the word "fornicator" – heaven knows why!'

'Is Prentiss a fornicator?' Slider asked.

'Oh, good heavens, it's not for me to say!' Medmenham cried. 'Though if he were, one shouldn't be surprised. I mean, he's an architect. What's that old rhyme? *Roads and bridges, docks and piers, that's the stuff for engineers. Wine and women, drugs and sex, that's the stuff for architects.*'

'You seem to be trying to suggest', Slider said, 'that Prentiss was Phoebe Agnew's lover.'

'Do I? Oh dear, I'm sure it wasn't intentional,' Medmenham said with artificial blankness.

'Did he often visit?'

'I believe so. She often talked about him and I'd seen him in there from time to time. As I said, they were old friends. She'd known him even longer than me.'

'Did he always visit alone, or did his wife come too?'

'I never saw Noni there, but of course I didn't watch her door every hour. But Phoebe went to their house too, so she saw Noni there. It was all above board. For all I know, they met for lunch every day.'

The blue eyes were round and expressionless and the lips were pursed like a doll's. It was hard to know what he was trying to suggest or not suggest.

'Did Phoebe have lovers, that you knew of?'

'I wouldn't be surprised,' he said. 'I don't know of anyone specifically, but I mean she was a gorgeous woman, with that lovely hair, and skin like a newborn babe, though she never really bothered much about glamour, knocked about in a pair of old leggings and a floppy jumper. I said to her many a time, you've got legs most women would die for, darling, yet you never, ever show them – and between you and me,' he added confidentially to Swilley, 'she was one of those lucky creatures who never even had to shave them. But she wore trousers *all the time,*' he tutted. 'Still, she never had any shortage of men admiring her. And not only for her intellect, fabulous though it was.' Again, the bland stare. 'I'm sure she had all the affairs she wanted. Not that I knew anything about them. She was always discreet. No names, no pack drill. I certainly never heard her mention any man's name, or heard her name coupled with anyone else's in that context, by anyone.'

On their way back upstairs, Norma said to Slider, 'Was he for real, do you think, boss? Bit of a Tragedy Jill, wasn't he?'

Slider frowned thoughtfully. 'There was something going on underneath his words – or at least, he wanted us to think there was. That's the trouble with actors, I suppose – you can never tell when they're acting.'

'He's only an ex-actor,' Norma pointed out.

'That might very well be the worst kind. What did you make of him.'

'He struck me as possessive. Phoebe was *his* best friend, and she oughtn't to be anyone else's.'

'Hmm. What a life she led, with Lorraine upstairs and Medmenham downstairs, both knocking at her door at all hours, yearning to unbosom themselves.'

'It was her choice,' Norma said unkindly. 'What was she doing living there anyway? I see her as leeching off them as much as vice versa – surrounding herself with sad acts who made her feel important.'

He dropped behind her as they met people coming down. 'But surely she was a big enough name already, without that?'

'No-one's ever important enough in their own eyes,' Norma said. 'We're all insecure. It's only a matter of degree.' She climbed faster than him, and her wonderful athletic bottom bounced just ahead at eye-level, leading him ever upwards. Better than a banner with a strange device. She stopped on the landing and waited for him. 'I couldn't get my head round his kit. Those trousers and that sweater were smart and expensive, but then he tops it off with that whiskery old weasel.'

'Harris tweed,' said Slider, glad for once to be sartorially better informed than one of his minions. 'It lasts for ever, but it costs a small mortgage in the beginning. So it's of a piece with the rest.'

'Oh,' said Swilley. They pushed through the swing doors. 'Maybe that's what he spends his money on, then. If he's a protected tenant, he won't be paying much rent. He'd be a fool to move out of that flat. It makes you feel quite sorry for the Sborski character.'

'Hmm. You know, there's something not quite right about Medmenham. Something he's not being straight about.'

Norma raised her eyebrows. 'I should have thought almost everything.'

'Seriously. There's something wrong about his story.'

'Yes, he didn't seem convinced by it,' Norma agreed. 'And if he was going to see his dear old mum, why not wait till the weekend, instead of taking a day off for it?'

'Why indeed?' Slider said. 'I think I could bear to know whether he did go and see her last night. He's hiding something. Or—' he added with frustration, 'he wants us to think he is.'

'Don't start that,' Norma warned, 'or you'll drive yourself nuts.'

'But even if he is hiding something,' Slider continued, pausing at his door, 'I can't really see him as the murderer. I mean, why would he? And even if he did it, he'd hardly tie her up and rape her, would he?'

Norma looked thoughtful. 'I don't know about that bit. But if it's a motive you want, there's always jealousy.'

'Jealousy?'

'Well, he obviously adored her. She was just the type – a big redhead, a faded star – just the sort they go for. And if she preferred butch men to the sort of sensitive love he could offer – well, that type of jealousy can be worse than the other sort.'

'Interesting,' Slider said.

CHAPTER FOUR

De mortuis nihil nisi bunkum

Phoebe Agnew's parents, it seemed, were both dead, and her next of kin was her only sister, Chloe, married to a Nigel Cosworth and living in a village in Rutland.

Atherton was impressed. 'It's quite hard to live in Rutland. Turn over in bed too quickly and you end up in Leicestershire.'

The local police were breaking the news to her. Porson had held off from issuing a press statement until that was done, so the media frenzy had not yet materialised. The paragraph in the *Standard* did not name Agnew, only said that a well-known journalist had been found dead at her home in West London and that the police were treating the death as suspicious. The late editions of the tabloids were still running the ongoing search for two teenage girls who'd run away with some ponies that were going to be slaughtered ('The story that has everything,' Slider said), while the broadsheets were obsessed with another Government minister sex scandal and the Balkan crisis in about equal proportions.

'I suppose the *Grauniad* will run the obituary tomorrow,' Atherton said. 'After all, she was one of theirs. And I suppose when the details get out they'll all be panting for it. We'll have the Sundays crawling all over us. The rape angle always gets 'em.'

'Her having her hands tied doesn't make it rape,' Norma pointed out. 'She had dinner with this geezer, and they were old mates. It was probably how they liked to do it.'

'Well, said geezer is obviously the next port of call,' Slider said. 'Have you located him?'

'Josh Prentiss? Yes, he's still at work,' said Norma. 'D'you want him brought in?'

'You haven't said anything to alert him?' Slider asked.

'No, boss. I just asked for him, said it was a personal call, and got myself accidentally cut off when they put me through.'

'Good. I'd like to confront him myself. First reactions and so on. Meanwhile, I'd like someone to go over and talk to his wife, get her slant on it before she knows what he's said. Yes, all right, Norma, you can do that. Anyone who's not house-to-housing can make a start on going through her paperwork. You've got it all here now?'

'Sackloads of it,' Anderson said.

'Weeks of work,' said McLaren.

'There's one thing, guv,' Mackay said. 'You know there were two filing cabinets? Well, they were stuffed so full you could hardly get them open, all except for one drawer. In that one the files were hanging quite loosely. The desk drawers were the same – jammed full of papers. It occurs to me that maybe some big file was taken out of that one drawer by chummy.'

'Possible. Any way of knowing which one?' Slider asked. 'Labels on the drawers? Was the stuff alphabetical or anything?'

'You kidding?' Mackay said economically.

'Okay,' said Slider, 'keep that in mind as you go through. Try to classify the stuff and see if there's anything obviously missing. It may not mean anything, though. There were a lot of papers loose on the desk, as I remember, and they might have been what made the space.'

'Anyway,' Anderson said, 'if it was a sex thing, he's not going to go looking through her files, is he?'

'Probably not,' Slider said, 'but it's as well to keep an open mind.'

It hadn't snowed, but the sky had remained lowering, and its unnatural twilight had blended seamlessly with the normal onset of winter dusk. It seemed to have been dark all day, with the lights in shop and office windows making it darker by contrast. 'It's like living in Finland,' said Slider gloomily.

Atherton glanced at him. 'SAD syndrome,' he said. 'Sorry Ageing Detective.'

'Oh, thank you!'

Rush hour was winding itself up. Illuminated buses glided past like mobile fish tanks; the wet road hissed under commuter tyres, so that, with your eyes closed and a certain amount of good will, you could imagine you were on the piste. Prentiss's office was in a new block in Kensington Church Street – prime real estate these days, especially as it had a car park. Somewhere to leave a car in central London was becoming more valuable than somewhere to lay your weary head. The time would come when it would be cheaper to hire someone to drive your car round and round all day and jump in when it passed you.

When they were finally ushered into Prentiss's large and expensively furnished room, he was standing behind his desk and talking on the phone while he looked out of the large window onto the ribbon of lights, gold and ruby, that wound down to Ken High Street and up to Notting Hill. He gestured them to seats while continuing with his conversation; behaviour that Slider, perhaps unfairly, couldn't help feeling was an executive ploy for impressing them with how busy and important he was.

At last Prentiss slammed the phone down in its cradle and said, 'Sorry about that, gentlemen. What can I do for you?' He didn't sit down, suggesting that whatever they wanted, it wouldn't take him very long to sort it out and be rid of them.

He was a tall man in his fifties, and broad under his pale grey suit, which even Slider could tell was fashionable and expensive. He was not fat, but heavily built and with a certain softness around the jowls and thickness in the lines of his face that was not unattractive, given his age, merely adding to his authority. His beautifully cut hair was fair, turning grey, and brushed back all round to give him a leonine look, which went with his straight, broad nose and wide, lazy hazel eyes. Altogether he seemed a commanding and handsome man, the sort women would fall for badly. A man who could kill? Perhaps, Slider thought, if the reason and circumstances were right. He looked as though he would be single-minded in pursuit of his own ends; and whatever he did, he would prove a formidable opponent. Or at least – Slider amended to himself, wondering if there wasn't a trace of self-indulgence about the mouth and the softness – he'd always make you think he was.

Slider introduced himself and Atherton, and proffered his ID, which Prentiss waved away magnanimously. 'I'd like to speak to you about Phoebe Agnew,' he said.

The gaze sharpened. 'What about her?'

'You are a friend of hers, I understand.'

'Phoebe and I are very old friends,' he said, a faint frown developing between his brows. 'There's no secret about that. I've known her since college days. We've worked on many a fund-raiser together. Why do you ask?'

Defensive, thought Slider. 'Would you mind telling me when you saw her last?'

'I certainly would,' Prentiss said.

Slider raised his eyebrows in his mildest way. 'You have some reason for not telling me?'

'I am not going to answer any of your questions until you tell me why you're asking,' Prentiss said impatiently. 'So either come out with it, or I shall have to ask you to leave. I'm a busy man.'

'You haven't heard, then', said Slider, 'that Miss Agnew is dead?'

Prentiss didn't say anything, but he stared at Slider as if looking alone would suck information out of him.

'I'll take that as a "no",' Slider said.

'Dead?' Prentiss managed at last.

'Murdered,' said Slider.

Slowly Prentiss felt behind him and lowered himself into the high-backed leather executive chair. 'You can't be serious.'

Genuine shock, or an act? Poke him and see. 'No, I go round telling people things like that just to see how they react,' Slider said.

That roused Prentiss. 'What the devil do you mean by coming in here with that attitude? Are you trying to be funny? Do you think this is a game?'

Slider faced him down. 'I most certainly do not. A woman has been murdered, and I never find that in the least amusing. As to attitude, perhaps we can examine yours. I'd like you to answer some simple questions instead of wasting time with ridiculous power-play.'

'How dare you!'

'It's my job to dare. When did you last see Miss Agnew?'

Prentiss seemed taken aback. Perhaps no-one had spoken sharply to him since he outgrew his nanny. 'But I – I don't understand. Phoebe's dead? How? How did it happen?'

'I'd rather not go into that at the moment.'

Prentiss shook his head. 'I can't take it in. It's not possible. And surely you can't be suspecting *me* of anything?'

'I haven't got as far as suspecting anyone yet. You may have been the last person to see Miss Agnew alive. I'd like to know about that.'

'I haven't seen her for weeks!' Prentiss protested.

Slider felt Atherton beside him quiver with pleasure. 'You went to see her yesterday,' he contradicted firmly.

The lion's eyes widened. 'What makes you say that?' he asked with careful neutrality.

Slider only smiled gently. 'You went to see her yesterday,' he repeated. 'Now, would you like to tell me about it, or shall we continue this conversation elsewhere?'

With another stare, Prentiss swung the swivel chair round so that he was facing the window, and left Slider his back to look at for a long moment, while he marshalled his thoughts, perhaps, or reorganised his face. When he swung back, he was in control again, but he looked grave, and suddenly older.

'I don't know what all this is about,' he said. 'Please, tell me the truth. Phoebe was my oldest and dearest friend. Is she really dead? She was really murdered?'

'I'm afraid she was,' said Slider.

'Dear God,' said Prentiss.

Slider pressed him. 'Please answer my question, Mr Prentiss.'

He swallowed and licked his lips a few times, seeming to come to a decision. 'I did go to see her yesterday,' he admitted, 'but I don't know how you knew. It was just a spur-of-the-moment thing – I dropped in on her on my way somewhere else. I was there less than half an hour, and she was fine when I left her. I don't know any more than that.'

'Give me some times,' Slider said.

'I don't know exactly, but it would be about eight o'clock. I mean, I must have got there about eight and left about twenty, twenty-five past.'

'I see,' said Slider in troubled tones. 'You're quite sure about that?'

'I've just said I can't be exact, but that was about the time.'

'The problem is, you see,' Atherton joined in, 'that she told a witness yesterday morning that she was expecting a visitor, and we have witnesses to the fact that there was someone there with her between six-thirty and seven. Now you say you called without warning and not until eight o'clock.'

'That's right.' He paused, frowning with thought. 'It must have been someone else,' he concluded. 'She must have had another visitor.'

'Did she say, when you saw her, that she'd had a visitor?'

'No, but – well, if it wasn't me, it must have been someone else, mustn't it?'

'Where were you for the rest of the day – at work?'

'No, as it happened I was working from home yesterday. I do that sometimes to get away from the phones.'

'How did Miss Agnew seem to you?' Slider asked. 'Was she in her normal spirits?'

'I don't know – yes, I suppose so.'

'What did you do?'

'Do? We chatted about this and that. I had—' Something seemed to strike him.

'You had what?'

'I had a drink,' he said slowly.

Slider smiled inwardly. He's remembered the whisky glass, he thought. 'Anything else?'

'Phoebe had one as well,' he said in that same distant tone. And then he snapped back to normal. 'Anyway, that's all I can tell you. She was perfectly all right when I left her.'

'Where were you on your way to, when you called in?'

He hesitated. 'I was going to a meeting.'

'At that time of night?' Atherton asked.

He looked lofty. 'A ministerial meeting. The business of government is not nine-to-five. As you probably know, I am the Government's special advisor in inner city development.'

'Yes, I did know that,' Atherton said. Slider was glad at least one of them read the newspapers. 'And who were you going to see?'

'Is it any of your damn business?' Prentiss snapped, getting some spine back.

Slider took it up. 'Well, yes, I'm afraid it is. You must see that, as you were with the deceased at such a crucial time, we have to check your story. I'm sure you wouldn't expect us to do otherwise, given that Miss Agnew was your friend.'

A pause. 'I went to see Giles Freeman,' he said at last. 'Does that satisfy you? I'm sure', he added with heavy irony, 'you'll accept the word of a Secretary of State, won't you?'

The words *not on a bet* jumped to mind, but Slider went on, 'What was your relationship with Miss Agnew?'

'I've told you, we were old friends.'

'Were you lovers?'

Prentiss burst to his feet. 'Look, I'm tired of your damned impertinent questions! My best friend is dead, don't you understand that? Can't you imagine how I must feel?'

Slider was unmoved. 'Nevertheless, I have to ask you, were you lovers?'

'No, we were not!'

'You were just good friends?'

'Perhaps your imagination is so limited that you can't conceive of a man and a woman being friends, but that's not my problem!'

Slider stood up. 'Thank you for your frankness, Mr Prentiss. I do have to ask you if you will come to the station and let us take your fingerprints and a blood sample for comparison.'

'For comparison with what?' he snapped.

'We need to eliminate any traces you may have left around the flat,' Slider said evenly.

He looked shaken. 'And if I refuse?'

'Then I should wonder whether you had something to hide. I know that if my dearest friend had been murdered, I'd want to do everything I could to help bring the murderer to justice.'

'I don't need you to lecture me on the duties of friendship,' Prentiss said, but after a moment he added, 'When do you want me to come?'

'As soon as possible. Now, if you can. We can give you a lift back with us.'

'No, I'll go in my own car, thank you,' Prentiss said.

'Is that the XJS?' Atherton asked with car-spotting eagerness. 'Dark blue? Reg number something-FRN?'

'Yes,' Prentiss said, slightly puzzled. 'You like Jags?'

'I like all cars,' Atherton said.

'So, Mr Prentiss, are you coming now?' Slider asked.

'I'll follow in five or ten minutes. I've some things to clear up here first.'

When they were out in the car park, Atherton gave a soundless whistle. 'Quite a set up. The rent of that place must really hurt. Then there's the Jag – and he was wearing some serious cash. His suit looked like a Paul Smith.'

'Paul Smith?' Slider queried.

Atherton smiled kindly. 'Like Armani, only more so. Cutting-edge stuff.'

'Thank you,' Slider said humbly. 'So, bank account left aside, what did you think of him?'

'Guilty,' Atherton said. 'Lied straight off about having seen her. Nervous, evasive, falling back on the old lofty arrogance to try and get out of answering awkward questions.'

'He's an architect. Maybe he can't help being arrogant.'

'Still, given she was his best friend, shouldn't he have been more surprised and upset that she was dead?'

'Maybe he is, but doesn't show it,' Slider said.

'Don't be perverse,' said Atherton. 'You're just seeing both sides, as usual. You think he did it.'

'His story may be true. Why shouldn't she have had two visitors?'

'It'll be true just as soon as he's phoned his old friend Giles Freeman to give him the script, which is what he's doing right this minute, by the way.'

'Perhaps. But I can't stop him without arresting him.'

'Ah, yes, and he's not a person to arrest unless you're sure. Too many friends in high places.'

'What is he, a dustman?'

'Laugh it up, guv,' Atherton warned. 'It doesn't stop at Giles Freeman, you know – though that'd be bad enough. Freeman's one of the Coming Men and doesn't like anyone to get in his way. But more than that, the Freeman set has the key to Number Ten. In and out like lambs' tails.'

'You terrify me,' Slider said.

'You're a political ignoramus,' Atherton told him affectionately. 'How do you manage not to know all these things?'

'I don't get time to read the papers.'

'That's dedication.'

'Apparently Prentiss didn't either – or not the *Standard*, since that's the only place it appeared.'

'Her name wasn't mentioned in that anyway,' Atherton pointed out.

'True. But wouldn't you have thought someone would have phoned him and told him? He must know plenty of journalists, and the word must have got round by now.'

'Maybe they don't like him. All right, what now?'

'Back to the factory. With any luck, Norma will have got something from his wife that we can work with.'

In the car, Atherton said, 'What about the tying up, guv? Do you think it was a sex game that went wrong? Do you see him as the bondage, S&M type?'

'There's no point in wondering until we find out if the finger-marks and semen were his.'

'How much d'you want to bet?' Atherton said.

'I'm not a betting man,' Slider said. He glanced at his colleague sidelong, wanting to ask him about the horse-racing thing, and then deciding it was none of his business. Lots of people gambled. It wasn't a crime.

* * *

Campden Hill Square was on a hill rising steeply from the main road, with a public garden in the centre graced by massive plane trees. Fog now draped their bare branches like cobweb, and made fizzy yellow haloes round the street lamps. The steepness and the narrowness of the houses gave it a Hampsteady feel to Swilley. The houses looked unstable, as though they might topple like dominoes and send two hundred years of architecture rumbling out into the Bayswater Road in a lava flow of bricks and slates. And good riddance, in her view. She had as much respect for old London architecture as the Luftwaffe.

The door of Prentiss's house was opened by a small, slender woman. In the gloom of the unlit hall she lifted her eyes to Norma's height with darting apprehension. Her brown eyes, thick dark hair and very white skin reminded Swilley of a lemur.

'Mrs Prentiss? I'm Detective Constable Swilley of Shepherd's Bush CID. May I come in and talk to you?'

She said it in her most pleasant and unthreatening tones, but Mrs Prentiss seemed to be struck breathless and wordless. She moved her lips and made an uncompleted gesture of her hands towards her chest, as though her lungs had sprung a leak. Swilley, afraid she was going to faint, reached out and held her elbow. 'Hang on, love. Sorry if I startled you. You'd better sit down.'

But Mrs Prentiss shook her off and turned away to lean against the banister of the steep, curving staircase, which was all there was in the hall, apart from a glimpse through an open door of a dining-room. The hall was papered in dark green, a William Morris print Swilley just about remembered from her childhood. It was worn in places, and gave an air of shabby gloom that Swilley had come to associate with a certain sort of wealthy person, as if they felt themselves to be above anything as mundane as refurbishment. It was what she would have expected in a place like Campden Hill, and she had no patience with it.

The impatience now spread to Mrs Prentiss, who she felt was time-wasting, and she said firmly, 'P'raps you could do with a brandy. Tell me where it is and I'll get you one.'

Mrs Prentiss lifted her head. 'No, I'm all right now. Would you like to come upstairs to the drawing-room?' She led the way, walking with a peculiar, rigid gait and holding on to the banister carefully. 'I've put my back out,' she said, evidently feeling some explanation was due.

'Backs are bastards,' Swilley acknowledged with bare sympathy. 'How did you do it?'

'It's an old problem. Comes and goes,' said Mrs Prentiss.

The drawing-room, on the first floor, ran the full depth of the house from front to back, with folded-back doors in the middle. The double room was panelled, had two vast marble fireplaces, and was furnished with large and well-used antique pieces. The panelling had been painted in the dull greyish-green that the National Trust had vouched for as authentic eighteenth century; the drops of the chandelier had that dim lustre, like slightly soapy water, that proved them original; and even Swilley's uninformed and unappreciative glance could tell that the paintings on the walls hadn't been bought or sold in a very, very long time. There was real money here, old-established money, the sort that took no notice of fashion. This room had probably not looked much different in all the years it had existed. Swilley couldn't think how they could bear it.

Mrs Prentiss crossed to a side table on which stood a tray of decanters and glasses. 'I think I will have something. What about you?' she asked with her back to Swilley. Her voice sounded strained.

'No, thanks. Not on duty,' Swilley said.

Mrs Prentiss poured something brown – whisky or brandy – into a glass and threw back half of it, and only then turned to face her. 'Please, won't you sit down? I'm sorry I made such a fool of myself.'

'That's all right,' Swilley said, sitting down. 'I suppose I can look a bit scary.'

Mrs Prentiss lowered herself carefully onto one of the hard settles, opposite her, and sat on the edge of the seat, very upright, nursing the oversized tumbler in her lap. Everything about her seemed neat and complete, from her short-cropped, thick, shining hair to her slender, well-shod feet. Now, with the aid of light, Swilley could see she had the beautiful skin – colourless but glowing, like alabaster – that sometimes went with dark hair. Together with her small, symmetrical features it made her look unnaturally young, though she was obviously in her forties. No, not young so much as un-aged, out of step with the stream of time. A ruined child, Swilley thought unexpectedly: like something out of an old black-and-white film, the beloved but neglected only child, maintaining, in its well-stocked nursery, the exquisite manners that concealed a brooding sorrow. There was a feather of blue shadow under her eyes, as though she were very tired or unhappy.

'It isn't that,' she said. She gave Swilley a searching look. 'I suppose you've come about – about Phoebe?'

'Oh, you've heard?'

'My husband told me. He rang me this morning. I'm just so shocked.'

'You've known her a long time, haven't you?' Swilley asked.

'She was my oldest friend. We were at university together.'

'Oh, really? Which one?'

'University College, London. We were both reading English,' Mrs Prentiss said. 'We took a liking to each other the first day, when we were all milling about wondering where to go and what to do. You know what it's like – if you're lost, you always want to latch on to someone, so that at least there are two of you in the wrong place. Not that Phoebe was, for long. She always knew exactly what she should be doing. I tagged along with her, and after that we always hung around together.' She smiled with an effort. 'We used to sit on the sofa in the corner of the English Common Room in Foster Court all day, and make terrible critical comments about the other students. Phoebe was frightfully left-wing and radical, and they all seemed so conventional: tweedy sixth-formers, Young Conservative types. We thought we were being witty, but it got us a reputation. Some of the others called us *Les Tricoteuses*.' She glanced at Swilley to see if she understood the French. 'We didn't mean any harm. To tell the truth, I barely understood half the comments. But Phoebe led and I followed.'

'And how did your husband meet her?' Swilley asked. 'Through you?'

'No, not really. Josh was at UCL too, reading architecture,' she said. 'We all met through Dramsoc – the Drama Society. I wanted to act – I'd been to stage school – so I joined it straight away, and Phoebe came along just for fun. Josh joined because – well, anyone who was anyone at UCL had to be in Dramsoc.' She smiled with faint self-mockery. 'It was a hotbed of preening student *poseurs*, though of course one only realises that with hindsight. But anyway, that's how we all met. We liked the look of him. He seemed much more sophisticated than the other male students. He had an air about him, of belonging to a larger world. What he saw in us—' She shrugged. 'Phoebe was stunning, of course – that gorgeous red hair and those eyes. Intelligent, too – she was a brilliant student. And so witty – that fabulous stream of words! Everyone was in love with her. I don't know what she saw in me. I was dull and plain beside her.'

If she wanted contradiction, Swilley thought roughly, she'd come to the wrong shop. 'Who knows what friends see in each other? It just happens, doesn't it, friendship?'

'Yes, of course,' Mrs Prentiss said. 'It's a kind of love, and love is unaccountable. At any rate, Phoebe had beauty and brains, though she wasted them, in my opinion. Josh had looks, brains, charisma, *and* a private income – quite the Golden Child. The only talent I ever had was for acting, and even that's proved not to be such a huge talent. I don't suppose you remember me in *Des Res*?'

'I didn't watch it. I think I may have seen a bit of one episode, but it's not really my sort of thing.'

'It wasn't anyone's sort of thing,' Mrs Prentiss said bitterly. 'Yet I suppose in a way it was the high point of my career. High point and death knell. Everyone thinks if you get a sitcom you're made for life, but when it's a stinker like that . . .'

Swilley was not interested in a career post-mortem. 'So at university you went around as a threesome?' she prompted. 'Or was it more two and one?'

'We were a threesome. But when we graduated Phoebe sort of disappeared for a while, and that's when Josh and I started to get close.'

'Disappeared?'

'Oh, I don't mean mysteriously,' Mrs Prentiss said. 'I just mean we lost touch for a while. Three or four years, it must have been. I was in London, trying to get my career moving, and Josh was with a firm of architects, also in London, so we still saw each other. And in the end, of course, it was us who got married. When Phoebe reappeared, we became a threesome again, but with Josh and me the couple within it.'

'Do you know where she was or what she was doing in that time?'

'I imagine she was involved in some protest or other – she was always marching and demonstrating. I don't know where in particular. She didn't live anywhere permanently at that time. When she came back to London it was just the same, just lodgings, and sleeping on other people's floors. She was still a student at heart.'

A touch of disapproval? Swilley wondered. The materialist's contempt for the idealist? 'You didn't agree with her ideas?' she asked.

'Oh, I don't want you to think that,' Mrs Prentiss said hastily. 'Of course Josh and I are *convinced* socialists, always have been. But Phoebe was always much more radical than either of us. I was always willing to sign petitions and make donations, but I never went in for direct action the way she did. I was more interested in my career. And Josh had doubts about some of her pet causes. She was rather hot-headed, and sometimes she didn't examine the issues before jumping in. She was so passionate about things. She and Josh used to fight like cat and dog about some of her ideas – but it never touched their friendship. That goes too deep to be affected by a difference of opinion.'

Swilley nodded encouragingly. 'It sounds marvellous, a friendship like that. So did you see a lot of each other?'

'Oh, you know how it is,' Mrs Prentiss said, looking faintly embarrassed. 'Marriage, children, careers – there never seems to be enough time for getting together with your old friends, does there?'

Swilley declined to party. 'How often did you see her?'

'I suppose – about half a dozen times a year. But we talked on the phone a lot,' she added hastily, as though her dedication had been questioned. 'There was never any sense of being apart, however long it was.'

'When did you last see her, can you remember?'

'She saw the New Year in with us. We had a little dinner party – just family. Our children both made it home, for a wonder. Josh and me, Toby and Emma, Josh's brother Piers, and Phoebe.' She looked at Swilley. 'We counted her as family. The children used to call her Aunty Phoebe when they were little. Toby's twenty-two now and Emma's twenty. They have their own lives, of course, so we don't see so much of them. He's a company analyst for an investment firm. Emma works for a magazine group – followed Phoebe into journalism, you see. Phoebe helped her get the job. She always loved my two as if they were her own children.'

Swilley accepted all this patiently, thanking God she was

not the sort of woman who had to define her life by her husband and children. 'At your dinner party, did Phoebe seem in her usual spirits?' she asked.

Mrs Prentiss frowned in thought. 'Oh, yes, I think so. I mean, she always had a lot on her mind, but she didn't talk about anything out of the ordinary. She chatted to the children about their lives, argued with Josh about the Government, had a flaming row with Piers – but that was par for the course.'

'What was that about?'

'Oh, goodness, I can't remember. Something political – the homosexual age of consent, was it? I think it might have been that. They were always arguing – it didn't mean anything. I mean, actually, Phoebe argued with everyone.' She opened her eyes wide. 'I don't want you to think there was any malice in it. It was late in the evening and they'd both had a lot to drink so instead of just debating they started shouting at each other. But Josh told them to shut up because it was nearly midnight, and when Big Ben struck everybody kissed everybody else and it was all forgotten.'

'Did she usually drink a lot?' Swilley asked.

'Well, she *was* a journalist,' Mrs Prentiss said. 'She always was what I'd call a hard drinker, though I've never seen her drunk since our student days. I don't mean she was an alcoholic.'

'But?' Swilley prompted. Mrs Prentiss looked enquiring. 'You sounded as if you were going to say "but".'

'Oh.' A pause. 'It's just that the past few months I've thought she was drinking more than usual. She doesn't get drunk, but once or twice when she's come over we've sat talking and she's just gone on drinking, long after I've had enough and—' she gave a little, nervous laugh, 'frankly, long after I've wanted to get to my bed.'

'Do you think the heavier drinking was to do with some problem she had?'

Again the hesitation. Mrs Prentiss gazed towards the dark

window, which showed only a reflection of the lighted room, nothing beyond. 'I wondered whether she had something on her mind that she wasn't telling me about. She's been – less lively and cheerful these past few months. More thoughtful. But then,' she turned the direct, dark eyes on Swilley frankly, 'there's her age to consider. The Change is not easy for anyone.'

Too genteel, Swilley thought impatiently, to use the m-word. 'You must all be about the same age,' she suggested.

'Phoebe and I were just two months apart. My birthday's February the eighth, and hers is April the eighth. Josh was born in June, but the previous year.' She emptied her glass with a sudden movement. 'I'm talking too much, aren't I? I'm forgetting why you're here. You don't want to know all this stuff.'

'It all helps to build up the picture,' Swilley said. 'She never married?'

'No,' said Mrs Prentiss. 'It never seemed to be something she wanted. Her career and her political interests filled her life. I asked her once, when we were in our thirties, if she wasn't worried about the biological clock ticking away, if she didn't want children before it was too late, and she said, "I can't think of anything I want less than a husband and family."'

'But she had boyfriends, presumably?'

Mrs Prentiss shrugged. 'Men always wanted her – she was so beautiful and exciting. She had affairs from time to time, but they were just casual. Even when we were younger, men were just an add-on in her life. Her career was everything.'

'I'm wondering, you see, who would have had a reason to kill her,' Swilley said. 'Do you know the names of any of her recent affairs?'

'No. I don't think she's had anyone recently,' Mrs Prentiss said. 'The last one I know of was last summer, a man she saw for a couple of months. But she came to a garden party of ours in August alone, and said she'd got fed up with him, and she hasn't mentioned anyone since.' She looked straight into Swilley's eyes; she sat very still, enviably free from the human propensity to fidget, her hands folded together, back straight; revealing her distress at the murder of her friend only by a certain rigidity in her shoulders and face.

'Would she have talked about it more to your husband, perhaps? I understand he dropped in on her at her flat sometimes.'

Mrs Prentiss eyed her tautly. 'Why shouldn't he? It was a three-way friendship. There wasn't anything underhand going on. Josh and Phoebe were friends in just the same way that Phoebe and I were.'

'I wasn't suggesting anything,' Swilley said blandly, 'but it's interesting that you jumped to that conclusion.'

Mrs Prentiss flushed. 'It isn't the first time suggestions have been made. We live in a tabloid world.'

Swilley gave a faint shrug. 'At any rate, your husband was probably the last person to see her alive. He visited her yesterday evening.'

'Who told you that?' Mrs Prentiss asked sharply.

'We have a witness,' was all Swilley would give her.

'Well, your witness is wrong,' Mrs Prentiss said firmly. 'Josh was here all yesterday evening.'

'Then how do you account for his car being parked in her street?'

She didn't even break stride. 'It wasn't there yesterday, I can assure you. Your witness must have seen another Jaguar. They're not exactly rare.'

'You're quite sure your husband was here all evening?'

'All evening and all day as well. He was working from home yesterday. He never left the house at all. Surely', she said, her eyes widening, 'you can't be trying to suggest that Josh had anything to do with it? That would be ludicrous. He loved Phoebe as much as I did. Please don't say anything like that to him: it would break his heart.'

'I'm not suggesting anything,' Swilley said calmly. 'A witness said he was at the flat yesterday and we have to check that statement. You must understand that. There's no need for you to get upset.'

'My best friend is murdered, and there's no need for me to get upset?' Mrs Prentiss cried hotly. 'I suppose it's all in a day's work to you, but you can't expect the rest of us to be so completely callous. And then to accuse my husband of being the killer!' Her voice shook.

'Mrs Prentiss, if he visited her, she might have said something to him that would help us, that's all we were wondering. Nobody's accusing anybody of anything.'

'Well, if that's what you want to know, why don't you ask him?'

'Oh, we will,' said Swilley.

CHAPTER FIVE

Mallard imaginaire

The bitter cold didn't last long. By next day a normal English winter had reasserted itself: mild, overcast, with a fine prickling drizzle from a blank and whitish-grey sky.

Hollis, updating the whiteboard, said, 'You've chosen a right funny time o' year to get married, Norma. You'll want to get the plastic wedding dress and white wellies out.' He was the other detective sergeant on Slider's firm, an odd-looking man with bulging green eyes, a ragged moustache, and a strange, counter-tenor voice with a Mancunian accent. His oddities made him a successful interviewer: people were so mesmerised by his face and voice, he got things out of them without their noticing.

Norma shrugged. 'Least of my problems. I'm just hoping this murder doesn't turn out to be a sticker. I've got enough on my plate without that.'

'Lots of nice overtime to pay for all the booze we're going to drink at the reception,' Mackay pointed out.

'If you think any of you lot are getting invited you've got a screw loose,' Norma said brutally.

'If you think we'll get paid for the overtime, ditto ditto,' Hollis added.

There was a brief and electric silence. Budgetary restraints had curtailed quite a few investigations recently, and much unpaid overtime had been worked, not without grumbling.

Atherton, a folded-open newspaper in his hands, looked

up. 'Don't say that, Colin. Please don't say that. I dropped a packet yesterday on Maurice's three-legged pony. Shy Smile!' he said witheringly, with a glare at McLaren.

McLaren shrugged, his mouth full of pastry. 'I never said she'd win,' he bubbled flakily. 'I said she'd walk it.'

'So she did, while the other horses ran gaily past her,' Atherton said bitterly. 'I've got to recoup my losses. Anybody got any tips for Lingfield Park?'

'Never mind the bloody racing,' Mackay said impatiently. 'What about this overtime thing? I can't afford to work for nothing. I haven't paid for Christmas yet.'

'And I've spent a packet on timber,' said Anderson, the DIY fanatic. 'Ever since I gave the wife a nice bit of tongue-and-groove in the kitchen, she wants it all over the house.'

'Must we discuss your sex life first thing in the morning?' Swilley complained.

'Overtime or not,' Hollis said, 'if we don't clear Agnew up in short order, the press'll string us up by the goolies. It's in all the broadsheets today. She wasn't just one of theirs, remember, she was anti-us, so they'll be watching us.'

'Talk about feeding the hand that bites you,' said Atherton.

'We shouldn't have to investigate it at all,' McLaren said resentfully. 'She spent her life slinging mud at us and chumming it up with the slags we put away – serves the cow right if one of 'em turns round and offs her. Why should we care? Good riddance to bad rubbish, I say.'

Norma made fierce shushing gestures at him. Porson had come in, with Slider behind him, and was standing just inside the door, his vast eyebrows drawn down in a frown like hairy venetian blinds. 'Irregardless of who she was,' he announced into the sudden silence, 'I expect my officers to give of their best at all times. Whether the victim is male or female, black, white or tangerine, straight or as crooked as a bottle opener, it's irrevelant to me. In my department everyone goes Club Class. Do I make myself crystal?'

There was a dutiful murmur of agreement, which evidently only went skin deep with some of them. Hollis asked a question that was on everyone's mind.

'Sir, are we going to take this case all the way, or is it going up to AMIP?'

Porson didn't seem to want to be cornered. 'I've been trying to get hold of Peter Judson of AMIP to get that very point straightened into, but he's been proving a bit illusory so far. However, the ball is certainly on our plate for the time being.'

The troops stirred Hollis like a gentle breeze in a wheatfield. 'Only, I can see a scenario, sir, where we do all the work, and then AMIP jump in at the end and claim the credit.'

Porson frowned. 'Yes, well, I don't want to get bogged down on hypotheoretical points—'

'But sir—!'

'Now, you know me, lads,' Porson said firmly, lifting his hands. 'I don't mince my punches. I promise you, Mr Judson will get short shift from me if he tries to prevassilate over this one. In the mean time,' he looked round from under threatening eyebrows, 'let's just get on with the job we're paid to do. It's in the papers this morning, so we'll all be under the telescope from now on.'

'Sir, what about overtime?' said Mackay, his credit card statement writ large all over his face.

The eyebrows went up and down a bit, and then Porson said, 'I shall do everything I can on the renumeration front, I promise you that. But we've got a result to get, and I don't want superfluous attitudes undermining our professional reputation. When push comes to the bottom line, the Job is about service. I think you all know what I'm talking about.'

It made a good exit line, but it left a roomful of muttering complaint. They all knew what he was talking about. He was talking about unpaid overtime again.

'It's like everything in this bloody Job,' Mackay grumbled.

'All the money goes on show, so there's nothing left for getting on with the bloody job.'

Even Hollis, usually silent and loyal, joined in. 'Queen Anne front and a Mary Ann back. We haven't even got enough wheels.'

The troops were slumped in various dispirited attitudes around the room, like marionettes waiting for Slider to pull their strings. 'Right, boys and girls,' he said briskly, 'let's get on with it. In the case of Phoebe Agnew—'

'Slagnew,' McLaren corrected bitterly.

Slider paused. 'Look,' he said, 'I know you're sore about some of the things this woman wrote in life—'

'Like, all of them,' Anderson agreed.

'But she's dead now, and it's our job to find out who did it. So I'll say it again slowly for the hard of thinking: it doesn't matter who she was or what she did, the law is the law for everybody. Anyone who thinks differently can come and see me afterwards with his P45 in his hot little hand and we'll have a chat about it. Savvy?'

There was an unwilling mutter of agreement.

'Right,' Slider said. 'Let's go. Phoebe Agnew was forty-nine, unmarried, lived alone in a rented flat—'

'Why?' Atherton said. 'She must have been making plenty.'

'Not everyone wants to own property,' Norma argued. 'And we've been told several times that she had a mind above material comforts.'

'I'd like to know, though,' Hollis put in, 'what she did spend her money on. If she didn't have a fancy pad or a lot o' Nicole Farhi suits, it begs the question. I'd like to see a fat savings book.'

'Who wouldn't?' said Mackay.

'Okay,' Slider said, 'that's one thing to look for amongst her papers. But it's probably not important. Robbery from the person or the premises does not seem to have been the motive. She had a visitor, on the evidence of both neighbours – Lorraine Peabody and Peter Medmenham. Medmenham saw Josh Prentiss's car parked nearby at about eight p.m., and Prentiss admits he was there between eight and eight-twenty or thereabouts, but denies having been there earlier.'

'Neither witness actually saw a visitor earlier,' Hollis pointed out. 'Peabody heard music and the street door banging at around seven, and Medmenham says Agnew said the visitor was there at six forty-five and wouldn't let him in; but she might've not wanted Medmenham in the flat for some other reason.'

'True,' Slider allowed. 'But as against that there's the meal. Could Prentiss have eaten a two-course dinner in half an hour?'

'Why not?' said McLaren.

'Not everyone's in your class, Maurice,' Swilley said kindly.

'I don't see the problem,' Anderson said. 'Prentiss admits he was there at eight, and we haven't got an exact time for the murder, so what does it matter whether he was there earlier or not?'

'What matters,' Slider said, 'is finding out what happened. Prentiss lied to us at first about having been there at all. Then he admitted he was there, but only for twenty minutes. He denies having had sex with her—'

'But sex with her was had,' Atherton completed for him.

'And as an added complication, we've got two different versions of where he was on Thursday. He says he was at home until around seven forty-five, at the Agnew flat eight to eight-twenty, and at a meeting with Giles Freeman in Westminster from nine until after midnight. But his wife says he didn't leave home at all that day.'

'We know his wife was lying about some o' that, because we know he *was* at the flat,' Hollis said.

'Also,' said Swilley, 'she said Prentiss told her about the murder yesterday morning—'

'Whereas he put on a good show of not knowing about it when we interviewed him yesterday afternoon,' Atherton finished.

'Well, there's no mystery about why he'd lie,' Hollis said, 'but why would she? To protect him?'

'Obviously. She thinks he did it, throws herself into the breach.'

'Does a wife leap to the conclusion that her husband's a murderer just like that?' Slider queried. 'And if so, why would she defend him?'

'Fear,' Swilley said. 'She might be next.'

'Did she strike you as fearful?'

'Maybe. She didn't seem at ease, anyway.'

Slider moved on. 'How are you getting on with checking Prentiss's movements after he left the flat?' he asked Hollis.

'Not well,' Hollis said. 'I can't get near Giles Freeman. He's got more wrapping round him than an After Eight. The best I've managed is his press officer – and he's cagey as hell. Can't say, no comment, have to check on that. Everyone's going to "get back to me" and no-one ever gets.'

'Keep trying,' Slider said. 'Freeman's got to come across, if he doesn't want a slap for obstruction.'

'Can you slap a Secretary of State?' Atherton asked doubtfully, eyeing his mild-looking boss in his ready-made suit. In the power-dressing league he packed all the force of a digital watch battery.

'I can slap anyone,' he said heroically. 'But this whole Prentiss business is a mess. The trouble is, we know he was there and he admits he was there, but there's no reason why he shouldn't have been there. It doesn't make him the murderer, all his lies notwithstanding.'

'We've got the finger-mark on the whisky glass and the semen,' Hollis said.

'He's covered himself for the finger-mark,' Slider pointed out. 'If the semen comes back his we might have a different picture. But in the meantime, I think we'll have to at least entertain the notion that Prentiss didn't kill her. Give it tea and biscuits, if not a bed for the night. So what else have we got?'

'I'd go for Wordley,' McLaren said. 'Okay, maybe she done him a good turn, but he's got form as long as your arm.'

'He's got no form on sex crime,' Mackay demurred.

'There's always a first time,' McLaren said. 'If you ask me he's an evil psychotic bastard who'd kill anyone without a second thought, just for looking at him sideways.'

Swilley shook her head. 'You're a prat, Maurice. Would an evil psychotic bastard who raped and strangled a woman who'd done him a good turn bother to use a condom, and then throw it tidily down the lav?'

'And not check it had been flushed away properly?' Atherton added.

'Why not?' McLaren defended his brainchild. 'Barmy is barmy. You can't account for nutters.'

'By all means look into him,' Slider said generously. 'Find out where he was and how he felt about Agnew.'

'Maybe he despised her, and hated being done good to,' Atherton said. 'I know I would. But would she have cooked him a nice supper?'

'We don't know the diner was the killer,' Swilley said, and sighed. 'In fact, if Prentiss is telling the truth about seeing her alive at eight, he couldn't have been.'

'Unless the supper was eaten after Prentiss left,' said Atherton. 'People do eat later in the evening in some strata of society,' he informed her kindly. She stuck her tongue out at him.

'Or Prentiss et it,' said McLaren. 'Or there was another visitor we don't know about.'

'The meal is a blasted nuisance,' Hollis said.

'And probably not even important,' Atherton concluded. 'Can chicken be a red herring?'

'Thank you, we won't go down that byway,' Slider said hastily. 'What else?'

'Boss, I'm still not happy about Peter Medmenham,' Swilley said. 'There's something not right about his story. I think there's something he's not telling us.'

'There's probably a lot he's not telling us. What the average citizen doesn't tell us would make the Internet sag. But follow him up,' Slider said. 'Until we get confirmation on Prentiss one way or the other, there's no need to stop at him. In fact, it seems to me the only way forward is to find out exactly what was going on, that day at the flat and in Agnew's life in general. Let's get some street witness, find out if anyone was seen entering or leaving. Talk to her work colleagues – find out what she was involved in recently. Go through her papers, see if anything shows up missing. And, of course, check the pedigree of everything we've been told so far. Test every statement, follow every lead—'

'You sound like a chorus from *The Sound of Music*,' Atherton complained. 'It's still Prentiss for me.'

'Even if it is,' Slider said, 'I'd like at least to know why he did it.'

Slider came out of the washroom and bumped into Norma.

'Oh – I was just looking for you, boss.'

'Haven't you gone home?'

'Apparently not,' she said gravely. She turned and fell in with him as he walked back towards the office. 'I've managed to get hold of Medmenham's dear old white-haired mum, and guess what?'

'He didn't go down there on Thursday night?'

'In one! And she hasn't been ill – fit as a fiddle, she said. Sounded quite indignant about it. Must have made a mistake, she said. Never had a day's illness in my life, young woman, all that sort of thing. And she wasn't expecting him, either. He turned up about eleven on Friday morning and said he wanted to take her out to lunch. So she drove them both into Chelmsford and they had lunch in a restaurant and she saw him off on the train.'

'That's a long way for him to go just for one meal,' Slider said.

'She said, "He's such a good son, always thinking of little treats for me." Said it before I even asked.'

'Ah! So she thought it was odd, too.'

'I'd guess she did. Also, I checked with the *Ham and Ful* and Martin, the editor, said the notion of having a day off doesn't apply to Medmenham because although he's a regular he's a freelance, so he can choose his own hours.'

'What would we do without bad liars?' Slider smiled. 'So what, I wonder, was he up to on Thursday night? Easiest way to find out is to ask him, I suppose.'

Norma looked serious. 'If he killed Agnew, sir, he's a dangerous man.'

'Is that you worrying about me, WDC Swilley?'

'Somebody's got to, and Jim's gone home.'

'I'm not sure I like that juxtaposition,' Slider said. He walked with her through the CID room, passing her desk on the way to his office. There was a thick file on it. 'What's this?'

She blushed. 'Oh, I was passing the time between phone calls looking at menus. I still haven't sorted the caterers out.'

The file, he saw, was neatly labelled 'Wedding' in Swilley's firm black capitals; and reading no unwillingness in her posture, he opened it and found it full of orderly paperwork, everything from correspondence with the organist over the choice of music to comparative quotations for marquees.

'You're going about it like a military campaign,' he said. For some reason he found that unbearably touching.

'I don't know any other way,' she said, and for a moment her voice was uncertain, and her look as she met Slider's was horribly vulnerable. 'Tony laughs at me, but – you have to be organised about things, don't you?'

'Absolutely,' he said, feeling like Steve Martin. 'It's going to be the end of an era, you know, you getting married.' Expect earthquakes, comets, two-headed calves, he thought; the very globe would gape in wonder – but it didn't seem quite polite to say so. 'So, is it all coming together all right?'

'I wish!' She regained her old ferocity. 'I hate caterers! They start off telling you you can have anything you want, but they've got three standard menus, and you're going to end up with one of them. Whatever you say, there's a problem with it, or it's not advisable and, blow me, there's the standard menu back under your nose. It's like *Alice Through The Looking Glass.* As fast as you walk out the door, you find yourself walking back in through it.'

'So that's why food at weddings always tastes the same,' Slider marvelled. 'Those caterer's prawns, exactly like new-born baby mice. The rubber chicken.'

'I *said* no chicken,' Norma gnashed. 'I said duck. I *swear* we agreed on duck. And when the confirmation arrived, it was down as chicken. What do you do?'

'Keep fighting,' Slider said. 'It's your wedding, not theirs. But shouldn't your parents be doing all this?'

'Don't be silly, at my age? Anyway, my parents are dead.'

'What about Tony's?' She made a face. 'Don't you like them?'

'Oh, they're very nice. All his family are terribly nice – but—'

'Dull?'

'Dull?' It burst from her. 'They're like dead people without the rouge! Boss, d'you think – d'you think I'm doing the right thing?'

Slider spread his hands. 'How can I answer that? Look, you love Tony, don't you? Well, that's the only important thing. Weddings are something you do for the sake of other people. Weddings are hell, but it doesn't mean the marriage isn't right.'

She opened her eyes wide. 'Gosh, that sounded so brill! Did you just think of it?'

'It was pretty good, wasn't it?' Slider said modestly. 'Just hang in there, Norma. We're all behind you.'

'Some of you are more help than others,' Norma said, closing the file with a sigh. 'I asked Jim if he'd help me choose the wines, seeing he's such a wine buff. He said I'd need a Mâcon with the chicken. I was writing it down, when he said, "Yeah, I've watched you, you're a messy eater."'

'Atherton's a pain in the khyber sometimes,' Slider agreed. He patted her shoulder and headed for his office, but she called him back.

'Boss?' He turned, to encounter the unfamiliar vulnerable Norma again, lurking in those usually marble eyes. 'I don't suppose – I mean – are you doing anything on the sixth?'

He turned fully, surprised. 'Are you inviting *me* to your wedding? I thought you didn't want any of us there?'

'I don't want the others. They laugh at me.'

'They don't.'

'All right, not laugh, exactly, but—' She frowned, searching for the words. 'They don't think of me as a real person at all. I'm just old Norma Stits – like a cartoon character.'

Slider knew, uncomfortably, how far this was true. 'They're a bit scared of you, that's all.'

'I didn't ask them to be scared of me,' she said fiercely. 'Why can't they just accept me? I accept them, I don't judge them by their revolting bodies and nasty habits. But to them I'm a freak. Well, I won't have them at my wedding, sneering and sniggering.' Slider couldn't think of anything to say, and in his silence her ferocity drained away. She became diffident. 'Anyway, I know it's short notice and everything, but I wondered if you'd – if you'd give me away?'

He was so surprised he didn't answer at once, and she hurried on, blushing painfully.

'I mean, say no if you think it's a cheek to ask, but my Dad's dead and the nearest thing I've got is a cousin I've never liked, who's got dandruff and BO and terrible teeth. I don't want him. Tony's Dad's offered, but that doesn't seem right to me. It ought to be someone of mine. And you – well – you're practically like family. In a sort of way. I mean . . .'

He had to say something to check this painful embarrassment. 'I always knew there was some reason you never made a pass at me,' he said, smiling slowly. 'I assumed it was respect for my rank, but now I see it's because you thought of me as a different generation.' Now she smiled too, shyly. 'I'd be honoured to do it. Thank you for asking me.'

'Thank you, boss,' she said, and, hugely daring, darted a kiss at his cheek.

'And now you'd better go home,' he said, mock-sternly, because someone had to get them out of this before they both burst into tears.

'Right, boss.' She sat abruptly at her desk and bent her head, shuffling her papers together in a terminal sort of way.

Slider marched himself off into his office.

Mâcon, indeed!

CHAPTER SIX

Things can only get bitter

Peter Medmenham opened the door to Slider and said without a great deal of surprise, 'Oh, it's you.'

'You know why I'm here?' Slider said sternly.

'Yes. My mother rang me.' He managed to scrape up a bit of indignation. 'You had no right to call her without my permission.'

'Don't be silly, of course we did,' Slider said, and Medmenham's balloon collapsed. 'And we wouldn't have had to bother her if you hadn't lied to us in the first place.'

Now he only looked miserable. 'You'd better come in,' he sighed, and stepped back.

Medmenham's flat was a very different affair from either of the other two. A great deal of money and thought had obviously gone into it. The narrow passageway beyond the front door ought, Slider knew from other houses like this, to have been dark and damp-smelling. In fact it was brightly lit from sunken halogen lamps in the ceiling and smelled faintly of pot-pourri. The walls were white, and the single piece of furniture in view was a delicate mahogany side table of breathtaking simplicity and elegance – Georgian, Slider thought – on which stood a narrow glass vase containing a single scarlet gerbera, spiky and stunning against the white wall.

Medmenham led the way past two closed doors – bedroom and bathroom, presumably – to the room at the back.

This was the living room, with the kitchen beyond in a new glass-roofed extension, divided from the sitting-room, American style, only by a counter. The kitchen was blisteringly modern, all pale ash and chrome, with a wicker-fronted drawer stack, a lot of expensive stainless-steel equipment on overhead racks, and a huge stone jar filled with dried rushes on the floor by the door.

Everything was tidy and put away, except that on the counter stood a large Gordon's bottle and a heavy-bottomed cut-crystal glass, and a small chopping-board with half a lemon and a short knife lying on it.

The sitting-room was decorated in the sort of spare, minimalist style that depended on a very high quality of workmanship to make it succeed. Again the walls were white, and sported a series of black-and-white eighteenth-century political cartoons in huge white mounts and thin gold frames. The polished floorboards were covered in the centre with a large square carpet, very thick and blackberry purple. There was an enormous sofa covered in coarse white material, with lavender-coloured scatter cushions, and a heavy glass coffee table on which stood a single purple orchid in another tall skinny glass. The only other chair was an expensive-looking leather recliner which faced the state-of-the-art television set in the corner. Behind the TV was a cabinet which seemed to have been specially designed to house four video recorders – for his job as reviewer, Slider supposed. Evidently he didn't watch Channel 5 – but then, who did?

'You've really put some work into your flat, haven't you?' Slider said in admiring tones.

Medmenham seemed pleased. 'Do you like it?'

'You obviously have very good taste,' Slider said. 'But I wonder you should do so much when you don't own it. I mean, I suppose you must have had to pay for all the building work yourself?'

'Goodness, you don't think Sborksi would *ever* put his

hand in his pocket? I know,' he said, looking round, 'it's probably a bit foolish of me, but the rent is so low, and I'm comfortable here, and my surroundings are so important to me. Things grate, don't you find, if they're not *just so*? And I never intended to move again, so what did it matter?'

'You never intended – does that mean you intend now?'

Medmenham waved him graciously to the sofa, and stood facing him, clasping his hands together as though he were going to recite. 'I don't know. All this business – poor Phoebe – it's so unsettling. I wonder if I'll be able to bear it here now, thinking of her being – you know – up there.' He rolled his eyes at the ceiling. 'And, of course, not having her there to talk to will make such a difference. We always planned to grow old together.'

The lighting in the room came from artfully placed lamps and was designed to be flattering, but even so Slider could see the age and weariness that had come to the plump face. Medmenham had bags under his eyes that even a BA stewardess would have rejected as cabin luggage.

'You were very fond of her?' Slider suggested.

'I thought I'd made *that* clear,' said Medmenham.

'I thought you'd made a lot of things clear, until it turned out you'd been lying,' Slider said sternly.

He made a fluttery movement of his hands. 'Oh, Lord, don't make a big thing of it! I'm not up to it. I can't tell you what a state I've been in these last few days! Look, would you like a snort? Frankly, I'm not going to get through the next half hour without a drinkette. Gin and ton?'

Slider accepted, and having handed him a gin and tonic very nearly large enough to wash in, Medmenham took his own replenished glass and retired to the leather recliner, where he tucked one foot under him girlishly, took a good mouthful, swallowed, and shuddered.

'That's better! Not', he added firmly, 'that I want you to think I'm a boozer. Normally it's moderation in all things, but things aren't normal, are they? And frankly, dear, it's ruinous to the complexion. Oh, I know, don't look! I must look shocking. I've been weeping like a waterfall, and no sleep; but I just haven't had the heart to put any slap on. I've said to Phoebe many a time, you and I just can't go on drinking at our age the way we used to – well, you know what journalists are like, first cousin to a bottomless pit as far as alcohol's concerned; but when you're young you burn it off, don't you? And just lately darling Feeb's been hitting the White Horse a bit hard. I mean, I said, you're not Lester Piggott, darling! But the past few weeks it's been sip, sip, sip like a dowager. So depressing! Not that she can't hold it. Always a perfect gentleman. But you can't punish yourself like that and get away with it for ever.'

This was a promising vein, but Slider had other seams to mine first. 'Let's get back to what you were doing on Thursday evening,' he said.

Medmenham raised his glass to his lips defensively. 'Oh, must we? Look, I know I told a teensy little porkie pie, but, honestly, it's nothing to do with all this – nothing to do with poor darling Feeb. It's purely my personal life, which is so utterly ghastly at the moment I wouldn't trouble anyone with it. I promise you I know nothing about what happened upstairs, other than what I've told you.'

'You have to understand, Mr Medmenham, that I have to verify every statement that's made to me. When people tell me lies I have to assume they've got something to hide. Especially when they can't be accounted for at the time of the crime.'

'Well, you can't suspect me of murder,' he said, almost gaily, and then, looking shocked. 'You don't? No, really, look at me! I'm the human equivalent of a cosy eiderdown. Born a duvet and I'll die a duvet! Even on stage I'd never cut it as First Murderer. *Please* tell me you don't think I'm capable of such a horrible thing!'

'I think you capable of anything you put your mind to,' Slider said seriously, and he saw his words give Medmenham pause. He drank, put his glass down on the counter top and folded his hands together in his lap.

'What do you want to know?' he asked without affectation.

'How much of what you told me yesterday was true? Did you see Miss Agnew at six forty-five? Did she say she had a visitor?'

'Oh, yes, all that was true.'

'But you didn't see the visitor? Or hear his voice?'

'No. There was music playing in the background. Quietly. Vivaldi, I think.'

'So she might have been alone.'

'But then why wouldn't she have asked me in?' Medmenham looked suddenly shrewd. 'Oh, you think I'm a chattering nuisance and she might just want to be rid of me? But I assure you, she was quite capable of telling me she wanted to be alone, and often did. We had a very frank relationship. "Sorry, Peter darling, things to do. Bog off, sweetheart." No, it wasn't that. There was someone else in there: you can *feel*, can't you, when a house is empty? You just *know*. And the way she opened the door only a little bit and stood there in the gap: she didn't want me to see who it was.'

'Why do you suppose she would do that? Was she usually secretive about her visitors?'

'Well—' He thought. 'Not *secretive*. She didn't go into graphic detail about her sex life, and I didn't ask. But she didn't go out of her way to hide the fact when she had visitors.'

'So if it was Josh Prentiss, for instance—'

'Well, why should she try and hide Josh from me?' he said. 'I've known Josh for yonks.'

'It was you who told me that's who was visiting her,' Slider said patiently.

Medmenham put a hand to his cheek. 'You're right! I did say that. Because I saw his car outside. It doesn't make sense, does it?'

'That's what I was thinking.'

He looked at Slider and went a bit pink. 'You think I'm lying? But I'm not! It all happened exactly as I told you, up to that point; and I did see his car in the street. It's only about where I went afterwards that I didn't tell the truth.'

'Well, suppose you tell me the truth now, and we'll see how we get on,' Slider suggested kindly.

'Oh, we can be sarcastic when we try!' Medmenham complained. 'Well, look, I'll tell you, since you make such a thing about it, but it's very painful for me, and I hope you won't repeat it to anyone. Can I trust you to be discreet?'

'If it has nothing to do with the case, I will do my very best,' Slider said.

Medmenham sighed. 'And I suppose that's all I'll get out of you. You're very *hard*, you know. Well, after I'd been up to see Phoebe and she said she wasn't coming down, I came back down here and thought I'd just hole in for the night and watch some television. I'd put the tape in for *Red Slayer*, but I thought I ought to watch that new thing on the Beeb, *Windermere*, though frankly, love, it sounded like the usual old drivel – ess and vee lightly wrapped in panoramic views. So predictable! It would never have got made at all if it hadn't been set in the Lake District. Dear old Auntie's regional promotion plan! I don't know why they don't just give them a Tourist Board grant and be done with it. Well, long story short,' he responded to Slider's look, 'I was just about to change into my kimono and slippers when the phone rang.' He stopped.

'Please,' Slider said, 'the suspense is killing me.'

Medmenham sighed. 'I suppose I've got to tell you. All right, it was Piers.'

'Peers?' With all the Government connections of Josh Prentiss in the background, Slider's mind offered him a section of the House of Lords.

'My *friend*.' He gave it an emphasis to show he was talking about more than friendship. 'And, to be perfectly frank and honest, Josh's brother.'

Slider got the spelling at last. 'Oh, I see! Piers Prentiss?'

'Do you know him?'

'Never met him.'

'I wish I never had. The heartache that little wrecker's given me!'

'How did you know him?'

'Oh, I met him through Phoebe and Josh, of course. I've been to the Prentisses' house to parties and things. Sometimes escorted Phoebe when they wanted the numbers kept even. Always fancied him, but we didn't get together until a couple of months had gone by. Then it was a case of why didn't we do this before? We were made for each other – or at least I thought so. Not that it's been a bed of roses. He's not the easiest man to get on with, let me tell you! But I thought we were settled for life. Then about two months ago, or a bit more, he started acting strangely. Blowing hot and cold. Not phoning. Breaking dates. I thought, hello, I thought – because we've been there before, dear, believe you me! Our life has not been a garden path, by any means. No, I thought, it's got a little something on the side, that's what's going on here! Well, I let it go, because these things happen, and least said, soonest back under the duvet. I thought it would burn itself out and we'd be all right again. That's usually the best way. But then came this phone call. Out of the blue. Not so much as a "brace yourself, love."'

'He was breaking it off?' Slider asked, hoping to move the story on.

'Breaking it off? I'd like to break his off!' Medmenham cried with tiny rage. 'And doing it like that, the little bitch, on the phone! I *had* been expecting to be seeing him, you see. We *were* supposed to've spent Sunday together. But then he phoned me on Wednesday to say he had to go on a collecting trip up north somewhere – a country house sale on Monday, with the viewing on Sunday. He's in the antiques trade, you see. Well, that rang true. Sunday and Monday are the days most antiques shops shut. But he said he was going up on the Saturday night so as to get to the viewing early and put some reserves on, and that made me a bit suspicious, because he'd never done that before. Still, I didn't say anything. And then he phones me at seven o'clock on Thursday to say it's all over and he's got someone else and it's the real thing this time. He hadn't been going to go away at all – he planned to spend the weekend with the new one. They'd arranged it Wednesday night – he'd been there, the new one, spent all day Thursday with him, and he'd just gone, so Piers had got straight on to me to tell me it was all over.' He stopped a moment. 'I'm sorry, I'll have to have another drinky. It makes me shake just thinking about it. What about yours?'

Slider declined, and watched as Medmenham got up and mixed himself another G and T. Had it not been Josh Prentiss's brother, he would have been impatient with all this detail, but as it was, he was listening with mind agog. If Piers had done him wrong and it was Phoebe who'd brought them together in the first place and Phoebe was making the beast with two backs with Josh – well, could that add up to enough to make Medmenham snap? Except that the rape still seemed a bit unlikely.

Medmenham returned with his drink, but didn't sit down. He wandered about restlessly, sipping, touching things. Slider prompted him. 'So Piers told you it was all over. What next?'

'Naturally I argued with him. Told him this new thing was a flash in the pan. He says he's known him a while, but it was just ordinary acquaintance before – well, I thought, tell that to the marines! I know the symptoms. I've been dumped on before, believe you me! Anyway, it's obvious that Piers has just been dazzled by a young turk in a Donna Karan suit and Gucci shoes. So different from tweedy old *moi*. He wouldn't say who it was, but he went on and on about how wonderful he was in frankly tedious detail. I said why all the secrecy? Tell me his name. And he said the new one wanted it kept secret, forbade him to tell anyone. I said, love, if he's ashamed of you, but he said no, it was that his career was at a delicate stage. He's going to be frightfully important, and when he is, he'll come out in the open about the relationship.' Medmenham sniffed. 'Piers is such an innocent, he shouldn't be let out alone. One can see why he's gone doo-lally over this power dresser. What *he* sees in Piers is another matter! Seal my lips for *that*, dear, because nobody likes a bitch. But anyway, I wasn't taking it lying down, pardon the pun, because I just *know* it isn't going to work and I'd like to save Piers heartache if I can, despite the way he's treated me, so I said, "Is he with you now?" and Piers said he'd just left. So I said, "Then let me come up and see you. You owe me that, at least, to tell me to my face." Because of course I thought if I could see him I could talk him round. He argued a bit, but I wore him down. I think he was quite glad really, because he was never the slightest use at being on his own, Piers wasn't. I think one should be a world unto oneself. I'm happy as a lark with my own company. But Piers has to be with someone every minute. I suppose that's what the problem was with *us*, because I wasn't there enough of the time. Not that we couldn't have worked that out. Anyway, after a bit he said all right, I could come if I wanted but it wouldn't make any difference. So I went.'

'Went where?' Slider asked.

'To see *Piers*,' Medmenham said irritably, and then, 'Oh, you mean *where*? Well, Chelmsford, of course. He's got the shop there, and a dear little cottage, very *bijou*, stuffed with the most *precious* things. I mean, Chelmsford's Outer Mongolia as far as I'm concerned, anything beyond the Angel Islington just doesn't *exist* for me, but he finds it convenient and it's only forty minutes on the train, and when he wants to stay in London he's got a room at

Josh and Noni's, if he's not with me – or someone else, the slut, as I found out to my cost! But don't let's think about that. So anyway, I caught the 9.02, just like I told you – you see, I did tell you the truth, except for some bits that didn't matter – and he met me at the station. We went to a wine bar – what? Oh, Ramblers, it's called. We had a spot of manjare and some drinkie-poos and then we went back to the cottage. I thought everything was all right again, but in the morning, just when I was squeezing the oranges for breakfast, he said as calm as you like that it was still over and that now he'd told me to my face there'd be no call for us to meet again.'

'That must have been upsetting for you,' Slider said mildly. Medmenham seemed to be trembling with rage.

'Upsetting? He'd played me for a complete patsy! I felt like a – well, I felt *used*! I threw the orange juice at him, that's how mad I was – and I'm not a throwing person usually, too conscious of the mess. So it ended up with a flaming row, and I marched out of there and slammed the door. It was dreadful,' he confided, 'because when I'd calmed down a bit I realised I'd have to walk to the station, and with my feet that was no joke! But then I saw a bus coming with Danbury on the front, and I thought of the dear old Aged P, and flagged it down. Quite an adventure, because I never go on buses – well, one doesn't, does one? Normally the Mum collects me from the station and takes me back – she's a marvel, seventy-nine and still driving! She was a bit startled when I turned up, but I said I wanted to take her to lunch, and that way she drove us into Chelmsford and I ended up being dropped at the station, so my poor old feet didn't take the punishment.'

'Didn't she ask you why you'd suddenly appeared?' Slider asked.

'You don't know the Mum. Naturally she suspected I'd flown to her arms from some little *crise* or other, but she'd never ask. Just took it in her stride. She was always wonderful like that. When I first came out to them, my parents, she said she'd always suspected and she loved me anyway, and she talked to Dad like a Dutch uncle to make him accept it – though I don't think he ever really came to terms. Well, fathers don't, do they? Have you got any kiddies, love? I can tell you're married.'

Slider wasn't going to be drawn. 'So you had lunch with your mother and got her to take you to the station?'

He shrugged. 'Like I said. I brooded all the way down on the train, and then when I got to Liverpool Street I picked up the *Standard* and there I saw the para and found out about poor darling Feeb. Well, you can imagine! I was so shocked I thought I'd faint.'

'And when you found out, what was the first thing that went through your head? Who did you think must have done it?'

'Well,' he said, shaking his blue head reluctantly, 'just for a teensy-weensy instant I thought it might have been Josh, because I knew he'd been there – and also, I suppose, because he was Piers's brother and just then I was willing to believe anything bad about a Prentiss. But then I couldn't think of any reason why he'd want to kill her – I mean, they were old, old friends – so I thought it must have been one of those drug addict loonies, like I said to you, breaking in at random. I mean, no-one's safe now, are they?'

'But apart from not being able to think of a motive,' Slider pursued with interest, 'you didn't think Prentiss wasn't capable of such a thing?'

'Oh, I'd think he was capable of it all right,' Medmenham said easily. 'He's a very ruthless man when it comes to getting his own way. I could quite see him murdering someone if they'd become inconvenient, and not thinking twice about it. But he'd do it cleverly and I bet he'd never get caught. But he and Phoebe were very close, so I put it out of my mind.'

'Were they lovers?'

He hesitated. 'D'you know, I don't really know? She never said so one way or the other. Maybe they had been at one time – no, I really couldn't say. It was funny really, they were more like—' He paused, thinking it out. 'I don't know, brothers or something. Or an old married couple. Very close, but almost too close for sex, you know? But then, I've always had my doubts about Josh. He's always played the great butch omi-about-town, but there's just something about him – I wouldn't be surprised if he wasn't a closet queen. Ooh, slap my wrist for gossiping! Still, they say it's in the genes, don't they, and there's Piers to take into consideration.'

Slider thought of the softness he had suspected in Prentiss – a hint of petulance and self-indulgence, it had come across to him. Medmenham seemed to have picked up on the same thing. And it was interesting that he had said that Josh and Phoebe were like brothers, rather than brother and sister.

Well, if Medmenham's story was true, it looked as though he could be ruled out as the murderer, and that was one strand untangled. *If* it was true – and if Prentiss's story was true – and if they weren't in it together. That was enough ifs to make a cult movie.

'I shall have to take steps to verify your story,' he said. 'Which means I shall have to speak to Piers Prentiss.' Medmenham looked dismayed. 'But if he agrees with what you've said, there's no reason why anyone else should know anything about it.'

'Thank you,' Medmenham said a little stiffly. 'The whole episode was horribly humiliating to me. Of course, we're no stranger to pain of that sort, but, well, one doesn't court it, does one? And then,' he seemed to remember suddenly, and sagged a little, 'the way it ended, with darling Feeb being killed . . . I'd like to put it completely behind me as soon as possible.'

'One more thing,' Slider said, 'you said that she had been drinking heavily just recently. Did you get the impression she was worried about something?'

'Definitely,' he said, sitting up straighter. 'She had something on her mind that was gnawing at her, that's what I thought.'

'Did she tell you what it was? Hint at it in any way?'

'No, not a dickie. I said many a time, tell all, heart face, you'll feel better. Don't bottle it up. But she just laughed and said there was nothing wrong and changed the subject. But she was *brooding*, that's what. Something was preying on her mind, and if she'd *only* trusted her Uncle Peter,' he mourned, 'all might have been well.'

CHAPTER SEVEN

Britannia waives the rules

Slider was in the hall putting on his coat when the flap on the letter-box lifted and vomited a pack of letters onto the floor, like a heron regurgitating fish. He picked them up and shuffled through them. A few minutes later, wondering why he hadn't left, Joanna came out from the kitchen and found him standing there, motionless. The printed heading on the paper held in his hand was IN THE DIVORCE REGISTRY. His head was bent, the thin sunlight coming in through the glass panel of the front door back-lighting his hair in a pre-Raphaelite way. Not for the first time, she wished she could paint.

She leaned gently against him from behind, and he lifted the paper to show her.

'It's the Decree Absolute,' he said.

'So I see.' He said nothing more, only stood there like a sad lamppost, and after a bit she said, 'How do you feel about it?'

'I don't know. Strange.' He hauled a great sigh up from his socks and said, 'It's so bald. The End. Sixteen years of marriage.' He turned to face her and she slipped her arms round him inside his coat. 'I'm a free man,' he said, trying to sound glad about it.

'This is my dangerous moment,' she said lightly. 'Any minute now you'll realise that free means you don't have to settle for me either, and off you'll flit like a butterfly to more exotic flowers.'

'Yes, you should worry,' he advised her. 'I'm such a fickle man.'

'It's all right to be upset,' she mentioned. 'I won't be offended.'

He rested his face against her hair and closed his eyes briefly. It was a gesture that needed no thought. She was his mate now, she was home, and everything he did with her or without her took place in the context of her, automatically, as once it had – though without the same pleasure – in the context of Irene. She was now *selbstverständlich*. And because of that, this piece of paper didn't have the impact it might otherwise have had. He didn't feel upset, he just felt strange. And guilty, of course, but that was endemic. And he couldn't help wondering how Irene would be feeling, receiving her copy of this same document, and opening the envelope in Ernie Newman's house, perhaps in her predecessor's kitchen, waiting for her predecessor's electric kettle to boil.

Joanna squeezed him a little tighter, reading his thoughts effortlessly. 'You ought to ring her, perhaps? It must be a hard moment for her, whatever the circumstances.'

He kissed her gratefully. 'Yes. I will. When I get to work.'

Not here, not from his-and-Joanna's phone. Joanna smiled inwardly. That was male tact. There were so many things he thought she minded, out of some elderly and elaborate code of chivalry he had learned young and never forgotten; and they were hardly ever the things that she really did mind, she who had been breadwinner and decision-maker to herself all her adult life, husband in her own household, without the luxury of a Norman Rockwell aproned wife's sensibilities.

'Yes, do that,' she said in benison. 'I'll see you tonight.'

At the door he turned. 'Have lunch with me?' He knew she was not working.

And she knew he had a murder case. 'Will you have time?'

'For you, always.'

'All right. I'll ring you later and check,' she said, hedging his bets.

The phone was ringing as he reached his desk. It was Freddie Cameron.

'You're up early,' Slider said, switching the receiver from hand to hand as he shed his coat. It was good navy wool, but so old it had gone almost white along the seams. There were men who cared about overcoats and men who didn't, and that was just the way it was.

'I've done your post, old dear.'

'What, this morning? Don't you ever sleep?'

'No, yesterday. *Servissimo*. I'm up to my ears in bodies and I'm going to be in court for the next couple of days, so I thought I'd better put in a bit of overtime. Martha was not amused.'

'I should think not. That way lies divorce and madness.'

'Anyway, I put your report in the mail last night,' Freddie said, with a shrug in the intonation, 'and I've called to give you the edited highlights. Talking of which, I see you've been getting big coverage in the papers.'

'Not me personally.'

'All the broadsheets have had fulsome obits on the Agnew,' Freddie said. 'Career appraisals. Highlights of her campaigns as a mercenary in the justice war. Farewells from journalists and editors. Personal tributes from showbiz personalities and Queen's Counsels – which are much the same thing, of course. An endorsement from Ronnie Biggs—'

'Eh?'

'Just testing if you were listening. They don't seem to have published the fine details of the murder, though, which shows extraordinary restraint.'

'An appeal was made to keep them out,' Slider said, 'but I think they're showing solidarity because she was one of their own, rather than for Mr Porson's sweet sake. But if we don't get home sharpish with the streaky rashers, they'll forget their promises soon enough.'

'Is the case still with you or is AMIP taking it?'

'All AMIP's taking at the moment is aspirin.'

'Ah, the 'flu epidemic.'

'They flew, they have flown. It's down to me and my little chums. So, tell me, was it strangulation?'

'It was indeed. Strangulation with some force. The hyoid was fractured, and there was considerable damage to the thyroid and cricoid cartilages with severe localised bruising and extensive petechiae above the ligature.'

'Any idea what that was?'

'A narrow band of material. Probably a tie, possibly a folded scarf – something of that sort.'

'Pair of stockings?'

Cameron chuckled. 'Tights, dear boy! A good feminist would never wear stockings. And, no, the texture was wrong for tights. The material was smooth. I'd plump for the tie, if you put a gun to my head. Nicely available, for one thing. Carry it in – and out – round your neck.'

'If you could get the knot undone,' Slider said.

'There was no knot,' Freddie said. 'The killer relied on strength and determination. And there were some other points of interest. The strangulation was carried out from behind, which was not what you'd expect from the position of the corpse.'

'Are you sure?' Slider said. 'No, silly question, of course you are.'

'You can see by the comparative depth of the bruising,' Freddie explained. 'The ligature was placed round the neck, crossed over at the back and pulled tight. Now, if the ends had been pulled by someone standing in front of her, the crossed part would have dug into the neck at the back, but in fact the pressure is all at the front. So that means . . .' He paused, inviting comprehension.

'Yes, I see,' said Slider. 'It's pretty difficult to strangle someone from behind when they're lying on their back on the bed.'

'Ten points,' Freddie awarded him approvingly. 'And when you add the intriguing little fact that the wrists were tied after death—'

'What?'

'Dead men don't mark,' said Freddie. 'The ligature round the wrist was tight, but there was no bruising. However, from the distribution of hypostasis, she was put into the position we found her in immediately.'

'So she was strangled somewhere else in the room,' Slider said, 'and then put on the bed and tied to the bedhead to make it look like a sexual assault?'

'That's a viable hypothesis,' Cameron said. 'There was, in fact, semen in the vagina, but there's no bruising or any other sign of forcible penetration. I've sent a sample off to be typed, as well as the sample from the condom. Though I doubt we'll get much from the condom – too dilute.'

'We don't know', Slider said, 'that they are from the same person.'

'I don't like to contemplate that scenario,' Cameron said. 'But we have a bonus ball: there was some tissue under the nails of the left hand. She managed to scratch her assailant: not deeply, just a surface abrasion, but enough to give us a tiny sample. I've sent that off to the genetic boys, too. Let's hope it matches one or other semen sample.'

'Let's definitely hope that – and further that it matches Prentiss,' Slider said, 'otherwise it starts getting complicated. Oh – was the sexual penetration post-mortem?'

'No way of telling,' Freddie said. 'Not a nice thought, that.'

'No,' said Slider. 'Not that it would have mattered to her once she was dead.'

'True. Still, at least the condemned woman ate a hearty dinner,' Cameron went on, 'with wine and spirits. I've secured the stomach with contents, in case you want it analysed.'

'I can pretty well tell from the kitchen what she ate,' Slider said. 'There's no reason to think she was poisoned or drugged?'

'Nothing in the pathology, though there are plenty of things that don't show up unless you look for them. So unless you want me to go through the whole pharmacopoeia from Astra to Zeneca—'

'No, not at this point.'

'She seems to have ingested a large quantity of alcohol, which might have made her easier to strangle. D'you want a blood test for the volume?'

'Hold off on that for the moment. I need the semen and tissue typed, and we've got to think about budget.'

'Sooner you than me,' Cameron said. 'Well, I must away. I've two to do at Guy's, before the Old Bailey.'

'Complicated case?'

'That fire in Hendon. Arson stroke murder. Four bodies and a dispute over identity. A pathologist's life is not a nappy one. Let me know if there's anything else you want.'

'A holiday in the sun,' said Slider promptly.

'A holiday? Ah, yes, I had one of those once,' said Freddie.

He heard Swilley's voice in the outer office, saying good morning to Anderson, who was first in. Anderson hardly spared time for a hello before offering yet again to take her wedding photos.

'You don't want to have anything to do with those professionals,' he said earnestly. 'They charge a bloody fortune. A century plus just to turn up, and a tenner a time for the pix. And half of 'em are in league with villains. They give the tip-off about when the house'll be empty, and a gang goes in and cleans out all your wedding presents.'

'Yeah, thanks, Tony, but I really think—'

'Straight up! There's this snout of mine, he used to be in on a shutter scam before he went straight, told me all the wrinkles. He was the fence. Made a fortune. Toasters, microwaves, food mixers—'

'An electric fence, then?'

'You gotta use your loaf, Norm,' Anderson urged. 'I'll do you a real nice job. Did I ever show you my sister's wedding pix? I did this thing off the top of a ladder, with her on the grass and her dress spread out all round her. She looked just like a flower—'

Slider had had enough. He went out to rescue Swilley, and, basking in her look of gratitude, told her about his visit to Medmenham.

'Well, that sounds a bit more like it,' she said.

'Yes, plenty of free-flowing detail to comfort a policeman's doubts. I would still like some confirmation from someone outside the triangle, though. This wine bar they went to – Ramblers. It would be nice if anyone there remembered our couple and could put an approximate time on it. It would be nice to have someone in the case whose word we could trust.'

'Okay, boss, I'll get on to it. D'you want me to chase up Piers Prentiss?'

'No, leave him be. I want Medmenham's story checked first. If it's okay, there's probably no need to touch Prentiss junior.'

Back in his office, he took a moment before he plunged into the rest of the day's work to call Irene. The phone was picked up at the first ring.

'What were you doing, crouching over it?' he asked.

'I was just passing when it rang,' she said. She sounded defensive.

'Are you all right? I got something in the post today.'

'Yes. So did I.'

A silence. 'How do you feel about it?' Slider asked awkwardly.

'How do you think I feel?'

Something in her voice warned him. 'Have you been crying?'

'What if I have? It's a big thing, after all these years. Someone ought to feel something.'

'I'm sorry too,' he said. 'It was never what I . . .' He couldn't say wanted. '. . . anticipated. When I married you, I really thought it was for good. But things change.'

'*People* change,' she said, as though that were something else.

'Yes. We're both different now,' he said carefully. 'I just phoned to see if you were all right.'

'That was nice of you.' He couldn't tell if she was being ironic or not.

'I do care about you, you know,' he said. 'I want you to be happy. And also—' This was more delicate territory. 'Well, I phoned because I wanted to say thanks. That I appreciate all you did for me all those years. I wanted to say – I'm not sorry that we married.'

'Yes,' she said, and the line vibrated with perilous emotions. 'Me, too. Thanks for saying that. We had some good times, didn't we, Bill?'

'We did,' he said, though for the moment he couldn't think what they were. Except the children. They were definitely a good thing. 'Will you tell the children?' he asked.

'I suppose so. When they get back from school. I think they'll take it all right. I mean, they must know it was about due.'

'Do you think', he asked diffidently, 'it would be a good idea if you and I were to take them out somewhere together next weekend? Just the four of us. If I can get the time off.'

'To celebrate?' Irene said, with a twist of lemon.

'Of course not to celebrate,' he said. 'To reassure them. To show we can still be all right together, even though – well, you know. What do you think?'

'It might be nice,' she said cautiously. 'But I won't say anything to them yet, in case you can't get the time. I wouldn't want them to be disappointed.'

If she had learned one thing in the years she had been a policeman's wife, it was not to plan ahead.

Atherton came in, looking as if he had been out on the tiles.

'Late night?' Slider asked casually.

'No, early. Early, early hours.'

His breath had the vinous sting of heavy consumption. Slider thought if he took a breathalyser test right now his drive in to work might take on a whole different complexion.

'Nice to be able to afford debauchery,' Slider said.

'You have yours laid on at home,' said Atherton.

Slider wasn't sure what he meant by that. Had the dog been up to his old tricks? But he didn't feel up to pursuing it. 'I've had Freddie Cameron on the phone,' he said, and passed on Freddie's report.

Atherton's greyness was shed instantly. Alert, eyes wide, he sat on Slider's window-sill and crossed his arms into thinking position. 'Wait a minute, wait a minute, this is weird! He has sex with her, using a condom, because he's a careful boy – or she's a careful girl – and chucks the debris down the lav, presumably as per usual habit; relaxed enough about it anyway not to check that the corpus voluptae is safely off on its journey to the sea. Then he has sex with her again, without precautions. Then gets her drunk, strangles her, and arranges her on the bed to make it look like a stranger-rape, despite the fact that his semen is inside her, ready to finger him as the rapist.'

'It doesn't make sense,' Slider agreed, 'but we don't know what order things happened in. Maybe it was sex with condom, then more drinks, then unprotected sex because they or she were merry enough not to care.'

'Then strangulation,' Atherton acknowledged, 'but why the rape scenario?'

'Not thinking clearly. If he was drunk too . . .'

'But if he was trying to make it look like a random rapist, he ought to have faked a break-in as well. A stranger wouldn't have known that you could slip that lock.'

'He would if he tried,' Slider said.

'Yes, but Prentiss wouldn't know that we'd realise that. If someone's faking something they daren't get that subtle, in case the other side misses it.'

'I'll just sit here and let you argue yourself into a corner,' Slider said. 'There are yet other scenarios.'

'Sell me one,' Atherton invited.

'Sex with condom, drinks, quarrel or whatever, strangulation, and then bondage sex with the corpse, because that's what he really likes, or as an act of revenge – humiliating her when she couldn't fight back.'

'You've got a nasty mind,' Atherton complained. 'But necrophilia does at least make more sense than the set-up idea. Anyone who'd do that would be mad enough not to care about leaving the semen behind, and wouldn't need to fake a break-in. But Prentiss didn't have a scratch on his face, did he?'

'It needn't have been the face,' Slider said. 'It could as easily be the neck, or it might be hand or arm, trying to loosen his grip. Or it might have been the bare body while they were bonking. And in any case, Freddie says it's a tiny tissue sample – nothing more than a slight abrasion.'

'I suppose she was too drunk to fight much,' Atherton said. 'I didn't like the woman, but she's gaining my sympathy point by point.'

'But remember, we don't know yet that the semen is Prentiss's, or even that both lots are from the same person. Prentiss may have noshed, made love and left, and the murderer came in afterwards for the rest of the sex. Or someone else might have been responsible for the condom and Prentiss for the rest.'

'And meanwhile we've got an unverifiable alibi for him, and a wife who gives him an alibi he apparently doesn't want.'

Slider smiled faintly. 'Life is fun, isn't it?'

'So what're you going to do, guv?'

'Have a crack at Giles Freeman myself, and get Porson to try and hurry the DNA results. We're stuck without them. Meanwhile, you go and have a bash at Mrs P. Your famous charm and sexual magnetism might get something different out of her.'

'Okay.' He stood to go. 'What's this about you giving the fabulous Norma away at her wedding, by the way?'

'How the hell did that get out?' Slider said, startled.

'Oh, it isn't out. Norma told me. Wanted to crow over me, I think. But I told her you wouldn't go if I wasn't there.'

'And she believed you?'

'Not entirely,' Atherton admitted. 'She called me a lying, weaselling scumbag. So I'm relying on you to get me an invite, guv.'

'Why should I?'

'Could you bear to think of me being humiliated in that way?' Slider nodded grimly. 'Could you live with yourself afterwards?'

'I could try.'

'You wouldn't enjoy the wedding without me. It'll be nothing but strangers there.'

'My job, of course, doesn't accustom me to meeting strangers.'

'Ah, but it's different in a social situation,' Atherton said. 'You need me as a buffer. Look, I'll get your sandwiches every day. I'll be good for ever. Go on, go on, get me an invite, *pleeese*!'

'The furthest I'll go', said Slider, 'is to ask her why she doesn't want you there.'

Atherton shuddered delicately. 'No, no, I'll pass on that. There are some things it's better not to know.'

After a frustrating interval, Slider, too, got as far as Freeman's press secretary, Ben McKenzie.

'I'm sorry, Giles Freeman doesn't talk direct to anyone,' he pronounced.

'What's he got, a mouth at the back of his neck?' Slider asked irritably. 'I don't think you understand, Mr McKenzie, I'm conducting a murder enquiry—'

'No, *you* don't understand,' McKenzie interrupted him firmly. 'We're talking about the Secretary of State, a member of Her Majesty's Government, not some crackhead off the streets.'

'I don't care who he is, he has to answer my questions,' Slider said. 'He must confirm or deny Prentiss's alibi, and make a statement to that effect. I can come myself and interview him, or send one of my officers, or he can come here and do it, but one way or the other it has to be done, and done today.'

'Today? Absolutely out of the question! Giles has got a completely full diary. Even if he were to grant you an interview – which I stress is highly unlikely – I couldn't fit you into his schedule anywhere, not any day this week.'

'Do you want a writ for obstruction slapped on him?'

McKenzie's voice grew rich with irony. 'Perhaps you don't know that Giles Freeman is a *close personal friend* of the Home Secretary. Now are you really telling me you want to blackmail the personal friend of the man who ultimately controls your career?'

Slider smiled happily. 'Are you really telling me that you want the papers to know that the Home Secretary interfered in a high-profile murder case so that his friend could avoid his clear legal and moral duty to help the police?'

There was a beat of silence. 'You'd sink so low as to go to the press?'

'You can always try me and see,' Slider said pleasantly.

'I'll get back to you,' McKenzie said tersely; and then added, as if driven to it, 'I hope you don't live to regret this conversation, Inspector. We don't take kindly to underhand tactics.'

The line went dead.

McLaren came to the door. 'Guv, you got a minute?'

'If I had one of those I'd be a rich man,' said Slider sternly. McLaren was used to his style, and took it as an invitation to come in. Slider looked up. 'What's that on your shirt?'

'Chocolate,' McLaren said, after due consideration.

'You're a health hazard,' Slider said. 'Why can't you eat without spreading devastation in all directions? What d'you want, anyway?'

'It's about Micky Wordley. I've been round his gaff—'

'On your own?'

'It was just a friendly visit,' McLaren protested. 'I wasn't looking for trouble.'

'You might have got it just the same. For Chrissake, McLaren, you're not in this job to get your head blown off!'

McLaren spread his hands. 'Wordley's not that much of a head-banger. He's not going to blow me away just for asking questions, is he? Anyway,' he hurried on before Slider could answer, 'I didn't get to see him. He's done a runner.'

'Gone?'

'Had it away beautiful. Kelly – his girlfriend – says she's not seen him since Wednesday night.'

'Oh?'

'Yeah, some bloke come round about half nine on Wednesday night and they went off together, and he's not been back since.'

'Some bloke?'

'She says she doesn't know him, but I'm working on that,' McLaren said. 'You could see she was scared stiff. Anyway, a snout of mine says he's heard Wordley's mixed up in something big.' He cocked his head hopefully like a pigeon waiting for bread.

'Something big could be anything,' Slider said.

'That's right,' McLaren said, taking it for confirmation. 'Kelly knows he's up to something with this other geezer, and I reckon if I work on her I can get it out of her. She's got a soft spot for me.'

Slider blinked. 'Well, I suppose a lot of women are fond of animals. But look, if there's any truth in it, that's he's mixed up in something big, it's far more likely that he's planning another robbery, given his form, and given this mysterious other bloke. He's not likely to take a chum along with him when he goes a-murdering.'

'It could be a robbery,' McLaren said, with an air of stretching a point about as far as it would go. 'But if that was it, why would he stay away? Kelly says he's never done that before. He likes his home comforts. The only times he's stopped out like that was when he's been on one of his benders.'

'So what's your point?'

'He's gone out on the piss with this bloke. Next day, still under the influence, he's gone round Agnew's place and offed her in a fit of temper.'

Slider thought a moment. 'And tied her up afterwards to fake a rape?'

'It didn't have to be a fake, did it, guv?' McLaren said intelligently. 'The sex could've been post-mortem. He's the kind of nutter that'd enjoy something like that.'

'Is that what his girlfriend says?'

He shrugged. 'He's got some very funny ideas, according to Kelly. And he likes a bit of bondage. Anyway, she's like a cat on hot bricks – she definitely knows something. If I just lean on her a bit—?' He made it into a question.

'All right, you can follow it up,' Slider said. 'We ought

to keep an open mind that it might not be Prentiss. And if Wordley's disappeared we may as well know why.'

'Thanks, guv.'

'But be careful,' Slider added as McLaren retreated. 'Wordley's a dangerous bastard, and he won't like you messing about with his girlfriend's head. Don't go sticking your face into a hornet's nest.'

'I'm not scared of him,' McLaren said.

'If you had any brains you'd be scared,' said Slider.

CHAPTER EIGHT

Lies, damned lies and ballistics

Mrs Prentiss was a long time answering the door, and Atherton was ringing for the third time, purely in the cause of being thorough, when it opened.

'Mrs Prentiss? I'm Detective Sergeant Atherton of Shepherd's Bush CID.' He showed his ID.

'My husband isn't home,' she said.

'I know. It's you I want to speak to.'

'I've already told another detective – a woman – everything I know.'

'WDC Swilley. Yes, but there've been further developments, and I'm afraid I really do need to ask you some more questions. May I come in?'

She stared at him for a long moment, and then sighed and stepped back. 'All right. Do you mind if we talk in the dining-room? I'm not too good at stairs yet. That's why I was so long answering the door.'

She walked ahead of him with the stiff and too-upright gait of the back sufferer.

'Oh, yes, you hurt your back, didn't you?' Atherton said. 'My colleague told me.'

'It's an old trouble that comes and goes,' she said. 'I hurt it in a fall years ago.'

'Horse-riding? Skiing?' Atherton asked conversationally.

'Ballet. I used to be a dancer.' In the dining-room – green silk Regency-stripe wallpaper, dark Edwardian furniture, and a lot of heavy silver that needed cleaning – she pulled out a chair and sat carefully, letting her trousered knees relax outwards in the approved Alexander method.

Atherton sat catty-corner to her and laid his large, smooth hands on the table, and she looked at them in the way that people in a railway carriage will automatically look at a dog or a child: a way not to meet strangers' eyes. In the dark room, the sidelong light from the window pooled in the patina of the old mahogany, showing up an even film of dust, like pollen on the surface of a pond. There was a faint fragrance of past pot-pourri and dusty carpet, underlined with damp and a hint of candlewax. A bit like a church, Atherton thought: hassocks, cassocks, incense and rot.

Mrs Prentiss looked haggard. Swilley had said she appeared younger than her age, but the shadowed eyes and drawn face before Atherton now had all their years on show. She was suffering; and she was apprehensive. The liar flees when no man pursueth. But even apart from that, if your husband has murdered your best friend, you are entitled to look a bit on the seedy side – particularly when he hasn't been locked up yet.

'I suppose you know what I want to talk to you about?' he invited gently.

'The murder, obviously. I don't know what more I can say to help you.'

'Well, you see, we've got to get one or two things sorted out, haven't we? Because you told us that your husband was at home on Thursday evening, and that wasn't true, was it?'

'Wasn't it?'

Atherton smiled. 'Come on, Mrs Prentiss, you and your husband must have talked about this since we first interviewed you. You must know his story and yours didn't tally. He doesn't even pretend he was here all evening. Why did you say he was?'

She put her hands to her face as though her cheeks were

hot. 'Oh, I don't know! I was confused. Upset. A detective came to my door completely out of the blue and told me my best friend had been murdered. Was I supposed to be calm and collected?'

'But you said that your husband had already told you that Miss Agnew was dead.'

'Did I? Well, that doesn't stop it being a shock. And I'm not accustomed to dealing with the police. It frightened me to have that woman suddenly appear on my doorstep.'

'Hmm,' said Atherton, with a kindly, trying-to-understand tilt of his head. 'So because you were startled and upset by the news, you immediately jumped to the conclusion that your husband was the murderer and needed an alibi?'

'No, of course not! It wasn't like that,' she cried indignantly.

'Well, what was it like, then?'

'Oh, I don't know. I wasn't really thinking clearly. I was confused.'

'I don't think you were confused. I think you were defending him. It's a natural instinct in a wife, isn't it?' She didn't answer. 'But what were you defending him against, if you didn't think he did it?'

'Getting mixed up in it, I suppose,' she said, as if goaded into answering the unanswerable. 'I wanted to protect him from trouble – scandal – the newspapers. Anything like that could damage his career. I just wanted your colleague to know that Josh couldn't possibly have had anything to do with it. I wanted her to go away and leave us alone.'

'Yes, well, telling lies isn't the best way to stop us coming back, is it?'

She met his eyes at last, and hers were anxious, guarded. 'I suppose not. But as I said, I wasn't thinking clearly.'

He tried a shift of direction. 'Did you know your husband had gone to see Phoebe Agnew on Thursday?'

She hesitated, and there was something there in the dark

depths, he thought, something cautious. It was the look a suspect gave you when they didn't know what it was safe to say, how much you knew. His heart lifted, as it always did at the scent of guilt.

'No,' she said after a substantial think. 'But why shouldn't he? They were good friends. All three of us were good friends.'

'Did he often visit her without you?'

'I don't know how often he visited her, but there was no reason he shouldn't, or that he should tell me when he did. There was nothing going on between them, if that's what you're suggesting. Of course, that's bound to be the conclusion everyone will leap to, that they were having an affair behind my back, especially given the way she was found. But that's precisely the reason I wanted to protect him. Once the press gets hold of it, they'll turn a decent friendship into something sordid and underhand.' Her voice rose a little in agitation. 'Something commonplace and disgusting and deceitful!'

'I'm afraid we can't be responsible for what the newspapers print,' Atherton said soothingly. 'I wish we could. Do you know where your husband went afterwards – when he left her flat?'

'To see Giles Freeman, on Government business,' she said promptly.

'He told you that, did he?'

'Yes.'

'I wonder, then, why you didn't tell us?'

She looked away nervously. 'I didn't know at the time that that's where he'd gone. He told me on Friday night, after he'd spoken to you.'

'So what you're saying is that he went out on Thursday evening without giving you any indication of where he was going? Was that usual?'

'I'm not his gaoler,' she snapped.

'Quite so. But married couples usually say, "I'm off to

such and such a place, darling" when they get up and leave, don't they?'

'I don't know what other married couples do,' she said stubbornly.

'But weren't you a bit curious? Husband gets up and leaves the house without a word? And when you hear later that your best friend has been murdered you assume that's where he went and tell a lie to protect him?' She didn't answer. 'Mrs Prentiss, I have to press you on this point. Can't you see how odd your behaviour looks? I must know the truth. Did your husband say on Thursday night where he was going?'

She put her hands between her knees and squeezed them, hunching her shoulders. She looked like a cold bird on a winter branch, thin and vulnerable. 'I don't remember. It's all so confused. I was so upset about Phoebe it's driven everything out of my head. I expect he did say. He probably said he was going out on business, or going to a meeting. In fact, yes, I'm sure that's what he did say. He said he was going to a meeting at the Ministry, and that he might call in on Phoebe on the way. Yes, and I remember now, he said had I any message for her, and I said just give her my love.'

All this was less than convincing, Atherton thought; and why was she so nervous? Had Prentiss threatened her? Well, perhaps he wouldn't need to. Just being married to a man who had murdered your best friend must make you eager to please him. 'And what time did he go out?' he asked.

'I don't know. About half past seven, a quarter to eight maybe. I didn't notice particularly.'

'He was with you all morning and afternoon, was he? Did he go out anywhere else before that?'

'No, he was here.'

'What did he do all day?'

'He read some papers, did some writing. We had a late lunch. I don't remember in detail.'

'Where did he do those things? Was he in the same room as you all the time?'

'I don't understand.'

'If he wasn't actually in the same room as you all the time, he might have left the house without your knowing.'

'Of course he didn't leave the house,' she said robustly. 'I'd have known. Anyway, he didn't leave the room for long enough to go anywhere.'

'And what time did he come home on Thursday night?'

'I don't know exactly. It was very late, after I'd gone to bed. After midnight – nearer one o'clock I think. But that was usual, when he was on Government business. They often have late meetings when the House is sitting.'

'Did he ring you at all that evening?'

'No.'

'You were in all evening?'

She looked startled. 'Of course I was. What do you mean?'

'I mean, were you in all evening? Did you go out? If you were out, you wouldn't know if he'd phoned.'

'We have an answering machine. But I was in all evening. And he didn't phone. Why should he?'

Atherton was silent, letting her stew, letting her relax. Then he said, 'A little while ago, when you were talking about the trouble the newspapers would make for your husband over his relationship with Phoebe Agnew, you said, "Especially given the way she was found". What did you mean by that?'

A stillness came over her. 'I don't understand.'

'Well, how *was* she found? What aspect of the way she was found made you think it would cause trouble for your husband?'

'I don't know what you mean. I don't remember what I said. But it's obvious the papers will make trouble for him when they know he visited her that night, won't they? Everyone always assumes the worst.'

* * *

Joanna phoned. 'About that lunch—'

'Oh, Lord, I'd forgotten. I think it's going to be out of the question,' Slider began.

'It certainly is. I'm cancelling,' said Joanna. 'Some work's come in. The Grossman Ensemble. A concert in Woburn. Rehearsal three-thirty to five-thirty, so I'd have to leave around one at the latest.'

'Leave earlier and don't rush,' Slider advised.

'I did think of it,' she admitted. 'Some of the others are meeting at the Sow and Pigs for lunch on the way.' This was a pub at Toddington, just off the M1, handy for musicians on their way to dates in the north. Slider had learned that there were 'musicians' pubs' which everyone in the business knew and frequented – places with good food, real ale and an accommodating landlord.

'Have lunch with my blessing,' he said. 'Just promise to think of me when you're enjoying yourself.'

'Well, I think I should stop off,' she said, 'because the guy who gave me the date, Gerhard Wolf, will be there, and I'd like to buy him a pint to thank him.'

'Do I know him?' Slider asked. She had pronounced the surname the German way, but wolf was as wolf did in any language.

'I don't think you've met him. Tall, skinny guy, foxy eyes, long blond hair and an earring?'

'I know so many who fit that description,' Slider said. Fox and wolf? This was getting worse. He forced himself to be noble. 'If you chum up to him, maybe he'll get you some more work.'

'Oddly enough,' she said, 'that had occurred to me. How's the case going?'

'With the speed of evolution.'

'So fast?'

'That's how long it takes to get a DNA report back.'

'You know what DNA stands for, don't you?' Joanna said.

'Eh?'

'The National Dyslexics' Association.'

'Go away, Marshall. Go and play some music or something.' As he put the phone down, Atherton came in, rubbing his hands. 'You look pleased. How did it go?'

'Loyal little wifie is dropping him in it as fast as she tries to bail him out.' He recounted his interview with Mrs Prentiss. 'First she says one thing then another. She didn't know where he went and then she did. Obviously he's come home after talking to us and given her a rocket for giving him the wrong alibi. Now she's so confused she can't remember what story they're going with.'

'We don't know that,' said Slider.

'Oh, Mr Caution! All right, but she has been lying, and she was obviously trying to protect him, and what would she need to do that for if he wasn't guilty?'

'Did she admit she was trying to protect him?'

'Yes, she did, as it happens. And here's something odd,' Atherton added. 'She said she wanted to protect him from getting involved because the media would assume he and Agnew had been having an affair—'

'Makes sense.'

'Yes, but listen, then she added, "especially given the way she was found" – the way Agnew was found.'

'Oh?' said Slider.

'Later on I asked her what she meant by that, and she waffled and said she didn't remember saying it; but it must surely have been a reference to the fact that Agnew was found half naked and tied to the bedstead, *à la* sexual games. And that's a detail that hasn't appeared in the newspapers yet. So how did she know, unless Prentiss told her?'

Slider made an expressive face. 'You think he boasted to her about the way he did the murder? The two women were friends, remember.'

'Would you put it past him?'

'She might not have meant anything in particular by it,'

Slider demurred. 'It's amazing how little people manage to mean by anything for ninety per cent of their lives. Still, it does look like another piece of evidence against Prentiss.'

'Together with the fact that he told her on Friday morning about Agnew's death and pretended to us that he didn't know. Have you managed to penetrate the Freeman barrier yet?'

'Not yet,' said Slider.

'They stick together, these types,' said Atherton. 'That'll be why Prentiss has got the missus to go with the Freeman alibi – he's betting we won't be able to check it one way or the other.'

'But what puzzles me most is why Prentiss should think a meeting with Freeman constitutes an alibi anyway,' said Slider. 'He could just as easily have killed Agnew first. We don't have an exact time of death.'

'He probably doesn't know that. The general public mostly think we can pinpoint the time of death to within minutes,' Atherton pointed out. 'Still, he'd have done better from the beginning to say he was at home all evening. I wonder why he didn't? He didn't know we were interviewing his wife at the same moment. In fact, if he'd called her earlier on Friday to tell her about Agnew's death, as she says he did, he could have fixed the alibi then.'

'If he'd been anything of a gentleman he'd have left her out of it altogether.'

Atherton looked amused. 'I should have thought, my dear old guv'nor, that murdering Phoebe Agnew pretty well ruled him out of the gentleman stakes. I'm sure they said something about that on my first day at Eton.'

'You were never at Eton,' Slider objected.

'Josh Prentiss was,' Atherton said soberly.

Porson paced back and forth across his room, his face looking older and more ghastly by courtesy of the fluorescent strip light that was needed to augment the thin winter sunlight. He must have been scratching his head in agitation, for his toupee was askew, and the line of natural hair revealed seemed greyer than it had been yesterday.

'You've really opened up a kettle of worms now,' he said, giving Slider a harried look. 'I've had Commander Wetherspoon on the phone, literally bursting a blood vessel. It seems Giles Freeman's evoked the Home Secretary's support and the Home Secretary's got straight on to the Commissioner. He was incrudescent with rage, I can tell you. You can't go around issuing threats to a member of HMG, Slider, not if you value your pension. What were you thinking of?'

'I was thinking of the case, sir.' Slider remained sturdily unrepentant. In the first place he knew he was right; and in the second place, Porson was one of the old school, and no actor into the bargain. 'Does the Home Secretary believe Cabinet Ministers are above the law?'

'No-one's above the law,' Porson said.

'Except the editor of a tabloid newspaper?' Slider amended.

'I'm glad you think it's funny,' Porson snapped. 'Why the hell didn't you come to me when this Freeman type wouldn't come across? I could have passed it up to Mr Wetherspoon to get the Commissioner to tell the Home Secretary to put official pressure on him. It's being side-passed makes Mr Wetherspoon go ballistic, and between you, me and the bedpost it's him we've more to fear from than the Commissioner in all his glory. He's in the best position to retaliate. He can make our lives a mockery just by lifting his little finger; and it's no secret he doesn't like you.'

'That's a cross I'll have to bear, sir,' said Slider. 'And if I'd gone the long way round, via the official channels, would I have got a result so soon?'

Porson's crest went down, and he sighed and scratched his poll. 'No, you wouldn't, and that's an indispensable fact. Well, I've done my bit by reprimanding you. In fact, I told Mr Wetherspoon I was on your side. It gets on my goat, this attitude that you have to pussyfoot round people just because they've got themselves installed somewhere up the higher arky. We shouldn't have to ask permission to talk to someone in the pursuit of duty, no matter who they are. As it happens,' he added confidentially, 'the Commissioner doesn't like being leaned on any more than Giles Freeman, and especially not by a portentious little shit like McKenzie. He backed you all the way.'

Slider couldn't conceal his surprise. 'The Commissioner did?'

'Oh, yes. He told the Home Secretary that Freeman's got to come across or he'll be prosecuted just like you, me or Rosie O'Grady. And come across he has.'

'I'm glad, sir.'

'But you've certainly stirred up a mare's nest in Government circles,' Porson went on, shaking his head sadly. 'The fact of the matter is that Freeman has categorically denied that Prentiss was with him that evening. Blown his story sky high. And Prentiss, in case you didn't know, is a special advisor to the Government. A chum. A member of the inner sanction.'

'I did know it,' Slider said.

'Well, you see what you've done. One spoke on the wheel of power has placed another spoke in a very embarrassing position. Involved him in potential scandal. You've forced them to decide between Freeman and Prentiss, and they don't like it.'

'*I've* forced them? It's Prentiss's fault for lying.'

'In the real world, yes,' Porson said. 'But the Government likes people to sing from the same hymn sheet. And Prentiss is valuable to them and they don't want to lose him. They already had their heads to the grindstone trying to work out a way round the problem, when you shoved your size nines in and brought it to a crisis. Now too many people know about it, and they'll have to drop Prentiss, which pisses them off more than somewhat. You're a marked man, Slider.'

'I'll try hard to care, sir,' Slider promised.

'Yes, well,' Porson said. He cleared his throat, looking at Slider reflectively. 'You're not interested in politics, I take it?'

Slider shook his head. 'I've never had the time.'

'The higher you go, the more it matters,' Porson said. 'But times have changed, and none of us can afford to ignore the political aspic of the Job any more. It affects all of us, right down the line to the coalface. So next time there's a problem of this sort, bring it to me first. Do you savvy?'

'Yes, sir,' said Slider. 'What's happening about Freeman? Is he going to make a statement?'

'It's on its way. You can take it as read that Prentiss didn't visit him that evening and precede on that assumption.'

'Good. I can't say I'm completely surprised. But it gives me some ammunition against Prentiss. If we could just get the DNA profile back quickly—' He looked hopefully at his boss.

'I'm on to that,' Porson barked, 'so you needn't give me the Battersea Dogs' Home treatment. Given who Prentiss is, and the press interest, I think it's important enough to justify some positive budgetary outlay. I'm prepared to pay the lab the extra for the quick result. As soon as we get the confirmation we can jump on him, before he finds any other political trees to hide behind. Meanwhile, there's no harm in keeping some pressure on about his lies. If he's talking to us, he can't be talking to anyone else, can he?'

'Right, sir.'

Porson nodded dismissal. Slider, on his way out, paused to say, 'Sir? Thanks for backing me up.'

'You're at the sharp end. You shouldn't have to worry about politics,' Porson said. 'That's what you've got me for.'

He looked old that morning, but, for all his oddities, impressive. A totem carved in enduring granite; a giant in a world of pygmies.

CHAPTER NINE

The food, the cad and the bubbly

The result on the semen was waiting on the desk when Slider got in the next day. He took it through to the office.

'How'd you do it, boss?' asked Swilley. 'Only yesterday they were pretending they'd never heard of us.'

'Undue influence and bundles of used fivers,' Atherton suggested.

'Mr Porson flashed his legs and suddenly we were first in the queue,' said Slider.

'So what's the score?' said Mackay.

'They couldn't get anything from the condom – the sample was too dilute,' Slider said. 'But the semen from the vagina matches Prentiss's blood sample.'

'I always knew he was lying,' Swilley said with satisfaction. 'What about the tissue under the nails? Did that come from him too?'

'The result of that test hasn't come back yet,' Slider said. 'Bit of administrative confusion. Mr Porson asked for the semen result and they evidently separated that out.'

'Still, if the semen's Prentiss's, we've nailed him in that lie,' Swilley said.

'And of course you all know now, don't you,' Slider said, looking round and gathering attentions, 'that Giles Freeman has made a statement that he didn't see Prentiss that evening, and that there never was a meeting scheduled. In fact the House was sitting and there was an important division, so there is no doubt Prentiss made it up.'

'Ah, what it is to have friends!' said Atherton.

'But look here,' Slider said, 'the fact that Prentiss has been proved lying about these things doesn't make him the murderer. He admitted all along that he had been at the flat—'

'Not quite all along,' Atherton said. 'Only after we told him his car had been seen.'

'All right, almost all along,' said Slider. 'Of course this new evidence makes it look more likely that he did it – he certainly behaves as though he's got something to hide – but let's keep an open mind. I want you all to go on with searching her papers and talking to the neighbours and her colleagues. Anyone got anything to report on those fronts yet?'

They went through the most useful so far. 'Early days yet, guv,' Hollis summed it up.

Slider looked round, frowning. 'Where's McLaren?' Nobody answered. 'Has he said anything more about Wordley's whereabouts?'

'Not to me,' said Hollis, 'but I know he was going to talk to that Kelly again, Wordley's girlfriend, last night.'

'Well, keep me posted. It certainly won't hurt to know what Wordley's up to, even if it isn't anything to do with the case.'

'What're you going to do now, boss?' Swilley asked.

'Talk to Prentiss again,' said Slider. 'And this time we'll do it here, on our territory, just to concentrate his mind.'

Josh Prentiss looked every inch a man whose entire life was swirling down the kermit before his very eyes. Sex, power and charisma had abandoned his fleshy face with the suddenness of seaside bathers at a shark alert. Now the face looked merely baggy, and the eyes were pouched and exhausted. His expensive clothes seemed to sit sadly on him, as if they'd sooner be anywhere else. In the institutional drabness of the interview room, where the smell of guilt, mindless crime and cheap trainers had soaked into the distemper, his designer chic looked as out of place as an orchid in a beer bottle.

When they arrived at his office, Prentiss was looking sick and a little dazed, but nodded meekly and without hesitation when they asked if he would accompany them to the station to help them with their enquiry. He had not screamed for a solicitor, which was out of character for a man in his various positions, and Atherton had looked sidelong at his boss when Slider gently insisted he ought to have one. Of course, from the police point of view it was always nicer to conduct an interview without the tortured mind of a legal representative hobbling the progress; but what boots it a policeman if he gains the whole confession and loses his case on procedural quibbles?

At the station, Prentiss had accepted the offer of a cup of coffee, but when it was placed before him he only looked at it blankly, as if such a thing had never come in his way before. Well, perhaps it hadn't, Slider reflected. In Prentiss's world, coffee was probably a delicious aromatic stimulant made from freshly ground roasted arabica beans. Maybe he'd never been presented with a dingy ecru liquid that smelled of rancid laundry and been expected to swallow it.

When the brief, Philip Ainscough, arrived, Slider and Atherton took their places and faced him and Prentiss across the table that had heard more futile lies and feeble excuses than a regular army sergeant. Prentiss looked up from his stunned contemplation of caterers' revenge, and said abruptly, 'I've been a complete fool. I realise that now. I should have told you the truth from the beginning.'

'It's always a good idea,' Slider said mildly.

'Is it? Always?' Prentiss said with some bitterness. 'Is one always believed? I think not. The press and the public believe what they want to, regardless of the truth.'

'We're not the press or the public,' Slider said. 'And we've got ways of testing whether something's true or not. For instance, let's start with where you were on Thursday evening. You told us that you were at a meeting with Giles Freeman, but that was a lie, wasn't it?'

'Yes, it was a lie,' Prentiss sighed. 'Look, do you mind if I smoke?'

The reply in Slider's mind, 'I don't mind if you burn' was withheld in favour of a *go ahead* gesture of one hand.

Prentiss drew out and lit a cigarette with hands that trembled slightly, but when he spoke, his voice was calm and reasonable. 'I did lie to you about where I was on Thursday night, but I did it to protect someone who has nothing to do with this business. I hoped you wouldn't check up, given who my alibi was. I mean, if you can't trust a Cabinet Minister, who can you trust?' Atherton made a slight choking noise, and Prentiss looked at him and frowned. 'Well, I suppose I should have known better.'

Ainscough spoke. 'You realise that by approaching Giles Freeman in the way you have done, you've ruined Mr Prentiss's career?'

'I should have thought he did that himself when he killed Phoebe Agnew,' Slider said.

'You'd better be careful what you say,' Ainscough warned impassively. 'You could be looking at a civil action. And if you're not going to conduct this interview in a proper fashion, my client will withdraw his co-operation.'

Slider shrugged slightly and turned to Prentiss. 'Let's clear up this business of where you were first.'

Prentiss took a long suck at his cigarette, blew out a shaky cloud, and then said, 'I went to see a young woman with whom I'm having an affair. That's why I lied about it. I didn't want her dragged into all this. And I didn't want my wife to know.'

Atherton stirred and gave Slider a look. *Not that old*

chestnut again! Prentiss caught the look and a spot of colour appeared in his cheek – indignation, or shame?

'What's the young woman's name?' Slider asked.

'Maria Colehern,' Prentiss said. 'She's my secretary. Not at my firm – I mean, my secretary in my capacity as Government special advisor. We've been seeing each other for a few months now. She has a flat in Kensington – one of those service blocks in Phillimore Walk.'

'Write the address down,' Slider said, pushing a pad over to him.

Prentiss obeyed. 'I suppose', he said, looking from Slider to Atherton and back, 'you'll have to check it with her, but I do hope you'll be discreet. Maria's done nothing wrong, and it would be unfair to make her lose her job over this.'

Slider raised an eyebrow. 'I think we've got a bit beyond "unfair" now, haven't we?'

Prentiss stared a moment, and then burst out, 'I didn't kill Phoebe! Why won't you believe me?'

'Because', said Slider, 'we found Phoebe Agnew tied to her bed, naked from the waist down, and with your semen in her vagina. It seems a fair conclusion to me. What would you think?'

'Don't answer that,' Ainscough said quickly. 'You are not to ask my client to indulge in speculation.'

But Prentiss hadn't attempted to answer. He went white and fumbled the cigarette to his mouth and sucked on it like an asthmatic on an oxygen mask. He drew in so much smoke that when he tried to speak he could only cough, spouting spasmodic clouds like a dragon with hiccups. At last he gasped, 'It's not possible. You must have made a mistake.'

'No mistake,' Slider said. 'You kindly gave us a blood sample, if you remember, and we've run a genetic test on the semen. So unless you've got a twin brother, we've got a match. You had sex with Phoebe Agnew and then killed her, didn't you?'

Get outta that one, sucker, Atherton thought happily.

Prentiss opened his mouth, but Ainscough snapped, 'Don't answer that.' He looked at Prentiss hard and then said, 'I'd like to talk to my client alone for a few minutes.'

Slider and Atherton left them alone. When Ainscough recalled them, he seemed a little puzzled and uneasy. 'My client has agreed to continue with this interview, though against my recommendation,' he said. Prentiss smoked in silence, his face turgid with thought. 'I must warn you again to be very careful of the language you employ. Remember my client is here voluntarily.'

'All right,' said Slider, 'shall we start again? Let's have an account of all your movements on Thursday, starting from when you got up in the morning, and this time, make it complete and true. Remember that we will check everything.'

'There's nothing to check,' Prentiss said at last. His voice sounded faint and hoarse, though that could have been from the heat of the smoke. 'I got up about seven, and did the usual things, showered, dressed, had breakfast, read the papers. Then I did some work—'

'Where?'

'Where?' He looked surprised at the question.

'Where did you do your work?'

'At home. In the drawing-room. It was only reading – some reports on brownfield sites. I read and made some notes, looked at some drawings. We had lunch quite late – about half past three. Then I—'

'What did you have for lunch?'

'Chicken. Why the devil d'you want to know that?'

'You never know what might be important,' Slider said neutrally. 'Go on. After lunch?'

His eyes moved away from direct contact. 'I did some more work. Then I changed and went out. I left at about a quarter to eight. I'd told Maria I'd be there at eight, but when I left the house I decided on an impulse to drop in on Phoebe on the way. I got to Phoebe's at about eight and left again at about twenty past. And I got to Maria's about half past. I had supper with her and eventually left about a quarter to one and was home at one, or just before.'

Slider listened impassively until Prentiss stopped, and then asked, 'When you left home – at a quarter to eight, you say – where did you tell your wife you were going?'

'I said I was going to see Giles Freeman, of course.'

'I thought you were going to tell me the truth?' Slider said sternly.

'It is the truth,' Prentiss said.

Slider made an impatient movement. 'Now *I'll* tell *you* what really happened. You had chicken that day all right, but you had it with Phoebe Agnew. She cooked you supper, chicken casserole and tiramisu, with plenty of wine, and coffee and brandy to follow. Then you had sex with her. Then at some point you quarrelled. The quarrel escalated, and you strangled her. Realising the position you were in, you arranged the body on the bed with the hands tied to make it look like a rape attack, and left. You assumed no-one would know you had ever been there, but unfortunately for you someone identified your car parked nearby.'

'You're crazy! I don't know what you're talking about,' Prentiss said. 'None of that happened. No, it's all right, Phil. It's complete nonsense and they know it.'

'When we came to see you on Friday afternoon,' Slider continued implacably, 'you pretended you didn't know Phoebe Agnew was dead—'

'I didn't know! That was the first I'd heard about it.'

'But your wife meanwhile had stated to another of my officers that you telephoned her on Friday morning and told her the news.'

Prentiss said nothing to that, though his lips rehearsed a few unfinished words.

'We're going to end this interview right now,' Ainscough said.

Slider ignored him. 'You really should have briefed your wife better. First of all she said you were at home all evening. Now she says you went out saying something vague about business. She didn't know anything about the Giles Freeman story until you told her on Friday night that that's what you'd told us. And the most foolish thing of all is that your Giles Freeman story and your present story about your mistress aren't alibis at all, because there's no evidence about what time on Thursday Phoebe Agnew was killed.'

Prentiss looked like a man in deep shock. 'But – but she must have been killed after eight-thirty,' he said faintly.

'Josh,' said Ainscough warningly.

'And what makes you think that?' Slider asked quickly, to get it in while he still could.

'Because she was fine when I left her.'

'That's enough,' Ainscough said. 'Unless you're prepared to charge my client, we're leaving. Don't answer any more questions, Josh.' He put a hand on Prentiss's shoulder and he stood up, still looking blank and shocked.

Slider had one more try. 'Mr Prentiss, you've told us nothing but lies from beginning to end. Can't you understand that we check everything, that your lies will always be found out? You're an intelligent man, you must see that nothing but the truth can help you now. Tell me the truth. What have you got to lose?'

'Nothing,' he said slowly. 'My career's already gone, and my marriage—' He shrugged, and turned to Ainscough. 'It's all right, Phil. I've got nothing to hide, and I want to get it straight with them. Otherwise this thing will drag on and on. I know what I'm doing.' He sat down again and faced Slider. 'Look, you're on the wrong track altogether. Phoebe and I didn't have a sexual relationship. We never did. We really were just friends. To tell you the truth,' he added, 'she wasn't my type. She was too hard and masculine – and far too much of a slob. She was a great friend, though – a great mate, if you like. She and Noni and I have been friends since university days, but it was Noni I married. Noni's the sort of dainty, feminine woman I find attractive. If you knew anything about me you'd know that was the truth. If you're going to check with Maria you'll see what sort of person she is.'

Slider only nodded expressionlessly.

'Noni's my type,' Prentiss went on. 'She's been a wonderful wife. Smart and pretty. Superb cook. Entertains my friends and business colleagues. An absolute mainstay – the sort of wife and home-maker a man in my position needs. Phoebe's never cared for anything like that. She'd scoff at the idea of taking second place to a man or supporting him in his career. Her own career is all she cares about. And she despises domesticity. She lives in a state of chaos, her clothes are always held together with safety pins, and she's never cooked for me or for anyone in her life. She lives on take-aways. The idea of her cooking supper for me is ludicrous – you simply don't know how ludicrous!'

'She cooked for somebody on Thursday, or didn't you notice?' Slider said.

Prentiss looked distracted. 'No, not really. I mean, there were a lot of dirty plates and things in the kitchen, but that was the way it always was. They could have been there for days, for all I knew.'

'You went into the kitchen, then?'

'No, I just saw as I went past the door that there were dishes stacked up. I didn't go in. Why should I? But it was typical of Phoebe, that's what I'm saying. Noni would never tolerate mess like that – and I like an orderly home.'

'Yet,' Slider pursued, 'despite all the perfections of your wife, you still had to have a mistress?'

Prentiss reddened. 'Are you going to sit in judgement on me?'

'I warned you not to go on with this,' said Ainscough.

'I'm trying to find some consistency in Mr Prentiss's story, that's all.'

'It's all right, Phil,' said Prentiss.

'No, it isn't. If you insist on ignoring my advice then I'm of no use to you. Perhaps you'd like to instruct someone else.'

Prentiss thought a moment and then said, 'All right, you can go. I'll do this on my own.'

'I most strongly urge you not to.'

'Your advice is noted. But I'll do this my way.' When Ainscough had left them, Prentiss gave Slider and Atherton a strange look, part angry, part pleading. He appeared to have braced himself for something, but Slider hadn't any hope it was a confession. Prentiss seemed to have regained his confidence since the low point when Slider had told him his alibi was not an alibi. Had he thought of something – some device for getting out of trouble which, significantly, perhaps, he did not want his brief to hear?

'Okay,' he said, 'I didn't want to tell you this before because it's personal, and I didn't see why the intimate details of my life should be pored over by strangers – but, though I love Noni and she's a wonderful wife, we haven't had sex for a long time. Not for a couple of years. She's been depressed ever since her career flopped. She was in a sitcom and it was panned by the critics.' He paused and looked to see if they knew what he was talking about.

'Yes, we heard about that from someone else,' Slider said.

'Right, well, you must understand how hard that was for her. It ought to have been her big break, and in fact she hasn't worked since. Naturally, she's been very low. And she's getting to a difficult age for women.'

Ah, that was it, Slider thought. The inconsistencies in the story were to be laid at the door of Mrs Prentiss's menopausal irrationality.

'Well, I've been as supportive of her as I can,' he went on, 'but it hasn't been easy. My own career takes up a lot of time and energy; and, frankly, I'm a man who needs a sexual outlet.'

He appealed to them, man to man. Slider and Atherton remained unappealed to, and Prentiss was bounced back into his exposition as off a wall.

'Well, I don't apologise for that,' he said. 'I've always been discreet, and never given Noni anything to complain about. And as for Maria, I assure you she knows the score and she's quite happy with the situation. So where's the harm?'

Slider refused to specify. 'What has this to do with your actions on Thursday?' he asked neutrally.

'I'm coming to that,' Prentiss said. He lit another cigarette from the stub of the first, drew on it and coughed a little. 'Look, I don't like telling you this, but I have to, otherwise you won't understand, and you won't believe me. On Thursday, right from the time we had breakfast, Noni seemed to be in a funny mood.'

'In what way, funny?'

'I don't know, she seemed a bit edgy and excited. I couldn't tell what was going on with her. I was trying to read and she kept interrupting, trying to start up conversations. Talking about the news and my Government job. She asked about holidays, and when we were going to have the children over and so on and so on. I did my best to be patient with her but she was making it hard to concentrate. In the end I had to say that this was a working day at home, and I didn't want to be disturbed, and she shut up and went off.'

'Off?'

'Oh, just pottering round, the way women do. I thought maybe she was sulking, but when she called me to say lunch was ready she'd obviously got over it because she seemed quite happy. Almost—' He frowned, seeming to search for the right word. 'Almost flirtatious. She brought me a glass of champagne first. I said, what's the occasion, and she said, nothing, I always used to like a glass of champagne as an aperitif, and had I changed. I said I still had work to do that afternoon and she said, oh you've got a hard enough head to take it. Flattering me, you know?'

'Go on.'

'Well, she'd done a delicious chicken and rice dish for lunch – she really is a super cook – and at that point I thought, what the hell, the poor love probably needs the company, stuck here alone all day with nothing to do, so I gave in and we had an excellent bottle of burgundy with it. She was being as entertaining as she knew how – chatting and laughing. She has immense charm when she wants to use it. Anyway—' He hesitated, and looked down at his hands. 'Anyway, after lunch she – we – we went to bed.' He was silent a moment, and Slider didn't prompt him. 'It was the first time for a couple of years. She said she hadn't been a good wife to me lately and she meant to make it up to me in the future.'

Another silence, and he looked up unhappily. 'It put me in a difficult position. I mean, I'd got used to the way things were, and I was quite happy with my arrangements. The last thing I want to do is to hurt Noni, and I do love her – there couldn't be a better wife – but the fact of the matter is—'

'You don't fancy her,' Atherton suggested.

'It's not that,' he said defensively. 'I want you to understand. Maria and I – I'm deeply involved with her. I can't give her up. But I knew I'd feel bad about it if Noni and I were also – if we were lovers again. And there was her mental state to consider – Noni's. I've told you she's been very depressed. If she was making an effort to come out of it, and I rejected her, or she found out about Maria after I – oh,' he finished, goaded, 'you must *see*!'

Slider nodded. 'So with all these worries about your wife on your mind, you decided the best thing was to pop out and visit a couple of your mistresses.'

Prentiss reddened and half rose. 'Look, I don't have to take this sort of abuse!'

'Oh, I think you do,' Slider said. 'You invite it, it would be rude not to take it.'

Prentiss was so shocked by this response he hardly knew what to say. 'Do you think this is funny?' he said at last, incredulously.

'No,' said Slider, fixing him with a hard stare. 'I've seen the body of Phoebe Agnew. I don't think there's anything remotely funny about it. So please sit down and stop blustering. I'm trying to get at the truth.'

Prentiss subsided, but he looked angry and disconcerted. 'I don't understand you at all. I'm here voluntarily. I'm doing my best to help you, but I can walk out of here right now and leave you to stew in it, and I will do if you don't start showing me a bit of respect and common courtesy. You're a public servant. And you must know I'm a man of influence. Do you want me to make a complaint against you? Don't you value your career?'

'Let's not talk careers, Mr Prentiss,' Slider said. 'Let's remember why we're here, and what I already know. Now, tell me what happened after you made love with your wife.'

He breathed hard, but answered after a moment. 'I fell asleep. When I woke up it was half past six. I was annoyed because I hadn't done all the work I'd planned to do, and I'd told Maria I'd be round at eight. I jumped up to go and shower, and Noni asked where I was going. She said, "You're not going out, are you?" I said I had to, and she got upset. She felt that after what had happened I ought to stay with her. She asked me who I was going to see and said I should cancel it and I got angry and said it was Government business and she ought to know by now what was important, and she said did that mean *she* wasn't important – well, you know how women go on. Before I knew what was happening I was in the middle of a row. The last thing I wanted to do was quarrel with her, especially—' He hesitated.

'Especially given where you really were going,' Slider

suggested. 'She made you feel guilty and that made you angrier.'

He shrugged. 'You know what women are like,' he said again. 'I will say that was one thing about Phoebe. She never behaved that way. She had a mind more like a man's. That's why I went to see her, really. When I was in the car and starting off for Maria's, I decided to call in on Phoebe and ask her advice about the situation. I didn't know what to do about Noni, and I thought Phoebe could give me an impartial view.'

'Did you tell your wife you were going to call on her?' Slider asked.

'No, of course not. I told you, it was spur of the moment. I didn't think of it until I was driving off.'

Atherton spoke. 'But your wife told me today that you said you were going to call in on Phoebe and asked her if she wanted to send any message.'

'That's not true.' Prentiss shook his head in a goaded way, and drew again on the cigarette. It was burning too quickly, and the glowing lump of tobacco at the end detached itself and fell, landing in the untouched and cooling coffee. Prentiss looked down in vague surprise, and then reached for his lighter. 'I don't know why she said that,' he mumbled through the lighting operations.

'I think I do,' Slider said. 'She was trying to protect you as a loyal wife would. Trying to make us believe your relationship with Phoebe Agnew was innocent.'

'But it *was* innocent.'

'Don't forget', Slider said, 'that we know differently.'

CHAPTER TEN

Faurés a jolly good fellow

It was the early hours of the morning when Slider got home. The streets were empty, shiny with incipient frost, the sky black without feature behind the yellow street light. The houses looked two-dimensional and unreal. It was a bleak time of day, and winter sunrise was too far off to inject a ray of hope.

The streets were parked both sides as far as the eye could see: everyone was at home and accounted for. He had to cruise to find a space several streets away, and then walk back. The parked cars seemed to be sleeping too, tucked in snugly at the kerb; he imagined a windscreen eye half-opening as he passed and then drooping closed again.

He turned a corner, into a better-off street. The security conscious owners had fitted intruder lights, and because the front gardens were so short, he set them off from the pavement, like a row of bathchair colonels on the promenade waking one after the other: 'What? What? What?' He yawned as he walked, and yawning made him shiver. Oh, for bed, for the blissful sleeping heat of Joanna's body, for that wonderful moment when you check out of your brain and slip child-naked into the warm black waters of oblivion!

She woke as he came into the bedroom. 'Huh? Wasser time?' she muttered.

'Sshh! Just after four. Go back to sleep.'

'Huhnn,' she said. He pulled off his clothes and slid in

under the covers, cold as a stone, hesitating to touch her. But she reached behind her and pulled him against her scorching flesh, draping her legs over his and rubbing his cold feet with her warm ones. Sighing, he sank into her back, and thought that this was probably the most inexpressibly wonderful sensation life could afford.

Five minutes later she said, 'Can't sleep?'

'How could you tell?'

'I can hear you thinking.'

'I'm sorry, I didn't mean to disturb you. Go back to sleep.'

'No, it's all right,' she said. 'I'm awake now.' She rolled over to face him, and he went onto his back, taking her on his shoulder – their talking position. 'You're very late. Is it the case or another woman?'

'What would I do with another woman?'

'Remind me in the morning and I'll draw you a diagram. So what's happened?'

'We brought the prime suspect in for a little chat,' Slider said. 'We've matched the semen in the vagina to his blood type, and his Westminster boss has blown his alibi.'

'Oh, good. You arrested him?'

'No, he was just helping us with our enquiries. It's not always the best idea to arrest them. Once you do that, you're on the clock and all sorts of rules apply.'

He told her of the long interview with Prentiss, in its various stages. 'While we were talking to him I sent Hollis round to see Maria Colehern, and she confirmed that Prentiss had been there on Thursday night at the time he stated. Not that that was any surprise – if your mistress won't back you up, who will? But Hollis liked her. He believed she was telling the truth.'

'But?'

'It doesn't help him,' Slider said. 'He seemed terribly relieved and grateful when she backed him up, but it doesn't help him at all. She can't be his alibi if we don't have a definite time for the murder, and if he's the murderer he ought to know that.'

'Don't you think he's guilty?'

'Yes, I think he's guilty as hell, but I can't make up my mind if he's playing a long game, or just stupid. He doesn't *seem* stupid, but if he wanted an alibi, why didn't he use his wife? She tried to give him one, but her evidence is so compromised now we can't take her word on anything. Why did he say from the beginning he was at Agnew's flat just for the half-hour? If he was going to deny the rest – including having sex with her – why not deny it all?'

'Maybe he knows someone saw him,' Joanna said. 'Or maybe he doesn't know whether she told anyone he was coming, so he's trying to cover all eventualities.'

'Yes,' said Slider, 'you could be right there. And of course it has worked to an extent. It's tied our hands. We know he was there and he admits he was there but that doesn't prove that he murdered her.'

'Even with all his lies?'

'His lies suggest he had something to hide, but that's not enough,' Slider sighed.

'So what does he say he was doing there?' Joanna asked.

Slider told her what Prentiss had said about his visit.

Phoebe Agnew hadn't seemed surprised to see him. 'Phoebe was the sort of person you could just drop in on,' Prentiss explained. 'She never minded. Liked it, in fact. It wasn't as if she was the houseproud sort who needed advance notice so that she could put her best foot forward. Well, you've seen her place. It was always a tip – like a student bedsit. In fact, in some ways she still lived like a student. She never minded what time of the day or night it was, she was always ready for a drink and a chat.'

Phoebe, he said, had got the whisky bottle out straight away, and he'd accepted a glass and told her his problem over Noni and Maria.

'She seemed in a bit of an odd mood, though,' Prentiss said. 'Distant. Distracted, maybe. At times she hardly seemed to be listening to me. To tell you the truth, I think she'd had a lot to drink,' he added, 'and she was putting away the whisky at an alarming rate. She refilled her own glass and offered me a top-up before I'd taken more than a sip or two. And after that I saw her fill up a couple more times.'

'Are you saying she was drunk?' Slider had asked him. A woman sleepy with drink would struggle less when she was strangled, of course.

'Not really. She always could hold her drink like a man,' Prentiss had said, 'but she has been drinking more heavily these last few weeks. I had words with her about it at New Year – asked her if she realised how much she was getting through. She told me to mind my own damn business. Anyway,' he went on, 'on Thursday night when I'd told her my problem she didn't say anything, just sat there sipping at the blasted whisky, so I asked her if she'd been listening to me. I said, "Just say if I'm boring you and I'll go." And she flared up and said, "Oh, stop being such a prima donna! You think the world revolves around your penis!"'

'It was brave of him to tell you that,' Joanna commented.

'I think he was telling us how exasperating Agnew could be,' Slider said, 'and inviting our sympathy for murdering her.'

'Go on,' Joanna said. 'What did he say next?'

'He said it had suddenly occurred to him that maybe Agnew was starting the menopause too, and that that was what was making her irritable and irrational. So he decided to be patient and kind with her, because she couldn't help it, poor cow.'

'Patronising bastard!' Joanna exclaimed. 'What d'you mean, starting the menopause *too*?'

'He'd wondered if his wife's odd moods were partly

from the same cause, because she and Agnew were the same age.'

'How you men do harp on about hormones!'

'Never mind the "you men" business,' Slider said sternly. 'Anyway, Prentiss said he asked Agnew very kindly and calmly if there was something bothering her, and she said, "I've got a problem that makes yours pale into insignificance." So naturally Prentiss asked her what it was, and she said, "I wish I could tell you, but I can't." Prentiss pressed her a bit, said surely she could tell him, he was her oldest friend, and hinted that with all his friends in high places he might be able to help her.'

'Sensitive,' Joanna said. 'Doesn't miss an opportunity for self-aggrandisement.'

'Well, he said that Agnew just snapped at him, "You're the last person who could help me with it." So he shrugged and let it go.'

'And what about his own problem? Did he get her advice?'

'No, he said she seemed to think it was trivial and irrelevant. She said, "You get yourself into these things, try thinking how the other people involved feel", which he said annoyed him because that was exactly what he was doing, trying not to hurt either the wife or Maria Colehern.'

'It's a bugger when women don't recognise a compassionate, self-sacrificing man when they see one,' Joanna agreed. 'So did you believe all that?'

'Oh, yes, there was too much detail for him to have made it all up; and his annoyance with Agnew showed through clearly, which is presumably not what he would have wanted. I can see him losing his temper because she didn't understand him and kept claiming her own problems were worse. And I suppose it explains why he persists in denying he had sex with her: he thinks being her lover makes him more likely to kill her than being a detached platonic friend.'

'Well, he's not wrong there, is he?' Joanna said. 'If she

were just a platonic friend he'd shrug off her moods and leave her to it. So where do you go from here?'

Slider moved restlessly. 'We've got to find more evidence. We've got the house-to-house still going – if someone saw him coming out in a dishevelled or agitated condition, that might help.'

'What did Maria Colehern say about him when he arrived on Thursday night?' Joanna asked.

'That he seemed normal enough. Perhaps a bit subdued and preoccupied, but no more than she would expect from a man with his business and political commitments.'

'Well, he might have enough self-control to fake normality in front of her, given that he was relying on her for an alibi.'

'But it *wasn't* an alibi,' Slider fretted.

'Maybe you've missed something that was meant to fix the time of death,' Joanna said. 'Think of it: he left some subtle clue that you haven't cottoned on to, and he's being driven mad with frustration, not able to point it out to you without dropping himself in it!'

'A pleasing thought,' Slider said. 'Anything that could make that bastard writhe . . .'

'What else?'

'What else can we do? Find out more about his relationship with Agnew, I suppose. The thing is, I can't quite see him murdering her on what he's told us so far. Getting mad and smacking her, perhaps; but to strangle a big strong woman like that, even if she is drunk, takes enough time for an angry man to think better of it, if he hasn't got a really adequate reason. Especially a man with as much to lose as Prentiss. There must be more cause between them than that; and if we can nail the *why*, and present him with it, we might shock him into confessing.'

'How will you go about that?'

'We've still got all her papers to go through – something

might emerge. And meanwhile, there's his and her nearest and dearest to winkle at.'

'Good. You sound better now you've decided what to do.'

'It's relieved my mind to talk, but I'm sorry I've woken you up,' he said. 'D'you want to get a couple of hours now?'

'You're wide awake, aren't you?'

'To tell you the truth, I'm absolutely starving,' he confessed.

'Then it must be breakfast time,' she said, starting to get up.

'But it's only five o'clock!'

'What's an hour or two between friends? Anyway,' she added, suddenly serious, 'I want to talk to you.'

'Uh-oh! What have I done?'

'Let's get some food going first.'

While he made toast and tea, she scrambled eggs and, in deference to his hunger, grilled several rashers of bacon. The smell – surely the best in the world, especially early in the morning – got his juices going so that he was almost frantic by the time they sat in their dressing-gowns at the tiny kitchen table. They ate with cheerful daytime clatter, just as if the accumulated sleep of the rest of London wasn't lapping at the walls of the house like a reproachful tide.

'So, what have you got to tell me?' he asked. 'How was the concert, by the way? I haven't really seen you to talk to since then.'

'It was nice,' she said. 'Fauré and Schumann. Musicians' music.'

'Isn't it all?'

'Not by any means. Some of the things the public like to listen to, we don't like to play. And vice versa. The best music is both. Brahms, for instance. But I digress.'

He reached across the table for her hand. 'I like it when you do that.'

'Stop mucking about, Bill Slider. I've got to talk to you seriously about Gerhard Wolf.'

'Aha! I knew I ought to worry about a man named after a predator. Do you think it's going to lead to more work for you?'

'Nail on head, with a vengeance,' she said. 'The thing is, you know how tough things are at the moment?'

'Yes, you've told me,'

'I haven't told you everything. The orchestra's got virtually nothing until April. Our Government grant is being "discussed" at the highest levels, which means they want to withdraw it, or merge us with one of the other Big Four orchestras. And worst of all, we may be losing the summer opera tour.'

'You didn't tell me that,' said Slider.

'It's so grim to contemplate I didn't even want to think about it until it was certain one way or the other. But the fact is the opera company's losing money, and the only way they can economise is to cut out the big operas, particularly on tour. They're talking about only taking a chamber orchestra this year.'

'But if they take fewer musicians, you'll still be one of them, surely?' Slider pleaded. 'You're number five.'

'No, I don't mean they want to cut us down to chamber orchestra size. They want to drop us completely, in favour of a chamber orchestra. The Academy of St Paul's is the front runner. So you see,' she concluded bleakly, 'if we lose the summer tour, it means we'll only have something like four months' work a year. No-one can live on that.'

'But you do freelance stuff.'

'When I can get it. There's less and less of that around, too, and more and more musicians going after every job. The fact of the matter is, Bill, that I can't earn enough to live on.'

He was silent. He ought to be able to say, never mind, darling, I'll keep you, but that just wasn't true. He could barely afford to keep himself. Once all the deductions were taken out – tax, National Insurance, the maintenance for the kids, pension contributions, life insurance, payments on the car – he only just had enough left for his food and petrol and so on. In fact, because he was living with Joanna in her flat, he didn't even pay a proper share of those expenses. The contents insurance, for instance, and the council tax she paid – and she covered the whole telephone bill, though he gave her half the gas and electricity.

While the children were at school he was never going to have enough to keep Joanna; and as a Detective Inspector he could neither earn overtime nor take on a second job to boost his income. He could see why some officers, often with more than one ex-wife and family to pay for, got into debt and turned desperate.

'So what has this Wolf person got to do with it?' he asked at last. He had an awful apprehension about where this might be going.

She closed her fingers round his in the manner of a nurse about to exhort a patient to be brave. 'He's offered me a job.'

'In the whatsname – the Grossman Ensemble?'

She nodded. 'They've got a fantastic schedule – dates right into next year, regular bookings for festivals all over Europe. Recording contracts too. Wolfie's brought the musical standard up to a level where all the best conductors want to be associated with them; and Adela Pronck, the general manager, is just a total diva when it comes to publicity and getting bookings. She's had enquiries from all over the world in the last few months. You know what it's like – when you're hot, you're hot. Word goes round and before you know where you are, managements are fighting each other to get you.'

'It's a compliment, then, that they want you?' Slider said, trying to sound positive.

'Yes, it is. And I won't even have to audition. Wolfie's an

old mate – he knows my playing. That's why he called me to fill in in Leeds. And Adela never interferes with artistic decisions, so if Wolfie says I've got the right sort of sound and flexibility, it's a done deal.'

She stopped abruptly, as if she had suddenly heard her own voice. Slider felt cold through to his bones, despite the bacon and eggs. 'You sound as if you've made up your mind,' he said.

'No, I haven't, not yet,' she said. She bit her lip. 'It's an opportunity I can't afford to miss. But it would mean living abroad. They're based in Amsterdam. Most of the concerts are in Amsterdam and Frankfurt. And the recording sessions. And they tour a lot, mostly in Germany, Holland, Belgium and Switzerland, and there are American and Australian tours coming up, and Hong Kong in October. Sometimes they come to England,' she added on a failing note. 'As you see. But not often.'

'Yes, I see,' he said. There didn't seem anything else to say.

'It's a fabulous opportunity,' she said.

'Yes, I see that.'

'Bill, what am I supposed to do? If I take the job I'll have to live in Amsterdam. There's just no way I could travel back and forth.'

'How long would it be for?' he asked.

She shrugged. 'It's a permanent job. I don't really see myself living in Amsterdam for ever, and if the business picks up over here again of course I'd want to come back. But – well, it'd be a few years. At least.'

'So what happens to us?' he asked at last.

She took a deep breath. 'That's the problem I've been trying to think around ever since Monday night.'

'I thought you had something on your mind.'

'The only solution I can come up with is that you come with me.'

'What?'

'Come with me. Come to Amsterdam. Make a new life with me abroad.' She squeezed his hand again, to stop the negative she saw gathering like snow slipping down a roof. 'You've got nothing in particular to keep you here, have you? Your old house is sold, and now your divorce is through—'

'My children aren't nothing,' he said.

'I didn't mean that, but how often do you see them anyway? Once a month? You could fly back once a month to visit them – once a fortnight if you wanted.'

'But what if anything happened – an emergency? How would Irene get in touch with me?'

'There are telephones,' she pointed out. 'Amsterdam's not the end of the world. You could get back in a few hours—'

'A few hours!'

'You're being unreasonable. Would you refuse to move to Wales because it would take you a few hours to get back in an emergency?'

'Wales would be quite different.'

'Would it? Amsterdam's no further, really. Just because it's a foreign country—'

'That's not the point. Anyway, I wouldn't move to Wales either.'

'Wouldn't you? Not even if it was the only way for us to be together?' He was silent. 'Please, Bill, don't reject it out of hand. At least think about it.'

'I *am* thinking about it,' he said. 'Amongst other things I'm thinking what the hell could I do in Holland?'

'The same as you do here.'

'Don't be silly. Policing is completely different over there. I could be a policeman in Wales if I could get a post, but I could never learn a whole new system of law in a foreign country – and they'd never take me at my age anyway.'

She saw the truth of that, though reluctantly. 'Well, you could get some other job, then.'

'I don't speak Dutch.'

'You could learn.'

'I'm not qualified for anything else. The only thing I know how to do is what I do. And anyway, I don't want any other job,' he finished on a burst of honesty. 'I like what I do.'

She drew back her hand. 'Why should it be my career that gives way to yours? If a man gets promoted and moves, he expects his wife to go with him. Well, this is a tremendous promotion for me, and it means moving a few hundred miles. Are you going to stand in my way?'

'It's not a matter of that.'

'Well, what is it a matter of?'

'Jo,' he said painfully, 'I just don't see how it can be done.'

'You mean you're prepared to give me up, just like that?'

'I'm not giving you up. But it's an impossible decision to make.'

'It'll have to be made, one way or another,' she said, 'but not now.' She stood up, pulling the empty plates together. 'This is not the time to discuss it. I can see how it will end if we go on now.'

'I don't see—'

'Please. We'll talk later. Just think about it, will you? You can do that much.'

'I am thinking,' he said.

She turned away to dump the plates on the draining board. 'I'm going to take a shower.'

CHAPTER ELEVEN

Braising with fake hams

He got back to work bathed, shaved and clean shirted, but unrefreshed, his mind raw with this new galloping doom that was suddenly bearing down on him. The missing lab report on the tissue sample from under the victim's nails had caught up with reality and was lying on his desk. He opened it one-handed and read it as he sipped the first unsatisfying cup of machine tea of the day.

'Oh Nora,' he whimpered. Bad to worse. The skin sample was not a genetic match with the semen and blood. The person Phoebe Agnew had scratched was not Josh Prentiss. '*Bloody* Nora.'

'Sorry?' said Swilley from the door.

'Nora, not Norma,' he explained. 'Get Atherton in here, will you.'

'He's not in yet.'

Slider looked at his watch. 'Where the hell is he?'

'I don't know, boss. He hasn't phoned in that I know of. D'you want me to ring him at home?'

'Yes, do that. He might be ill.'

She hesitated, and then said, 'If he's not at home, I know where he might be.' Slider raised his eyebrows. 'At least, I know where he was on Sunday night, and he was late in Monday morning.'

'If you want to say something, say it,' Slider suggested.

She looked away. 'You know I don't gossip. But I know

how you feel about Jim and Sue. I like Sue myself. And I happen to know Jim was out with Tony Hart on Sunday night because I saw them together.'

'Oh,' said Slider.

Hart was a WDC who had been on loan to his firm a while back, at which time Atherton had seemed to have a thing going with her. He was now in what was supposed to be a steady relationship with Joanna's friend and colleague, Sue Caversham; but Atherton had always been a serial bonker, and nothing had been more surprising than the idea of him settling down with one woman. How Atherton ran his private life was his own concern, of course, but Slider couldn't help knowing that if Sue was made unhappy, it would upset Joanna. Equally, though, he couldn't run his firm on that basis.

'Well, that's none of my business,' he said.

Swilley gave a faint shrug. 'If he's not at home, d'you want me to ring round for him?'

'No, leave it,' Slider said. 'How are you getting on with checking Medmenham's story?'

'It's all right,' she said. 'I sweet-talked the local boys into doing it. That wine bar, Ramblers – they call it Benders. Heart of the Essex gay scene, but fairly up-market. They don't have any trouble there. Anyway, Prentiss and Medmenham are well known, and the staff confirm they were in there on Thursday from about ten right through to closing at half past eleven.' She looked enquiringly at Slider. 'It doesn't rule out one of them going back to London in the early hours but . . .'

'But it's unlikely, unless they're involved in a deep plot. At least we can interview Piers Prentiss with a bit more confidence. What's that in your hand?'

'First report on the latents from Agnew's flat,' she said. 'The prints on the whisky glasses belonged to Prentiss and Agnew, but the wineglasses and cutlery and the edges of the plates had all been wiped clean.'

'Yes, Lamont told me that at the flat.'

'Oh. Well, they're still going through the lifts – there were a hell of a lot, as you know – but they've found two lots that don't belong to Agnew, Medmenham, Prentiss or the girl upstairs. One set was on the edge of the unit the hi-fi stands on, left hand, half a palm and four fingers, as if he's leaned on it while he's doing something with his right.'

'Changing the music or pouring coffee?' Slider suggested.

'Could be. Oh, and we've checked with Records and it's not Wordley's either.'

'Well, he's smart enough to wear gloves if he's there for felonious purposes. What else?'

'Fabric smudges on the front door and the lounge door, as if they'd been held by a gloved hand, or through a handkerchief,' Norma said promptly. 'Someone trying to let himself out without leaving a mark. But, boss, if whoever ate dinner with her was trying to cover his tracks, doesn't that rule out Prentiss? He didn't mind leaving his marks on the whisky glass.'

'Maybe he just forgot the whisky glass.'

'Yes, but I mean, he didn't deny he'd been at the flat, so why should he mind if it was him ate the meal?'

Slider frowned in thought. 'I don't know. Unless he didn't want it to be known that he was there earlier – something to do with the time of death, maybe.'

'His wife says he didn't leave home until after half past seven—'

'If we can believe anything she says.'

'But if she was telling the truth,' Norma persisted, 'it fits with him saying he left home at a quarter to eight, and if he got to Colehern's at half past eight, the window he could have been at the flat's too small for him to've eaten the meal. He could still have killed her, but he couldn't have got outside a casserole and trifle job as well as all the rest.'

Slider rubbed his head. 'I wish we could have checked

his stomach contents on Thursday. If Prentiss wasn't the one who ate the supper, then he must have come after the eater, because he said the kitchen was stacked up with dirty plates, and the only ones that were in there were the casserole and tiramisu lot. Which means the eater couldn't have been the murderer or Agnew would have been already dead when Prentiss got there. But if the eater wasn't the murderer, why did he try to get rid of his finger-marks?'

'God knows,' Swilley said. 'This is the nuttiest case I ever worked on. But we know *someone* else was there at some point because of the tissue under the nails and now the rogue fingerprints on the unit.'

'But we don't know that that was the murderer, or even that it was the person who ate the supper,' Slider concluded. 'Someone not connected with the meal could have leaned on the unit for some reason. And she could have slightly scratched someone by accident.'

Swilley nodded. 'And also, whose was the condom, if it wasn't Prentiss's? And why does Prentiss still insist he didn't have sex with Agnew?'

'You identify the questions all right,' Slider said. 'I wish you'd identify some answers as well.'

'Well, maybe the murderer had nothing to do with the meal at all. Maybe he came after both the eater and Prentiss had been and gone, and for some reason he fiddled about with the cutlery and things, and then realised what he'd done and went round wiping anything he might have touched.'

'Why would he touch the cutlery?'

'Maybe Agnew asked him to help her clear up. Maybe it was all still on the table. He helped stack it and carry it out to the kitchen, murdered her, and then had to wipe his traces away.'

'Very obliging murderer,' Slider said. 'Why didn't he murder her first and save himself the trouble?'

'Maybe he didn't mean to kill her. He did it on an impulse,

and then got in a panic, tried to remember what he might have touched.'

'I suppose that makes more sense. Faking the rape scene looks like panic. But Prentiss said the dishes were already in the kitchen.'

'Well, listen, boss,' Norma said eagerly, 'it could still be Prentiss. Suppose he went round there for a shag. They're having a drink afterwards and he sees all the dirty plates still lying about, and blows her out for being a slut. They clear up the stuff together, but he goes on nagging and the row develops and he loses his rag and murders her. Then he thinks, shit, I've got to cover my tracks. He wipes everything he can remember touching, chucks old Aggers on the bed and ties her wrists, puts his gloves on to let himself out because he's clever enough to think of that. But then, when you come round asking questions, he remembers he didn't wipe the whisky glasses, so he makes the best of a bad job and says yes, he was there, but only for half an hour and a drink – knowing that we'll find that out anyway.' She looked at him hopefully.

'I love it,' he said. 'It explains everything except why he keeps denying the semen.'

She shrugged. 'Denied it to start with because he thought it made him look too tasty. Now he's stuck with it and doesn't know what else to do.'

'And the skin under the nails, and the other fingerprints?'

'You said yourself they might be nothing to do with it. Someone who called earlier, nothing to do with anything. Might not even have been the same day.'

'But if the skin was still there under her nails at the time of death, it would mean that she hadn't washed her hands since. Okay, she lived in a tip, but she didn't strike me as a dirty person.'

He remembered suddenly a witness from another case, one Sandal Palliser, saying there were untidy people who were personally clean, and dirty people who were models of tidiness: that tolerance of one did not necessarily mean tolerance of the other.

'Yeah,' said Norma. 'Well, I dunno.'

Slider caught an echo. 'You said there were two sets of alien finger-marks?'

Norma roused herself from thought. 'Oh, yes. The other set was on the flush handle of the loo – points to you, guv.'

'I have my uses,' Slider said modestly. 'Are they the same as the others?'

'No. It's a right thumb, and Bob Lamont says it's a woman's – very small, anyway.'

Slider frowned. 'This gets worse.'

'So she had a female visitor,' Norma shrugged.

'Yes, but if the thumb-mark isn't overlaid, it means no-one used the loo after that, so it must have been late in the day.'

'You don't think the murderer was a woman?'

'I wouldn't have thought a woman was strong enough to strangle Phoebe Agnew, unless she was a very big woman.'

'And it was a very small thumb.'

Slider shook his head in frustration. 'There must have been a lot of coming and going all within a small space of time.'

'Like a bleedin' French farce,' Norma assented. 'Well, there's a stack of statements about people seen in the street, from the door-to-door and volunteer witnesses. Maybe some of them will come good.'

'We can hope,' Slider said.

'Meanwhile, where do we go from here, boss?'

'I think we go and see Prentiss's brother,' said Slider. 'But first, I've got some phone calls to make, and I'll have to bring Mr Porson up to speed. Do me a favour, will you?' He pushed the plastic cup away from him in distaste. 'Get rid of this and bring me some proper tea from the canteen. I can't think with my tannin levels dropping like an express lift.'

'Cuppa rosy. No prob,' said Norma obligingly.

Atherton was not at home. Slider hesitated, and then rang Sue. As soon as she answered he wished he hadn't called, because if Atherton was out on the pull, there was nothing he could say to her that wouldn't drop him in it.

But while he was agonising, she said easily, 'If you're looking for Jim, he isn't here.'

'Oh, right,' Slider said.

'Hasn't he turned in to work?'

'Well, he's a bit late. I just wondered . . .' Slider said vaguely. 'I expect he's on his way.'

Unexpectedly, she chuckled. 'You're such a rotten actor. It's one of the nice things about you.'

'What do you mean?' he prevaricated.

'He's been off tom-catting somewhere,' Sue said, still in that amused voice. 'You know it and I know it, and you're wondering whether you've got him into trouble, while at the same time feeling sorry for me.'

'It would be a bold man who felt sorry for you.'

'Hmm. Well, I suppose you mean that for a compliment. But you might as well know, Jim and I had a big row on Saturday, so he's punishing me. I did the shopping, you see, and I got the wrong sort of ham and ruined his quiche. It was in a packet instead of on the bone – a heinous crime, apparently.'

'Oh dear,' said Slider.

'He was mad as fire,' Sue said. 'It was quite funny, really.'

Slider worried she wasn't taking her sin seriously enough. We all have our little ways, and a man's vanity can reside in many places. Kick him in it, and you're socking around for a smack in the puss. He said cautiously, 'Well, he can be a bit pernickety, but after all, he is a very good cook.'

'That's praising with faint damns, all right,' Sue said, and Slider recognised it as an Atherton phrase. Language mutation was one of the signs of a real relationship, and obscurely he felt better about them.

She went on, 'Anyway, the bloody old ham was just the surface excuse. Underneath, it was the same old row rehashed. You know, the one about commitment?'

'Oh,' said Slider cautiously. It was a word no man liked to hear, even applied to someone else. Like 'castration', just the sound of it made you cross your legs and fidget.

'I want us to move on a stage and he's hanging back. So we quarrel. That's what it's really about.'

'He's been on his own a long time,' Slider said.

'So have I. It isn't easy for me, either. Believe me, I understand the problem. But—' She hesitated. 'Seriously, Bill, I am a bit worried about him. I know he's squeamish about the idea of settling down, and we fight a lot, and that's healthy. And we have ways of punishing each other, and a lot of the time it's half in fun. But underneath I think he's under a lot of strain. Have you noticed it at work?'

Slider felt uncomfortable with the direction the conversation was taking. He was only just learning to discuss himself with Joanna; discussing Atherton with Sue was a breast-baring too far. Besides, he was Atherton's boss as well as his friend, and he couldn't discuss his performance at work behind his back. 'Well,' he said, trying to think of a way not to answer.

But Sue answered for him. 'This gambling, for instance. You must have noticed. I think it's a sort of lashing out. He likes wine too much to waste it by getting drunk, and I won't let him upset me with the threat of other women. So what's left? I think the gambling is him saying, look, I'm being bad. He's doing it to spite me.'

'Why should he want to do that?' Slider said robustly. Why did women think everything a man did was because of them?

'Oh, because I'm there. Like Everest.' It was another Atherton expression. 'He's wound up tight as a watch spring and it has to come out somewhere, and I'm just handy. But I really am worried,' she went on. 'He's getting through a lot of money, and now there's this buying a racehorse thing – had he told you about it?'

'He did mention something about it.'

'He's going to put all his spare into it, and I'm sure it's a scam.' She sounded quite different now, not amused, but chilled and anxious. 'I just know he's going to get really burnt, and I don't know how he'll cope. I wish there was something you could do.'

'Look, Sue—'

'Bill, he's your friend. I know men don't like to interfere in each other's lives, and I know you being his boss makes it a bit delicate, but I really think he's close to cracking up, and I can't get near enough to help him. I'm a newcomer in his life, and, anyway, he's made me the enemy over this, so anything I say will only make things worse. If he gets caught and made a fool of, it's really going to hurt him – not just financially, though that's bad enough. Can't you *please* see if you can help him?' She paused a beat, and added almost inaudibly, 'I do love him.'

That she was shy of saying the words aloud touched him. 'I'll try,' he said. 'But I don't know – he's a very private person, you know.'

'Yes, I know that,' she said, and the amusement was back in her voice.

'He may not like me interfering.'

'If anyone can, you can,' she said. Her confidence did not improve his. 'And you've a right to, if it's affecting his work. At the moment I've no right.'

'I wouldn't say that exactly.'

'He would,' Sue said succinctly.

* * *

'Right,' said Slider, emerging into the office, 'let's have the latest so that I can report to Mr Porson.'

'Still trying to follow up the various sightings in the street,' Hollis said, gesturing to a tottering heap of reports. 'We've got everyone from Lord Lucan to Shergar. A scruffy man in jeans and a state of agitation running away. That'd be all right if it wasn't Prentiss. Someone standing watching the house – unfortunately, that was a woman. A smart man doing up his tie as he walked along. I quite like him, because he had something under his arm, a briefcase or a paper or something, and if we are missing a file, that could be it. But he sounds too young to be Prentiss. Nothing hotter than that yet.'

'Okay, keep it up. What else?'

'One of the journos from the *Guardian* got in touch to say that Agnew'd been working on a special project recently,' Mackay reported. 'Something of her own – not for the paper. Very secretive about it – wouldn't say what it was, but he says she seemed worried about it. She hinted it was very important stuff and that it would be bad news if it fell into the wrong hands. That's all I could get out of him,' he apologised. 'But if it was that important maybe there *was* a missing file and that's what she was killed for, and it was just coincidence that Prentiss went round there.'

'Maybe,' said Slider. 'Have another go at this bloke, in case he knows more and just isn't telling. And ask around some of her other contacts. Ah, McLaren, how's your Wordley idea getting on? You've been out of the office a lot. What have you got to show for it?'

'Not much, guv,' McLaren admitted. 'I had a couple of goes at Kelly, and she's given me a description of the geezer Wordley went off with. She says he was a big bloke, mid-thirties, a slaphead with an earring in the top of his ear. She still swears she doesn't know his name, and I believe her now. Says she thinks she's seen him somewhere before but can't place where. But she's obviously shit scared of him and Wordley. I don't want to hang around her too much in case it gets back to him and gets her in schtuck.'

Slider nodded. 'Nothing on where Wordley is?'

'No, but I've had info he was drinking in that club, Porky's, in the Shepherd's Bush Road Wednesday night. Well, that's only five minutes from Agnew's flat.'

'It's a long way between Wednesday night and six-forty-five Thursday evening, when she was seen alive by Peter Medmenham.'

'Yes, guv, I'm working on that,' McLaren said. 'Wordley's not an easy bloke to forget, but a lot of people are scared of him, so it takes time to track him.'

'And what about a motive? Or are you sticking with motiveless violence?'

'Well, there's this stuff Andy was just saying about something she was working on that was worrying her. And Medmenham said she was worried and she'd been drinking heavier recently. Suppose it was something to do with Wordley? She got him off that blag, didn't she, but say she'd found some more evidence that said he did it after all? That'd fry her brains all right, wondering whether to come clean and drop him, or hide it and live with her conscience?'

'Supposing she'd got one,' said Swilley.

Slider shifted impatiently. 'What's your point?'

'Point is, guv, it would give Wordley the best motive to off her,' McLaren said.

'It's a lot of supposing,' Slider said.

'It's more motive than we've got for Prentiss, which is none,' McLaren pointed out. 'And Wordley's a slag with a record for violence.'

'Blimey, you sounded almost intelligent then, Maurice,' Swilley said admiringly. 'You've got to hand it to him, boss.'

'All right, you can stay on it, McLaren, but watch your step. Anything else?' Silence. 'Well, if that's the magnificent total, I'd better just take it to Mr Porson, and hope he doesn't throw a fit. I suppose you all saw the papers today? We're on trial on this one. Keep at it.'

When Slider got back from Porson's office, Atherton had arrived. Slider sucked him into his office with a look.

'I'm sorry I'm late, guv,' Atherton pre-empted him.

'Where were you?'

'I had a bit too much last night and overslept,' Atherton said. Slider noticed he didn't say too much what.

'Is that it? That's your excuse?'

Atherton shrugged gracefully. 'What can I say? I could spin you a line—'

'Well, do,' Slider invited. 'At least a good, four-ply, industrial-weave lie would make it look as if you had some respect for me.'

But Atherton wasn't playing. 'I'm sorry,' he said again. 'I know it's not on, and it won't happen again.'

Slider was stumped. There was nothing in that smooth carapace he could address. Having been cast in the role of boss, he could not speak as friend. He would have to find a different way in. 'It had better not,' he said. 'Well, now you're here, I want you to come and interview Piers Prentiss with me. I was going to take Swilley—'

'Swilley? It doesn't take much, does it? One little slip – and after I've given you the best years of my life!' Atherton cried dramatically.

It was a crack in the armour. 'Where were you, anyway?' Slider tried. 'You look like hell.'

'Wednesday's my flower arranging class,' Atherton said, papering it over. 'So how come Prentiss junior? Have I missed something?'

'If you'd been here, you'd have known.' Slider brought him up to speed. 'Porson's quite keen on Wordley, but obviously Prentiss is still front runner, so the next step is to try and get some more information on his relationship with Agnew – and, we can hope, what she was working on – from a safe source. Hence Prentiss's brother. I nearly went without you,' he finished.

'Yes, I'm sorry,' Atherton said, and he sounded genuine this time. 'It really won't happen again. I'll buy you lunch as my penance.'

'It will be a penance. We're going to Essex, remember.'

CHAPTER TWELVE

Primrose path

Piers Prentiss's home was called Primrose Cottage. 'And you can't get more *bijou* than that,' Atherton said. It had half submerged beams and little lattice windows, and round the small, low door a rambling rose grew, which would presumably look divine in summer but at the moment merely lurked thornily waiting for someone's eye to put out. To complete the picturesqueness, the ancient roof was as wobbly as an auntie at a wedding, and the chimney leaned perilously out of true.

'I wonder what holds that up?' said Atherton.

'Probably roadworks somewhere,' Slider said vaguely.

The cottage was in what had once been the high street of a village just outside Chelmsford; but the village had been absorbed, stuck to the town by bland blobs of infill – new 'vernacular' housing as tasteless as sticking-paste. Now the row of mediaeval dwellings, some of them with downstairs fronts converted long ago to shops, stood braced at one end by a petrol station, and at the other by a raw-looking supermarket already in the process of being out-evolved by a greenfield superstore just off the A12.

The building next to Primrose Cottage was an antiques shop with 'Prentiss' over the window in tasteful gold lettering on dark green. The window display was of china, glass, old wooden boxes, silver and jewellery, and a couple of porcelain-faced dolls. Beyond were some handsome pieces of furniture and other, more eclectic items: a pair of leather riding boots on wooden trees, a spinning-wheel, a Victorian child's tricycle and, on the wall, framed classic cinema posters.

'Cinema posters are very collectable these days,' Atherton said, peering in with a hand shading out the light. 'I'm looking for one myself: Sean Connery and Marilyn Monroe in *Gentlemen Prefer Bonds.*'

'Eh?'

'It's the one where she sings *Diamonds Are For Ever.*'

'I know it well,' Slider said. A middle of the road shop, and probably successful, he concluded: everything looked clean and well tended, and there were no depressing boxes of unsaleable junk, the usual hallmark of desperation. There was a 'closed' notice hanging on the door. He looked at his watch. 'Lunch hour. He said on the phone he eats at home. It looks as though he doesn't keep an assistant.'

They rang the doorbell of the cottage, and waited on the narrow pavement while the local traffic pottered by behind their backs in an unhurried but constant stream.

A barking got up from within, and a moment later the door was opened and a pair of small wiry dogs leapt up like clay pigeons being fired. They sprang with all four feet at once, barking with staccato endurance, timing it so that one took off as the other landed, to get the maximum coverage. But they were not showing their teeth, and the blunt end was eagerly a-twitch, so Slider assumed they meant no harm and turned his attention to the human accompanying them.

'Piers Prentiss?' he asked. He held up his brief and introduced them.

'Yes. Hello,' the man replied. 'Down, dogs! Shut up! Don't mind them, they don't bite.'

Piers Prentiss was as tall as his brother, but thin instead of massive, drooping a little at the shoulders, perhaps the reaction to living in Primrose Cottage, where the clearance was less than generous. His face was interestingly gaunt under the same leonine growth of hair, but cut rather longer, brushed back all round, and completely white. It made a startling contrast to the tanned skin and brown eyes, a shade darker than Josh's, and he carried his head self-consciously, as though inviting comment. Slider guessed he had gone grey very young and made capital out of it; now, however, the lines of his face had caught up. He had the same short, broad nose as his brother, but his mouth was wider, thinner and looser, giving his face a downward drag that made him look older than Josh, and somehow more aesthetic. A mournful and thoughtful lion, not much of a threat to the wildebeest.

His kit was expensively country casual: loose-fitting dark brown corduroy trousers and a forest-green lambswool sweater with an open shirt collar peeking out at the top; a gold signet ring and an expensive-looking gold watch weighted his long, delicate-looking hands. There was nothing in the least fey about his clothes, but they had the effect of making him look precious, perhaps by contrast. He looked as though he was just standing around inside them, and would have been surprised to discover that anyone thought they were his. In the same way, if you had ever seen him at a bus stop, you would have assumed he was looking for a taxi. This was a man you could not imagine on public transport; Josh would take a bus without a second thought if it suited his purposes.

'You want to talk to me about Phoebe,' Piers Prentiss said. Slider assented. 'You'd better come in. I'm just having my lunch – do you mind? I have to open the shop again in half an hour.'

He led the way down the narrow, flagged passage towards the back, and Slider and Atherton followed, with the dogs' heads appearing regularly at their elbows, like people trampolining behind a wall. It was dark inside the cottage and smelled of damp brick and furniture polish, and Slider caught a glimpse through a door of gleaming wood and old chintz, before being led into the low-ceilinged and dog-smelling kitchen at the back. The reedy sunshine outside bounced off the diamond-paned windows, doing nothing much for the illumination inside. The kitchen looked like an advert from a Smallbone catalogue: no expense had been spared to make it look like the real thing, only better. There was a great deal of exposed brick, interspersed with white painted plaster; dark beams across the ceiling, red-brown quarry tiles on the floor; expensive pine units with black iron hinges and handles, and a huge dresser filling one whole wall floor to ceiling.

'Lovely and warm in here,' Slider commented.

'It's the Aga,' Prentiss said, gesturing to where it sat fatly under the long, low inglenook. 'Sadly the chimney isn't up to much, so it's only electric.'

'What you'd call ohm on the range,' Atherton murmured.

Fortunately Prentiss didn't hear him properly. 'Yes, there must have been a range there, but the previous owners removed it. But to me, the space just cried out for an Aga, so I heeded the cries. I mean, if you've got an inglenook, flaunt it, I always say.'

It was plain what Piers had been doing when they arrived. In the middle of the kitchen was an old pine table on which stood a stoneware bowl half full of yellow soup, spoon akimbo; a rustic-looking wholemeal loaf on a bread board; and butter and cheese crocks, next to which lay the folded-open *Guardian*. It looked like a still-life group; or the Smallbone ad again.

'Would you like some?' Piers offered, gesturing vaguely towards it. 'Lentil soup – home-made. There's plenty.'

'No, thanks all the same,' Slider refused for them both. 'But please don't let us stop you.'

'All right, I won't,' said Piers, resuming his seat. 'Make yourselves at home.'

Slider and Atherton pulled out chairs and sat at the table. The dogs had stopped bouncing in favour of a lengthy and committed smelling of their shoes and trousers. They were terriers of some sort; their square faces and grizzled curls reminded Slider disconcertingly of Commander Wetherspoon, especially as they stared at him with the same dispassion. It made him feel he was on trial.

'So, what do you want to know? It's a terrible business about poor Phoebe. There was a big spread about her in the *Guardian* on Monday – was it? – or Tuesday. I hear,' he twinkled gravely at them over his spoon, 'you've been grilling my brother about it. He's thinking of suing you for wrongful arrest.'

'He wasn't arrested. He was—'

'—helping you with your enquiries, yes,' Piers finished for him. 'You can't sue for that: that's what I told him. Poor dear, he was mortified. He was on the phone last night, keening like an Irish peasant for his lost career – his political career, I mean – because the Government can't bear anything that looks the least bit like sleaze, so poor Josh will be out on his ear before you can say floccinaucinihilipilification.' He paused a beat to see if they appreciated his style, and meeting intelligent interest, he seemed to relax a little and expand. 'I said, love, you don't want to work for that bunch of crypto-fascist asses anyway.' He pronounced it *arses*. 'But of course the tragedy is that he *does*. The architectural stage was never big enough for Josh. The *stage* stage wasn't. Well,' he took and swallowed a spoonful of soup demurely, 'I suppose there's always Europe.'

His voice reminded Slider of dried flowers: a faint, odourless ghost of some great past vigour. He moved his hands as he spoke, as though trying to help the failing voice along, but his gestures had the slow, underwater impotence of the running-dream. Still, talking was obviously very much his thing, for which Slider gave inner thanks. All he had to do was to filter out the useful grit from the river of words. He settled himself, exuding ease and not-being-in-a-hurry.

Atherton, noting the posture, resigned himself to a long session.

'Your brother was never on the stage, was he?' Slider asked, on the back of Prentiss's last comment.

'Not an act*or*,' Piers said, striking an attitude, 'and yet, surely an actor *manqué*? Always wanted to be centre stage – always *was* centre stage, let's face it – but without the nuisance of learning lines.'

'He joined the Drama Society at university, didn't he?'

'However did you know that? Yes, he did – though of course in any university, joining Dramsoc has everything to do with social popularity and nothing to do with the theatre. But Josh could have been a thespian if only he'd had the self-discipline. He has real talent, you know. He dissipates it.'

He smiled, and his rather lugubrious face was translated: the charm and pulling-power of his brother were there, but diluted, like September rather than July sunshine.

'On the other hand,' he went on, 'if it comes to the parable of the talents, Josh would say I've buried mine under a bush. We were both born with every advantage, and look at our relative positions now.'

'You come from a wealthy family?' Slider slipped the question in as undisturbingly as an otter slipping into water.

'Oh, yes. Family pile in leafy Buckinghamshire – not too many acres, though. Grandpa and Father were both ambassadors, so they preferred their wealth portable.'

'So you must have spent a lot of time abroad?'

'Oh, no, we stayed at home in good old England.'

'Who looked after you?'

'We had nannies and so forth until we went to school. But we had super holidays with the parents – up until Mummy died. That was when I was eleven. After that we didn't go and stay with Father because there wouldn't have been anyone to supervise us. But there were always relatives around. And Granny lived in the South of France – we stayed with her quite often.'

'You went to Eton, like your brother?' Atherton asked.

He nodded. 'Eton, Oxford and the Guards was the family tradition – until Josh broke it. After Mummy died, he was always getting into rows with Father. First he refused to go to university at all, and then instead of PPE at Balliol he chose architecture and UCL. Father dropped down dead with shock – well, almost.' He made a deprecating gesture. 'It was heart, but in fact he died in May 1972, just when I was about to do my finals. Still, I like to think it was Josh's rebellion that brought it on. Makes the story so much more symmetrical, doesn't it?'

He brooded a moment, crumbling a piece of bread in his fingers. There was some hostility buried here, Slider thought. Simple sibling rivalry?

'So,' Piers said abruptly, coming back, 'brother and I inherited the family fortune between us. As soon as probate was through, Josh used his to buy his own firm and the house in Campden Hill Square. Such foresight! Everything he now has and is stems from that first sensible investment. I, on the other hand,' he went on with an airy gesture, scattering crumbs, 'used my half to allow me to live comfortably without having to take the antiques business too seriously. It's moot whether the shop keeps me or I keep the shop. Now *whose*, I ask you, was the wasted talent?'

'I hope that's a rhetorical question,' Slider said. Worldly success versus elegant living: was that the issue between the brothers? Piers wanted his comment to sound ironic, wanted his audience to conclude from his denigration of his lifestyle that he thought it superior; but underneath, did he really feel that he was a failure, and that Josh had scored on all fronts?

'Oh, goodness, I wouldn't force you to take sides!' Piers said. He seemed to have been distracted from his lunch. The soup was cooling and congealing around the neglected spoon, and all he had done with the bread was to make a mess on the table. Now he pushed his chair back with a final air. 'What about some coffee?' He stood up, and the dogs, who had gone off trouser duty and were curled together on a beanbag in the corner next to the Aga, lifted their heads hopefully. 'You'll have some coffee?'

'I'm afraid we've kept you from eating.'

'Oh, no, don't worry. I never eat much at lunchtime, anyway. Besides,' he looked down at the bowl with sudden dislike, 'I loathe lentil soup. One might as well eat cardboard boxes.'

'I thought it was home-made,' Atherton said, amused.

Piers looked at him. 'Not by *me*. Good Lord, I'm *nothing* of a cook! No, I have an absolute treasure who comes in. My "lady who does". She cleans, cooks, soothes the brow when fevered, and looks after the doggies when I'm away travelling – doesn't she, woofies? Doesn't dear old Aunty Marjie look after my wuffle-buffles, then?' The dogs looked adoring and waggled their bottoms ecstatically. 'The trouble is,' he added in a normal voice, 'that she's *frightfully* keen on wholemeal nourishment and regular bowel movements. Just like an old-fashioned nanny! So, let me whisk away this *abrasive* nourishment—' He swept the soup bowl up, 'and put on some nice, evil, caffeine-loaded coffee. How do you take it? Why don't you two chaps go and make yourselves comfortable in the drawing-room, and I'll bring it in. Too sordid, sitting in the kitchen with the left-overs!'

The change of room was not a change for the better, for the drawing-room was chill and smelled of mushrooms, but at least it was a chance to have a look round.

'This bloke's a babbling brook,' Atherton complained when they were alone. 'We'll be lucky to get out of here before Easter.'

Slider raised his eyebrows. 'In a hurry? Got some major appointment you've been keeping from me?'

'I thought we had a date,' Atherton said. 'You, me and a

couple of pints of the amber foaming.' The dogs pattered in and stood just inside the doorway watching them. 'Watch out, guv,' Atherton hissed. 'Two people in dog suits at twelve o' clock. Don't touch the silver.'

Slider was making a round of the framed photographs which decorated almost every surface. Here was a 1950s black and white snapshot of the Prentiss boys aged about ten and six, with, presumably, their mother and father, standing together on a windy clifftop. The children's faces seemed a nice blend of the parents' different features, with Josh perhaps favouring his spectacularly beautiful mother slightly more, and Piers his rather long-faced father. Even at that age Josh was the more physically attractive, and looked straight at the camera with the winning smile of one who had no doubts he would be liked. Piers seemed to be drawing back, pressing against his mother, his eyes sliding uncertainly sideways, his smile required and perfunctory. Always overshadowed by his brother, Slider thought. A slight rearrangement of the same genes, and you had less of everything – good looks, charm, confidence and success. A first-class and a second-class son. There were things to be said, after all, for being an only child.

Josh featured in lots of the photographs. Here was another of the two boys together, this time kneeling with their arms round two Weimaraners; now a formal picture of them, mid teens, standing behind their seated father with a hint of pillars and chandeliers behind them – some embassy or foreign palace? Another, in their late teens and leaning on the rail of a ship. Here was a wedding photograph, Josh in morning suit and Noni thin as a rail and vividly dark in full white fig, Piers with top hat in hand, head turned, looking out to the side of the picture as though he didn't belong to the group.

Those that didn't feature Josh were of Piers – alone, with dogs, or with various men; the various men alone; and the progress of some children who Slider assumed were Josh's son and daughter. He was interested to note that there was no photograph of Phoebe Agnew anywhere – and also none of Peter Medmenham.

He was just working his way round to the piano and the last crop when Piers Prentiss came in with a tray, preceded by the smell of coffee. 'Here we are! Now let's sit down and be comfortable.' He saw Atherton glance at the clock and said, 'I'm not going to worry about opening the shop again. I hardly ever get passing trade on a weekday anyway, and everyone else knows to try here if the shop's shut. So we can take our time.'

'I was just looking at your photographs,' Slider said. 'I hoped you might have one of Phoebe Agnew.'

'There's one on the bookcase,' Piers said. He put down the tray on the coffee table and crossed the room, and then paused, puzzled. 'Well, that's odd. There was one here. It's gone. It was a rather nice one, of Phoebe, Josh and me in Josh's garden. What on earth could have happened to it? I suppose Marjorie must have moved it.' He made a rapid scan of the room, and shrugged. 'I'll have to ask her what she's done with it. I've got lots of others, though, unframed. I'll get the box out if you like. But first – coffee.'

He poured and handed it, and then from a cupboard in the chimney corner produced a bottle of Caol Ila. 'You'll indulge in a little *pousse-café*? Do you care for malt whisky?'

'I'm rather a fan,' Slider said. Atherton refused, on the grounds that he was driving, and Piers poured two large ones, and then took an armchair facing them, with the dogs at his feet. 'I didn't see any photos of Peter Medmenham, either,' Slider said, when they were settled. He sipped his malt, and noticed with mild satisfaction that Piers drank more deeply of his. 'He told me that you had been friends for many years.'

'Oh, poor Peter!' Piers said, but sounded quite detached about it. 'Did he tell you that our ways have parted?'

'He seems to hope they haven't really,' Slider said.

'Yes, that's what Thursday's little visit was all about. I'd spent Wednesday night with Richard, and we'd planned to have the weekend together, and I couldn't risk Peter barging in on us, so I decided it was time to tell him it was over. Then he insisted on coming over on Thursday night to persuade me that my new love was just a fling, a will-o'-the-wisp leading me from the true path.'

'And it isn't?'

'No,' he said, quite serious for once. 'If you'd seen how sorry Richard was to leave me on Thursday morning, you'd know. I'm sorry about Peter, because we've been together a long time, and I hate to hurt anyone, but the thing with Richard is on a different plane altogether. That's why I took down the photos of Peter. Richard didn't like them being there. I explained it to Peter and tried to be nice about it – I even offered him the photos, frames and all, which was generous because they were solid silver and rather nice – but he just got hysterical and started throwing things—'

'The orange juice?'

Piers raised his eyebrows. 'Oh, he told you that, did he? It made an awful mess – orange juice is so sticky! I was furious. And then he just walked out.' He finished his whisky and reached for the bottle. 'Top-up?'

'I'm all right, thanks.'

'But Peter always was too emotional. He says it's the artistic temperament but you can put *that* another way and say it's pure theatrics. He plays to the gallery the whole time. Richard's so different. He's serious. You'd never believe he was only twenty-eight. He's made me see how superficial Peter always was. And if we're talking talent,' he added emphatically, opening his eyes wide, 'Richard's in a whole different class. To have got as far as he has at such an early age—' He stopped. 'This is all confidential, isn't it?'

'Unless there's anything that bears on the case.'

'Oh, well I'm sure it doesn't. But Richard doesn't want anyone to know about him and me, and he made me swear not to tell anyone. And I haven't, until now, but this is different, isn't it? But we have to be discreet, because when I tell you that he's Giles's junior minister – do you know Giles Freeman?'

'Only by name,' Slider said.

'Best way,' Piers snorted. 'He's the most utterly poisonous toad in the whole Government! Career mad, like all of them, but he's ruthless, and wildly jealous of Richard, naturally, since it's obvious to the most meagre intelligence – a category Giles only just manages to scrape into – that Richard has more talent in his little finger than Giles has in his whole repulsive body! So naturally he's afraid that Richard is going to oust him; and there's a certain amount of homophobia involved – Giles makes a point of being Norman Normal. Anyway, he's just longing for Richard to lose his footing. He daren't move against him openly because Richard has the PM's ear, but if there were a scandal . . .' He looked anxiously from one to the other. 'So we have to be discreet. I hope I can trust you?'

Atherton raised an eyebrow. 'I wouldn't have thought that sort of thing was a problem any more,' he said. 'After all, it's not a crime. And there are lots of gay MPs, aren't there – and several in the Cabinet, come to that. Why should Richard Tyler be worried about your relationship?'

Slider felt a surge of gratitude as Atherton slipped the surname in for his benefit. Now at last he knew who they were talking about. He didn't manage to keep up with the intricacies of politics, the way Atherton did, but even he had heard of Richard Tyler, the party's golden boy.

'The relationship isn't the problem,' Piers said sharply, as though he had been very much afraid that it was. 'But any adverse publicity – you know what this Government's like. So we've always been discreet. We make a point of not being seen in public places together. And Richard phoned me on Friday, the moment he heard about Phoebe's death, and said that in view of my connection with her through

Josh we must be doubly sure to keep our relationship an absolute secret. The slightest hint of being mixed up in anything undesirable could ruin his career – and Richard's one of the real high-flyers,' he added proudly. 'He'll be in the Cabinet if the next reshuffle goes the way it's expected. And then – well, the sky's the limit, provided he keeps his footing. He could be the youngest ever prime minister.'

Slider recalled that only a few weeks ago a Cabinet Minister had been sacked for what had been called an 'error of judgement' in a Birmingham knocking-shop. It was the same sort of euphemism as a footballer 'bringing the game into disrepute', meaning, when it came down to it, being mentioned in the newspapers in anything but a flattering context. Yes, the need for discretion was obvious, though Slider thought it a touch of paranoia too far to worry about merely knowing the brother of a man who had been questioned by the police about a murder.

But despite having been enjoined to absolute secrecy, Piers was only too eager to talk about his new love, and as he sipped his way down the malt, he grew more expansive and descriptive, hardly needing Slider's little prompting questions to keep him going. He wanted to tell, and Slider saw something of the truth of what Peter Medmenham had told him, that Piers craved company, and was not happy with his own. The opportunity was all the justification he needed to unpocket himself.

In fact, as the story unrolled, Slider began to feel sorry for Piers Prentiss. He had met Richard Tyler through his brother's involvement with the DOE – some political drinkie-do or other – and it was clear that he had been bowled over by the dynamic young man with the friends in high places. What Tyler had seen in Piers was naturally pure conjecture, but Atherton, with more knowledge of the protagonists than Slider, suspected that it had less to do with the heart than the head. Piers was brother to Josh, who, at the time of first meeting, had been very hot in Government circles; Piers knew a great many showbiz personalities, which could be useful to an ambitious politician; Piers was independently wealthy, and political success never came cheaply.

Slider's different knowledge, of the way these affairs went, read between the lines and gathered that Piers had been Peter Medmenham's boy for a long time, and was now enjoying the heady sensation of having a boy of his own. He had been the junior partner and was now the senior, the one flattered and looked up to for his greater knowledge and experience. There was pride in having been chosen by such a demigod; and, it had to be suspected, there was some satisfaction in having swapped Peter's ageing flesh for Richard's young firm stuff.

But Richard was not going to be constant and available as Peter had been. Already the change of partner had left Piers lonely and rather lost, and being sworn to secrecy was depressing him, when he longed to publish his success and be seen arm in arm with Apollo at opening nights and fashionable restaurants. When the time came and the golden boy dropped him, as he had dropped Peter, he was going to be very lonely indeed. The number of times he assured them that the new relationship was the real thing and would last for ever, suggested that Piers knew that time was not far round the corner.

It was all very sad; but apart from confirming Medmenham's alibi, it didn't get them any further forward on the case, so as soon as a pause presented itself, Slider said, 'You were going to show me a photograph of Phoebe Agnew.'

'Oh, Lord, yes – d'you know, I'd completely forgotten what you came here for,' he said lightly. 'Poor Phoebe.'

Poor Phoebe indeed, Slider thought. He hadn't yet met anyone who seemed genuinely devastated by her loss. Perhaps that was her own fault, but his natural bent was to side with the underdog, and he didn't like to think that anyone should leave the fretted globe without some tears shed for them, even if they had made policemen's lives a burden during their tenancy.

CHAPTER THIRTEEN

Half an oaf is better than low bred

Piers Prentiss went away to fetch photographs, and when they were alone, Atherton said, 'Obviously it's bye-bye lunch. I assume you are going somewhere with this?'

'Nice of you to assume that,' Slider said.

'Sorry, I didn't mean it the way it came out.'

'We've got him talking now. You never know what will emerge,' Slider said. 'I just feel that somewhere in the silt at the bottom of the Prentiss pond is the information we need to understand what happened. We can't ask Josh because we can't trust what he tells us, but if we stir Piers's mud—'

'I see,' Atherton said. 'You're draining the moat to catch a mackerel.'

'Exactly: setting a sprat to catch a thief. But actually I'm trawling rather than fishing. I don't know what I want to catch, but I hope I'll know it when I see it.'

'You have been listening to *What's My Metaphor*,' Atherton announced. 'Tune in next week for—'

He broke off as Piers's footsteps sounded outside the door. He came back in with a large cigar box in his hands. 'Here we are.' He glanced from one to the other as if to guess what they had been doing while he was away. 'Can I get you some more coffee before I sit down? Sure? Right, well, let's see what we've got here.'

The box was full of photographs, and Atherton felt a

doomed premonition that they were going to have to look at every one; but Piers shuffled through them as if looking for specifics. He handed one across to Slider. 'That was in the spring of '69. On our way to an anti-Vietnam rally. Goodness, we were young!'

Atherton leaned across and Slider held it between them. Both Prentiss boys, familiar now from other photos, sitting on a wall; Josh in the middle with his arms round the thin, dark Noni on one side, and on the other what must be Phoebe Agnew, with Piers at the end of the row beside Noni, looking as if he wasn't sure how he'd got there. Tagging along, just tolerated – the fate of younger brothers.

All four were wearing jeans, and the boys had girly haircuts like embryo busbies, as was the fashion then. Noni, neat and tidy, with short-cut hair, make-up, and a smart jacket over her jeans, sat with her knees together and her hands in her lap, looking like an office worker rather than a student. Phoebe had a magnificent, if unkempt, mane of curls which seemed to blow in a wind all her own; her many-layered clothes looked shabby and untidy, and Slider would have bet that her fingernails were dirty; but she stared out into the world with the bright-eyed challenge of Xena the Warrior Princess, and the others paled into insignificance beside her – even Josh. While his arm round Noni's shoulders looked possessive and protective, the one round Phoebe's looked as if he was trying to hold down a wild horse with a piece of garden twine.

'They were all in their first year at university. I was still at Eton, of course. Father was furious that they got me involved – I was only sixteen. But of course it was Phoebe's idea first and last – everything always was. She was the political one. Whether it was Vietnam or Chile or nuclear weapons, there she was, protesting. Josh went along for the fun, and because it was the done thing for students – and to annoy Father, which was practically his mission in life in those days. Noni was never really interested in politics at all, but where Phoebe led, she followed.' He brought out another photo. 'Here they are – best friends. I think that must have been at the Notting Hill Carnival.'

The two women with a crowd in the background; Phoebe's arm round Noni's shoulders, bowing her a little as she leaned forward to the camera, her mouth wide open in a shout or exaggerated laughter, the other arm in the air with the fist closed round a can – only Coca-Cola, though. The wild corkscrew curls waved around the vivid face in sharp contrast to the neat dark head and reserved expression of her companion.

'I wonder what brought them together?' Slider said. 'Was it a case of "opposites attract", do you think?'

'Yes, poor Noni, she does look a bit overshadowed, doesn't she?' Piers said, taking the photo back. 'And when you look at what's happened since, Phoebe's always outshone her. Her acting career never really took off, in spite of everything Josh could do. When they were first married, he made a point of courting producers and directors – though between ourselves he enjoyed every minute of it,' he added archly. 'He always loved the luvvies – still does. And of course, they love him – which is why he's got an award for set designing, while Noni's got nothing.'

'When did they marry?'

'April 1970. Straight after graduating, Josh got himself into a firm of architects and started making friends with the world, and Noni got herself into LAMDA, and then they got married. Father was furious. He wanted Josh to marry one of our set: Noni was a suburban nobody. He'd always planned to buy Josh a house when he married, but that was all off when he married Noni. Josh didn't care – he liked showing he could do everything by his own power. So they lived in a dreadful little rented flat in Earl's Court to begin with – not that I thought it dreadful at the time, of course. I'd just started at Oxford and spent my weekends and every hour I could with them.

My dear, the glamour of that pair, to a callow, pimply student!'

'What was Phoebe doing?'

'Heaven knows. She was off somewhere, protesting about something,' he said, throwaway. 'None of us saw her for years. She just dropped out of our lives. Meanwhile, Josh shot up the career ladder and Noni got nowhere. I think that was one of the reasons she got pregnant in the end. Having babies gave her an excuse not to be chasing parts and not getting them.'

He looked thoughtful, as if something had occurred to him. Slider waited to see if it would come out, and then said, 'So when did Phoebe reappear in your lives?'

'That must have been in 1973 – the anti-Pinochet protests, was it? She was lobbying MPs when Josh bumped into her and invited her home, and the three of them more or less took up where they left off. Except that Phoebe was still living a sort of nomadic life, going wherever there was a cause, all her belongings in one rucksack, sleeping on people's sofas – just like a student.' He seemed not to approve of this behaviour. 'She didn't get herself a flat until 1985, after the miners' strike collapsed and she decided to settle in London.' He smiled suddenly. 'You see how dear Phoebe's entire life has been shaped by political events?'

'I see,' Slider confirmed. It was like watching one of those 'The Way We Were' movies. 'Go on.'

'Not much more to tell. Toby was born in 1976 and Emma in '78, so Noni had the perfect excuse to stay home until 1983 when Emma started school. Then Phoebe persuaded her to try and restart her career. Josh by that time had quite a lot of influence and she got parts all right, but she never really broke through, poor thing. Then in 1990, Phoebe won the Palgabria, and Noni got pregnant again.'

'You think there may have been some connection?' Atherton put in.

'Mm, well,' said Piers, 'perhaps I shouldn't say it, but I did have a very naughty thought. It did occur to me to wonder whether she hadn't been a teensy bit jealous of Phoebe from time to time. But it's silly, really,' he dismissed the idea with a wave of the hand. 'Noni would have hated the life Phoebe led, and she was never interested in politics. She was just born for wife-and-motherhood. The last pregnancy turned out badly, though. Poor thing, she miscarried, and because she was over forty by then she blamed herself, though I think the quacks said that was nothing to do with it, it was just bad luck. Anyway, she went into a fearful depression: she was just a wreck for years, until Phoebe encouraged her to pull herself out of it. So she tried again with her career, and she seemed to be doing all right in a quiet way, until she did that dreadful sitcom and had a spectacular flop. Then she just gave up – and who can blame her?'

'So, when was she a dancer?' Atherton asked.

'A dancer?'

'She told me she used to be a ballet dancer.'

Piers shook his head. 'No, you must be mistaken.'

'She said she had a fall while dancing and injured her back. The trouble recurs from time to time.'

'Never while I've known her,' Piers said. 'If she's ever had a bad back she's never complained about it. But I think she did ballet lessons when she was a child,' he added on the thought. 'Maybe that's what she meant. She's never danced professionally.'

Slider picked up the thread again. 'Tell me about your brother's relationship with Phoebe Agnew,' he said. 'Were they more than friends?'

'Much, much more,' Piers said promptly. 'But if you're asking me if they were lovers, the answer's no. Phoebe wasn't his type.'

'That's what he said.'

'There you are then,' Piers said triumphantly, starting on his fourth malt. 'No, what you have to understand about Josh is that these ferociously butch types really don't *like* women. They need to have them around as trophies, but at heart they're afraid of them. Noni was just right for him – the sort of fluffy, ineffectual female that he could dominate and protect. If she'd been successful at her career it might have been different – but there was no danger of that,' he added with unconscious cruelty. 'But he could never get the better of Phoebe. She was fully his equal. Of course, once he accepted that, he found her a better friend than any man could ever be to him, because really butch men don't trust other men either, do they? They see them as rivals. Shocking, isn't it?' He twinkled again, with half an eye on Atherton. 'The poor things are so alone. Crushing women and trumpeting at other men, stamping their feet and competing all the time. No wonder they have ulcers and heart attacks. Testosterone is not a happy bedfellow.'

'Perhaps the strain of his career—' Slider began, provoked by God-knew-what consideration into defending Prentiss to his own brother.

'He was never any different,' Piers interrupted briskly. 'Even as a boy his idea of relaxation was to play some madly competitive sport. He was a rugger blue at UCL, did you know?'

'It didn't come up in conversation,' Slider said drily.

'I've often wondered about those rugger buggers.' Piers seemed to have out-drunk any natural reserve. 'I mean, all that sweaty grappling and rolling in the mud – what's in it for them? Aren't they just a teensy bit too fierce in their protestations of manliness? But never mind! I'm talking too much. All I wanted to say was that Prentiss, R. J. was always one of life's ball clangers, right from school upwards.'

'R. J.?' Slider queried.

'Joshua is his second name. He and father had the same name, so he was called Josh to distinguish him. Anyway,' he resumed his plot, 'that's why Phoebe was so good for him. He could talk to her, tell her anything, discuss things with her without worrying that she'd use anything she learned against him. They fought like mad, but it was a healthy sort of quarrelling because it didn't affect their friendship – which it would have if they'd been lovers – and it didn't damage his career – which it would have if she'd been a man. That's why,' he looked full into Slider's eyes, his own now a little too shiny, like those of a stuffed animal, 'that's why you're way off beam if you think Josh had anything to do with her death. If it was *me* you suspected, there'd be more sense in it. When we argued, it could be nasty, as Noni will no doubt tell you.'

'You didn't like her?' Slider suggested.

'I like my women to be women and my men to be men,' he said. 'I don't like these ambivalent people. In the old days you knew where you were. Now all the edges are blurred and everyone's confused and unhappy. I blame co-education: takes away all the mystery.'

'Mrs Prentiss says you had a quarrel with Phoebe at New Year, at a family dinner party. What was that about?'

'You *have* been busy!' he said waspishly. 'It feels like sitting naked in a shop window, having you know all about my private life.'

'I'm sorry,' Slider said. 'I'm groping about in the dark, you see, as far as this case goes, and there's no knowing what may be important. What did you quarrel about?'

'About Richard, as it happened. She wanted me to give him up.'

'Why was that?'

'Oh, I suppose she was worried about Peter's heart being broken – I don't know. I don't think she said why, come to think of it. I was a bit naughty, really – shouldn't have told her. I promised Richard no-one would know. But Phoebe had a way of getting things out of you and – to be absolutely frank and honest, I was longing to tell *some*one. So I just let it slip ever-so-accidentally, and swore Phoebe to secrecy too, but for some reason she seemed really upset about it. I suppose she'd had too much to drink. Anyway, she lit into me and told me what I was doing with Richard was wrong and it must stop. I got annoyed with her and told her to mind her own business – I had quite a load on too – and we had a bit of a shouting match, until Noni got upset and Josh told us to shut up and asked what it was about. Well, we both felt a bit silly because we couldn't say, could we? So we shut up. Afterwards Phoebe apologised for being a buttinski, and I said I forgave her, and that was that.'

The dogs suddenly catapulted out of their semi-coma on the carpet at his feet and hurtled, barking like rapid gunfire, out towards the kitchen. There was the sound of a woman's voice, and Piers said, 'It's Marjorie, my domestic treasure. Coo-ee! Marjie! In here, darling!'

A moment later a woman appeared in the doorway. 'I didn't know you were still here, Piers. Oh, I see you've got company! Am I interrupting? Shall I vamoose?'

She was thin and athletic-looking in tightly fitting Lycra joggers under a heavy-padded ski jacket; perfectly made-up, professionally coiffed, and with a cut-glass County accent.

'No, come in and meet the chaps,' Piers said, getting up. He introduced Slider and Atherton and said, 'This is Marjorie Babbington, my lady who does.'

'How do you do?' The woman extended a beautifully manicured hand, noted Slider's rather blank look and said, 'Is something wrong?'

'No, not at all,' Slider said. 'You're not quite what I'd been imagining, that's all.'

She smiled. 'Did he portray me as old Mrs Mop? You are naughty, Piers! He's always playing pranks.'

Piers raised his hands. 'I just said you were a treasure, which you are – soothing the f.b., making me all those *delicious* soups! Marjie, darling, can you open up the shop for me now, instead of taking the doggy-wogs out? I've got to talk to the chaps about Phoebe.'

'Of course I can. Oh, gosh, wasn't it awful,' she said,

turning limpid grey eyes to Slider. 'Poor Phoebe! Have you any idea who did it?'

'They suspected Josh at first,' Piers said before Slider could answer.

'Oh no, poor Josh! He was devoted to Phoebe.'

'So was everyone, darling.'

'I know. She was so kind. Nothing was too much trouble for her. She helped Clive and me – my husband – when our son got into trouble,' she said earnestly. 'He got arrested with a lot of others at a rave in a barn, and Phoebe went to a great deal of trouble to see the right people and make sure he wasn't charged, because it could have ruined his chances of Oxford. I mean, he hadn't done anything, you know,' she added quickly, 'but some of the others had been taking drugs and it was guilt by association. I just don't understand how anyone could hurt someone so very kind. And you were only talking to her on Thursday, too,' she said to Piers. 'It's awful to think of, isn't it?'

Slider felt as if he'd been hit on the head with a woolly sock. He turned to Piers. 'You spoke to her on Thursday? Why didn't you tell me?'

'It didn't occur, that's all,' he said. 'Is it important? I only rang her to talk about Peter coming to see me. I wanted to ask her what sort of mood he was in. I told Marjie about it, didn't I, darling?'

She nodded. 'On Friday, when I was cleaning the kitchen.'

'What time did you ring her?'

'I don't know, really. About eight, half past, I didn't really notice. I'd been pottering about, thinking about Peter coming and wondering if there was going to be a scene, and then I thought he was bound to have talked to Phoebe about it so I gave her a tinkle. But she said she had someone with her and couldn't talk, so I said it didn't matter, and that was that.'

'Did she say who was with her?' Atherton asked. His

suppressed emotion showed in his voice, and Marjorie looked at him enquiringly.

'No. She just said, "Look, Piers, I've got someone with me. I can't talk now. Can it wait?" And I said, "Don't worry, it wasn't anything important", and that was that.'

'How did she sound?' Slider asked.

'Well, a bit unwelcoming,' Piers said. '*Not* happy to hear one's dulcet tones. And, if you want the honest, honest truth, a bit drunk maybe. I thought at first when she answered the phone that I'd woken her up, and then I realised it was probably Bacchus rather than Morpheus. She really had become a frightful toper in the past couple of months.'

'Please, think hard,' Slider said. 'Try to pinpoint the time more closely.'

'Oh dear, I can't. I just don't know,' he said, still not seeming to sense the urgency. But Marjorie Babbington's large eyes came round like car headlamps.

'It'll be on his phone bill, won't it? The itemised calls?' She looked at Piers. 'Your bill came yesterday, didn't it? I noticed the envelope when I picked up your mail from the mat.'

'How long were you on the phone?' Slider asked.

'Only a couple of minutes,' Piers said.

'Then it probably won't show,' Slider said. 'But it will have been logged by BT computer. We can find out.'

Now at last the penny dropped. 'But if it had been Josh with her, she'd have said so,' Piers said. 'Oh, my God!' His eyes widened. 'You think it could have been the murderer? Was I actually talking to her while the murderer was there?'

'It's a possibility,' said Slider.

They drove in silence for a while. 'Are you thinking what I'm thinking?' Slider asked at last.

'Were you thinking that there's never been a recording of the Dvořák symphonies to equal the Kertesz-LSO series of the late sixties?' Atherton said.

'No,' said Slider.

'Neither was I,' said Atherton.

Slider looked sideways at him. 'Is it my imagination or are you getting weirder? What I was thinking was if this phone call puts Agnew alive after, say, eight-thirty, it puts Josh Prentiss in the clear.'

'If you believe Maria Colehern. And if she really did notice the time he arrived.'

'Hollis believed her. But we'll lean on her a bit and see if she creaks. And try and get some outside confirmation of what time Prentiss arrived. Someone may have seen him.' There had been no point in wasting manpower on that before, when they had no definite time of death. 'If only this idiot had told us sooner that he spoke to Agnew on Thursday night, we could have done the asking while memories were fresh.'

'He *is* an idiot,' Atherton agreed. 'Stupid enough to invent a phone call that never happened, to get his brother out of trouble.'

Slider shook his head. 'The Marjorie woman agreed that he told her about the phone call on Friday. If he'd made it up to protect his brother, he'd have told us then.'

'He could have been waiting to see if it was needed.'

'Do you really see him as that cunning?'

'No, you're right,' said Atherton. 'He's educated, well-bred, but basically a clot.'

'I think the call will prove to be pukka,' said Slider. 'It remains to be seen what time it was. If it lets Josh out, it also clears Piers – I wish his name didn't rhyme with so much – and Peter Medmenham, since he couldn't have caught the 9.02 at Liverpool Street if he was murdering Agnew after half past eight, unless he has wings under his posh schmutter.'

'So what does that leave us with?' Atherton said restlessly. 'McLaren's pet theory about Michael Wordley?'

'McLaren is as thick as a whale sandwich,' Slider said, 'but maybe he's got a point.'

'He has – it's his head. Why would Wordley kill Agnew, the only person in the world who's ever loved him?' Slider told him about McLaren's missing file motive. 'Oh, that's why you asked Piers if he knew what Agnew was working on.'

'Yes.' Piers hadn't known. Slider sighed. 'I'm not convinced about Wordley. I'm getting less convinced all the time about Prentiss.'

'Despite his indisputable semen?'

'Well, we know he was there, but maybe all the supper-scoffing and sex-having was nothing to do with the murder. Maybe the murderer slipped in after all the other visitors had left.'

'In that case we'll be on this until next Christmas,' Atherton said. 'Couldn't we try and pin it to Giles Freeman? I've never liked him and there is the spare set of finger-marks to account for.'

'I'll let you go and ask for his prints,' Slider said. 'Tell him what you want them for, won't you?'

'Pass,' Atherton said with a shudder. 'No, I think I'm sticking with Josh. Probably the call was while he was still there. Agnew didn't let on to Piers who it was,' he anticipated Slider's question, 'because they'd been bonking and she didn't want anyone to know.'

'And he killed her because—?'

'Pick a reason,' Atherton shrugged. 'He's probably always loathed her. Why not? Oh, all right, if you want me to be logical about it – his political career is just taking off and she's going to get in the way. If she's known him all those years she probably knows something about him he doesn't want to get out. We just have to find out what it was. No, it's still Prentiss for me. He's the only one who makes sense of all the rest of it.'

'Well, we'll see,' said Slider. 'And then we'll know.'

CHAPTER FOURTEEN

Dial M for dilemma

Porson was pacing about, shaving his craggy chin with an elderly electric razor that buzzed feebly, like a fly on its back, as if it was barely up to the challenge.

'Where have you got with Prentiss? I've got to talk to the press and TV for the evening news, and it's going to get a bit hot under the collar if we don't find something positive to tell 'em. I've had Commander Wetherspoon on the dog again, and he didn't make pleasant listening.' He put down the razor and began struggling with the top button of his shirt. 'Wanted to know why we haven't charged Prentiss yet, after all the fuss we've made. He was more or less inferring that heads will roll if we don't come up with a result in short order.'

Slider hated having to do it to him. 'I'm afraid it looks as though Prentiss is out of the frame, sir.'

Porson did a creditable double take, and froze in the act of tightening his tie. 'What?'

'I've had the report from BT about the telephone call Piers Prentiss put through to Agnew on Thursday evening. It was timed from 8.43 to 8.45; Josh Prentiss arrived at Maria Colehern's flat at 8.30.' He saw the question in Porson's eye and added quickly, 'One of her neighbours saw him going in and confirms the time. A good witness. I don't think there's any doubt that when he left Agnew she was still alive.'

'Oh, good grief!' Porson cried. 'I'm not hearing this. I am

not hearing this. You mean to tell me that after a week on the case all you've done is clear the prime suspect? You've upset the Home Secretary – and the PM himself – for no reason? What am I going to tell the press conference? What am I going to tell Mr Wetherspoon? He'll have my balls for garters. And who's going to tell Prentiss?'

He stamped about and raged for a while, and Slider bent his head and bore it patiently. He didn't blame The Syrup. He was up at the sharp end when it came to censure, and would have to explain it all to a hostile news media gathering. Slider wouldn't have liked to be in his shoes and under those lights.

When he calmed down a bit, Porson sat down – unusually for him – behind his desk, and said, 'So where does it leave you? What have you got left to follow up?'

'There's Wordley, sir. McLaren's still looking into him. But we've got nothing on him, except that he's got a record, and that he's been missing since Wednesday night. And there's a mass of reports on people seen in the street and going in and out of houses. We've been working our way through them. Most of them will be nothing to do with the case, as always, but we may still turn up something. There are Agnew's papers, still being sorted. Something may turn up there. And we've got the team going over her major articles and campaigns, trying to find if there was a conflict of some kind that may have come back on her.'

'In other words,' Porson grunted, 'you're back at numero uno.'

'There's still the possibility', Slider said, 'that it was a random killing. Someone just broke in – the lock's easy to slip – and killed her for the hell of it.'

Porson looked at him sharply. 'But you don't think so?'

'It doesn't smell like that to me.'

'Nor to me,' said Porson.

'I mean, why would they tie her up like that afterwards – unless it was a joke?'

'The tying up aspect of the scenario is what puzzles me most,' Porson admitted. 'No record of those extra fingerprints anywhere, I suppose?'

'Nothing.'

Porson sighed. 'You'll just have to plod it out, then.'

'Yes, sir.'

'You realise, don't you, that Prentiss will probably sue us for destroying his career?'

Slider braved it out. 'I was just doing my job, sir.'

Porson shrugged. 'Best thing you can do is get your head down and get a result, double quick time. Meanwhile,' he stood up, the gloom intensifying on his granite crag, 'my unenviable task is to go and face the cerebos of the press.'

It turned out to be a long day. Prentiss – who in reason ought to have been pleased to be cleared – was not a happy bunny when the news was broken to him, and Commander Wetherspoon was not thrilled to have to be the one to break it. Telephone calls, press briefings, urgent conferences and carpetings followed. Slider was glad to have the bulk of Porson to cower behind. He was a funny old duck, but he stood by his men.

Slider was just putting things away, about to go home, when McLaren came in.

'Guv—'

'You still here? There's no overtime tonight, you know.'

'No, I been out talking to my snout,' McLaren said.

'You're a bleeding contortionist, you are.'

McLaren took it phlegmatically. 'He's got a line on the bloke Wordley went off with on Wednesday night. He reckons the description fits a geezer name of Tucker, Sean Tucker. Ex-bouncer. You know the sort, out-of-work Milk Tray man, all muscles and black roll-necks. Used to work down the Nineteen Club in Warwick Road – I busted him a few times when I was at Kensington.'

'He's got previous, then?'

'More form than a Miss World contest. Tasty as they come. Got sacked from the Nineteen for violent affray, and he's into serious naughties now. Nicked over at Notting Hill a while back for conspiracy to murder, but the CPS gave it away. Anyway, word on the street is him and Wordley's mixed up in something big.'

'Planning a robbery?'

'No, guv,' McLaren said with satisfaction. 'My snout says the word is they've done a murder.'

'Any word on who?'

'No, that's all he said, that Tucker and Wordley are mixed up in a murder.' He eyed Slider hopefully.

'It's a lead,' Slider acknowledged, 'but I've got reservations. Why would Wordley involve Tucker? It wasn't a two-man job.'

'Maybe he didn't know that,' McLaren said. 'She was a strong old doris, and gutsy. She could've put up a fight.'

'Faking the rape doesn't look right for Wordley.'

'He's thick enough to think it might help. And Tucker's always been a clever bastard. No, I can see him thinking it up, and laughing while Wordley does it. What about going round Tucker's gaff and giving him a tug? He lives over North End Road. Tucker's a toe-rag, he never minds shopping his oppos to clear himself. If we rough him a bit, he might drop us Wordley.'

'Well, it never hurts to roust them, I suppose,' Slider said. 'And he might at least know where Wordley is. I'll put it to Mr Porson tomorrow.'

'Tomorrow?'

'It's no good pouting at me, I told you there's no overtime tonight. Anyway, Mr Porson's gone home, and my voice is the last one he'll want to hear until he's had a good night's sleep. I'll speak to him in the morning and if he authorises the manpower we'll see about bringing Tucker in.'

'I was just gonna go on my own,' McLaren protested. 'Have a little chat.'

'Haven't you read the new Health and Safety guidelines? A trained officer is an expensive piece of equipment and you can't just chuck it into a situation without assessing the risk. More than any mother, the Metropolitan Police doesn't want your face altered. Tucker could be dangerous, and you're not going to roust him alone, and that's final.'

McLaren subsided into resentful mumbles. 'I go all out to get this red-hot lead—'

'Tucker will keep,' Slider said. 'If Mr Porson rolls for it, and the budget'll stand it, we'll have a go at him tomorrow.'

As a counter-irritant, trying to find a parking space in Chiswick was up there with the greats. Slider's first words as he came through the door were, 'If I have to park much further away, I might as well leave the car and walk to work.'

'Hello,' said Joanna, coming out into the passage. Her woebegone face reminded him of the situation he had left behind, and that living in Chiswick might soon be a thing of the past anyway. They looked at each other for a moment, and then he held out his arms and she walked into them.

He rested his weary chin on the top of her head and sought for something tender to say. 'What's for supper?'

'Sausage and mash,' she said, in the tone a farmer's wife might use to say, 'The cow's got mastitis, the hens are off lay and the goat's eaten your trousers.'

'I like sausage and mash,' he said, kissing her ear. 'Especially with fried onions.'

'There are onions,' she conceded. He nudged her face round and kissed her mouth. He had only meant to kiss, but he felt that instant arousal at the touch of her that still surprised as much as it delighted him. His love of her was so continuously, satisfyingly physical. He just wanted to be having her all the time. What was it about her, anyway? Why wasn't she followed everywhere by a pack of stumbling, drooling, lust-dazed men? Maybe it wasn't her, maybe it was *them*. The thought pleased him. There was a nice, kismet symmetry to it; a jigsaw-puzzle satisfaction. Slot their two pieces together and, lo, a bit of God's big picture emerged.

As he had continued kissing her while having these thoughts, the matter had now become urgent, so he started walking her backwards towards the bedroom, shedding his coat and jacket as he went.

Some time later he had a long, groaning stretch and said, 'Ah, that's better than sinking into a hot bath when you get back from work.'

'Gee, thanks,' she said, sitting up and pushing the hair out of her eyes. Some of the strain had gone from her face, so evidently it had worked for her as well. 'You can have one of those too, if you like.'

'I'm too hungry to wait that long. A quick shower will do.'

'All right, I'll go and put the potatoes on.' At the door she turned back and said, 'I suppose, man-like, you think that changes everything.'

'It did for me,' he said. 'Altered my profile, anyway.'

She grinned unwillingly. 'Rude,' she said, and disappeared.

When they finally sat at the table in the bay window of her sitting-room, a bottle of Côtes du Rhône had joined them, and was making itself agreeable all round. While they ate, he told her about the day's developments, and she listened in silence, not throwing herself into it as she usually did. When food and conversation both came to an end and they were left with only the last half glass of wine, she said, 'The problem hasn't gone away.'

'I know,' he said.

'I've just been going over and over it all day,' she said, 'and I can't see a way round.' She looked at him anxiously. 'I'm reminded again that now your divorce is through you're a free man.'

He didn't pretend not to understand her. 'After the proofs of love I've just given you?'

'Hot sex, agreeable though it is, doesn't necessarily mean lifelong commitment.'

'I was referring to eating your sausage and mash,' he said. And then, suppressing a self-conscious smirk, 'Was it really hot?'

'The earth', she assured him solemnly, 'outmoved a Travelodge vibrating bed.' And then she tacked off in her disconcerting way. 'It's always struck me as risky, having those things in California. All over the state, people must be missing earthquakes.'

'I've never been to California,' he said. 'Or anywhere in America. I'm just a home-body.'

'Which brings us neatly to the point. How's that for a link?' she said without pleasure. 'Bill, what are we going to do?'

'I love you,' he said. 'I know that's not an answer, but I thought I'd mention it.'

And she looked sad. 'That sounds like the sort of thing people say just before they split up.'

'I would never leave you,' he said.

'Which just throws it back on me. It's not fair. Why should I have to choose between my career and my man?'

'I'm not asking you to.'

'Yes you are. Implicitly.'

'Well, it's what you're asking me,' he said fairly.

'And you won't even consider it.'

How had they got back here so quickly? 'It's not that I won't consider it, it's that I don't see how it's possible.'

'It may be impossible for you to be a policeman in Holland – I have to accept your word for that because I don't know – but you could do something else.'

'Petrol pump attendant? Road sweeper?'

She glared at him, the rage of the trapped animal. 'If I stay, the same fate awaits me – or doesn't that prospect bother you? Probably not. There's a streak of the old-fashioned male in you that thinks a woman's job is less important than a man's. I suppose all men think like that, underneath. It's just the little woman amusing herself – harmless as long as the housework gets done.'

'Did I say that?' he protested, but mildly. He knew the rage was not really directed at him, but at the situation.

'No, but it's there all the same, the attitude. It's what you think even if you're not aware of it.'

'Like institutional racism?'

That made her pause. 'I'm sorry,' she said. 'That was unfair. But, Bill, I'm good at what I do! And what I do is *me.* If I stop playing the fiddle and get a job as a checkout girl—'

'But that isn't the option that's on offer, is it?' he said carefully. 'If you stay, you'll still play. You may have to take another job as well, to make ends meet, but you won't have to give up playing altogether.'

She stared. 'You *have* made up your mind.'

'No, I haven't, but—'

'I *want* this job! It's important. It's a fabulous opportunity for me, don't you understand? It's like – oh, I don't know – you being offered Assistant Commissioner or whatever.'

'But I don't want promotion. I just want to go on doing what I'm doing. I'm good at it. And what I do is me, too.'

She turned her face away miserably, twiddling the stem of her glass. 'I just can't see a way out.'

'I don't want us to part,' he said after a moment. 'The thought of being without you is – well – I don't know. I don't want to face it.' Inside his head the words flowed, powerful and passionate, but, man-like, all he could get out through his tight lips were crude wooden effigies of meaning. 'Don't try and make a decision now. Let's both think and try and find a solution.'

'I can't hold off for long,' she said. 'Wolfie's going to want an answer.'

'All right, but please, let's try and think of a way round it,' he pleaded.

She shrugged, which meant she'd try, but she didn't know what else there was to think. For that matter, neither did he. The realisation that he could lose her – or rather that they could lose each other – proved to him how strongly he had taken root in her. He felt shaken, loosened, likely to go over in the next strong wind. And yet, what solution was there? His foolish jealousies of the past, when he thought she might run off with another man, would have been a pleasure now, compared with the pain of this real dilemma.

He was disturbed mid-evening by a telephone call.

'That's my mobile,' he said. 'It must be work.'

Joanna, curled in the corner of the big, shabby leather chesterfield, staring at the television, grunted but didn't stir. On the screen a weather girl with straggly hair and wearing one of those Suzanne Charlton over-the-bum jackets (did they draw from a common wardrobe, like nuns?) was saying, '. . . but the watter wather will at least bring some warmer temchers, tickly in the wast.' Come back, Michael Fish, he thought. We forgive you the hurricane for the sake of your diction. Restore some 'e's to our forecasts.

He went out into the hall and stood by the front door, where the signal was better, to answer. The sepulchral tones of Tidy Barnet smote his ear. If a smoked haddock could speak, he'd sound like Tidy.

''Ullo, Mr S. That diction'ry bloke you was asking about, right?'

That would be Michael Wordley. Tidy, one of Slider's best snouts, had a way of avoiding using names. Telephones – particularly mobiles – were not secure, and his life was perilous enough as it was.

'I'm with you,' Slider said.

'You never warned me you 'ad anuvver bloke askin' questions,' Tidy said sourly. 'Tripped over 'im, didn't I?'

That would be McLaren's snout, presumably. 'I didn't know. One of my men had an idea and put the word out.'

'Yeah, I know 'im. The stupid one.'

'I wouldn't say that.'

'Useless as a chocklit fireman. His snout's a useless bastard an' all. Wouldn't know if you was up 'im wiv an armful o'chairs.' Tidy sounded unusually irritable.

'Sorry if it crossed your lines. My man's snout said dictionary man was involved in a murder.'

'Murder? That ain't what I 'eard,' said Tidy. 'Diction'ry went off Wensdy night wiv a certain party, call 'im Little Tommy, right?'

That would be Tucker. At least McLaren's snout got something right. 'Yes, I know who you mean.'

'Well, they're plannin' a bit o' biz between 'em. Goin' to turn over this rich tart's gaff, right? They was doing the clubs and boozers all Wensdy night, went 'ome well pissed Fursdy morning. Little Tommy's telling everyone he meets, the moufy div. Dictionr'y's not 'appy wiv 'im. They 'ad a row in Paddy's club in Fulham Palace Road about two o'clock.'

'Went home where?'

'Little Tommy's gaff. He lives wiv his mum down North End Road.'

'When was the job supposed to be done?'

'Fursdy,' said Tidy. 'They must a done it all right, 'cos I 'eard there was a lot o' tom come on the market sudden. More'n that I can't tell you.'

'Well, thanks,' said Slider. 'You've done a great job. If you can get anything on where the job was or what they did before and afterwards, I'd be grateful.'

'Yeah, I'll keep me ear out.'

'That other thing I asked you about?'

Tidy chuckled. 'Yeah, that's a queer one. Well, it ain't my field, but I laid it off on another bloke, and he'll give you a bell when 'e knows, right? Name o' Banks. Harry Banks, but they calls 'im Piggy.'

Slider was shocked. 'You never use names!'

'Yeah, well, 'e ain't in the business, is 'e? Got nothink to fear from Piggy Banks.'

Slider returned to Joanna. 'Trouble?' she asked.

'That was Tidy Barnet,' he said. 'I'm now expecting a call from a man called Piggy Banks.'

'Your life's one long episode of *The Magic Roundabout*, isn't it?' Joanna said.

After the disappointment over Josh Prentiss, Commander Wetherspoon was only too pleased to jump at Tucker, and being of the generation that loved kicking down doors and shouting, 'Go, go, go!' he recommended the Syrup to arrange a visit to the Tucker demesne on Friday. It proved unfruitful. Mrs Tucker, a phlegmatic, respectable but deeply stupid woman, was found in sole possession. She opened the door to them without waiting for them to kick it in, and confirmed quite willingly that Seanie had come home with Micky Wordley in the early hours of last Thursday morning, both of them a bit pickled. Micky had slept on the sofa. They had got up about one o'clock Thursday afternoon and Mrs Tucker had got them breakfast, a big fry-up, which was what Seanie liked when he'd been out drinking the night before. They'd sat about afterwards having a smoke and a chat, and they'd gone off about three o'clock, saying they were going down the club. No, they hadn't said which club, but Seanie liked the Shamrock in Hammersmith now he was banned from the Nineteen. And she hadn't seen them since.

Hadn't she been worried about that?

No, not really. Seanie was a big boy, he could look after himself. He often went off places. He'd come back when he wanted a clean shirt or something.

Did she know what he and Micky were planning to do on Thursday?

No, they never mentioned. She never knew what Seanie was up to. He was a big boy, he could look after himself.

Did she ever wonder where his money came from, given that he didn't have a regular job?

Oh, he was in business, her boy. She didn't know what sort. He bought and sold things, she thought. She didn't understand business. She left all that sort of thing to Seanie. But he was doing all right. And he was a good boy, very good to his mother. Gave her a lovely watch at Christmas. Second-hand it was, but a very good one, solid gold.

After a close search of Tucker's room and the rest of the house, which revealed nothing but a lamentable collection of pornographic magazines in a suitcase under Tucker's bed, they left. McLaren was elated, and shone in the glow of a prophet proved right.

Slider, however, was sceptical. 'Unless everyone's been holding out on us, I'd hardly call Phoebe Agnew a "rich tart" – and there's no evidence that she ever had a lot of jewellery. She was a confirmed dresser-down, from anything we know.'

'But these stories always get exaggerated,' Hollis pointed out, fairly. 'It's possible Wordley went and did her for some other reason, and lifted her watch or something in the process. Villains like him are daft enough to try and flog it afterwards.'

'Yeah, and we've still got my snout saying he'd been mixed up in a murder, *and* he's missing since Thursday,' McLaren pointed out.

'Well, it's all we've got at the moment,' Slider said, 'so you'd better get on with it. You and Anderson can go round the pubs and clubs and try and find out where they went. Ask all your snouts for information; and ask any of the fences who co-operate if there's been any jewellery through their hands in the past week. You could try Larry Pickett. He might come across, since tom isn't his field.'

After a morning poring over case notes and statements, Slider went up to the canteen for a late lunch, and with an air of what-the-hell, ordered the all-day breakfast. Sausage, tomato, bacon, egg and beans. The baked beans had reached that happy state that only canteen beans know, when they had been kept warm for so long that the juice had thickened almost into toffee. He sat down with it at a quiet table and laid the papers he had brought up with him beside the plate.

He hadn't been there long when Atherton appeared beside him with a tray.

'Can I join you?'

Slider grunted consent, and Atherton unloaded tuna salad and a carton of apple juice. Each of them looked at the other's lunch with horror.

'No fried bread?' Atherton asked, sitting down.

'They'd run out of the proper bread. Only had that thin sliced stuff. You might as well fry place mats.' He dipped a stub end of sausage in his egg yolk. 'Where've you been, anyway?'

'I just slipped out for a minute,' Atherton said. 'Personal time.'

To the bookies, Slider wondered? Atherton, too, had brought a folder up with him, and looking at it upside down Slider read the name of the racehorse consortium company, Furlong Stud, with the address near Newmarket.

'You're not really serious about that, are you?' he asked, a little tentatively.

Atherton swallowed. 'Of course. Why not? Look, you think everything to do with racing must be crooked but that's just paranoia. Thousands of people go into racehorse ownership every year.'

'And lose their money.'

'No,' Atherton said with a patient smile. 'It's an accepted medium of investment now. There've been articles in all the money sections of the papers. These people', he tapped the page, 'quote an investment return of twenty-four per cent.'

'Guaranteed?'

'Of course not guaranteed,' Atherton said. 'But it's not a pig in a poke, you know. We're all going down to see the horse tomorrow. You watch it on the gallops, time it against other horses. And the winning times of the various big races are all published, so you can tell if the animal's fast or not. It's all up front.'

'And how much are you putting in?' Slider asked.

'Fifteen each.'

'Fifteen hundred? It's a lot of money.'

'Fifteen thou,' Atherton corrected, faintly self-conscious.

'You're joking!'

'That's just to begin with. Look,' he added impatiently, 'with a return of twenty-four per cent there's no point in messing about with small change. You ought to come in on it with me. Look how much difference it could make to your finances.'

'I haven't got fifteen thousand,' Slider said, bemused.

'Nor'd I. I remortgaged,' Atherton said. 'You've got to help yourself in this life. If you can't make enough to live on one way, you have to try another.'

'Where have I heard those words before?' Slider said. 'No, wait, I read them – in the Bent Copper's Almanac.'

Atherton looked away, compressing his lips. 'There's no point in talking to you. You're prejudiced. Anyway, it's my business what I do with my money.'

'True,' said Slider lightly, to cool things down. But he was dismayed. This had the hallmarks of obsession about it, and looking at his colleague's face as he forked salad into it with rather angry movements, he could see the lines of fatigue and strain. Atherton had always been one of that blest band of coppers who rode the swell and seemed unperturbed at the end of each day; but since his serious wounding during the Gilbert case, he seemed to have joined the mortals.

Atherton had opened his file and was ostentatiously reading, so Slider turned to his own papers and tried to work out what the loose ends were. Prentiss denying having sex with Agnew on Thursday in the face of all evidence to the contrary was the most annoying: but Prentiss was out of it now. Even if he had lied about that, it seemed he had told the truth about the rest. None of the numerous street sightings seemed to have related to him, but the combination of the phone call and the witness at Colehern's flat put him out of Agnew's way before she was killed.

Prentiss said it wasn't him that had eaten the meal, and if he wasn't the murderer there was no reason to doubt his word on that; so who had eaten it, and wiped away his finger-marks afterwards? The same person who left the marks on the unit? In that case it wasn't Wordley. And then, what about the thumb mark on the flush-handle? How many people had there been swanning about that damned house on Thursday anyway?

And then something occurred to him. He shuffled through his papers for Bob Lamont's report. Why hadn't he thought of it before?

'It says here', he said aloud, 'that the thumb mark on the flush-handle of the loo was the only one.' Atherton looked up. 'It was clean apart from that.'

'But that was—'

'A woman's thumb, yes – but not Phoebe Agnew's.'

'Wiped clean?' Atherton said. Slider nodded. 'Who would do that, except for the murderer? But it doesn't make sense – if the murderer had been and gone, why would a woman go and flush the loo? And what woman?'

They looked at each other for a moment. 'I have an idea', Slider said unwillingly, 'that I really don't want to follow. It occurs to me that there's someone else, apart from Prentiss and Medmenham, who's been lying to us from the very beginning.'

'Loyal little wifie?' Atherton said, screwing up his face at the idea.

'She said Prentiss had told her Agnew was dead on Friday morning; but he seemed not to know about it when we spoke to him on Friday afternoon. We assumed he was lying, but if he didn't kill her, he was probably telling the truth. In that case, how did she know Agnew had been murdered?'

'Yes, and what about that business of her referring to the way the body was left?' Atherton said eagerly. 'If Prentiss didn't do it, he couldn't have told her – so how did she know?'

'She might possibly have learned that some other way,' Slider said, being absolutely fair, 'though in that case why shouldn't she have said so? But then why was she so keen to give Prentiss an alibi?'

'Maybe she wasn't. Maybe she was trying to cover herself. If she was his alibi, he would be hers.'

Slider shook his head. 'That doesn't make sense. If Prentiss didn't know he had to cover her, he would tell a different story – as in fact he did.'

'Maybe she hoped she could get to him before we did, to coach him.'

'Still no good. When their stories did finally agree – after they'd had time to collude – it still didn't cover her for the necessary time. He was at Colehern's flat, but where was she? At home and unaccountable.'

'Hmm,' said Atherton. 'But why should she want to kill her best friend? And would that little slip of a thing be strong enough to strangle a big woman like Agnew – especially when she had a bad back?'

'Probably not – unless Agnew was really drunk. I don't know. There's something there, I'm sure, but I don't know what. Mrs Prentiss has been acting strangely from the beginning.'

'Well, both Prentiss and Piers said she'd been depressed. Maybe it's nothing more than that. Unconnected irrationality.'

'Maybe,' said Slider. He got up, picking up his papers. 'I'll see you later,' he said vaguely.

'You haven't finished your sausage,' Atherton protested.

'Hmm?' Slider said.

'Stick it behind your ear for later,' Atherton suggested.

'Okay,' Slider said, evidently too preoccupied to understand what was being said to him.

CHAPTER FIFTEEN

Albie senior

Eltham Road had a Saturday quiet about it, the sleeping cars of the at-home workers lining the kerbs with an air of having their eyes shut tight. Do not disturb. Slider had to park dangerously near the corner, but there wasn't much traffic about. He just hoped no boy-racer in a BMW came round it too quickly.

Atherton was, even now, probably, driving down to view his wonder-horse; Slider was on his own, without his usual sounding-board. The idea that had been growing on him over the past eighteen hours seemed so far out he could have done with a sceptical audience to tell him whether he was cur-dog hunting, or on a scent.

The house opposite Phoebe Agnew's flat was one of the unmodernised ones, shabby and dirty-curtained. The January light was as pale and sticky as aphid's milk, but the man who answered the door of the area flat blinked up at Slider like a purblind pit-pony. He was tiny, collapsed together by age, and wrinkled like a relief map of the Himalayas.

'I'm Detective Inspector Slider from the Shepherd's Bush police,' Slider said carefully and clearly, holding up his ID. 'Can I come in and talk to you?'

It took a while to sink in – you could almost see the *wait* symbol in his eyes as his underpowered computer struggled to boot up – but then he smiled a pleased, shy smile of tea-stained china teeth, and said, 'Oh yes, that's right, come in, thank you very much.'

The door opened straight into the sitting-room. The room smelled of paraffin, and had a superficial, smeary warmth that did not quite mask the cavernous dank chill underneath. There was a variety of grubby rugs covering the floor, a pair of sagging brown armchairs bracketing the fireplace, and a Utility sideboard bearing an ancient radio with a chipped plastic dial. A small television stood on a square plant stand with barley-sugar legs, and there was a gateleg table against the wall with an upright chair on either side of it.

Clutter fouled every surface, heaps of old newspapers mouldered in corners, and on the mantelpiece sheaves of letters and bills spouted from behind a square electric clock whose art-deco face had a peach-mirror frame which dated it to the 1930s. The fabric had worn off its flex, and the bare wires showed through, dangling down the side of the fireplace to the unreconstructed Bakelite plug in the skirting.

The paraffin heater was milk-bar green, chimney-shaped, and stood on the hearthstone. The old man saw Slider looking at it, and said, 'Bit pongy, is it? I don't mind the smell o' parafeen meself. Some do. It's a nice, clean smell, to my mind, like the smell o' tar or queer soap. Any road up, it works out cheaper'n the electric.'

'It takes me back,' Slider said. 'We had them at home when I was a boy.' It hadn't been the smell of the paraffin he had been sniffing warily, but of the old man himself. His grey flannel trousers were much stained, and the various layers of clothes on his upper body – vest and shirt and knitted waistcoat and jumper and cardigan – were all grubby and food-spotted; his thin hair, carefully combed back in a Ronald Coleman, looked as if it hadn't been washed for weeks. He smelled terrible; but he stood alert as a pre-war pageboy, ready to spring into action, clearly pleased with Slider's presence, as though it were a social visit.

'Make you a cuppa tea, sir?' he said next.

Slider didn't want to think what might lurk in the kitchen regions. 'No, thank you. That's very kind, but no,' he said firmly. 'I just want to talk to you about—'

'That lot oppo-site,' he finished for him smartly. 'Hanythink I can do to 'elp, I'm most willin'. One o' your gentlemen 'as been here already.'

'Yes, I know,' Slider said. He thought the old boy would enjoy a bit of formality to make him feel important, so he took out a notebook and flipped it open. 'It's Mr Singer, isn't it?'

'Singer, that's right, sir, like the sewing-machine. Albert Singer. Won't you sit down, sir?'

The upright chairs looked less lethal, but Mr Singer was gesturing towards one of the fireside models, and Slider resigned himself and sat, keeping to the front edge so as not to have to lean back into its sinister embrace. The old man hovered attentively until Slider was down, then murmured, 'Thank you very much', and placed himself nippily in the other, hitching at his trouser legs as he sat until the pale, spindly shins gleamed above the grey socks and crimson bedroom slippers.

'Now, Mr Singer, concerning Thursday night last week—'

'Yessir, Thursday night, that's right,' he interposed eagerly.

'You mentioned that you saw a woman behaving strange-ly.'

'That's right,' Mr Singer said, fidgeting with pleasure. 'I mentioned it to the gentleman as come before, only 'e wasn't too int'rested in a woman, wanted to know about a man.'

Slider nodded. That was DC Cook, on loan from Ron Carver's firm, who hadn't had the patience to probe further. *Did you see a man? No? All right. No, we're not interested in a woman.* The resentment of having to work on some other firm's case, plus an old man like a troglodyte living down a smelly hole, had sent him skipping over this piece of evidence like a stone on a pond. Cook's ingrained training, however, had ensured that he made a bare note that Singer had said he saw a woman acting suspiciously, for which Slider could now be thankful.

'I 'ave to say I never pertickly noticed a man,' Mr Singer went on. 'I mean, there's people up and down the street all day, any number of 'em. I couldn't say one way or the other about any pertickler man. But this woman stuck in my mind.'

'I'd like you to tell me about her,' Slider said. 'Do you remember what time of day it was?'

'Course I do! Thursday night it was, about twenty to nine. I 'ad *The Week in Westminster* on, an' I was waitin' for nine o'clock to turn over to the Weld Service. Listen to that a lot, I do, the Weld Service. They talk proper, like the old days on the BBC – not like the modern lot, can't hardly understand a word they're saying. Gabblin' and funny accents. I don't mind a Jock or a Paddy or the rest of 'em,' he added fairly. 'Met a lot of them in the Services, in the war. They're all right. But not on the BBC, to my mind. Oughta talk proper on the BBC.' He paused, lost. 'I ferget where I was.'

'It was twenty to nine—'

'Oh, yes. Thank you very much. Well, like I said, I'm waitin' to turn over for the news hour at nine, see.' He looked anxiously at Slider. 'This is how I know what time it 'appened, you understand?'

'Yes, I understand. Please go on,' Slider said.

'Right,' Mr Singer said, reassured. 'Well, I'm not reely listenin' to *The Week in Westminster*, see, an' I'm standin' at the winder lookin' out.'

'It would have been dark outside,' Slider said.

The old man nodded approvingly at his quickness. 'That's right, sir. What I do, sometimes, is I 'ave the curtains closed, an' I stand atween them an' the winder, see? Cuts off the light. I can see out, but no-one else can't see me.'

'Why would you do that?'

'Oh, just lookin'. No 'arm, is it? Weld goin' by, sort o' style.' Slider nodded. 'Anyway, I see this woman. She's standin' by the pillar at the top o' my steps, leanin' against it, sort of, looking at the 'ouse across the road.'

'The house where the murder happened?'

'That's right,' Singer nodded. 'Ten minutes, it must o' been she stood there, just lookin'. Ever so still, she stood. Unusual that. People fidget about, mostly, when they stand, but she stood stock still, just like a soldier.' It had plainly impressed him, for he paused to replay the image in his mind.

'And what happened next?' Slider prompted after a moment.

'Well, something must of 'appened, because she like stiffens, as if she's seen something; then she moves away from the pillar a little bit and looks down the road, like she's watching somethink. She stays lookin' in that direction for a bit. And then she goes back to watching the 'ouse. An' after about anover five minutes, she starts across the road.'

'Could you see that from down here?' Slider asked.

'Well, sir,' the old man said, leaning forward and hitching again at his trousers in his eagerness – they were practically up to his knees now – 'I can't see the road, that's true, because of the angle and the cars, but I *can* see the door of the 'ouse oppo-site, on account of it's up the steps. And I see her go up to the door and go in. Try for yourself,' he added on a happy thought.

Slider went to the window. The area wall straight ahead hid the road but, yes, he could see two thirds of Phoebe Agnew's front door. Probably the old man, given his lack of height, would only see half of it, but it would be enough to see the head and shoulders of a person going in.

'Can you say more exactly what time that was?'

'Well, sir, no,' Mr Singer said regretfully. 'Not exactly. But near as I can say it would a' bin between ten to and five to. It wasn't long afore the wireless give the time at nine o'clock, and I 'as to turn over.'

'You didn't see the woman come out?'

'No, sir. I left the winder, see, when I turned over for the news hour, and then I never went back. But she never come out afore nine.'

Slider nodded. 'Well, that's very helpful, Mr Singer, thank you.'

'Thank *you*, sir. Glad to 'elp.'

'Now, can you describe the woman to me?'

He shook his head sadly. 'I couldn't see her face – too far away, and she 'ad 'er back to me most o' the time. But I'd say she was young. Slim. Short 'air—'

'Light or dark?'

'Dark,' he said certainly. 'She 'ad trowsis on, but not them jeans, dark ones. And proper shoes, not them trainers. She looked like a lady,' he added. 'Y'know what I mean? Not one o' these modern girls, all bits an' pieces, hair like a rat's nest an' no manners.'

Slider nodded. 'I think I know what you mean.'

'An' she stood still as a soldier. I'll never forget that.'

'One last thing, Mr Singer – do you live here alone?'

'Yes, I do, sir, since the wife went. Passed on nearly ten year ago. I manage all right but—' He looked round as if suddenly struck by his surroundings, and gave a little, deprecating smile. 'I dunno what she'd think o' the way I keep the place. But it's not in a man's nacher to be tidy, is it, sir? That's what I reckon. Wimmin are nachrally tidy. Looking after us, an' tidyin' up, it's in their make-up. That's why they're no good at inventin' things. There wouldn't be no jet engines nor motor cars nor anythink if it was left to them, 'cos they only see what's in front of their eyes, an' as soon as a man makes a mess, they wanna tidy it up. But you can't make somethink without makin' a mess, now can you? It ain't reasonable. That's why you never get no wimmin inventors.'

'You could be right,' Slider said. He made a firm gesture of leaving. The melancholy chill was creeping into his bones.

'Well, that's what I think, anyway,' Mr Singer said. He saw Slider to the door. 'I 'ope you get him, sir.'

'I hope so too. You've been a great help, thank you,' Slider said.

As he climbed the steps, up out of the Stygian cave and into the sunlit uplands of normal street level, he was followed by a heartfelt and slightly wistful, 'Thank *you* sir, very much.'

He moved away down the street a little, aware that he would be watched as long as he was in sight. He noticed that, as in many streets of this vintage, the street lights were staggered on alternate sides of the road. There was one almost right outside the Agnew house, which meant that across the road, outside Mr Singer's, there was none. Someone standing at the top of Mr Singer's steps would have been in comparative darkness, watching a door in comparative light.

Maria Colehern's flat had an intercom at the street door. When she answered, he asked for Josh Prentiss. 'Is he staying with you, by any chance?'

'If you're the press,' she answered snappily, 'you can go away. I'm giving no more statements.'

'It's not the press, it's the police. I'm Detective Inspector Slider, and I want a quick word with Josh Prentiss. Is he with you? I know he's not at home or in his office.'

There was a long pause, as if consultation was going on, and then her voice came back. 'All right, come up.' The release buzzed violently.

The building was of luxury flats, built in the thirties and now extremely expensive. Either Maria Colehern's job was more important than he had realised, or she was independently wealthy. As he stood outside her glossy door in the cream-painted hall on the thick green carpet, the door to the next flat silently opened four inches and a face inspected him through the gap. When he turned his head towards it, the door closed two of the inches, but the inspection went on. This, presumably, was the neighbour who vouched for Prentiss's arrival.

Maria Colehern opened her door and looked quickly past him, down the corridor. 'Oh, you are alone,' she said. 'I thought it might be a trick.'

She was extremely attractive: slim, with a sharp-featured, high-cheekboned face, and very glossy dark hair in a bouncy bob held off her face with an Alice band. She was wearing a short mulberry skirt over navy opaque tights, and a skin-tight black Lycra top under an enormous mauve mohair sweater with the sleeves turned up. Her legs were superb, her hands long and beautifully manicured, her make-up subtle and perfect. She looked both very feminine and very capable. She also looked very cross.

'I'm sorry to disturb you,' Slider said in his mildest manner, with a smile that would have disarmed an ICBM. 'It won't take long.'

'We've been badgered to death,' she said shortly, and then, turning towards her invisible neighbour, said loudly, 'All right, Mrs Romescu, thank you, there's nothing to see.' The neighbour's door snapped to. 'Come in,' she said to Slider.

Inside it was amazingly spacious, with a huge hall and glimpses through open doors of large airy rooms furnished with antiques. The air was warm and dry, and smelled of furniture polish, cedar, Miss Colehern's perfume (Estée Lauder, he thought) and, at a level almost below detection, that ghost-memory of chicken soup with barley that haunts all pre-war service flats, as though the shades of a hundred Jewish Mammas live in the air-conditioning vents, sighing over modern eating habits.

Maria Colehern led the way into a drawing-room with a parquet floor partly covered with a thick pink and cream

Chinese rug and what looked like French Empire furniture. Slider itched to examine the fabulous bronze group on the marble mantelpiece and the watercolours on the walls, but Miss Colehern had turned in the middle of the carpet to face him with the air of one who was not going to ask him to sit down.

'What is it you want?' she asked. 'I'm not sure if he'll speak to you – or even if he should, without a solicitor. I'm sorry to sound inhospitable, but our lives have been turned upside down, and I really don't think—'

'It's all right,' he said. 'It's not more trouble. I just want a piece of information.'

Her lovely lips parted for more objections when Prentiss came in behind Slider. 'Josh, I was just saying I think you ought to have Philip here if—'

'It's all right, I'll talk to him,' Prentiss said. 'It's the quickest way to get rid of him.'

Slider turned. It was a very different Josh Prentiss from the bedchamber ace he had first met: this one had crashed and burned and his propeller was six feet into the tarmac. He was unkempt, deeply haggard, and smelled of last night's drink, which he must have taken in plenty.

Prentiss must have read his own appearance in Slider's eyes because a bitter look came over his face. 'I didn't think you'd have the nerve to turn up again,' he said. 'Haven't you done enough? You've already destroyed my life – what more do you want? My political career's over, my firm's had orders cancelled, my wife's thrown me out, my chances of the Oscar are now zilch, and last night a Hollywood producer turned down a design he was crazy about a week ago. I've become untouchable, and it's all your fault.'

'Your wife's thrown you out?' Slider said, picking the bit that interested him.

'She thinks I'm a murderer,' he sneered. 'I wonder how she got that impression?'

'Did she actually say so – that she thinks you killed Phoebe Agnew?'

'Well, let me see. She looks at me with horror, shrinks away and screams "Don't touch me", and says she can't live under the same roof with me any more. What do you think that means?' Despite his ironic delivery, Slider could see the genuine distress underneath.

'I'm sorry. It's been an upsetting experience for everyone. But there are one or two things I need to confirm with you.' He went on quickly before any more objections could be voiced. 'You told me that Phoebe Agnew seemed to be worried about something that last day. Are you sure she didn't tell you anything about what was on her mind?'

'What's this, a new line you're pursuing? You've really convinced yourself I didn't do it?'

'I don't think you did it,' Slider said patiently. 'And if you'd been completely frank and honest with me from the beginning, I probably never would have. Now please, will you answer the question?'

'No, she didn't tell me. She said she wished she could but she couldn't.'

'I wonder why she couldn't tell you? Was there any area of her life she had previously kept secret from you? Do you remember coming up against a barrier like that at any point in your past friendship?'

'No,' he said. 'We talked about everything – or at least, I thought we did. She wasn't a reticent person. She had no taboos.'

'Have you any idea what she was working on recently? We've had a hint that she had a big project, something important and possibly dangerous.'

He frowned. 'Apart from her regular stuff for the papers, you mean? No, the only thing I knew was that she'd been working on a book.'

'A novel?'

'Of course not. A biography. I don't know whose, but

it would be someone political, no doubt. But she'd been writing that for – oh, six months at least. I don't think you could call that important, except to her, and I don't see how it could be dangerous.'

'No,' Slider agreed. 'I know she was never married, but did she ever have a—' Slider fished around for the right words. 'Was there a "one great love of her life", do you know? A major romantic entanglement?'

'No,' Prentiss said. 'Not that I ever heard about. She was the most unsentimental person I ever met. She liked love affairs – the sex part – but they never seemed to touch her emotionally. I never knew her to be "in love" in that way. Certainly she never mentioned anyone. Why do you ask?'

'It's the meal, you see,' Slider said. 'She cooked a two-course meal for someone, and you said it was ludicrous to suppose she would have cooked it for you. So who did she do it for?'

'I can't think of anyone she'd cook for,' he said blankly. 'She'd take a bullet for you if you were her friend, but she hated cooking.'

'Do you have a key to her flat?'

Slider slipped the question in and Prentiss seemed about to answer automatically and in the negative, when he thought of something and paused.

'As a matter of fact,' he said reluctantly, 'I have got one.' He was actually blushing, and Maria Colehern looked at him in concern. 'But I didn't use it that day.'

'Josh, I really think you ought to call Philip,' Miss Colehern began urgently.

Slider shook his head at her. 'It's all right. I really *don't* think he did it. But I can see', he went on, to Prentiss, 'that it might have looked incriminating if you'd mentioned it before.'

'I wasn't hiding the fact,' Prentiss protested. 'I'd just forgotten about it. Phoebe gave it to me ages ago, when she was going abroad for a couple of weeks and I thought

I might like to use her flat while she was away.' His eyes pleaded, and Slider understood that he had wanted to take a woman there, which was not a thing to mention in front of Maria. 'But I'd completely forgotten I had it. And I *didn't* use it that day.'

'Where is the key now?'

'At home, I suppose,' he said. 'We've got a key rack in the kitchen behind the door with all the spare keys on it, and I hung it on there. I haven't touched it since.'

'Did your wife know whose key it was?'

'I don't know. She may have. It might have come up in conversation, or Phoebe might have mentioned it. I really don't know. It wouldn't matter, anyway. We have neighbours' keys and friends' keys and the children's. It would have been quite natural to have Phoebe's.'

'Your wife used to be an actress, I know, but was she ever a dancer?' he asked next.

Prentiss seemed puzzled by the new direction. 'She did ballet as a child, but that's all. She was never a professional dancer, if that's what you mean.'

'So, this old injury to her back – where did that come from?'

'Old injury—' he frowned, and then his face cleared. 'Oh, you mean this present trouble she's got? It's just a pulled muscle, that's all. She slipped coming down the stairs and twisted it saving herself.'

'When was that?'

'Friday morning,' Prentiss said.

'Did you see it happen?'

'No, it was while I was at work. Why?'

'So when you went to work on Friday morning she was quite all right? No backache?'

'No. Well,' he added, 'she was still in bed when I left for work, but when I got home on Friday evening she was hobbling around in agony and she told me then that she'd done it that morning. Why are you asking? What's this about?'

Slider shook his head, pushing the question away. 'There is one last thing I want to ask you, and then I'll take myself out of your hair.' He looked up and found Maria Colehern's eyes on him, intent and troubled. She was an intelligent girl, and she seemed to be running somewhat ahead of her seedy old mate with his booze-sodden synapses. Slider realised that he needed to get her out of the way. What Prentiss chose to tell her afterwards would be his affair. 'I'd like to ask you this one question in private, if you don't mind,' he said to Prentiss. 'If Miss Colehern would be so kind as to excuse us?'

She didn't like it, but since Prentiss didn't object, she could only brand him with a searingly significant look, and leave the room. When they were alone, Slider said to Prentiss, 'I have to ask you this again, and I want you to be completely honest with me. I can't impress on you how important it is that you tell me the truth. Did you have sex with Phoebe Agnew that Thursday?'

Prentiss looked annoyed. 'No! How often do I have to say it?'

'We found your semen in her.'

'It wasn't my semen. You made a mistake. I didn't have sex with her.'

'And that's the truth? Please, it's important.'

'She and I didn't have that sort of relationship. I only ever did it with her once, way back when we were students, at a post-finals party. One of those spur-of-the-moment things on a heap of coats in someone's bedroom. I told her the next day how sorry I was, and that I'd never have done it if I hadn't been extremely drunk – though she was no more sober herself. Anyway, that was thirty years ago, and we never did it again. I doubt whether she would even have remembered it – it's certainly not something I ever think about. And that's the truth. It was always Noni and me. How can I convince you?'

'I'm convinced. Thank you,' said Slider unhappily.

* * *

Norma was waiting for him outside the station, looking elegant in trousers and heeled boots and one of those loose, wrap-around overcoats that only tall women with good figures can wear. She climbed in beside him, her cold cheeks pink, bringing a whiff of Eau de Givenchy with her, and said, 'Hi! Where are we going?'

'To see Mrs Prentiss,' Slider said. 'Thanks for coming in.'

'Pleasure. I'm only fretting myself to death over the wedding at home. Only a week to go.' She hunched her shoulders. 'So what does Mrs P know?'

'More than she's telling us, that's for sure. I don't understand it all yet.' He remembered a line from a book – he couldn't now remember which one – in which the author described a character as 'standing as still as only a soldier or an actor can'. Slider knew that stillness. It had reminded Albert Singer of a soldier, but, 'She was an actress,' he said aloud. 'It's important to remember that.'

'It is?' said Norma.

Slider didn't hear her. He had doubted Peter Medmenham at first, thinking that you never knew when an actor stopped acting. And Medmenham thought Noni Prentiss a sound actress. 'If I'm right, Mrs Prentiss has been playing a very long game indeed,' he said.

Norma caught the tone of his voice. 'You don't think *she* did it?'

'It's the same old question of who do you believe? She said Josh phoned and told her that Phoebe was dead, but he appeared not to know about it until we interviewed him. We believed her, so we thought he was lying. Then there was her remark about "the way the body was left". If he didn't divulge that little detail to her, how did she know it? And there's the question of her bad back.'

'The old dancing injury?'

'Except that she's never been a dancer – and Josh says

she had no old injury. She told him she hurt it slipping down the stairs on Friday. But it occurred to me that most people who hurt their backs do it trying to lift something heavy.'

Swilley was there. 'Oh. But if she hurt it on Friday—?'

'She was still in bed when he went to work on Friday morning. So it could have been already hurting – he wouldn't know.'

'And there's the female finger-mark inside the flat,' she remembered. 'If she says she's never been there, and it proves to be hers . . .'

'Yes,' said Slider. 'And Josh says he really didn't have sex with Phoebe Agnew on Thursday.'

'But—'

'You have to ask yourself, who else had access to his semen apart from him?'

Swilley's face curved in distaste. 'Oh, good God!'

Slider said nothing more, and she did not break the silence. It was too horrible to discuss. If he was right, it was something close to monstrous.

The house was silent. 'No answer,' Swilley said at last, when she had knocked and rung extensively. 'She must be out.'

'She's in there,' Slider said abruptly.

Norma glanced at him, and shrugged. There was no arguing with instinct. She looked up at the house. The landing window was partly open. 'Did you hear that cry of distress, sir?'

Slider followed her gaze. 'Could you get up there?' he said in surprise.

'Drainpipe. Easy.'

'All right. God help us if the neighbours are watching. It seemed like a very loud cry for help,' he said for the record, and added, 'If she's there, be careful. She might be desperate.'

Swilley slid out of her coat, handed it to Slider, and swarmed with light, muscular ease up the drainpipe, which had been thoughtfully placed in a more trusting age nicely adjacent to the window. It was a sash window, and there were a few heart-stopping moments as Swilley struggled to push it up one-handed, and Slider imagined her falling, the drainpipe breaking, or Noni Prentiss appearing like Norman Bates in a wig and stabbing her through the window.

But at last Swilley got it up enough to wriggle in and disappeared. A moment later the front door opened and she let him into the hall. 'No sound anywhere,' she whispered. 'Maybe she's asleep – or out.'

Slider stood a moment, his senses prickling. 'Downstairs,' he said.

He led the way. The narrow, dark stairs bent at the bottom into the subterranean gloom of an eighteenth-century basement kitchen. It had been knocked through into one room, front to back, which gave it a window at each end; but both windows were below ground level and, as the saying goes, twice fuck all is still fuck all.

Swilley shivered, wondering how people could live like this. The kitchen floor was stone-flagged, the cupboards were old pine painted grey-green, and there was a big, battered pine table in the middle, so it probably looked much the same as when it was first built. All very desirable in a certain stratum of society, but Swilley was a Möben girl at heart. It was at least warm, with an Aga in the chimney, where the original range would have stood. She had shivered from distaste, and the suspicion that gloomy basements always meant beetles.

Slider stepped out off the stairs into the kitchen, and at once there was a rush of movement. Noni Prentiss had been pressed against the wall beside the staircase and now flung herself at him. Her right hand was upraised, and even this poor light was enough to glint melodramatically off the blade of the large butcher's knife clenched in her fist as it swept downwards.

CHAPTER SIXTEEN

Origin of the specious

Reaction was instant and instinctive. Slider heard the movement and was side-stepping and turning even as Swilley launched herself from her vantage point one step up, grabbing the wrist of the knife hand as she brought the attacker down. Swilley was tall and strong and Mrs Prentiss small and slight and it was over, there and then. Mrs P disappeared under Swilley's body, Slider was knocked out of the way, and the Kitchen Devil went scooting off across the stone floor and under the table like an electric rat.

Mrs Prentiss had made no sound before Swilley got her; she could make none after, with the breath knocked out of her; but she writhed with the strength of desperation until Slider said, 'Keep still, or you'll hurt yourself. Just stop struggling and we'll let you up.' At the sound of his voice she became still, and when Slider had retrieved the knife and put it out of harm's way, Swilley rose and helped her up, still keeping hold of her wrist.

'You're hurting me,' Noni said. Her face was deathly white, gleaming faintly in the basement gloom like a peeled hard-boiled egg.

Slider nodded to Swilley to let her go, and she rubbed her wrist with the other hand but made no other movement. She was trembling so much it almost beat the air, like wings.

'I'm sorry we startled you,' Slider said.

She looked at him with glazed, unseeing eyes. 'I thought it was him. I thought he'd come back.'

'You mean your husband?' She swayed, as if she was going to faint. Slider pulled a chair out from the table and guided her to it. 'So you were going to kill him too, were you?'

'I thought he'd come to get me,' she said.

'Come to get you? Why? Because you threw him out?' She only stared. Slider pulled out another chair and sat down facing her. 'Why did you throw him out?' She didn't answer. 'Mrs Prentiss, look at me. Why were you trying to kill your husband?'

Swilley had been looking in cupboards, and had found a bottle of Sainsbury's brandy. She poured some into a tumbler and brought it over to show Slider, who nodded. She put it down in front of Mrs Prentiss, carefully closed her icy hand round it and said, 'Drink some of this. It'll make you feel better.'

In a few minutes the bolting terror had subsided in favour of a lower-key mixture of fear and misery. Slider observed her with interest. If Josh was looking haggard, this was a woman who had been all the way to hell and only halfway back. It fitted with his suspicions; now he had to find the best way of getting her story. If she had killed Phoebe Agnew, it must have been in the grip of emotions so powerful they might well rob her of speech, even of reason. Better to come to it indirectly, he thought, and from a long way back. This jump wanted long, wide wings, or the horse would refuse.

'You've had a hard few days,' he said at last. 'You've been living with a terrible secret. But it's over now. The secret's out. I know you were at Phoebe Agnew's flat that Thursday. I know what you did there. Now it's time to tell me everything in your own words, and get it off your chest.' He nudged her hand. 'Have some more of that. That's right. You're not afraid of me, are you?' She shook her head slightly. 'Good. So, then, tell me everything. Begin with you. Tell me all about you.'

It took a little coaxing and some gentle, probing questions before she began. But then it all came out, slowly at first, but with growing fluency: a story of love and of love mistaken, of the shadow that killed it and the crop of bitter jealousy that grew up in its place.

Anona Regan had been an only child, cherished daughter of rather elderly parents. Her mother was thirty-eight when she was born, her father seven years older. He was a cobbler by trade and had his own small shop in a respectable working-class suburb of London. By the time Anona was growing up the business was doing well enough for him to hire an assistant and keep his hands clean attending the counter; a change that conferred the perilous gentility of white-collarhood on him and his family. His wife had never worked. They lived in a neat maisonette which she kept spotless; she made her own and her child's clothes, cooked the plain, unimaginative meals of the fifties, and always put on her hat to go shopping.

Anona grew up a quiet, well-mannered, docile child, bending like sea-grass to the languid tides of the elderly household; the sort of little girl in hair-slides and white socks who never had any difficulty in staying clean, who played nicely on her own and could be relied on at any meal table not to spill or speak with her mouth full. At school she gave no trouble to teachers, and occupied the unexceptional place towards the bottom of the top third.

She had a little girl's passion for ballet, and since it seemed to Mrs Regan a wholly proper, feminine interest, Anona was allowed to begin dance lessons. It proved something for which she had a talent, and though she passed the eleven-plus and could have gone to grammar school, she pleaded in a quiet way to audition for a local well-known stage school, and was allowed. There she did solidly well, though not brilliantly – the hallmark of her life – and since, unlike many of the other pupils, she was also reasonably good at the academic lessons, the headmistress said it would be the sensible thing for her to go to university, just for insurance. With a degree, she would always be able to get a job if the stage failed her.

Anona never resisted the sensible, and her parents were proud and bewildered at the idea of a child at university, something that was becoming more common by 1966, but was still outside their frame of reference. The shop was doing less well – people were throwing away shoes and buying new ones now, instead of having them mended – and there was no longer an assistant; but Mr Regan, sixty-three, said a man with his own business never had to retire. He learned how to work a machine for cutting keys and engraving dog medals, and so managed to scrape up the money to supplement Noni's grant.

Quiet, clean, obedient Noni went to UCL in the October of 1966. Decades always have a time-lag, and the sixties, in the sense that history thinks of them, were just really getting under way. London was finally breaking free of the massive undertow of the war: the last of the bomb-sites were built over, there were goods in the shops and money to buy them, restaurants were opening to serve exotic food a world away from gravy and two veg, and young people were having notice taken of them in a way that was bound to go to their heads.

At UCL Anona Regan met Phoebe Agnew, who was so different from her, and who seemed to represent everything exciting about that magic decade. It was hardly too much to say that Noni fell in love with her. Phoebe was wild and beautiful, with her strange, loose clothes and unkempt mane of red curls. Phoebe smoked, drank, and talked incessantly, said unconventional things, used swear words, understood politics; laughed out loud, spoke to lecturers as if she were their equal, and addressed members of the opposite sex with teasing frankness. She even, Noni suspected, *had* sex. Most of the girl students talked about having it, but like Noni shied away from the awful reality, Phoebe didn't talk about it much – brushing the subject only casually in passing – but that seemed only to confirm the idea that she knew enough about it first hand to take it or leave it.

Phoebe was also brilliant, a top scholar with a real talent for writing, and she knew what she wanted to use her writing for. Other students were reading English because they had been good at it at school and couldn't think of anything else to do. They supposed, vaguely, that they would eventually become teachers. But Phoebe already had a track record in political activism and journalism. Why, that summer of 1966, before even starting at university, she had wangled her way into a trip to Chile, organised by a militant student group, to build a youth centre; and while there she had actually managed to get an interview with Allende, the Marxist leader of the land reform party. The interview appeared in the official Students' Union newspaper, and was subsequently reprinted in the *Socialist Worker* and précised in the *Guardian*. Thus Phoebe proved to her impressed fellow students that she not only knew what she wanted to do, she was getting on with doing it.

It was not to be wondered at that Noni was fascinated by this vivid extrovert. What Phoebe saw in her was less obvious. Perhaps it was the attraction of opposites; or perhaps Phoebe saw that Noni was not quite as much of an opposite as it appeared. For Noni was different from the other students. She too knew what she wanted to do, and she had a talent: that became apparent when they joined Dramsoc. Not everyone who joined wanted to act: it was the fashionable society to belong to, and was therefore a means to meet the most interesting members of the opposite sex. But plays were put on, and members auditioned for parts. Phoebe got one because her intellect dictated that she would succeed at what she undertook; Noni got the lead role because she could *act*. Phoebe's respect for Noni grew; Noni copied Phoebe's style in a quiet way, and the two girls achieved a small local fame together.

Josh did not audition for plays. Josh had joined Dramsoc so that he could have the pick of the women students; and the pick of the Dramsoc members, as far as he was concerned, were Noni and Phoebe.

At first it was an equal relationship. The three of them were drawn together, and took to hanging around and going out as a threesome. 'At least, that's what I believed,' said Mrs Prentiss. So far, she had told her story in a dreamy undertone, as if it were the history of someone quite detached from her. But now a bitterness began to creep in. 'I thought it was the three of us. But I see now it was always Phoebe. Always. Always. Right from the beginning.'

'You mean – her and your husband?' said Slider.

She nodded slowly, the now empty tumbler held in both hands before her face. 'How could I compete with her?'

'Weren't they just friends? He said it was a purely platonic relationship.'

'He told you that? What a *liar* he is! A man can't be "just friends" with a woman. It doesn't happen. I should know – God, I've lived with it all these years! All the Sophies and Stephanies and Carolines – all his secretaries and researchers and whatever else he liked to call them! Well, I put up with it. In a way, it didn't matter, because he didn't care a jot about them, the little sluts. But Phoebe – how could I bear that? It was different with her. He loved her.'

'Have you any evidence that they had a physical relationship?' Slider asked.

'Evidence?' She opened her eyes wide. 'You should have heard how he talked about her! He praised her to the skies. "Phoebe was so different – Phoebe understood – Phoebe had a real intellect." Not like poor stupid Noni, oh no! And he was always ringing her. They'd talk for hours on the phone. He asked her opinion. They had lunch together. He was always dropping in on her. And you ask me if I had any evidence?'

'It could still have been platonic—'

'Men and women don't have platonic relationships,' she said flatly. 'Not in the real world.'

There seemed no way of arguing with that. 'But she was your friend too,' Slider said.

'We did everything together at college. And afterwards she was always there. She helped me, advised me. I trusted her – she always knew better than me what to do. She had a – a *grasp* of things. I've never been clever like Phoebe, but she said I had something more important, that I had talent.' She rocked a little, mourning her friend. 'She did everything for me, sorted out all my troubles. If it wasn't for her, I wouldn't even have had Toby and Emma. Josh never wanted children – he hated his own father too much. But I wanted them so much. She told me just to stop taking the pill. I would never have dared. But she said he'd love the children once they were there, and of course he did. And when he found out what I'd done, she stopped him being angry with me. Took him away and talked to him and wouldn't let him shout at me. She always loved Toby and Emma; and they loved her. They called her Aunty Phoebe. She used to pretend to tell them off about that, but she loved it really.'

She rocked harder, and the tears began to slip out. Slider kept very still, letting the story come.

'Then when Emma went to school, it was Phoebe persuaded me to take up my career again, and made Josh use his contacts to get me on. He would never have bothered if she hadn't nagged him. He never thought my career was important. But Phoebe believed in me. She said I could be great – and I *was* good, I was!'

She met Slider's eyes in an appeal, and he nodded. 'I know you were.'

She seemed appeased, and went on. 'She always backed me up. When I got pregnant again and Josh wanted me to have an abortion because he said I was too old, she blew him up. She said I must have the baby. She was always dead against abortion. She fought him tooth and nail and made him change his mind – anyway, made him leave me alone about it,' she amended. 'He was never really persuaded.'

'Maybe he was worried about your health,' Slider suggested.

She shrugged the intervention away. 'She wanted that baby so much, almost as much as I did. When I lost it, it was her that cried. I couldn't cry – it was all locked up inside me. But I couldn't have got through if it wasn't for her.'

She paused and wiped the tears from under her eyes with her fingers and, finding her nose was running too, rubbed it on the back of her hand – an unconscious reversion to the childhood state before appearances mattered, showing how far from her normal poise she had fallen in the crash of what had been her life.

'It sounds as though she really was your friend,' Slider said. 'She must have loved you.'

Noni stared at him. 'Yes, that's what I thought. But I see now it was all an act. It's only in the past few years I've started to realise what was really going on. Now I know what a fool I've been. She was playing me along, while she and Josh carried on behind my back. It was them all the time, the two of them, heads together, laughing at me. I was the outsider.'

'But it was *you* he married,' Slider said.

'Yes, and how he regretted it!' she cried bitterly. 'He only married me because she'd gone away somewhere. The moment she came back he brought her home, and after that they started their game of making a fool of me. *That's* the real reason she made me have the kids – to keep me out of the way. She was jealous and wanted him to herself. I didn't see it at the time, but I see it now.'

'But you said she really loved the children – and they her.'

'Yes. She did. I suppose she couldn't help it. Oh, I don't know! Leave me alone, can't you! She's dead now, and it's all over. It doesn't matter any more. Nothing matters any more.'

She began to cry in earnest, putting her face into her hands. It was plain she was deeply confused about the situation; that she had loved her friend and even now, having convinced herself that there had been an affair going on, didn't want to believe it.

Slider saw how the layers of emotion – of love and admiration, of hurt and jealousy – had been confounded by a basic lack of understanding, an inability really to see what Phoebe Agnew had been about. A woman like her was so different from Noni that her motives must always have been a mystery. What you don't understand, you can only interpret according to your own lights. So, there could be no friendship without sex between a man and a woman; and an unmarried Phoebe could only have been jealous of and therefore hostile towards Josh's wife Noni. Add to that Noni's emotional breakdown following the loss of a child and the failure of her career, and the comparison of that with Phoebe's burgeoning success, and you had a seething cauldron of love and hatred that could easily spill over into action.

Probably it went all the way back to university, when Noni had wondered what clever Phoebe saw in her, and the seed of doubt was planted. Perhaps the soil was already fertile: didn't they say that all actors were insecure? That they became actors to escape from themselves into personae that they could control? And then Phoebe had to go on from strength to strength, winning fame and awards, while Noni never made it to the top, and had only her marriage to comfort herself with. And even in that one poor sphere of achievement, all she had to hug to herself, it seemed Phoebe outshone her. Josh liked Phoebe better, praised her to his wife. Naturally the wife came to think that a philandering stud like Prentiss must be having an affair with her. So the stage had been set for the action in which Anona Regan was sure she could play the leading role with conviction.

The tears were subsiding now. Swilley had found a box of tissues on the dresser, which she put down before Mrs Prentiss, and mopping up was now taking place.

'Tell me what happened on Thursday,' Slider said.

The story came out painfully. Despite Joanna's caustic comments, Josh Prentiss hadn't been wrong about Noni's being at a difficult age. She had started to have menopausal symptoms and was feeling unhappy, unloved and unattractive, especially as she and Josh had fallen into a pattern of hardly noticing each other. He was busy with his career, and she had nothing much to do, with the children gone, her own career in ruins, and her husband from home more and more of the time.

But on Thursday he had said he would be home all day – he hadn't mentioned his intention to go out in the evening – and following the hallowed advice of women's magazines through the ages, she had decided to try to make herself attractive to him. She began by taking an interest in his work and making bright conversation; but when he dismissed her rather testily, she had turned to plan B and concocted a delicious meal for him. It, or the wine that accompanied it, had done the trick, and she had been able to persuade him into bed, where they had engaged in the first sexual congress in many a long moon. So her chagrin and fury had been all the greater when he jumped out of bed and rushed away afterwards with what she thought was a lame excuse. She felt spurned.

Left alone, she had brooded on her wrongs and, as she had done more and more lately, blamed Phoebe for all of them.

'So you went round to her flat. Oh, yes, I know that,' Slider said. 'You were seen going in. There's no point in denying it.'

Mrs Prentiss sighed. 'All right. I went to have it out with her,' she agreed on a downward note.

'You didn't know your husband was going there that evening?'

'He said he was going out on Government business. I knew that was a lie. I knew he was going to see a woman. But I didn't think it was Phoebe. He never tried to hide it when he was going to see Phoebe – he just told me straight out.'

'So what happened?' Slider asked.

'I walked round there, but when I got to the door I could hear voices inside. A man's voice. She wasn't alone.'

'Did you recognise the voice?'

'No, I couldn't really hear well enough. I could just hear it was a man. So I—' She paused for a long time, her eyes fixed on some internal horizon. 'I gave it up and went home,' she concluded feebly.

Slider leaned forward a little. 'That's not true,' he said sternly. 'I thought you were going to tell me the truth?'

'I am,' she said faintly.

'You didn't just go round there to talk to her, did you? You wouldn't have needed the key for that.'

'The key?'

'The key to Phoebe Agnew's flat.'

'I don't know what you're talking about,' she said, but she was looking at him now. She seemed appalled and fascinated at the same time.

'You took the key to her flat, which she had given your husband long ago, and which hung on the rack alongside those to your children's flats. Did that seem like an insult to you? Anyway, you took the key so that you could slip in without her hearing. And what else did you take with you? A pair of tights, was it?'

Noni's lips moved, but no sound came from them.

'Phoebe never wore tights, did she? She *always* wore trousers, so the odds were she didn't even possess a pair. Anyway, you could hardly have taken time out to search for them when you got there, so you took your own. You knew she'd been drinking heavily recently, and you thought that with luck she'd be pretty well out of it by half past eight, so if you let yourself in you could creep up on her and get something round her throat before she knew you were there.'

'I wouldn't really have done it,' Noni whispered, her face drawn with horror. 'You can't, can you? Not how ever angry you are, you can't kill a person – not unless you're mad.'

'But you were mad,' said Slider. 'Mad with jealousy. This woman who had been your friend had outshone you all your life, and now you thought she'd stolen your husband from you. So killing Phoebe Agnew wasn't enough. You wanted to punish your husband as well – your husband who had made love to you that afternoon, and then left you to go to his other woman. You had to kill her, and make it look as though he had done it. You had to make it *absolutely certain* that he would be charged with the murder. When did you hatch your monstrous plot, Mrs Prentiss? And how did you get hold of the condom full of your husband's semen?'

Mrs Prentiss stared at Slider as if he were the hangman approaching with the noose. 'I didn't—'

'And then, when we came to question you, to make absolutely sure we'd suspect him, you told lies about where he was, so that when we found out they were lies we'd think you were trying to protect him. Everything you said to us, that sounded so innocent, was meant to incriminate him. A very long game you've been playing, Mrs Prentiss, and it almost worked. But you were careless. You left your fingerprints behind. We've found your fingerprints – in a flat you say you've never been in.'

She went cheese-coloured and doubled up, and Swilley came round the table to take hold of her neck and push her head down between her knees. 'Take it easy. Don't try to sit up. Breathe slowly and deeply – that's right.'

When she had recovered enough to speak, she said falteringly, 'You're wrong, so wrong—'

'I don't think so. That's how you hurt your back, shifting her body to the bed. You had no old back injury. And you told your husband you'd slipped down the stairs.'

'That's true, I did say that. But I didn't kill her! Listen,' she said desperately, 'and I'll tell you.'

It was like a madness that had taken hold of her, she said. When Josh got out of bed, saying he was going out, she had felt as though he had slapped her face. After making love as they had, she had thought he would spend the evening with her. She asked where he was going, and he said it was Government business. She screamed that that was a lie, he was going to see some woman. He lost his temper and yelled back. Then, apparently realising that arguing was only slowing him down, he calmed down and repeated that it was Government business, and added that the only woman he ever saw apart from her was her best friend Phoebe. Presumably he thought that would allay her jealous fears. Instead it had convinced her that Phoebe was at the bottom of all her troubles.

'He went into the bathroom to shower, and he threw the used condom into the waste-paper basket in there,' she recited tonelessly. 'I saw him do it before he shut the door. He never put them down the lavatory. He said it blocked it up. The basket has a bin-liner in it. When he'd washed and changed he went downstairs without a word, and I lay there in bed, looking at that bin. I could just see it, inside the bathroom door.'

'So you went and got the condom out again.'

She nodded slowly. 'It came to me all at once, the whole plan. I thought I'd kill her and then put his semen in her so that there was no way he could deny he'd been with her. I had a little plastic syringe I'd got from the vet years ago for giving the cat his medicine. I used that to get the semen out. I put a pair of tights in my pocket, and took the key and walked round there.'

'Go on. What time did you get there?'

'About half past eight, I suppose. I don't know exactly. I went to the door first and listened, and heard the voices inside. So I knew he was still there. I went and stood across the road where I could see the house and waited. It was then I started to calm down. I realised I couldn't do it. You can think of killing someone, you can want to, but when you actually face them alive – you can't really, can you? I wanted her dead, but I'm not that ruthless. So I was going to give it up and go home, when the door opened and I saw him come out.'

'Saw who come out?' Slider asked quickly.

'Josh, of course.' Her voice hardened. 'Seeing him come out started it all up again. I imagined them in there together, talking, laughing, making love. I wondered how many other times he must have gone to her without telling me. I could just see them, laughing about me and how easy I was to fool. I *hated* him then.' She stopped abruptly.

'So what did you do?' Slider prompted.

'I waited a long time to make sure he'd really gone, then I went across and let myself in quietly. Crept into the sitting room. And there she was, sitting in the chair, dead. It was so horrible! I can't tell you.'

She stopped for a bit, trembling, leaking tears, while she wound herself up for the rest. Slider waited, patient as nemesis, the awful sympathy that invites confession.

'I realised, you see, that I'd been living with a murderer. I've been living with him ever since. Can you imagine what that's been like? Every day, wondering whether he'd come home and do the same thing to me. I kept seeing her in my mind's eye – her face all swollen, that mark round her neck . . . If he did that to her, what might he do to me? When I heard you coming just now, I thought it was him, come to get me.'

'I see,' Slider said.

'That's why in the end I went through with the rest of the plan. I thought if I just left her like that he'd never be caught. I knew he was clever. He'd get out of it somehow.'

'You could have told us what you knew,' Swilley said.

Noni had forgotten she was there. She looked at her blankly and then said, 'How could I? He'd have found out and killed me. And what if you hadn't believed me? It would be just my word against his. So I did the rest of it, to make sure he got caught. It was horrible, horrible – I can't tell you! And now you've let him go! Why did you arrest him and then let him go?'

'Go on with your story,' Slider said. 'What happened next?'

She hunched her shoulders, pressing her clenched fists against her breastbone in a defensive pose. 'I thought I should die. In that room with her, looking like that. He must have done it with his tie, I suppose. And she was still warm.' She closed her eyes and swallowed, and her throat clicked. 'He'd done it only minutes before. She'd been alive only minutes before, and now she was dead. I'd never seen a dead body before. I think it made me a little bit mad. Otherwise I couldn't have—' She shuddered.

'Tell me,' said Slider.

'I dragged her over to the bed. She was so heavy, I had a terrible job getting her up onto it. That must be when I hurt my back. Then I took her clothes off – just the bottom ones. Tied her arms to the bed rail. And put – put the semen in her with the syringe.' She met Swilley's gaze. 'I had to make sure he was caught – and it didn't matter to her any more. And I threw the condom into the loo. No-one but me would know he didn't do that. I almost flushed it away – reflex reaction – before I stopped myself. Stupid.' She shook her head.

Slider's mind was reeling. 'That's when you left the finger-mark,' he said. All the brain-ache this woman had given them! 'But don't you realise, if he had done it using a condom, there wouldn't be any semen in her?'

She looked blank. 'No,' she said faintly. 'I never even thought of that. Stupid of me.'

'I suppose you didn't do badly for a first attempt,' said a grim Swilley. 'Did you wipe your finger-marks off everything else before you left?'

'I didn't touch anything else. I was very careful. I pulled my sleeve over my hand to open the door on the way out.'

Slider pulled himself together. 'Is this the truth you've told me now?'

'The truth,' she said, out of the blackness where she watched the endless reel of her own private X film: the appalling thing she had found; horror and guilt at what she had been prepared to do; horror and fear at discovering her husband had done it; the week she had spent living with it, with him, and wondering what was going to happen next.

'Do you wear contact lenses, Mrs Prentiss?' Slider asked.

She lifted her eyes to him, faintly surprised. 'No. I have glasses for driving, but I don't wear them otherwise.'

'You're short-sighted, then?'

'Only a little.'

'You were watching the house from across the road, and it was dark, and the street lamps aren't very bright in Eltham Road. You saw a man come out of the house that you thought was your husband, but it wasn't. No, I mean it. By the time you reached the house your husband was some distance away, in someone else's house. We have witnesses.'

'It was him. I saw him.'

'No. Your husband didn't kill Phoebe Agnew. He has an alibi. The person you saw come out of the flat was only someone who looked like him,' said Slider with awful pity.

She was silent a long moment as it sank in. 'Oh, dear God, what have I done?'

'What you've done', Slider said, 'is to interfere with the scene of a crime and seriously impede our investigation, while attempting to incriminate your husband for something he didn't do. Perverting the course of justice is a grave criminal offence for which the maximum penalty is ten years' imprisonment.'

Mrs Prentiss stared as another layer of desperate realisation was uncovered in her mind. 'I was so sure it was him,' she whispered. And then, 'What happens now?'

'You'll have to come with us to the station and make a complete statement. After that we'll decide whether charges will be laid against you,' Slider said. Swilley glanced at him, noting his distracted tone of voice. He was going through the motions here, but his mind was already galloping off, trying to work out the next step. If it wasn't Prentiss and it wasn't Mrs Prentiss, who the hell was it? They weren't just back at square one, they hadn't even got the board out of the toy cupboard yet.

CHAPTER SEVENTEEN

First among equines

'Damn and blast,' said the Syrup, quite mildly, all things considered. 'That's what comes of working weekends.'

'Swilley's taking her statement now,' Slider said. 'As far as charging her's concerned, I think she's pretty near the edge already—'

'Yes, well, that's not your decision to make,' Porson said sharply. 'Perverting the course is a very serious matter indeed, and not something to exercise leniency over. Besides, we've already got the Home Secretary in a right two-and-eight about Josh Prentiss and Giles Freeman. And this is a government that likes to be seen as above repute. Caesar's wife and all that. They don't want any more scandal.'

'I doubt whether charging Prentiss's wife with trying to stick him with the murder will absolutely kill all scandal stone dead, sir.'

'Don't be satirical, Slider. In your position, you can't afford it. We're a week into the investigation and what have we got to show for it? You've gone at Prentiss like a bull at a china gate, and now we're left with egg all over the carpet and a hostile press praying for our blood! We've got off lightly so far, but the Sundays have had all week to sharpen their pens, and they'll have the knives out for us all right. So you'd better have some plan of action up your sleeve, or there's going to be some pretty derisory comments made higher up the echelon, I can tell you.'

Slider tried not to shrug. What else could he have done but follow up the obvious leads? But bosses had to yell at you: they had bigger bosses upon their backs to bite 'em. 'Well, we know that there was someone else there on the Thursday,' he began, 'because of the finger-marks—'

'Oh, thank you very much!' Porson barked. 'An insightive comment, given that we know she didn't strangle herself! Is that what I gave up my afternoon's golf for?'

Porson played golf? Slider stared at him absently, wondering whether he wore a cap, and how he kept the rug on on windy days. Porson, fortunately, did not note the direction of the stare, only that it was blank. 'Yes, well, you look as if you could do with a bit of time off yourself,' he said more kindly. 'You're played out, laddie. When you've finished with Mrs Prentiss, you'd better go home. Give the old grey matter a rest. Have a shit, a shave and a shower and come up with some new lines to follow up.' His eyes followed Slider to the door, and he added, 'We can still hope for something on Wordley. I'd really enjoy nailing that sod.'

'I'll see what I can do, sir,' Slider promised.

Joanna had a rehearsal and concert at Milton Keynes on the Sunday, which was almost just as well, since he had some heavy-duty thinking to do. He was a long way down when the phone rang, and it took him a while to surface and get out to the hall to answer it.

'Bill? Chrise me, laddie, I thought you weren't going to answer. Asleep over the Sundays, were you?'

'Oh, hello, Nutty.' It was Nicholls, the uniform sergeant on duty. 'No, I was thinking, that's all. Took me a while to realise the phone was ringing. What's up?'

'We just had a phone call from Piers Prentiss. He had a bit of information for you. Didn't sound like much, but he seemed nervous as hell, so I thought I'd mebbe pass it on straight away.'

'You never know what might be important,' Slider said. 'What did he have for me?'

'He said he'd just remembered it – though I suspect he'd been a wee while working out whether or not to pass it on. But he said that while he was on the phone to your murder victim on the evil day itself – is this making sense?'

'Yes, go on.'

'Okay. While he was on the phone to her, he heard something in the background – in her flat, d'ye see? It was a pager going off.'

'Is that it?' Slider said after a pause.

'That's it, chum. Any use?'

'I don't know. You say he sounded nervous?'

'Aye, ahuh. Wettin' himself.'

'Well, then, evidently he thought it was important, though I can't quite see why for the moment. Unless he recognised the particular bleep.'

'Or he heard something else he hasn't coughed up yet,' Nicholls suggested.

'Yes. I'll give him a ring and ask. Well, thanks, Nutty. All serene down there?'

'Quiet as a church.'

Slider rang off, went to look up Piers Prentiss's number, and dialled. There was no answer. Slider was a little surprised – he'd have expected an answering machine. He rang Nicholls, and asked him to get Piers to ring him direct on his mobile, should he be in contact again.

As soon as he put the phone down, it rang again. This time it was Irene.

'Oh, God, I'm sorry. I was supposed to arrange something with you and the kids for the weekend,' he remembered.

'It's all right,' she said resignedly. 'I didn't tell them it might be on because I guessed it wouldn't be.'

'I'm really sorry. It's this case—'

'It's always a case. *You're* a case, Bill Slider! I sometimes think the Job is all there is to you. Take it away and you just wouldn't be there at all.'

It was too close to home, this comment. He thought of Joanna going to Amsterdam without him. 'I think you're right. Maybe I should give it up.'

She wasn't used to him agreeing with her. Even now she didn't want to hurt him. 'Oh, no,' she said. 'I didn't mean it. You're a good copper, and it's important work.'

'I don't know,' he said glumly. 'The Job's not like it used to be. And I start wondering whether there isn't more to life than this. I've always given you and the kids a raw deal. You've always come second to it.'

'No,' she said, defending him against himself. 'Maybe it wasn't always a bed of roses, but your job put food on the table, that's what matters.'

He smiled to himself. 'You're a very traditional woman, aren't you? There are things a husband does and things a wife does.'

'Well, I happen to think men and women were made that way, that's all, and these hard career women cause more trouble than they know. If they stayed home and cooked for their men and their children, the world might be a better place. There might not be so much crime to keep you working weekends.'

That was one very neat link. TV would love her. 'Look, we'll do it next weekend, definitely – all right?'

'If your case is finished by then.'

'If it's not, *I'll* be finished,' he said.

He looked at his watch when he put the phone down. Joanna wouldn't be back for hours yet. He wondered how Atherton's trip to Newmarket had gone. He could do with someone to talk to, he told himself; and if Atherton wanted to exercise his culinary skills on their behalf, he wouldn't object to that, either.

He dialled the number, and a cheery Atherton answered at once. Oh, hi! Yes, he'd had a great day, thanks. Of course, come on round. Had Slider eaten? He was just going to knock something up. Nothing special, just a store-cupboard job. No, it was all right. Well, okay, Slider could bring a bottle, if he liked. Red for preference.

Slider cleared up, left a message for Joanna in case he stayed late, and drove round, calling in at an Oddbins on the way for a bottle of Fleurie that he knew wouldn't make Atherton's eyebrow twitch. He was very tired and looking forward to a bit of comfort, and not prepared to have the door opened to him by WDC Tony Hart, dressed in tight ginger moleskin trousers and a white ribby sweater that left everything to be desired.

''Ullo,' she said cheerfully. 'S'prised to see me?'

'Surprised doesn't begin to cover it,' he said.

Atherton appeared behind her. 'Tony came with me to Newmarket,' he said. 'She's got a good eye for a horse.'

'Spent me formative years down bettin' shops,' she said. 'Me dad liked a flutter.'

'Get him a drink,' Atherton commanded her. 'I've got to get back to my chopping.'

Slider was divested of his coat and installed in an armchair with a glass of wine and Oedipus, the black former tomcat, kneading bread on his knees and purring like a DC10 about to take off. He glanced at the open door to the kitchen, and said quietly to Hart, 'Well?'

'Well what?' she bluffed.

He gave her a stern look. 'What are you doing here?'

She pulled a chair from the dining-table, reversed it and sat astride it, facing Slider. 'Listen,' she said broadly, 'I'm offered it on a plate, I'm gonna take it, ain't I?'

'Are we talking about the same thing?'

'You don't like me goin' out wiv Jim?' she said. 'Well, the way I see it, it's up twim, ennit?'

'He's seeing someone else.'

'All's fair in love an' war. This uvver bint can take care of 'erself – an' so can I.'

Slider shook his head wearily. 'It's none of my business. I just don't want him to get hurt.'

'Yeah, well, s'prisingly enough, I care about that an' all. What jer fink, I'm chasin' 'im for 'is money?'

Slider took the proffered side turning gratefully. His own emotional life was in enough strife not to want to get mixed up in Atherton's. 'Talking of which, what do you think of the racehorse scheme?'

'It looks all right. Dead posh stables an' everything. Nobs wiv nobby voices. Nice-lookin' gee-gees.' She shrugged. 'Personally, I fink he's nuts, puttin' all his dosh into it, but that's none o' my business. If he wants to chuck it about, that's up twim.'

'They told him there'd be a return of twenty-four per cent,' Slider said.

'If there was,' she said with unexpected shrewdness, 'evryone'd be in on it, wouldn't they?'

'Can't you talk him out of it?'

'Like I said, it's not my business.'

'If you really cared about him, it would be.'

The cheery, throw-away air disappeared like a conjuring trick. She looked suddenly upset. ''Course I care about 'im. An' if you ask me he's 'eadin' for a nervous breakdown. So what're *you* doin' about it? Don't dump it on me. *You're* the one who ought to've seen that coming. You're his boss.'

Atherton appeared with a plate of bruschetti. 'You two quarrelling? What about?'

'You,' said Hart, with an edge to her voice. 'Satisfied?'

'Oh, what it is to be loved,' he said, with one of his own. He handed the plate. 'Everyone wants a little piece of me, but there just isn't enough to go round.'

Slider gave Hart a hard look, and asked him conversationally, 'How was your horse?'

'Fantastic,' said Atherton. 'Brilliant. Ran like a hare – well, like a racehorse really. Bloody fast. Beat everything else on the gallop. Clever, too. As it passed us I heard it say to the horse next to it, "I don't know your mane, but your pace is familiar."'

'Seriously,' Slider pleaded.

'I tell you, it's good. Carrington – he's the boss-feller there – timed him while we watched, and the time's up there with the best. Everyone was very impressed.'

'What are the others like – in the syndicate?'

'All businessmen. All successful men in their own field. They wouldn't be going into it if it wasn't pukka. Like I told you, these days it's not a mug's gamble, it's a sound investment.'

'I don't see what "these days" has got to do with it,' Slider said, 'but – anyway, you're going for it?'

'Bloody right I am,' Atherton said. 'Eat all these. I've got mine in the kitchen.'

He departed. Hart looked at Slider. 'Pax?' she suggested. 'I fink he's a plonker parting wiv his akkers, and no-one ever got rich on the ponies, but it's his business, all right?' Her look hardened. 'And so am I.'

Slider remembered how when Hart had first joined them, Joanna had believed she fancied him, Slider. How wrong she had been proved! 'All right,' he said, 'pax it is.'

She crossed her arms on the back of the chair, pushing her bosom up under the sweater to sensational effect. Those ribs were never meant to take that sort of strain. 'So, how's *your* love life?' she asked casually. 'Married what'sername yet, Joanna?'

He didn't stay long at Atherton's flat. With Hart there, he couldn't talk much to him about the case, and no other conversation flowed easily between the three of them, despite Hart's efforts to amuse. They ate a soufflé ham and mushroom omelette with a salad and diced sautéed garlic potatoes – Atherton's scratch, store-cupboard meal –

and drank the Fleurie, and then Slider left them to whatever they were going to do together, which to judge by the way Hart wound herself round Atherton in the doorway probably wasn't a game or two of backgammon followed by the late-night movie and a cup of cocoa.

While he was driving home, his mobile rang, and he pulled over and stopped at the side of the road to answer it.

''Ullo, Mr S.' It was Tidy. 'I got a bit a gen for you.'

'Good man.'

'Turns out your two villains was involved in a murder after all.' Slider's heart jumped, but Tidy went on, 'Trouble is, it wasn't your murder.'

'What?'

'Yeah, well, this is 'ow it was. They done this job Fursdy arternoon, right, this old girl lives in 'olland Park. Your bloke 'ad got info she was gonna be at a weddin', so they could just walk in and out easy as pie. Well, Fursdy night they was out 'itting the 'igh spots, right? Celebratin'. Only Little Tommy, right, he's a moufy git, and he was talkin' it up big about the gear they'd got. So your bloke, Diction'ry, tells 'im to shut it. 'Ad a right ding-dong in this club down Earlsfield—'

'Earlsfield?'

'Well, they'd been travellin' a bit by then. That's where they'd fetched up. Anyway, they goes back to this flat wiv this other bloke they picks up at the club, game o' cards, few drinks, right? Then the row break out again. It all turns nasty. Your bloke's elephants, Little Tommy's a nutter, *'e* winds *'im* up, Little Tommy does 'im wiv a knife.'

'This is still Thursday night?'

'Yeah. Well, early hours o' Friday. They done the job about free o'clock time, an' they've been boozin' ever since. Now it's after midnight. So, anyway, Little Tommy sticks 'im an' as it away on 'is toes, right, so the other bloke, the bloke whose flat they're in, 'e dumps Diction'ry down St George's A & E and scarpers isself.'

'And that's where Dictionary is now?'

'I reckon. You'd better ask 'em. Or the local rozzers. Mr Nidgett, ennit, down Wandsworth nick? He'll tell you.'

Joanna came home shortly after he got back.

'Hello! Where've you been?' she said. 'I called you before I left.'

'At Atherton's. He gave me supper.' He didn't want to have to mention Hart's presence, so he hurried in with Tidy's phone call. 'So a rather tasty suspect has been taken out of the frame. Not that I ever really fancied him, but it would have been nice to clobber a real villain for this one.'

'I love it when you talk dirty,' she said.

'Wordley's in intensive care in St George's,' Slider said, 'and not likely to live, according to Derek Nidgett, the DI over at Wandsworth. They didn't know who he was to begin with – had no ID on him – but one of the porters recognised the bloke who brought him in and they eventually traced him back to his flat. So then he – the other bloke – saw the game was up and started rowing for the shore. Now they're looking for Tucker on an expected murder charge. But the upshot is that Wordley's accounted for from about six o'clock onwards, and we know Phoebe Agnew was still alive at a quarter to nine because that's when Piers Prentiss spoke to her. And in fact, that must have been only minutes before she was killed.'

He went on to tell her about the rest of his day, and Noni Prentiss's part in it.

'So what do you do now?' Joanna asked after a respectful silence.

He shrugged. 'Go back. Look into Agnew's life in more detail – if we can find it. Look for inconsistencies. Find out what she was up to.'

'You've wasted an awful lot of time on these Prentisses of various hues.'

'Yes,' he said feelingly. 'But we had to check out the

obvious people first. And at least now we know we aren't looking for someone who faked a rape to cover his tracks. Whoever strangled her left immediately. There was a report of a man with a file or something under his arm, fixing his tie as he walked along the road. That could be something. And there's this business of her telling a colleague she was doing some important work that might be dangerous.'

'Sounds like baloney to me,' Joanna said. 'What was she, working for MI5? I'll tell you', she added, putting the kettle on, 'what seems like an inconsistency to me. That bit about her persuading Mrs Prentiss to have the baby. These radical, feminist, anti-establishment, political types are usually fiercely pro-abortion, but you say Mrs P said she was dead against it. Cup of tea?'

'Yes, please.'

'And how was Jim?' she asked abruptly.

'He went to see his horse. He said it was fast. He's still determined to go through with it.'

'I know. I spoke to Sue a while ago. He'd just phoned her to tell her how wrong she was about it.' She looked at his unhappy face and added, 'Don't worry too much. If he took the trouble to provoke her about it, at least it means he cares about her opinion. He wouldn't bother to try and upset her if she meant nothing to him.'

'I suppose not.'

'It must have been after you left that he phoned her. How did he seem? Did you think he was miserable?'

Slider thought of Atherton bidding him goodbye, standing grinning in his doorway with Hart's elastic limbs wrapped round him, a glass of wine in his hand, and Elgar One on the CD player.

'Yes,' he said.

Swilley came into Slider's room. Atherton was perched on the edge of the window-sill, hands in pockets, legs crossed at the ankle, every inch the elegant, insouciant Englishman

– Richard E. Grant, but without the flurried awkwardness. He and Slider had been discussing the case; Slider, sitting behind his desk, seemed gradually to be being walled in by the piles of files, which were growing at the rate of Manhattan skyscrapers.

Swilley had more papers in her hand.

'Ah, here comes the lovely Norma,' Atherton said, 'on lissom, clerical, printless toe. Is that one of Hymen's lists you're entering?'

Swilley never encouraged him. 'Is that a burk I see before me?' she countered. 'Boss—'

'That's me,' Slider said, thinking it was time to get into the conversation.

'You wanted us to look for anomalies. Well, there's this. I don't know if it's anything,' she added apologetically.

'Anything could be anything. Fire away.'

'Well, you know there was a bunch of stuff on one of the chairs under a blanket?'

'Yes. I imagined she'd shoved it there in the course of clearing up.'

'You could be right. There was some recent correspondence and a telephone bill on top, so it could have been lying about waiting to be dealt with when she cleared.'

'And some clean underwear,' Slider added, 'which she hadn't had time to put away yet.'

'That's right,' Swilley said. 'So maybe she was interrupted or ran out of time or whatever, and just shoved it all under the blanket to get rid of it and make the room look tidy.'

'I wish I knew *why* she wanted the room to look tidy,' Slider said fretfully.

'To impress the person she cooked the supper for,' Atherton said.

'That's just the same question moved sideways,' said Slider. 'Anyway, go on. What have you found?'

'It's a letter from a female called Sula Brissan, dated Monday the eighteenth of Jan – so if she sent it first class it would have arrived on the Tuesday or Wednesday, depending what time of day she posted it. She says she encloses a copy invoice for the work done up to the beginning of December and she says, "I hope you won't mind my asking you to settle this outstanding invoice as soon as possible. You know that I was working almost exclusively on your project, and cash is always a bit tight after Christmas. Any time you want me to pick up the research again, I shall be more than willing." '

'And was it an outstanding invoice? Very large, or covered with gold leaf or something?' Atherton asked.

'Couldn't say. It wasn't there,' Swilley said.

'So Agnew was a tardy payer,' Atherton commented. 'Just what I'd have expected. She had a mind above material things.'

'It wasn't that she couldn't afford it,' Swilley said. 'She had plenty in her bank account. But that wasn't my point. The thing is, this letter suggests she's done quite a bit of work for Agnew, but I can't find the invoice or any trace of her – the Brissan woman – amongst the papers. You'd have thought there'd be a letter from her or another invoice or something with her address or handwriting on it, but no, nothing. Well, it just occurs to me that if there *was* a file missing from that filing cabinet, maybe that's where the Brissan stuff went.' She looked at Slider hopefully.

'And in that case, she might be in a position to tell us what Agnew was working on in the last few months,' Slider completed for her. 'Well, it's a thought. Where does she live, this female?'

'It's an address in Fulham.'

'Not too far. Okay, let's see what she's got to say. No, wait, not you,' Slider said to Swilley. 'I'd sooner have you on the files—'

'Who wouldn't?' Atherton murmured.

Swilley turned on him. 'If you've got something to say, say it out loud.'

'He can't tell talk from mutter,' Slider said kindly. 'Don't mind him. I'd like you to keep going through the papers. You', he turned to Atherton, 'can go and interview Miss Brissan.'

'Sounds like a drunken beauty queen,' Atherton said cheerfully. 'Me for that! Giss the address, oh blest police siren. Ta. If I'm not back in two days, send the RCMP.'

Slider translated with an effort. 'The Mounties?'

'No, a really cuddly motherly prostitute,' said Atherton.

Swilley watched him go. 'You shouldn't encourage him, sir, you really shouldn't.'

CHAPTER EIGHTEEN

We shall not all sleep, but we shall all be changed

Atherton had visualised Sula Brissan as tall, sveldt, young, and languid with unfulfilled passion. She turned out to be a brisk woman in her forties with short, thick grey hair; but she did have paralysingly lovely, deep-set blue eyes, and had evidently been sexy for so much of her life that she regarded Atherton with the unmistakable look of a woman who expects to be fancied. Obediently, he fancied her, so they got on well.

'Yes, I read about it, of course. It's terrible,' she said, making tea and loading the washing machine at the same time. To judge by the laundry, Atherton thought, exercising his detective skills, she had teenage children rather than little ones, which might not present such difficulties if she wanted to break out. On the other hand, there was a small baby to hand, in a car seat set on the floor; a steriliser/warmer stood on the window-sill, and a couple of bottles and teats were in the drying-rack. Atherton's signals were confused.

'And you've no idea who did it?' she went on.

'Not at the moment.'

'There was all that speculation in the papers about Josh Prentiss, of course,' she said thoughtfully. 'Poor Josh, it's buggered his career. Not that I like him much, but I'd never have thought he was capable of murder – and in any case, why Phoebe? They were old friends.'

'You know him – Prentiss?'

'I know just about everybody,' she said, without conceit. 'I was a Parliamentary researcher for years, and then I did all the Westminster stuff for IRN, before I went freelance.'

'So tell me, did Agnew and Prentiss make the beast with two backs?' Atherton asked.

'No,' she said with a pitying laugh at his naivety. 'It wasn't like that. Everybody knew they were just friends. It was a famous case – proof that platonic relationships can exist. No, they were like two old schoolfriends, or brother and sister, or something. She was more of a brother to him than his own brother, really.'

'You know Piers Prentiss as well?'

'I've met him,' she said. 'I don't know him well.' She handed him his tea in a mug. The kitchen was large and extended, untidy in the way of a much-used family room, and full of thin sunshine and the companionable noise of the washing machine and, in the background, the unheeded radio tuned to Capital. A fat Cyprian cat sat patiently at the glass-panelled back door, waiting to be let in. Middle-class family life in the nineties. 'So what did you want to know?' she said, leaning against the sink and sipping her tea.

'What was the research you'd been doing for her?'

'It was background for a political biography she was writing.'

'Biography of whom?'

She hesitated a moment. 'Oh well, she's dead now so I don't suppose it matters. But it was a big secret. Nobody knew except me and her. It was Richard Tyler.'

Atherton raised an eyebrow. 'He's a bit young for a biography, isn't he?'

She smiled. 'It's not how old you are but how much you've done. Look at all the biographies of the Beatles that came out as soon as they were famous, and they were even younger. She's been working on Richard for about six months now, ever since he became a junior minister. He's a remarkable person, and due to be remarkabler. Do you know about him?'

'That he's a member of the Freeman set and very in at Number Ten,' Atherton said.

'Oh, you do know your political gossip? I somehow never thought of policemen as being interested in things like that.'

'Most aren't. I'm unusual.'

'So I see.' A flirty look passed between them. Then the baby started crying; just like Jiminy Cricket. 'Well, if you know that much,' she said, putting down her mug and picking up the baby with a practised movement, 'you'll know that Whitehall is seething with factions. Ambition is rife. Richard's one of the young turks and the hottest tip for rapid promotion.' She slung the baby against her shoulder, supporting its bottom with one hand. 'He has a fabulous intellect and a photographic memory. He advises at the highest level, promotes the image, and disses the opposition – and I don't mean the official Opposition either, but the outs in the Party. He's known as a fixer, and he's got a publicity team that spins like Shane Warne on speed. *And* he's good-looking. No wonder the media love him. Well, you've seen all the Sunday supplement guff about him. They've even done his taste in interior decor – "the Tyler look", etcetera, etcetera.'

The baby, which had quietened when she picked it up, began wailing again. 'He needs changing, the little beast. Oh, don't worry, I won't do it in front of you,' she added with a laugh at his expression. 'Grandchild,' she explained. 'I thought I'd done with all this, but Nature kindly arranges a second go. My daughter's what the tabloids call a "working mum".' The baby, expertly jiggled, lowered the gain a notch. 'Where were we?'

'Tyler. You obviously think the world of him,' Atherton said.

She made a face. 'I don't have to like him to know he's

hot. My tip is that once the reshuffle's announced he's going to be the biggest media obsession since Princess Di. That's why it all had to be secret, Phoebe's book on him.'

'Why, had she uncovered some terrible secret?'

'No, nothing like that,' she said. 'For commercial reasons. Phoebe was a very prestigious commentator. If anyone had known she was working on it, they'd have tried to get in first and steal her thunder. It's cut-throat, the world of biographies. I can't tell you! The big political ones sell in the hundreds of thousands. I've researched for a few people, and believe me, if you get a good idea for the next subject, you keep it strictly to yourself.'

Atherton looked his disappointment. 'So all her secrecy and dark hints about her latest piece of work were nothing more than commercial prudence?'

'Why, what did you think?'

'Oh, that maybe there was some danger to her from what she was doing.'

'Oh, no,' she said robustly. 'She's not exposing the Mafia, you know! And Richard may be ruthlessly ambitious, but he's perfectly respectable. So are his people. An old political family. Steeped in it. His father and grandfather were both MPs and his mother was the daughter of a life peer and former Cabinet Minister. Funny how it so often does run in families,' she mused. 'Like actors, really. You have the Redgraves and Masseys and so on, and you have the generations of politicians, too.'

'I suppose in both cases, you get on as much through personal contact as talent,' Atherton suggested.

She grinned. 'In the case of MPs, much more! So what else did you want to know?'

'Who has the papers now – the work you and Phoebe had done so far?'

'She had it all. I don't keep copies of anything once I've sent it off. I suppose', she said regretfully, 'it'll all moulder in some police locker somewhere for ever, and someone else will eventually have the same idea and bring out their inferior Tyler biography.'

'Well, I suppose all the papers will be released to her next of kin sooner or later,' Atherton said. 'Which is her sister, I imagine.'

'I never knew she had a sister,' said Mrs Brissan. 'Maybe I should write to her and see if she'd let me have them.'

'You could try,' Atherton said. 'Tell me, did Richard Tyler know she was doing this biography?'

'I really have no idea. She never said one way or the other.'

'Isn't it usual to get the subject's permission?'

'Depends. There's the authorised biography, if the subject is controversial or powerful – gives it more weight. And if there's any chance of being sued for libel, it's best to get them to read what you've written and okay it. But otherwise you get more punch from launching it on an unsuspecting world – and you can get some brilliant publicity if the subject does object to anything. It's more fun that way if you've got the balls – and Phoebe certainly had them.'

'But she'd have had to have his permission to interview his parents, say, or look at his personal documents.'

'His parents are dead. And the work I did for her only concerned public records. Whether she asked him for anything else – as I say, I've no idea.'

'So you'd been working on this for some months – and then you stopped? Why was that?'

'Well, that was a bit odd,' Mrs Brissan said, frowning. 'She wrote to me in December to say that she didn't want any more work done. Just like that. No reason given. Naturally I rang her to ask what was going on, because I'd got quite involved in it. But she was very offhand, not like her usual self. I mean, we'd known each other for years, but she talked to me as if I was a stranger. She wouldn't say why she was stopping, just repeated that she didn't want any more work on it, and asked me to send anything I had outstanding, including any rough notes. She said she didn't want me to keep anything relating to the topic. I was a bit offended. I said, you don't think I'd pass them to anyone else after you'd paid for them, and she said she was sorry, she didn't mean to offend me, it was just that she had rather a lot on her mind. So anyway, I sent her everything I still had, plus my invoice for the work, and that's the last I ever heard from her. But she didn't pay the invoice, so I sent it again – just before she died. I suppose *that* won't get paid now. Not that it matters beside what happened to her, poor thing.'

'Well, thanks,' Atherton said, feeling they had come to a dead end. 'You've been a great help.' The baby was quiet again, and so that it should not have been a completely wasted journey, he added, 'Would you like to have lunch with me – my way of saying thank you?'

She gave him an infinitely knowing look. 'I'm a married woman.'

'I only offered you lunch,' he protested, lifting his hands.

'No you didn't – and thanks very much. When you're a mother of three, and a grandmother of one, it's nice to know you've still got it.'

'You've got so much you could take on a couple of assistants,' Atherton said, yielding.

She eyed him thoughtfully, and turned away to put the sleeping babe back in its carrier. 'Is there a Mrs Atherton?' she asked, her back to him.

'Not unless you're volunteering.'

'Not for all the tea in Lancashire,' she said. She straightened and turned. 'But you ought to get married. It can be lonely, being an ex-rake.'

Atherton staggered. 'Good God, you don't pull your punches, do you?'

'You and I understand each other,' she said. 'I've been there, done it – just ten years ahead of you. Don't get left behind, that's my advice. Married men live longer, and they're much less likely to commit suicide.'

* * *

'Richard Tyler?' Slider said. 'I wonder whether that was why Phoebe Agnew wanted to stop Piers seeing him? That row they had at New Year, you remember?'

'I don't quite see why,' Atherton said. 'I mean, if anything it would be beneficial to her, wouldn't it? Another personal contact with her subject – maybe access to more information. He might tell Piers stuff he wouldn't tell anyone else – and Piers is such a blabbermouth he'd let it all out as soon as she applied the single malt in sufficient quantities.'

'Yes, I suppose you're right. It would make more sense for her to encourage the relationship.'

'Anyway, I don't see that it helps us. Even if there were a file missing, and even if that was it, the only person who knew about it was Mrs Brissan—'

'According to her.'

'Quite. But Agnew hadn't even told her dear old mate Josh who the subject of her biography was, so it seems likely she *did* keep it secret. And why should it provoke anyone to murder her anyway?'

'You're right. In any case, it doesn't look as if that's the thing that was worrying her,' Slider said. 'She said to Josh she had a problem that would make his pale into insignificance, and that he was the last person who could help her with it, and it's hard to see how her research for a biography could fit either of those categories.'

'So what next?' Atherton asked.

Slider leaned back and put his hands behind his neck to stretch it. 'God, I don't know. There ought to be something in her papers, or somebody she knew or worked with ought to have known what this problem was. If she'd been worried and drinking more heavily for the last few weeks, you'd think she'd have told someone.'

'Maybe it was just the menopause after all,' Atherton said. 'All in her mind.'

'And she was murdered by telekinesis?'

'By a random lunatic.'

'Thanks. That's helpful.'

'Lunchtime, guv,' Atherton said. 'Give yourself a break. Feed the brain cells.'

'Yes, you're right. I am hungry, now you come to mention it,' Slider said, shoving his chair back and standing up. 'I fancy a big plateful of—'

Of what, Atherton was never to know – though he suspected chips – for the phone rang.

Slider picked up. It was Detective Inspector Keith Heaveysides of the Essex Constabulary. He was sorry to have to tell Slider that Piers Prentiss had been found dead in his shop this morning, and in view of Slider's recent interest in him, Mr Heaveysides wondered if he'd like to come along and pool information, hopefully to their mutual benefit. Pardon? No, it certainly wasn't natural causes, and there didn't seem to have been any robbery, either from the person or the premises. Yes, certainly. Not at all. They were all on the same side, weren't they? Not a problem. His pleasure entirely.

Slider liked Heaveysides straight away. He was one of those tall, full-fleshed, fair men who go bald right over the top very early in life, but keep a boyish face as if in compensation. He seemed a genuinely nice person, but yet to have survived in the Job with a name like his, he must have had a toughness, or at least an inner serenity, to survive the teasing.

He took Slider and Atherton into his office and gave them coffee (from his personal filter coffee machine, so it was drinkable) and biscuits while he filled them in on the story.

'It was his cleaner who found the body,' he said.

'Marjorie Babbington?' said Slider.

'Oh, you know her, do you?'

'We met her when we interviewed Prentiss at his house. She must be pretty upset.'

'She's holding up well. You know the sort – stiff upper lip. Anyway, she was doing the cleaning in the house this morning when someone comes knocking at the door. It's a local chap, name of Hewitt. He's gone past and seen the lights are on in the shop, tried the door and found it's locked, so he's called at the house in a neighbourly way to say did you know you've left the lights burning.'

'Was the closed sign up?'

'Yes, and he's a regular customer of the shop, so he knows it's usually shut on a Monday. That's why he wonders. So anyway, Babbington answers the door, Hewitt says blah-di-blah-di-blah, she says Prentiss isn't there. He says it's an awful waste of electricity so she says all right I'll get the keys and come and turn 'em off.'

'Where did she expect Prentiss to be?'

'Well, Monday being the closed day, he could be anywhere. She wasn't worried. If he was going away for any long time he always told her so she could look after the dogs, but as it was she thought he'd just popped out. So she gets the spare keys and goes in by the back door, and there's Prentiss lying dead behind the counter.'

'How did he die?'

'It looks as if someone knocked him down from behind with a blunt instrument, and then strangled him,' said Heaveysides. 'The ligature's been removed so we're no wiser about that, but the police surgeon said it was a smooth band, maybe a silk tie. Prentiss must have been groggy from the blow because he hardly struggled – just a couple of broken nails.'

'Break-in?'

'No, both the shop doors, front and back, were locked.'

'You said spare keys. What other sets were there?' Atherton asked.

'I was just coming to that,' said Heaveysides. 'Mr Prentiss had his own set on his own key-ring, which he kept in his pocket, and they were missing. We've had a bit of a search of the house, and immediate environs, but they haven't turned up yet.'

'I doubt if they will,' Slider said. 'And you say there was no sign of any robbery or theft?'

'Nothing as far as we can tell. Of course, in an antiques shop like that you don't know what was there to begin with, but everything looks all right. And Prentiss's money and credit cards were still in his pockets. It's a bugger,' he added feelingly. 'He was a nice old stick. Everybody liked him. You know that in places like this you can get a lot of prejudice and queer-bashing, but it never seemed to touch him. And this is a quiet community. We haven't had any violent crime here in years, leave aside the odd fight outside the pubs of a Saturday night.'

'Yes, it's a miserable business,' Slider said. He remembered his long talk with Piers, the shadow Prentiss, the B-side brother; conjured up the charm of his rare smile, the wry intelligence, the humour. Now it was all stopped, just like that, in an instant, in the twinkling of an eye. His corruptible must put on incorruption: but no-one had asked him if he was ready. His life, stolen from him, just like Phoebe Agnew's – and for what? What was the connection?

Heaveysides raised anxious eyes to Slider's. 'You've got something going on with Prentiss's brother, haven't you? Do you think the cases could be connected?'

'I have a nasty suspicion that they almost certainly are,' Slider said. 'But the brother's been cleared of our murder. It seems likely, on what you've told me, that whoever did this did our job as well. But I'm afraid we haven't a clue yet who that might be.'

'Ah, well, it goes like that sometimes,' Heaveysides said wisely. 'Would you like to talk to Babbington?'

'Thanks, that would be helpful.'

'I've got to get back to my own lads – but you'll let me know if you get anything that'll help me?'

'Absolutely. I'm grateful to you for letting me in on this. There's a lot wouldn't.'

'In my view, we're all on the same team,' Heaveysides said.

'I wish everyone thought like that,' said Slider.

Marjorie Babbington was white, rigid, and red-eyed, but she wasn't giving in.

'I'm sorry to put you through it all over again,' said Slider, 'but I'd be grateful if you would tell me what happened. I've had it from Inspector Heaveysides, but I may hear something slightly different from you, or you may remember a detail you didn't tell him.'

She said, 'I understand. I don't mind how often I tell it, if it helps catch whoever did this awful thing. How could anyone hurt someone like Piers? Do you think', she asked, meeting his eyes bravely, 'it was the same person that killed Phoebe?'

'I think it very likely.'

'Well, I hope you get them,' she said fiercely, 'and I wish we hadn't abolished hanging.'

'So, tell me, when was the last time you saw Piers?'

'Yesterday afternoon, when he was walking the dogs. He went past along the lane, and I waved to him from the kitchen window.'

'What lane is this?'

'The lane that runs behind our houses. You know I live a few doors down from Piers?'

'I do now.'

'Oh. Well, there's a lane that runs along the back of the whole row. Just a narrow mud track, really, too narrow for a car, but it gives access to our backyards. Anyway, he went by about, oh, half past three or thereabouts, walking the dogs. He waved back to me quite cheerfully. And that was the last time I saw him – until—' She couldn't finish it.

'All right,' said Slider soothingly. 'Tell me about this morning. When did you come to the house?'

'It was about half past nine. I came along the lane and let myself in at the back door—'

'Was it open or shut?'

'Oh, it was locked. He used to leave it open in the old days, but we had a spate of burglaries a few years back and I made him get into the habit of locking the house when he went to the shop. But in any case, the shop's closed on a Monday, so when I found the back door locked I knew he must be out. So I let myself in with the key.'

'What keys do you have?'

'Of Piers's? Only the back door. I always come in that way.'

'And what about the shop?'

'I don't have a shop key. Piers gives me the spare set if he wants me to look after it for him.'

'All right, go on. You let yourself in. How did the house seem?'

'Well, just as usual really. I didn't notice anything out of place. Oh,' she remembered, 'except that the dogs seemed unusually hungry.'

'They were in the kitchen?'

'Yes, on their beanbag. They rushed to me and jumped up and down, just as they always do, but then they went to their bowls and barked like mad and pushed them with their noses, the way they do when they want to be fed. Naturally I assumed Piers had fed them before he went out, so I just gave them each a Bonio. It's very wrong to overfeed dogs. Of course, now I think of it, they probably hadn't been fed since last night, poor things, but how was I to know?'

'You weren't, of course. So what happened next?'

'Well, I let them out to do their tiddles, and started my cleaning, as usual. Then Mr Hewitt came to the door and asked for Piers, and when I said he'd gone out, he said he'd left the lights on in the shop. I thanked him for telling me and said I'd go in and turn them off.'

'How come you didn't notice when you came past?'

'There are no windows to the shop at the back. The back door lets onto a sort of lobby with coat hooks and fuse boxes and the cloakroom, so you wouldn't see any light walking past at the back. Anyway, I got the spare set of keys—'

'Where are they kept?'

'In the bureau drawer in the drawing-room. I took them and went out the back way, to the back door of the shop, let myself in, and there was Piers lying behind the counter.' She stopped and drew a shaky breath. 'Of course, he couldn't be seen from the front door, or Mr Hewitt would have raised the alarm.'

'I'm sorry to put you through it, but how was he lying?'

'On his front. His – his face was turned sideways a bit. It was – swollen – and—' She stopped and put her face in her hands. 'I could see he was dead,' she said, muffled by her fingers.

'How was he dressed?'

She was a long time answering. At last she lowered her hands, in control again. 'Fully dressed. In his cord trousers and tweed jacket,' she said briskly.

'Did he look as if he had struggled? Were his clothes disarranged? Was anything knocked over?'

'No. The rug was rucked up a bit under him, but that was all. If anything had been knocked over, it must have been put straight again. And nothing seemed to be missing – except his keys, so they tell me.' She stared unhappily at her hands. 'I hate to think of him lying there all night like that, while the poor doggies waited and waited for him to come back.'

'Why do you think he was there all night?'

'Well, the police said – said he'd been dead for about twelve hours. And of course there was a light on in the shop last night.'

'Ah, you didn't mention that before,' said Slider. 'How come you saw that?'

'Oh, I didn't. It was Mr Hewitt. He said he'd taken his dog for a walk last thing last night – about half past ten – and he'd passed the shop on the way back and saw the light on then. Naturally he didn't think anything about it – why should he? But when he came by this morning and saw it was still on, he thought he'd better tell Piers he'd forgotten it.'

She looked enquiringly at Slider, who had lapsed into thought. Eventually he roused himself and said, 'You didn't notice anything in the house missing or disturbed?'

'Not really,' she said apologetically. 'I might have if I'd been looking for it, but of course I wasn't.'

'What keys were on the key-ring that Piers kept in his pocket?'

'The shop front and back and the house front and back.'

'So whoever took them could get in and out of the house without leaving a trace.'

'Yes, I suppose so – if the dogs would let them.'

'Are the dogs fierce?'

'Well, quite,' she said. 'If they don't know you. I mean, if Piers is there, or I am, they wouldn't hurt a fly, but if someone broke in – I know they're small, but with two of them they could be a real nuisance to a burglar.'

'And they were in the kitchen, but with the run of the house?'

'Yes, they—' Her eyes widened. 'There, now, you were right, I have remembered something that was different. The kitchen door was closed – the one between the kitchen and the rest of the house. That was always left open, but this morning when I went in it was closed.' She looked apologetic. 'I noticed it and didn't notice it, if you know what I mean. I mean, until you know something's important, you sort of dismiss it from your mind, don't you?'

'Yes, I know exactly what you mean,' Slider said. 'One

last thing, that photograph that went missing, the previous time we came to see Piers – did it ever turn up?'

Her eyes widened. 'No, it didn't, and that was odd, because he thought I'd moved it, but I certainly hadn't. I thought maybe it had fallen down behind something, but I looked when I was cleaning and didn't find it. So where it went is a mystery.'

When they had left her, Atherton said, 'What was that about the photograph? Was it important?'

'I've no idea,' Slider said. 'I'm just punting. Anything could be anything.'

'You don't know what's important until you know what's important,' Atherton agreed. 'So what do you think happened?'

'I suppose the murderer called on him last night and persuaded him to go over to the shop for some reason. Knocked him down, strangled him, and then went back to the house for something, using the keys from his pocket to let himself in and lock everything up after him. And shoved the dogs in the kitchen and shut the door while he looked for whatever it was.'

'Or maybe', Atherton said, 'he met Piers at the house, and shut the kitchen door before they went to the shop together. That way he could come back in the front without disturbing them.'

'It's possible,' Slider said, 'though he'd run more risk of being seen going in that way.'

'But I wonder why he left the shop lights on?'

'Oversight, probably. Or maybe he'd been careful not to touch anything, and didn't want to leave prints on the light switches. He could have let himself out with the key without having to touch the door, you see.'

'But then if he went to the house to rummage round he'd have had to have gloves, wouldn't he?'

'Well, we don't know that he *did* rummage round,' Slider

said. 'He might have taken the keys just to let himself out and lock the shop, and the kitchen door being closed was just a fluke and not related to anything. Which way's the incident room, do you suppose?'

'I'd bet that way. Want to thank Mr Heaveysides?'

'That, and to see if they'll let us have a rummage of our own through Piers's papers. Though I doubt whether it will reveal anything. I wish I knew what was going on,' he said sadly. 'This maniac has killed two people now, and it would be nice to know if anyone else is in the firing line before he gets to them.'

CHAPTER NINETEEN

Probably the best laugher in the world

There was the familiar blue-and-white barrier tape boxing off the cottage and antiques shop and the road and pavement in front of them, and a small crowd of the usual sort – shapeless women in C&A macs and headscarves, slovenly unemployed youths in trainers and scrub-headed ten-year-old truants astride mountain bikes of fabulous expense.

As Slider and Atherton were admitted through the barrier and walked towards the front door, Slider was surprised to hear his name called with some urgency.

'Mr Slider! Over here!'

It was Peter Medmenham, gripping the tape and staring at him with the urgency of a pointer. He looked out of place against the grimy background in his neat charcoal grey overcoat and yellow wool muffler. His shiny little feet were set in the gutter of the mud-streaked road, and a coating of fine mist droplets made his blue-white hair look dingy grey.

Slider went over to him. 'How did you get here?'

'The police telephoned Josh, and he called me right away, to let me know,' he said. 'I had to come.' He hadn't put on any make-up, and the cold had brought out the network of fine thread veins, red over the blue of his cheeks. He looked pinched and old. 'I should have been with him,' he said starkly. 'He phoned me yesterday. He's hardly seen anything of his new friend. I think he was lonely. But I wouldn't go. Pride, you see. And now he's—'

'I'm sorry,' Slider said, and he really, really was.

Medmenham shook the sympathy away. 'My own fault. They're saying it was a break-in. Is that right?' His eyes appealed, but for what, Slider didn't know. There was no comfort he could give this man one way or the other.

'I don't know,' he said.

Medmenham swallowed, reaching for words. 'I wonder – if you can ask for me. I can't get anyone to listen. His things – photographs, for instance. Just something of his to keep. If I could go in, just for a moment—?'

'I'm afraid that's not possible. But all his things will be released to his brother eventually. Why don't you ask him? I'm sure he'd let you have something.'

Medmenham shook his head again, as if Slider had said something hopelessly naive. 'It's awful to be kept out like this. Like a stranger. I should have been with him. It wouldn't have happened if I'd been there.'

'I must go,' Slider said. He turned away, and Medmenham's voice, lifted a little, followed him like a sibylline pronouncement on the damp air.

'He'd have left him soon, you know, the new one. Dropped him. It wouldn't have lasted.'

Slider glanced back from the door, and he was standing there at the barrier, as still as only an actor or a soldier can; small and upright, staring into the distance, the bright dab of pure colour at his throat marking him out from the surrounding browns, greys and sludges. He was as unlike as possible the rest of the crowd, the real natives of this place and this event. Some of them were looking at him, with curiosity and faint hostility, like sparrows just about to start pecking an escaped budgerigar.

It was fortunate that Slider was still at the house when the call came through from Shepherd's Bush that a Mr Henry

Banks wanted to meet him in a pub in Sudbury, because it was only about twenty-five miles from there, straight through on the A131. If he had started off back to London he'd have been going in the opposite direction.

There was Atherton to deal with, but one of the local boys offered to drop him at the railway station, and the trains from Chelmsford were frequent and fast. Atherton gave him a curious look as he left: it wasn't often that Slider did anything Atherton didn't know about. But Slider said it was a meeting with a snout of his – which was almost the truth – and a man's snout was sacrosanct, so he couldn't very well ask any more.

It was a slow drive, with the afternoon pootling traffic clogging up the roads: elderly Cambridges and Metros driven by old men in hats who could only just see over the wheel; cheap hatchbacks with rusty bumpers and the back door secured with string, driven by red-faced men who looked as if they might well have a pig or a crate of chickens in the passenger seat. They all drove at forty-five miles an hour in the exact centre of the lane and never looked in their rear-view mirrors, so it was impossible to pass them.

There was that melancholy feeling of all comfort ending that you only get towards dusk in the countryside in winter. The sky was pinkish along the horizon, the bare trees looked chilly, and here and there a lone rook flapped slowly home, straight as the crow flies. Loneliness breathed up from the brown furrows and the scattered, crouched houses. The oncoming dark seemed a menace to flee. You felt you had to get indoors as quickly as possible.

He thought of his own childhood home, the dank cottage with its garden full of cabbages and brussels sprouts and the drain in the kitchen that smelled of tea leaves. Suddenly he was ten again, and coming home across the fields, his feet weighted with mud and his cold legs aching so he could hardly get along, and the night mist beginning to be exhaled from the black water in the field drains. But indoors, if he could only get there, would be lights, and the furry, comfortable warmth of paraffin heaters, and Mum in the kitchen, where a mum always ought to be, getting tea. Women and food: how they locked on to your heart, taking it so young that if you had ever been properly loved and nurtured, you could never quite untangle them again. And did you ever, ever get over losing your mum? It seemed absurd after so long, and at his age, to be seized with such a yearning to go home; but she was gone, beyond reach, and a grown man wasn't allowed to feel like this.

The bricks and street lights of Sudbury came as a relief. It had been a pretty town, though like everywhere else now it had its rash of ugly little new houses creeping out over the outlying fields like psoriasis. It was years since he had been here, but he remembered his way about all right, as a pub man does, navigating from inn sign to inn sign. The Rose and Crown was one of those tiny beamed cottages, long and low with diamond-pane windows, sunk slightly below the pavement level, that look as if they've shrunk together with age, like little old women. He pushed open the oak door – probably five hundred years old, and how many unthinking hands had pushed it open in that time? – and stepped into the parlour. It had a red carpet and red velvet banquettes and beams everywhere, a game machine flashing its lights in a corner like someone humming to himself, and at one end a glorious log fire, just getting into its stride. There were two customers sitting on stools at the bar. One was talking to the landlord, who was obviously an old friend; the other was at the far end, near the fire, reading a newspaper.

'Afternoon,' said the landlord pleasantly. 'What can I get you?' His friend looked round as well, and half smiled; the reader didn't look up from his paper.

'Afternoon. A pint of Adnams, please,' Slider said, and drifted, as though of no purpose, down the bar, to station himself between the other two customers, but closer to the newspaper man.

The pint came. The landlord made a remark or two about the weather, looking at Slider keenly with copper's eyes, as though assessing where he came from and what he was doing here, and then politely left him and went back to his friend. Slider turned his back on them casually to look at the fire, leaning his right elbow on the bar. The man with the paper looked up. The paper, Slider could see now, was a sporting one; the man was small, thin, and deeply lined in the face, with an all-weather complexion and hands like wooden clubs.

Slider met his eyes and raised his eyebrows. The man nodded slightly. After a suitable pause, Slider said, 'Might have a bit of snow before the weekend, I shouldn't wonder.'

'C'n do with it,' he said, in a voice faint and hoarse with a lifetime of fags. 'Warm winter don't kill the bugs.' He had a Norfolk accent.

'At least there haven't been too many sporting fixtures cancelled, though.'

'There's always an upside and a downside.' The little man up-ended his pint and Slider took his cue.

'Get you another?'

'Don't mind if I do. Ta very much.'

When the landlord had refilled the glass and the little man had offered and lit a cigarette, they were licensed to talk without drawing suspicion; though Slider had the uncomfortable feeling that the landlord had no illusions about why the stranger in the well-worn suit had suddenly turned up at his pub.

There was nothing in the least porcine about Piggy Banks – it was evidently just one of those inevitable nicknames, like Chalky White and Lofty Short. 'You was wanting to know about Furlong Stud, then?' he asked in due course. Another couple of customers had come in, and the landlord was further off. On his way down the bar he had also turned on the background music, a courtesy Slider could normally have done without, but useful now. Had he done it deliberately?

'Yes,' said Slider. He made a polite gesture towards his wallet pocket. 'I expect you'll have expenses to cover.'

Piggy slid his eyes away modestly. 'Half a cent'ry'll cover it,' he said. 'Tidy's a mate of an old mate of mine who wants to do him a favour. Slip it me after so that lot don't see.' With a jerk of his head towards the rest of the population.

'I don't think there's much the guv'nor doesn't see,' Slider said, feeling he ought to warn Banks that his cover might not be impenetrable.

'He used to be one of your lot. Cozzer from down London. He's all right. I know him and he knows me. Anyway, Furlong. It's a scam, o' course.' He looked to see if Slider knew that.

'I thought it must be. Do you know how?'

'Ever heard of a horse called Hypericum?'

Slider shook his head. 'I'm not a racing man.'

Banks didn't seem to mind that. 'Smashing colt. Got everything – blood, bone, and a heart as big as a house. Unbeaten as a two-year-old, won the Queen Anne Stakes at Ascot and the Prix Morny at three, and the Canadian International. He was a real engine. Second in the Guineas and would've had the Derby, but they over-raced him and he broke down. After that he was never really sound. When he was fit, he could beat anything, but he'd go all right for a while and then break down again.'

He took a drag on his fag and had a long, sustaining cough. 'Anyway,' he began again, breathlessly, 'this codger Bill Carrington used to be Hypericum's trainer. He loved that horse. When they decided to sell it, he couldn't bear to see it go where it might not be well treated, so he bought it himself and left to set up his own place.'

'Where did he get the money?'

'Oh, he had a bit put by. He's not a bad trainer – had a few winners. Bit o' prize money stashed away. And he may have had a backer, I dunno. The new place, I reckon it was all meant to be legit. But it ain't that easy to get on, specially when you're starting up. And Hypericum – they don't call him that now, use his old stable name, Gordon – anyway, he didn't improve. Couldn't race him. So Carrington hit on this scam.'

'Which is?'

'Just a twist on the old ringer dodge,' Banks said, with a shake of the head that it should be so easy. 'A lot of what they do's legit. Breeding, training, racing. But when they get a horse that don't show, looks all right but ain't gonna get in the money, they set it up for the syndicate. Pull in a lot of daft city types with more money than sense, show 'em the horse in stables, and then on the gallop they bring out Hypericum. Dye his coat to look like the other. The mugs see him run, they think they can't lose. Carrington gets ten times the value of the horse, plus all the running expenses for a couple of years before they get fed up and jack it in. And the beauty of it is, the paperwork's all right as rain. Nowadays, with lip tattoos and microchips an' all, you'd have a job putting a ringer in a race. But the mugs, they bought a certain horse, that's what's in the contract, and that's what gets entered in the races. Beautiful.' He sighed over his pint. 'It'll break Carrington's heart when Hypericum gets too old, or breaks down for good. But he'll have had a good run for his money by then.'

'It sounds too simple to be true,' Slider said.

'Like all the best dodges,' Banks said wisely, 'it works on greed. The punter twists himself.'

'Greed, yes. The brochure said the investors could expect a return of twenty-four per cent,' Slider said.

Banks nodded. 'That's a little joke of Bill Carrington's. A while back, last year I think it was, there was a newspaper article about investing in racehorses. Everyone talked about it around the stables. And it said that on average you could only expect to get back a quarter of what you put in. So it's not twenty-four per cent *on* your investment, it's twenty-four per cent *of* your investment.'

Slider didn't know whether to laugh or cry. Banks was looking at him speculatively. 'You going to do anything about it?' he asked.

'What? Oh, no. It's not my field. I just wanted to save a friend of mine from making a fool of himself.'

'Glad of that,' Banks said. 'I done this as a favour, but I wouldn't like it to get about I been talking. Wouldn't do to make meself unpopular.'

'I won't tell anyone. You can trust me. Jockey, are you?'

'I was. National Hunt. Till I broke me hip. Big horse fell on me, going over the fifth at Aintree. Joey Jojo his racing name was, but we called him Socks. Big chestnut, two white legs be'ind like a Clydesdale. Lovely horse. Gor, could he jump! And kind? But he came down on me and broke me hip, and that was the end of me riding career. Still, I was the lucky one.'

'How's that?'

'They mended my hip, but he broke his leg, and they 'ad to shoot him.' He took a long pull at his pint. 'He was a lovely horse.'

Echo of Tennyson, Slider thought. She has a lovely face; God in His mercy send her grace. He slipped Piggy Banks his fifty, drained his pint, and left under the clocking gaze of the landlord, into the whizzing darkness of rush hour.

A little pricking rain had started, and it was cold. Everyone was hurrying home to their tea and telly, and the world seemed too big and dark and hostile. Slider's mind was full of other people's misery – Medmenham's, Noni Prentiss's, even Josh's – for who knew what emptiness his swaggering had been meant to hide? And the unavenged dead haunted him, their sadness the greatest of all, to be over and finished before their time, no more life for them, no more anything. He believed in ghosts – or shades, or furies, or something.

When he was very little, they hadn't had electricity at the cottage, and lamplight gave itself to believing in things half seen. His mother had said the dead watched over you and were nothing to be afraid of; but their eyes, whether reproachful or forgiving, were not what you wanted your darkness peopled with.

The other main road out of Sudbury, the A134, went almost through Upper Hawksey, the village of Slider's birth. It was as long as it was broad to go back that way, via Colchester instead of via Chelmsford, he told himself; and if he was passing within a mile of the cottage, he might just as well call in and see Dad.

Bumping carefully down the muddy, rutted track from the road to the cottage, he saw the light up ahead of him, the single square of the kitchen window, hanging flat on the absolute blackness beyond the headlights like a painting on a velvet wall. Pulling onto the parking space at the end, he saw that the square was pale red, light shining through the red gingham curtains drawn across the window. When he cut the engine and got out, there was that absolute silence that went with the absolute blackness, something you never got in Town, and which thrilled down his spine, like the evocative smell – Christmas trees and tangerines, for instance – that takes you straight back to childhood.

The kitchen door opened, spilling light out, and his father stood there in the doorway. He looked frail with the light behind him; his neck rose in cords from the worn collar that had been snug last time Slider had seen him. Slider was aware that he had not been down for some time, and he was seared with a panicky guilt. He would make time to come down more often; he would bring the kids to see Grandad; he would bring Joanna – Dad liked Joanna. He shouldn't let the Job blot out everything else.

'That you, Bill,' said Mr Slider – not a question, but a greeting.

'Hello, Dad. I was passing this way, so I thought I'd call in.'

Silently Mr Slider stepped back from the door to let him in. Not one for wasting words, wasn't Dad. Inside the kitchen was spare and spotless, much as it had been in Mum's day, but not dank any more – central heating had been installed long ago.

'How are you?' Slider asked, as one does.

'I'm not complaining.' Mr Slider regarded his son impassively a moment. 'Cuppa tea?'

'Thanks. I'm sorry I haven't been down for a while.'

'Busy, I expect.' He was wearing grey trousers and a grey lambswool sweater over a brown and beige check Viyella shirt which Slider recognised as one of his own which he had passed on to Dad when the collar got too tight for him. How many years ago? It had to be ten, probably more. The collar was rubbed white along the fold, and the sweater was darned at one elbow with a man's patient clumsiness; but everything about him, and about the house, was spotless, and as he walked past Slider to go to the gas stove, he carried only the clean smell of fabric softener. Slider felt a rush of desperate love. It wasn't necessary, you see, to be like Mr Singer! For all these years his father had kept house, tended his garden, gone out shooting rabbits and wood pigeons, cooked his tiny meals, slowly washed up and put away, and at the end of each day, retired to his neatly made, empty bed; never complained, paid his way, kept up standards, was no trouble to anyone. But what did he think, what did he feel?'

'How do you do it?' Slider asked aloud.

'Do what, then?' Mr Slider asked, putting a match to the gas.

'All this,' Slider said, waving a hand round the kitchen. 'Just keep going on, without her. Doing – things. How do you bear it?'

'You just do,' Mr Slider said. He settled the kettle over

the flames, and turned to regard his son with steady, faded blue eyes. 'You have to get on with things, don't you?'

One day, Slider thought, I'll look like that. His father's grey hair grew the same way, made the same shape as his own; they had the same eyes, the same build, except that Dad was now thin with age. He wondered suddenly, vividly, what Joanna would look like when she was old. 'Dad, I'm in trouble,' he said.

Mr Slider nodded. 'Thought it must be something.'

'I'm afraid I'm going to lose Joanna.'

'Ah.' Mr Slider stared thoughtfully a moment longer. 'Have you eaten?'

'No,' Slider discovered. He had been kept from lunch by the phone call, and hadn't eaten since. 'I'm starving.'

'I haven't had mine yet. Beans on toast, I was going to have. Suit you?'

'Fine. Thanks.'

'Sit down then. No, I'll do it. Can't have two women in one kitchen, your mother used to say.'

Slider sat and watched as his father pottered about, assembling the meal, knowing he would not be hurried, that the listening must wait until the meal was before them. Dad would always listen, but he liked to have something to occupy him while he did. Eyes must not be met while personal matters were being aired.

At last the plates were on the table, the knives and forks, the cruet, the cups of tea. 'Tuck in,' said Mr Slider.

And Slider told him about Joanna's job offer.

'How long's it for, this job?' Mr Slider asked when he paused.

'It's a permanent job. Years, anyway. Maybe for good.' He watched his father's hand reach out for the sugar-caster: a brown, old-man's hand, all knuckles, the fingers thickened from a lifetime's hard work. 'It's a wonderful thing for her, for her career. I just don't know what to do.'

'No, I see that,' Mr Slider said, stirring his tea. 'O' course, it's her decision, whether she goes or not.'

'But her decision will be affected by mine, whether to go with her or not.'

'That's right. You can't duck it that way,' his father said approvingly.

'But what could I do over there?'

'Get a job, I suppose. Other people manage somehow.'

'And give up the Job?'

Mr Slider knew enough to recognise the capital-letter distinction. 'Well, that's the other side of it, isn't it.' He looked up, suddenly meeting Slider's eyes, his usual impassivity softened by the hint of a smile. 'It's what you'd call a dilemma.'

Slider said nothing, only applied himself to the last of his beans.

'Thought I'd sort it out for you, did you?' Mr Slider said knowingly. 'Give you a quick answer. Rabbit out of a hat. I can't do that, son. I can only tell you that I like your Joanna, and I think she's good for you. Only time I've ever heard you laugh is when you're with her.'

'What?'

'Oh, yes,' Mr Slider nodded. 'I don't mean you don't smile or have a chuckle, you're not sullen, but it's only with her you really laugh out loud.'

'She makes me laugh,' Slider admitted.

'Your mother did me, too.'

'Really?'

'Oh yes. She was a very funny woman, your mother. In a quiet way.'

'I never knew that,' Slider said. He had loved his mother, but she had never struck him as a comedian.

'Well, you wouldn't,' said Mr Slider, gravely twinkling. 'Kept it for me. When we were in bed.'

Slider asked, a little shyly, 'Do you miss her?'

'Your mother? All the time. Every day.' He looked round

the kitchen as if he might see her, having mentioned her. 'Funny, I can't remember what she looked like, now, not really, but there's a hole where she ought to be.' He picked up his cup with both hands and sipped his tea. 'A job's just what you do to stay alive. There's good ones and not so good. But your wife's something else.'

The problem was back. 'But what could I do? The only thing I know is the Job. And there's my pension to think about.'

'Yes, you've got to think about that.' Mr Slider drained his cup and put it down, and began gathering the plates together. 'You stopping a bit? I was going to light the fire. We could have a game of crib and a glass of beer.'

'No, I've got to get back,' Slider said absently, too absorbed in his own thoughts to wonder what the alternative for his father would be.

'Ah, well,' Mr Slider said.

Slider dragged himself up. 'Let me wash up, anyway.'

'No, no, I can do it. Not much here.'

At the door, Slider said, 'Thanks for the tea. I wish you could have told me what to do as well.'

'Your trouble is, you always think too much,' Mr Slider said. 'Ask yourself, what does it say *here*?' He tapped himself on the chest. ''Cos that's what you'll have to live with.'

Slider smiled suddenly at this typical Dad-advice, and put his arms round his father in a quick hug. He felt all bones. They didn't often do this, which made it a bit perilous, but Mr Slider returned the pressure briefly, and gave his back one or two pats, as undemonstrative men do when emotions threaten to assert themselves.

CHAPTER TWENTY

Sense and Sensibility

Slider didn't feel up to telling Atherton about the racehorse business straight away. It would keep for now, he thought. He needed to get home to Joanna. She met him with determined brightness, and he took his lead from her. She cooked for them, and they ate, chatting lightly on neutral subjects, and then spent the evening gamely *not* talking about the problem. But probably neither of them could have said afterwards what they had watched on the television; and when they went to bed, they clung together as if it were their last night on earth.

Atherton was late in again the next morning, and when he did appear he looked more white and strained than ever. Slider eyed him with scant sympathy. 'On the slam again last night?'

Atherton shook his head. 'I've lost Oedipus.'

'Oh,' said Slider. 'What d'you mean, lost?'

'I let him out last night when I got home and he didn't come back. I went round the streets calling and calling for him but I couldn't find him. I went out looking again this morning – that's why I'm late. Sorry.'

'I'm sure he's all right. Cats go on the wander sometimes.'

'Not him. And he *always* comes when I call.'

'Well, he's an old cat, isn't he? They can get a bit contrary. He'll turn up again when he's ready. I expect you'll find him waiting on the doorstep when you get home tonight.'

Atherton shrugged, rejecting the comfort. It didn't seem the right moment to tell him about Furlong Stud and add to his troubles. Anyway, there was the case to consider. Slider called everyone together in the CID room and brought them up to speed on the Piers Prentiss murder.

'The MO looks similar, and there was no robbery of any sort so we have to assume a personal motive. I don't think it's going too far to suppose the two murders are connected.'

'Yes, but what's the connection?' Swilley said. 'There's Richard Tyler – she was working on his biography, and Piers was his new lover, but why should that make anyone kill either of them?'

'Yes, and if she'd been working on the Tyler biog for six months, why was she only worried and drinking heavily for the last few weeks?' said Atherton.

'Maybe she'd found out something about him – some nasty secret,' Hollis suggested.

'I should have thought that was a biographer's dream,' Atherton pointed out. 'It'd make her happy, not miserable.'

'Yeah, but if the papers are missing – all the stuff she did on Tyler,' Anderson began.

'Well, we don't know they are,' said Swilley fairly. 'We only know we haven't found them. She might have sent them to someone. Or be keeping them somewhere else.'

'Anyway, if a rival biographer had stolen the papers, I don't see why he would have killed her,' said Atherton. 'That's a bit extreme, wouldn't you say? I mean, I know the literary world is cut-throat, but surely not literally.'

'Anyway, she'd apparently stopped work on that,' Swilley said. 'Stopped her researcher, anyway.'

'We do know from several sources that she was deeply worried about something,' Slider said, 'and I think our best bet is that the murder's connected with that. But what was it?'

'It's got to be something in her life, some area we haven't uncovered,' Hollis said. 'Something she was involved in or someone from her past who had a grudge against her.'

'Yes, I can't believe it was just random,' Slider said. 'But it's hard to see what Piers Prentiss had to do with it. There doesn't seem to be any mystery about him.'

'Boss,' said Swilley, 'it seems to me the one big question mark we've got that we haven't gone into is what she was doing during those years after university when she was so-called missing.'

'Not much of a mystery there,' Mackay said. 'She was off protesting, doing the hippie bit.'

'Anyway, it's a hell of a long time ago,' Atherton said. 'Even if you could find out, I doubt if it would have any relevance. Who's going to hold a grudge for thirty years?'

'Well, you just never know, do you?' Swilley said, annoyed.

'And nor will you, unless you can find someone to ask.'

'Don't get snitty, you two,' Slider intervened.

McLaren, who had been scratching a bit of egg yolk off his tie with his thumb nail, looked up. 'You could ask her sister. We've not had a go at her yet.'

There was a brief silence, and then Swilley said, 'Maurice, that's a stroke of genius. All those things I said about you – I take 'em back.'

'You said he wasn't fit to live with pigs,' Hollis supplied obligingly.

'Well I was wrong,' said Swilley. 'He *is* fit to live with pigs.'

'Har har,' said McLaren. 'So what about it, guv?'

'Yes, why not,' said Slider. 'But not you. Swilley, you can go and see her.'

'Why does she get all the trips out, just because she's a bird?' McLaren said resentfully.

'I want you', Slider told him, 'to re-interview the witness

who saw the man tying his tie. Try and get a more detailed description from him, and if he thinks he can, get him in to do an e-fit. Atherton, you're good with women. You can go and see Noni Prentiss again, try and get a better description of the man she saw leaving the house. Hollis, we're going to go over everything we've got so far and look at it from the perspective of Piers Prentiss, see if anything clicks. And Mackay, get our notes on Piers Prentiss and Marjorie Babbington over to Keith Heaveysides at Chelmsford and make sure he keeps us informed of anything that comes up at their end – especially if it turns out that anything was missing from the house. Not goods and chattels, but papers of any kind. Come on, boys and girls, let's get cracking.'

The tiny county of Rutland had not only laboured under the disadvantage of being abolished and reinstated by successive governments, subsumed into Leicestershire and then exhumed again, but a large part of it had been drowned by the making of Rutland Water, a vast reservoir. Still, it was pretty country – quintessentially English shire country, of the green rolling hills, woods, river valleys, thick hedges and stone walls variety. Good hunting country – not that Swilley thought of that. She was a Town girl, and green was not her favourite colour. If she went too far from a tube station for any length of time she got the bends.

Phoebe Agnew's sister, Chloe Cosworth, lived in a new square stone house, slipped in amongst the old square stone houses, in Upper Hambleton, the village on the tongue of land that stuck out like a jetty into Rutland Water. The tongue had once been a steep hill, rising above Middle and Nether Hambletons, which accounted for its survival: its sister villages were deep under the water.

Mrs Cosworth was a tall woman in her fifties, as tall as Swilley herself; slim to the point of gauntness, and plain. She had a long face and bad skin – presumably from childhood acne, for it was pocked, and looked thick and puckered over her cheeks. She wore no make-up, and her lips were thin and grey; but her grey hair, cut short, was expensively layered, and her clothes, though dull, were also expensive, so it wasn't lack of money but by intent that she looked as she did – which was pretty well as different from Phoebe as it was possible to get. Phoebe had been beautiful, wild and untidy; Chloe was plain, conventional and neat.

The inside of the house was just as much of a contrast with Phoebe's flat. Everything seemed new and almost grimly clean and shining: reproduction antique furniture, John Lewis fabrics and plain-coloured, thick Wilton carpets. There was no speck of dust, nothing lying around, no newspaper or discarded shoe. It was like a brand new showhouse. The only personal touch was a surprising collection of china figurines, modern mass-produced ones of the sentimental girls-in-long-dresses sort that you see advertised on the backs of colour supplements. It seemed oddly out of character, for Mrs Cosworth was horsily brisk, and her husband, it quickly transpired, owned a very large engineering firm.

She was perfectly willing to talk, provided Swilley with coffee and a coaster depicting the middle bit of Constable's *The Hay Wain*, and settled down in the immaculate, bare living room to tell whatever Swilley wanted to know, and more.

'I haven't had much to do with Phoebe in recent years,' she said. She had a toneless voice, rather hard, accentless, as though it too had been purged and swept and redecorated like the house to show nothing. 'Our lives have always been very different, as you can probably tell. I never approved of the way she carried on, but blood is thicker than water, and I've always been willing to see her whenever she wanted to visit. But I suppose as we've got older we've got more set in our separate ways. It's not that we've fallen out, it's just that we don't get around to seeing each other.' She paused a moment. 'Well, it's too late now, of course.'

'Do you mind about that – that it's too late?' Swilley asked, curious about this impassivity.

'Of course I mind,' she said. 'Phoebe was all the family I had – apart from Nigel, of course, but you don't count a husband as family, do you?'

Swilley left that one alone. 'There were just the two of you? No other brothers or sisters?'

'Just us. Literally.' She glanced to see if Swilley wanted to know more and, seeing receptiveness, went on to tell, in clipped and unemotional tones, the circumstances. Chloe and Phoebe's father, headmaster of a private boarding school in Leicestershire, had walked out on his wife and family one summer day during the school holidays and was never seen again. It was one of life's great mysteries what had happened to him. Phoebe had always inclined to the theory that his bones were lying undiscovered at the bottom of some quarry or lake; Chloe believed he had simply gone off with another woman and successfully changed his identity – still fairly easy to do in the fifties. What their mother thought, she never divulged. The three of them were left particularly badly off, since until he was declared dead, there could be no question of a widow's pension; and the accommodation had gone with the job.

Mrs Agnew moved with her children back to Oakham, her home town, took rented accommodation and found a job. Phoebe was ten and Chloe twelve at the time. Swilley gathered, with a bit of reading between the lines, that Phoebe was her mother's pet and had also been her father's: she was very pretty, exceptionally intelligent, bright and lively. Chloe had gone to secondary mod, Phoebe to grammar school; Chloe was doing typing, shorthand and housewifery while Phoebe did Latin, philosophy and higher maths; and Phoebe had a gaggle of boys hanging around the school gates for her every afternoon, where Chloe had only one swain, a very dull boy called Barry, who had short legs and wore glasses and was a swot. The other boys called him Barold. She disliked him in a mild way, but since she was not pretty it was assumed, even by Barold, that she'd be grateful for his lordly attentions.

Chloe grew up believing in 'the baby's' superiority in every sense, and that the superiority must be nurtured by the rest of them. When their mother died six years later, probably of overwork and underinterest in life, it seemed natural to Chloe that she should support her sister.

'I'd left school at fifteen. I did a secretarial course and then started work with a local firm. But when Mother died Phoebe was ready to go into the sixth form and then on to university. It would have been a crime to make her leave and get a job. So we stuck together. I got a better job with more money, and Phoebe stayed on at school. Once she got into university, she got the full grant, naturally, so the strain was taken off, but it was a hard couple of years.'

'What did you think of her going off to Chile?' Norma asked, just out of curiosity.

'I never liked her political activities,' Mrs Cosworth said harshly. 'And frankly, they've been an embarrassment sometimes. Nigel never approved. He's very – conventional. He's fifteen years older than me, and his generation has strict ideas about what's right and wrong.'

'How did you meet him?'

'I worked at his firm. I was his secretary, in fact.'

How conventional, thought Norma. It's nice to hear of old traditions being upheld. He must have been attracted by her youth, she supposed, because she didn't seem to have any other charisma.

'We married in 1968, when Phoebe was still at university,' Mrs Cosworth went on. 'He was very good about helping support her, and giving her a home during the vacations. Not that she was home much – always off somewhere, to some peace camp or something.'

I bet she was, thought Swilley. Old Nigel must have been a good incentive to stay away.

'But she worried Nigel dreadfully. He was always terrified she was going to get into the papers or end up in gaol. In the end, of course, it was trouble of a different kind she got into, and that was just as bad in its own way.'

'What trouble was that?' Norma asked, though she had guessed.

'She turned up at our house one day and said, "Chloe I need your help. I'm pregnant." Just like that.'

'When was that?'

'It would be – oh, September 1969. It was tactless even by her standards,' Mrs Cosworth went on, 'because I'd just had a miscarriage.'

'Oh, I'm sorry.'

The eyes moved away. 'It was a bad one,' she said tonelessly. 'And I was never able to have a child afterwards. We didn't know that *then*, of course. Nigel was furious that Phoebe had dumped this thing on us, but I told him I was the only family she had and we had to help. So he offered to pay for her to have an abortion. He said any child of hers was bound to grow up a criminal so that was the best thing.'

My God, thought Swilley, as a world of pity opened up before her. She could see it all. The meek, cowed Chloe, grateful for having been married and still under discipline to her boss; the pompous, stiff-necked man without the slightest sensitivity to his young wife's feelings; the wild, red-haired beauty, full of passionate feelings about everything. Chloe, having lost her own child, was told she had to persuade her sister deliberately to do the same.

'What did Phoebe say to that?'

'She wouldn't do it,' said Mrs Cosworth abruptly, and stopped. Swilley waited. At last she went on, 'Nigel was surprised – he'd thought, being the sort of girl she was, she'd jump at the offer and be grateful. But she went absolutely mad, said it was murder, jumped down poor Nigel's throat. They had terrible arguments about it. Screaming matches. It was dreadful. In the end he said if she wouldn't have the abortion, he washed his hands of the whole business, and she could get out of his house, too.'

So that, thought Swilley, was the origin of the stance against abortion. She could imagine a hot-blooded girl like Phoebe Agnew, an intelligent girl, flying into a rage at the tactlessness of this man, flying to the defence of the sister who had worked to put her through school. 'So what happened?' she asked.

'In the end I persuaded him to let Phoebe stay until after Christmas. It was a dreadful time, though.' Understatement of the year, thought Swilley. She could imagine it. 'Then I helped her get into one of those mother-and-baby homes, in Nottingham. The baby was born in March 1970 and they arranged for it to be adopted.' She stopped again, staring at the illuminated plastic coals of the electric fire in the imitation Adam fireplace. 'She came to see me just after she'd signed the adoption papers. It was in the daytime, when Nigel was at work. She cried and cried and cried. I've never seen anyone cry so much. And then she stopped and blew her nose and said, "Well, that's that." And she started talking about Vietnam.' She shook her head. 'She never spoke about it from that moment onwards, and I don't think she ever cried again, for anything. At least, I never saw her. She just put it out of her head. I never understood how she could do that. And then Nigel came home and she got up and left. Not a word of thanks to him for all he'd done for her. She went off, and we didn't see her for a couple of years.'

'Do you know where she went?'

'To America, to join the anti-Vietnam movement. She was there until her visa ran out. Then it was back to Chile, I think, and then – oh, I forget. She was always off somewhere. She used to phone me sometimes, but that was all. She lived on a commune in Wales for a while, I think. She was such an embarrassment to Nigel. I sometimes half think she did it deliberately to annoy him.'

She said it idly, as if she didn't mean it, but Swilley wondered if she hadn't hit on a truth, or at least a part of it. A life spent not just protesting against man's general inhumanity to man, but against Nigel Cosworth's specific inumanity to the Agnew sisters.

'Eventually, of course, she settled down – or at least, she became a bit more respectable. Once she was established as a proper journalist and started to get famous, Nigel took to her a bit more, and she started visiting us again. Of course, he disapproved of her subject matter a lot of the time. Well, most of the time, if I'm honest. But she was very well thought of in her own circles, and he respected that.'

I bet he did, the nasty snob.

'I can't say they ever liked each other, but they were polite to each other – for my sake, I suppose.' She looked up. 'And now she's dead. Do you know who did it?'

'No,' said Swilley. 'I'm afraid we don't yet.'

Mrs Cosworth sighed. 'Nigel says it must have been one of her hippie friends. That living the way she did, it's only surprising it didn't happen before. He said—' She stopped.

'That it served her right?' Swilley suggested. She had a fair picture of the sort of conversation that went on between the Cosworths regarding the sister-in-law.

Mrs Cosworth didn't answer directly. 'He's a good man,' she said. 'He's just of a different generation. He never understood Phoebe. Well, frankly, neither did I. She was my own sister, but I never understood how she got to be so hard. She never seemed to have any feelings for anyone. She never married, you know, despite being so beautiful. Nigel said she wasn't like a woman at all, so it wasn't surprising no-one would have her; but it's my belief that plenty wanted her, she just didn't want them.'

'What about the father of the baby?' Swilley asked. 'Did she want to marry him?'

'She never said anything about him. I asked, of course, but she wouldn't even tell me his name. I never knew from that day to this who it was. Nigel said', she added, seeming to have lost some of her protective reserve about her husband, 'that she probably didn't know herself.'

Nigel, thought Swilley, was just a total peach.

According to the Nottingham police, the mother-and-baby home had closed down in 1975.

'It's interesting,' Swilley commented to Slider. 'There's just this window of about ten years when hundreds of thousands of babies went for adoption. Before that girls didn't have sex, or the boys married them. After that, they knew about contraception, or they kept the babies themselves.'

It had been a privately run home, but the premises it used were council-owned. In the absence of any other information, it was to be assumed that the records would have gone back to City Hall and stored somewhere there; but it would be a long job, as preliminary enquiries proved, to find anyone who knew where they were precisely, or would even be willing to look. The other way would be through the County Courts, or the Central Register, almost equally time-consuming.

'Does it matter, boss?' Swilley asked, when she came to report failure so far. 'I mean, what's the baby got to do with anything?'

Slider got up and walked to the window, and Atherton shifted over to make room for him. The short afternoon was fading, and the yellow of shop lights made the grey seem greyer. 'It occurred to me, you see,' he said, 'that the weirdest thing about her last day was that supper. This woman who hated cooking and lived a gypsy life in a reconstructed student bedsit. Who would she cook chicken casserole and tiramisu for? She even went out and bought a cookery book for the occasion. Who is the only person in the world who cooks for you, apart from your lover or wife?'

'Your mum,' Atherton said, getting there.

Swilley stared. 'You think she'd somehow traced her kid and invited him round for a nosh?'

'I can't think who else she would go to the trouble for. Lorraine Tucker said she was flushed and excited when she met her with an armful of groceries that day. And she tidied up the flat, which everyone says she never did, not even for a lover. If she wasn't in love, what else could it be?'

Swilley nodded slowly. 'It makes sense, I suppose. But how would she find out?'

Atherton came in. 'She researched. She was used to doing research, she knew how to go about it. And who had she been researching for the past six months?'

'Richard Tyler,' Slider said. 'A junior minister at the amazingly young age of twenty-eight. Which would mean he was born in 1970.'

'If we—'

'I did,' Slider anticipated. 'I phoned Mrs Brissan. March 1970, she said, according to the Parliamentary *Who's Who.*'

'A lot of people must have been born in March 1970,' said Swilley. 'Was he adopted?'

'I don't know. It doesn't say.'

'It would be a large size in coincidences,' Atherton said.

'Maybe not so very large,' Slider said. 'When girls gave up their babies for adoption in those days, they were asked if they had any stipulations about the adoptees – religion or particular interests or whatever. And the stipulations were followed when possible. Phoebe Agnew might well have stipulated that her child must go to politically conscious parents. It was the biggest thing in her life, then as later. And since she was an intelligent white girl, there would have been a lot of competition for her baby, so the agents would have been able to be choosy.'

'Okay so far,' Atherton said cautiously.

'Tyler's father comes from an old Nottinghamshire family, and his parents lived at Stanton-on-the-Wolds, which is less than ten miles from Nottingham. And Richard's the only child. If they couldn't have children of their own, and applied to adopt, they'd have filled Phoebe's requirements perfectly. I know it's all speculation, but it fits.'

Atherton wrinkled his nose. 'You think she started doing the biography as an excuse to find out if he was her son?'

'I don't think so,' Slider said. 'Why should she ever begin to wonder if he was? No, I would suspect it was the other way round. He was her biography choice because he was hot. Then, as she went into his background, she started to have her suspicions.'

'Another long coincidence?'

'Not coincidence – concurrence,' Slider said. 'People with the same interests tend to end up in the same place. Tyler was brought up by a political family, so he went into politics. That's natural. And he had the talent – that might be hereditary. Phoebe Agnew was a political creature and ended up in the same general circle, which is not, after all, such a large one that everyone doesn't know everyone else. And then she picked on Tyler for sound commercial reasons. Not coincidental at all, when you think of it – inevitable, rather.'

'She might also have been attracted to him without knowing why,' Swilley said. 'I read an article that said you are naturally attracted to people who look a bit like you.'

'Explains a lot about incest,' said Atherton. 'Does he look like her?'

'I've never studied him closely enough to find out. That's the thing about recognising people. You have to know what you're looking for before you see it,' Slider said.

'But I don't see how it helps us,' Atherton sighed. 'Why should anyone kill her for being Tyler's mother? And what about Piers? Where does he come into it?'

'Besides, boss,' Swilley said. 'I've just thought – it couldn't have been Tyler she did supper for, because Medmenham said when he spoke to Piers on the Thursday evening, he said his new lover had been with him all day and had only just left.'

'Yes, he did say that,' Slider said. 'But I've looked at the notes on our interview with Piers, and he told us that Tyler left on the Thursday morning. I wonder whether he told Piers to say he was there all day, in case he needed an alibi. But Piers was such a plonker he forgot by the time we came to see him.'

'What would he want an alibi for?' Atherton said. 'We know whoever ate the meal didn't kill her, because Josh Prentiss was there afterwards.'

'He might just not want anyone to know she was his mother. She wasn't exactly an asset, was she?'

'I don't know – eminent, prize winning journalist, all the right political connections—'

'But with a wild past, a scruffy lifestyle, and in any case not as eminent and respectable as his parents. And some people still think there's a stigma about being adopted,' said Slider.

Norma shook her head. 'I can't see her telling, if he didn't want her to. Why would she?'

'Are you kidding?' Atherton said, 'It would be a bombshell for her biography – certain best-sellerdom.'

'Yes, but she wouldn't sacrifice her own kid for money like that.'

Atherton snorted, and Slider intervened calmly. 'Still, he might want to keep any contact between them to a minimum, and it would probably cause comment if it was known he had been at her house. I can see how he might want that kept secret.'

'I suppose clearing up who ate the meal would be a help to us, even if he wasn't the murderer,' Atherton said. 'What are you going to do, guv?'

'Ask him, I suppose,' said Slider. 'If I'm right about this, and it was him she cooked supper for, he might have some other information that would explain the connection between the two murders.'

Atherton boggled. 'You're going to ask Richard Tyler – *the* Richard Tyler – if he's the illegitimate son of Phoebe Agnew?'

'Why not?'

'Lions' den time,' Atherton said. 'Sooner you than me.'

CHAPTER TWENTY-ONE

Red Slayer

It took a long time to get hold of Richard Tyler. Given the difficulties Slider had already caused by his pursuit of Giles Freeman, he felt he ought to clear it through Porson before he tackled him. He told Porson he just wanted to talk to Tyler about Piers Prentiss – background stuff, to see if he said anything that could suggest a connection between the two murders. He said nothing about any of the other possibilities he was pondering. If they were put up front, he'd never get an interview at all.

Everyone else had gone home by the time the phone rang with his permission. Tyler would see him that evening in his private office at the House. Slider received the news without joy. He had spent the waiting time making other enquiries and piecing things together, and for the last half-hour had been sitting alone and thinking, and his thoughts had brought him only darkness. He collected up his papers, shoved them into a folder, and went out. It was getting colder, as forecast. He looked up automatically to see if the sky was clearing, but of course in the middle of Town, with the street lights, you couldn't see the sky at night. Clouds or stars, they were equally hidden. The weather was what happened – you weren't allowed to predict it.

He was shown into Tyler's office at exactly nine-thirty. Tyler was standing behind his desk, talking on the telephone while with the other hand he flicked through a pile of papers.

His eyes registered Slider and he nodded, and freed his hand to gesture to the large leather chair on the other side of the desk, without breaking the rhythm of his speech.

Slider had a few moments to study him. The general look of Tyler was familiar to him from newspapers and the television screen, but of course in the flesh people have details to be taken in which make them quite different, close up, from their image. The rather long, smooth, pale face, and the dark brown hair slicked back with gel were what he knew, together with the exquisite suiting and elegantly dashing silk tie. What was new was that he was much taller than Slider had expected, and broad at the chest – Slider had gained an impression of slenderness from the TV, but Tyler was quite well built, and what he had taken to be padding in the shoulders was all him. The television also didn't do justice to the remarkably beautiful, luminous hazel eyes, or the firmness of the wide, narrow-lipped mouth. He had read descriptions of Tyler as 'feline' but that didn't really cover it. Feral, he thought; and ruthless. He was apparently very popular with women, and Slider could see why: he'd provide a safe but exciting ride, and look very, very good to be on the arm of.

Chronologically he might have been twenty-eight, but there was something in this man which had never been young, was as old as ambition itself. Close to, there was a hint of fox in the hair, though it was hard to see under the gel, and a spark of red in the eyebrows; and there were freckles on the backs of the pale hands. Large hands, they were, bony and strong, undecorated except for a thin, old gold ring on the left little finger. The fingers of the right hand drummed a moment impatiently on the desk as he spoke into the telephone, and then snapped a paper over with a sharp sound. Strong fingers, with short-cut, well-kept nails. Very clean.

He put the phone down at last. 'Well, Inspector, what can I do for you?' he asked uninvitingly. He looked at his watch. 'I can't give you long.'

'In that case,' said Slider, rousing himself from the clutches of his thoughts, 'I'll be direct.'

'I wish you would.'

'I'd like to know where you were on Thursday the twenty-first of January. Thursday week past.'

Tyler's eyebrows went up. 'That is not what you are supposed to ask.'

'You agreed to talk about Piers Prentiss,' Slider said, 'so I assumed you wouldn't mind telling me that.'

Tyler seemed to consider. 'Well, if you already know that I was with Piers all day that Thursday—' he began.

Slider interrupted. 'Ah, yes, I know that's what he was supposed to say,' he said apologetically, 'but you know Piers – or rather, you did. I'm afraid he blurted it all out. About you leaving on Thursday morning. He managed to remember to tell Peter Medmenham that you were with him all day, but by the time I went to talk to him, he'd forgotten your instructions.' The really scary thing, Slider thought, was how little impact any of this had on Richard Tyler's expression. His face remained impassive, his eyes bright and thoughtful. Whatever he would do, he would do, Slider felt. You might as well try and talk a lion out of eating you.

'I think you'd better leave,' was what he did eventually say.

'Oh no, don't say that! Because we've got so much to talk about. Look, to save you trouble, I'll tell you that I know you were at Phoebe Agnew's flat on Thursday. You left your fingerprints behind.'

'Impossible!' he said quickly.

Slider leaned forward a little. 'Because you wiped them all away?'

'Because I wasn't there.'

'Well, I admit you did a very good job,' Slider went on, as if he hadn't spoken. 'You've got a wonderful intellect and a photographic memory, as I've been told by several people.

You made a mental note of everything you touched so that you could wipe it afterwards. You even had the wit not to wipe the whisky glasses, which you knew you hadn't used, so that any prints there would incriminate someone else – Josh Prentiss, as it happens. You know Josh, of course?'

Something did stir in the amber depths then; but Tyler said calmly, 'You are talking complete drivel. Your statement is a nonsense for the simple reason that you do not have my fingerprints to compare with any you might have found at the flat.'

'You're right, of course. I'm just assuming the rogue set – the set that doesn't belong to anyone else – is yours. And you won't refuse to give me your prints for comparison, will you?'

'Certainly I refuse.'

'Oh. That makes things difficult. I can, of course, bring pressure to bear on you, but I wouldn't like to do that. It's much better if you do the thing voluntarily. Much better for your reputation as an MP to be seen to be helping the forces of law and order. And, after all, why shouldn't you have supper at Phoebe Agnew's flat? Nothing wrong with that, is there? She was your mother, after all.'

'I don't know what you're talking about,' Tyler said, but he sat down, rather slowly, behind his desk, and Slider felt a tired surge of triumph. If he really didn't know, he'd have thrown Slider out. But he wanted to hear – to know what Slider knew.

'Your date of birth and that of Phoebe Agnew's illegitimate child are the same. She gave her son to be adopted and the order went through the Nottingham County Court. Your parents lived in Nottinghamshire, and you were their adopted child. That's as far as I've got at the moment, but tomorrow I shall get a reply from the County Court records office and the two ends will be brought together, so it would be a waste of time for you to deny it. And why should you?

She was a mother to be proud of, wasn't she? A very fine journalist and a woman of intellect.'

'Go on,' said Tyler, without emphasis.

'Oh – well, all right. I suppose she discovered your identity in the course of researching for her biography of you – did you know about that, by the way?'

'No. I had no idea she was intending to write one.'

'I suppose she told you about it when she invited you to supper?' No answer. 'We have your finger-marks, you remember. On the unit in her sitting-room, the one under the window that the hi-fi sits on. I suppose you must have leaned on it when you poured coffee or something.' He demonstrated on the edge of the desk with his hand. 'Palm and four fingers.'

Behind the bright eyes a reel was being replayed. Slider's information was tested against memory. Tyler sighed, just faintly, and said, 'Since you seem to know so much, I will admit that she telephoned me at the office to invite me to supper. I refused, naturally, and then she said she had some important information that she had uncovered while researching my biography. Given her reputation as a journalist, I was inclined to give her credence, but I told her she must tell me what it was about there and then. She was unwilling at first, but when I threatened to put the phone down, she told me the same story that she seems to have sold to you, about her being my real mother – which is absolutely not true, by the way.' So, Slider thought, he's going to play the end game. 'I'm afraid the poor woman was demented. I don't know what was wrong with her, but I do seem to have an extreme effect on some women. She was obviously obsessed with me, but I think there was already some mental instability, and I've heard she drank very heavily. At any rate, I told her she was mistaken and put the phone down very firmly. And that's all I know.'

Slider shook his head slightly. 'I'm afraid that's not true.'

Tyler continued impatiently, 'It is a matter of public

record that I was in the House on Thursday night. There was an important division at seven-thirty and the whips were out. You will find my name entered amongst the Ayes. I think that must be conclusive enough evidence even for you.'

'Yes, I know you voted. I've checked that,' Slider said. 'Of course you left her alive. You dashed up to Westminster for the division, to make sure you were known to be at the House. But you weren't there earlier. It's an easy place to dodge around and not be seen in, so that even if no-one could swear to having seen you, no-one could swear you weren't there. You were in the division lobby at seven-forty, as everybody knows. And then you went back to Phoebe Agnew's flat.'

'Absolute rubbish. I'm not going to listen to any more of this,' Tyler said, but he didn't move. His shining eyes were fixed on Slider, and for all his experience, Slider couldn't tell what he was thinking or feeling. Perhaps all it was was vanity, the desire to hear himself talked about.

'You were there at the flat with Phoebe at a quarter to nine when Piers telephoned her. Piers told me all about it.'

'Piers couldn't possibly have known—'

'That you were with her? Why, because she didn't mention your name?'

'No, because I wasn't there,' he said calmly.

'While he was on the phone to Phoebe, he heard your pager go off in the background.'

'One pager is exactly like another,' Tyler said.

'Not quite. Each type has a different bleep. Obviously there are lots like yours, but the bleep he heard was that sort. He recognised it. He'd heard it before when he was with you. It troubled him so much when he finally remembered hearing it, because he couldn't think what you were doing there. Did he ask you on Sunday – this last Sunday, I mean? Did he put his worries to you?'

'Be careful what you say,' Tyler said. 'Be very careful.'

'Oh, I'll be careful. And there are no witnesses to this meeting, so it doesn't matter anyway, does it? But I have checked with your office, and they did call you on the pager at a quarter to nine that evening. Because no-one knew where you were – they thought you were in the House, but they couldn't find you. It's all making sense, isn't it?'

'Not the slightest. So what was I doing at the flat on this extraneous second visit, in your fevered imagination?'

'Phoebe Agnew had told you on your first visit what she wanted you to know – the thing that was troubling her so desperately for the last few weeks of her life. You had to dash off for the division, because there was a three-line whip, as you've agreed. But you couldn't leave it there. All the way up to Westminster you must have been thinking about the implications of what she said, and realising that if it ever got out, your career would be over. So you went back and killed her.'

Tyler gave a shout of laughter. 'What? Oh, this is very entertaining. I'm glad I granted you this interview. Go on. When you've finished, I'm going to have you removed, and I think you'll find your career is pretty well over, but I'd like to know how far your imagination stretches.'

'You were careful,' Slider said. 'You telephoned her to make sure she was alone – I've checked the records of your mobile, and the call is there. Afterwards you wiped away all your finger-marks – you even remembered to wipe the flush-handle of the loo, which was pretty smart of you, because that's one that's usually forgotten. There was just the one on the unit you missed, but no-one's perfect, are they? And you collected all the paperwork on yourself, which you'd got her to show you on the first visit – I suppose that's why you stayed to supper, wasn't it, to give you time to make sure you found out everything she had on you.'

'More,' said Tyler, leaning back in his chair. 'This is fascinating.'

'Unfortunately for you, you were seen leaving the second time. By two people. One of them saw you walking down the street re-tying your tie – the one you used to strangle her. He said you had a file or newspaper or something under your arm – the missing file, I suppose. Destroyed now, I imagine?'

'Imagine is right.'

'The other person saw you actually coming out of the house. Interestingly, she mistook you for Josh. And she was the one that moved the body, by the way. It must have been a terrible shock to you when you read the details of how the body was found.'

Something glinted in the depths of the golden eyes. 'Go on,' he said, but he wasn't laughing now.

'There's not much more,' Slider said, dully. He was very tired now. 'The next day, as soon as the news broke, you telephoned Piers to tell him to keep your relationship secret, just in case anyone put two and two together. But in the end you decided you couldn't afford to take the risk. If it got out, it would be the end of you. And Piers had confided his inconvenient worries to you. So Piers had to go as well.'

'Why on earth should I worry about my relationship with Piers being known?' Tyler said loftily. 'I am quite comfortable with my sexual orientation, and so, I can assure you, is the Party.'

'Yes, I know that,' Slider said. 'But they wouldn't be so happy about incest, would they? That's almost the last taboo, really, when you think of it,' he added conversationally. 'That, and possibly necrophilia.'

Tyler sat very still, staring at him, not in fear or anxiety, but it seemed in deep thought.

Into his silence, Slider went on. 'There were one or two little clues that put me on to it. Small things. Josh Prentiss's first name is actually Richard. He was called Josh to distinguish him from his father, another Richard. He and Phoebe Agnew had one sexual encounter, when they were both the worse for drink, at a post-finals party in June 1969 – that was when you were conceived. But afterwards Josh was quick to repudiate the encounter, and he was already attached to Anona Regan, Phoebe's best friend. So she didn't tell him. She never told him, in fact, just went away quietly, had the baby, and gave it up for adoption.

'I don't know whether she harboured a secret love for Josh all her life, or if she was just chastened by the experience. But after that she never let herself get attached to anyone. She concentrated on her career, and had casual affairs. But I imagine parting with her child was a deep vein of hurt. Then in the course of researching your biography, she discovered the truth about who you were. That was enough to make her thoughtful, but not deeply unhappy – after all, you were doing well in your chosen career, and she must have been glad to know how you had turned out. But then the unthinkable happened. You started an affair with Piers – he blurted it out to her at Christmas, even though you had impressed on him it was to be kept secret. Ironic, isn't it, that the only person he told was the one who really mattered.'

'Ironic,' Tyler said tonelessly.

'Though I dare say she would only have been the first of many – not the world's most discreet man. Anyway, it was from that time that she became more and more anxious, started drinking heavily, obviously wondering whether it would be worse to tell you or not tell you. At a dinner party at New Year, she tried to persuade Piers to give you up, but he was deeply smitten, and wouldn't hear of it.'

'Piers was very attached to me – and I to him,' Tyler said, with a creditable attempt at a little break in the voice.

'Yes, I can believe that,' Slider said. 'A colleague of mine remarked that people are often attracted most to the people who resemble them. And really, now I come to examine you, you do look more like your uncle Piers than your father Josh. That's often the way, isn't it – that children resemble their parents' siblings more than their parents. Same genes, different mix.'

Tyler wasn't looking at him. He sat very still, staring past Slider's head at the silk-covered wall.

'Finally, when it seemed that the relationship between you and Piers was not going to go away, she decided to break the silence of a lifetime and tell you. She thought if she told you the awful truth, you would simply break things off with Piers. But she couldn't resist having you to herself for a little while first. Doing for you what mothers do for their children, what she had never done for anyone – cook. She was so happy that day – a perilous sort of happiness, but still. I'm glad you gave her that, at any rate.'

Tyler's lips quirked and he made a curious gesture – almost a 'don't mention it' of the hand.

'You had to hurry away for the division, and while you were away you started to think of the danger to your career if ever any of this got out. You're a rising star, with everything before you. Someone even said to me you could be the youngest ever prime minister. You could kiss all that goodbye if ever the story were known. You could kiss your job goodbye, come to that – this is a government that won't stand for any scandal, as you of all people must know. Phoebe said she'd never tell, but could you trust her? And what would she write in that damned biography of hers? You realised then that there'd be no peace for you while she lived.'

A clock on the bookshelf struck tinklingly. Tyler had been slumped in thought. Now he looked up. 'Division,' he said.

'I've nearly finished,' Slider said. 'There's only Piers left now. The how of that's easy. He was always ready to see you, any time. And he would be easy enough to persuade to go over to the shop. I suppose you didn't want to be killing him with the dogs around. Did you take the opportunity to look round the house for any incriminating letters or documents? Was that why you shut the dogs in the kitchen? Oh,' he remembered, 'by the way, it was you that took the photograph of Phoebe with Piers and Josh from his sitting-room on the Thursday, wasn't it? To study her features, was it, to see if there was any likeness?'

'I have to go,' said Tyler.

'Piers was unlucky, really – there'd have been no need to kill him if he hadn't been your lover. Were you sickened by the thought that he was your uncle, and what you'd done with him? Once he was dead and gone, the fact that you'd ever slept with him could be forgotten, couldn't it? But I wonder if he would have been the last. What about Josh? Phoebe swore he never knew, but could you rely on that? And who else might have known? A secret has so many threads, trying to eradicate it is like trying to root out ground elder. You could have been embarking on a lifetime of murder.'

Tyler stood up. It seemed an effort; but once he was on his feet, he took control. His shoulders seemed to square, his face to firm. Ruthlessness did not come and go. You either had it, or you didn't.

'You are absolutely insane,' he said, 'and while it's been an experience to listen to you, I must warn you that to repeat any of this will bring the full force of the law down on your head. You have absolutely no evidence whatsoever for any of this nonsense.'

Slider looked up at him. 'She scratched you while you were strangling her. Such a slight scratch you might not even have noticed it, but we got enough tissue from under her nails for a DNA sample. I take it you wouldn't object to giving us a blood sample for comparison?'

Tyler's lips parted, but he said nothing.

'And you see, now we know who we're looking at, we'll get more evidence. You can't come and go around London without being seen. And the investigation into Piers's death is only just beginning. They'll find traces of you there.'

'You're mad,' Tyler said at last.

'No. I wish I were. On my way here, I thought perhaps I was, but now I've seen you, I know. If I was wrong, you'd have thrown me out long ago. But you had to hear me out, didn't you? Not only to find out what I knew, but because you love being the centre of attention.'

'You'll never make a case of this,' Tyler said, with absolute certainty.

'Won't I?' Slider stood up. 'Well, maybe I won't. But the main thing is, you know that I know. So if you should have any more thoughts about eliminating people who might know your secret, you'll put them aside quietly, won't you – the thoughts, I mean, not the people?'

And suddenly, shockingly, Tyler laughed; a big, ringing laugh like a golden bell. From a man who was invincible, who could fly. 'But you would be number one on that list, wouldn't you?' he said.

Slider only shook his head slightly, and turned away. There were a few seconds as he crossed the room to the door when his back was to Tyler, and the hairs on the back of his neck stood on end, wondering if there would be a silent rush of catlike feet behind him, and a soft, deadly blow, or two big white hands round his throat. But he made himself plod on without flinching, and then the doorknob was in his hand, and he was out and free.

And he told himself not to be silly, of course the man wouldn't kill him right there in his office. Or, indeed, at all. His fear was just the effect of mighty charisma on the mediocre man, that was all.

Porson was inclined to agree with Richard Tyler, that Slider had no evidence, that he was raving mad, and that it would never stick together into a case.

'The fact that he heard me out,' Slider said, swaying with weariness and emotional reaction, 'and the fact that he hasn't blown the Department sky high, point to his guilt. He ought to be screaming writs by now. The Home Secretary should be threading tiny cubes of me onto a skewer for kebabs. But he's said nothing.'

'He probably hadn't found a calculator with enough digits to work out the damages he's going to get,' Porson said. 'Don't count your chickens! When he gets a moment to spare he's going to hang your balls out to dry on the biggest, longest washing line in the world. And,' he added before Slider could speak, 'when he's finished, I'm going to have my turn in the laundromat. What the hell came over you? How could you go in there like that with this cockatoo story without checking it with me first? How long have you been in the Job? Have you forgotten everything you ever learned about proper procedure?'

'I didn't see how I could get any further with procedure,' Slider said. 'So I just had to face him with it to see if I was right. And I was thinking of Josh Prentiss. I couldn't be sure he wouldn't be next. This man is totally ruthless.'

Porson shook his head, lost for words.

'We'll get other evidence, sir. The DNA. The finger-marks. The street sightings. His phone records. He has no alibi. And we can prove that the relationship existed.'

'I don't think you understand,' Porson said, with a patience that was more unnerving than his rage. 'Whatever you can prove about his relationship with deceased or anybody else, or even his presence in the flat, you can't prove he killed her. It may be very heavily suggested by the circumstantials, but this is one case above all that the CPS won't take on without a cast-iron confession-plus-evidence. Even if you had a video of him actually in the act, I doubt if they'd touch it.'

'You mean, some people are above the law?' Slider said resentfully.

'No, just that sometimes you can't punish them in the normal way.' He eyed Slider a moment, thoughtfully. 'If you can convince me and I can convince the Commander, action will be taken. His career will be over, I promise you that. And that'll be as much punishment to a bloke like him as being banged up in the pokey.'

Unfortunate choice of words, Slider thought, with a tired surge of humour. But the old boy perhaps wasn't far wrong. And at the moment it was hard to care. Porson saw the heaviness of his eyes, and said, 'Go on, get off home now. And don't dilly-dally on the way.'

Slider hadn't a dilly or a dally left in him. He turned without a word and went.

The lights were still on downstairs in Atherton's *bijou* residence. Slider had remembered he still had to tell him about Furlong Stud and thought he might as well get all the pain over at once. When the door was finally answered, and Atherton stood there, framed by the light, Slider got it out quickly in a blurt.

'Look, I'm sorry to have to tell you this, but I've had some research done on your racehorse thing, and it turns out it's a scam.'

He got that far before he realised that Atherton wasn't listening – that there was, indeed, something far wrong with his friend. Was he drunk? Ill?

'Are you all right?' he asked.

Atherton didn't speak, only stepped back and sideways to let him in, shutting the door behind him. Everything in the little sitting room looked the same – no immediate evidence of doom or calamity. Slider turned again. 'What's up? You look funny.'

'It's Oedipus,' Atherton said.

'Still not come back? Well, don't worry too much. I'm sure he'll turn up.'

Atherton shook his head. 'I found him in the garden. Under the ceanothus.'

'Found him?' Slider registered the passive nature of the verb.

Atherton nodded. His mouth, shut tight, seemed to be a

strange shape; and then Slider saw with rippling horror that he was crying.

'He just – he just – crept away and died,' Atherton gasped, and then he sat down in the nearest seat and buried his face in his hands.

Slider sat, too, and waited a long time. The pain of seeing Atherton cry was very bad. It was the end, he realised, of something that had begun a long time ago, at the point of Gilbert's knife, or perhaps even before. Who knew how any of them paid the debt? It had to come out somewhere, the cost of the Job.

When the crying had eased a bit, he laid a hand on Atherton's rigid shoulder, and pushed a handkerchief into his fingers, and then went into the kitchen and took his time finding a couple of glasses and pouring some whisky, to give him time to mop up.

When he came back, Atherton looked pale and exhausted. He took the glass without a word and drank half of it.

Slider said, 'Where is he? Do you want me to deal with it for you?'

Atherton shook his head. 'Thanks. But, no, I have to do it. He was my—' He couldn't quite manage the end of the sentence.

'What will you do?' Slider asked after a bit. Atherton's back garden was tiny.

'I'll dig up the ceanothus and put it back afterwards. It was where he liked to sit.'

Slider nodded, and they drank in silence for a little while.

At last Atherton roused himself. 'You sorted it.'

'The case?'

'Nicholls phoned me.'

'Oh. Well, I don't know. It's not really sorted.' He was too tired to go into it now. He waved a hand. 'I'll tell you tomorrow.'

'Yeah. You'd better get home.'

'Do you want me to help you with—?'

'No. I have to do it. I'll do it tomorrow. Thanks, though.'

Slider eyed him. 'I don't like leaving you. Are you going to be all right?'

'Christ, it's only a cat,' he said roughly.

'No, it isn't,' said Slider. 'You should have someone with you.'

Uncharacteristically, Atherton looked away. 'D'you think – if I phoned her – Sue would come?'

Slider managed not to smile. 'She never goes to bed very early, does she?' he said seriously. 'Give her a ring.'

'Maybe I will,' Atherton said.

Getting into his car Slider thought, there are just some times when what a boy really needs is his mum.

Joanna was asleep when he got in, for which he was grateful. He didn't think he could bear another word, question or even sidelong look. He cleaned his teeth with a minimum of fanfare and slipped delicately into bed beside her, and she turned with a warm, woolly murmur into his arms but didn't wake.

But despite his tiredness, sleep didn't come to him. He lay in the tide of Joanna's breathing, feeling the world turn with him, big and slow, easing round the dark side; and thought of the people whose lives he had stumbled into, and whose pains and faults clung to him like sticky cobweb. He had achieved nothing, solved nothing, saved nothing; and that what had been done had all been for worldly ambition, without pity or humanity, exhausted him, as evil always had the capacity to do. It was Phoebe Agnew who came back again and again, and he wished he had not seen her face, discoloured and suffused. He was glad he hadn't seen Piers dead – at least he'd been spared that.

The Greeks thought patricide the worst sin. Well, let's hear it for matricide! For Phoebe Agnew, a woman he had never met. Her life had stopped when she parted with her baby: having declined motherhood she could not properly enter adulthood, but was doomed to go on repeating the same few lines over and over again, the ultimate perpetual student; growing older but never really up, until the day came when she met him again, and the circle was closed.

Josh Prentiss, a vain man, in love with his own youth, might well find the student irresistible; and if they hadn't actually had sex together all those years, well, that was the least of it. Noni had grieved that it had always been Phoebe, and perhaps she wasn't far wrong after all. Did Josh know, really, even if only subconsciously, how Phoebe felt? That he was the one man she had ever loved? Ha!

But he wished he didn't have an image of her, flushed and excited with her bagful of shopping, waiting for him to come to supper, her lost child. What had she ever done for him but save his life? And so he took hers. If you listen very carefully, you can hear the gods laughing.

He fell at last into an exhausted sleep, too dead for dreams, and woke with a start to find it was daylight. Wrong, wrong, his head shouted. He must have slept in.

'I let you sleep in,' said Joanna. 'You were dead to the world.'

He struggled up to sitting position. She was standing by the bed, in her dressing-gown, holding a mug from which a snippet of steam arose, like the irresistible wisp that used to drag the Bisto kids along to the haven of kitchen, mum and gravy. Oh, bugger, he had to stop thinking about that.

'Tea,' she said.

He took the mug and thanked her with a croak. She sat down on the edge of the bed with a serious look, and the functioning bit of his brain shouted *Uh-o, trouble! Bad talk coming*!

'Bill,' she said, 'I've been thinking. About this job offer of mine. No, wait,' she lifted a hand. 'Don't say anything. The fact of the matter is, I realise I haven't really been fair on you. Whether I take the job or not is absolutely my decision, and it was unfair of me to expect you to take responsibility for it. You can't make up your mind about the situation until I've made up mine, otherwise it's like me asking you to decide for me. So I've thought and thought, and I've taken the plunge.'

'Uh?' was all he managed to get out from his matted brain via his matted mouth.

She smiled a tense smile, as of one who has screwed herself up to the sticking point. 'I've decided what I'm going to do,' she said.

BILL SLIDER OMNIBUS

3 books in one volume

Cynthia Harrod-Eagles

ORCHESTRATED DEATH

Middle-class, middle-aged and, according to his partner, menopausal, Detective Inspector Bill Slider is never going to make it to the Yard. Passed over for promotion again, the last thing he needs in his life, or on his patch, is an unidentifable, naked female corpse.

A priceless Stradivarius and a giant tin of olive oil are the only clues in an investigation that takes the steely-eyed detective all the way from the exotic backstreets of Shepherd's Bush to far-flung Birmingham.

DEATH WATCH

When a noted womaniser dies in mysterious circumstances in a sleazy motel and the whole of his murky past comes to light, DI Bill Slider begins to question more than whether the game is worth the candle. Right is right, and indivisible. As soon as he's solved the mystery, and found out what the Neary boys and Gorgeous George are up to, Slider's going to have to start putting his own house in order . . .

NECROCHIP

Detective Superintendent 'George' Dickson's replacement by DS 'Mad Ivan' Barrington – a new broom determined to sweep clean – is all par for the course for DI Bill Slider, as he faces the unhygienic fact of a dismembered corpse in a catering establishment.

But there are still niggling questions to distract him: why didn't Barrington like Dickson? What is the mystery of the stake-out they once did together? And why is Slider's home life in almost perpetual crisis?

KILLING TIME

Cynthia Harrod-Eagles

Detective Inspector Bill Slider is back at work, plus a thumping headache – thoughtfully donated by the last villain he encountered – and minus Atherton, his friend and colleague, still in hospital with a knife wound where no gourmet should have one.

Slider was hoping for a quiet week. But erotic dancer Jay Paloma is murdered, only hours after complaining about poison pen letters, and Slider plunges into the seedy world of entertainment to question table-dancers, prostitutes, pimps and cabinet ministers. Did Jay's murderer also whack popular 'community cop' PC Cosgrove? What was Cosgrove's connection with prostitute Marion Brown? Who exactly was blackmailing whom? And why on earth would an animal rights group storm a tacky Shepherd's Bush night club?

With doubts over Atherton's recovery, his estranged wife seeking reconciliation, and Atherton's nubile replacement anxious to show him her testimonials, Slider has enough to prime his headache for the foreseeable future. But the old grey matter won't be denied: doggedly, and with a whimper, Slider starts to unravel the truth . . .

SHALLOW GRAVE

Cynthia Harrod-Eagles

Detective Inspector Bill Slider has always been keen on architecture – what Atherton calls his edifice complex – and The Old Rectory is the kind of house he would give anything to own. But the dead body of Jennifer Andrews, found in a hole on the terrace, rather spoils the view. It looks a straightforward case: Jennifer was a congenital flirt, and the hole was dug by her builder husband Eddie, who was violent and jealous. But questions remain unanswered. Why was Jennifer's body so unmarked? How did she reach her shallow grave unnoticed? And why would anyone want to be an estate agent?

As the investigation proceeds, it seems there is something rotten at the heart of the community surrounding the lovely old house. New suspects and motives keep crawling out of the woodwork, and when Slider finally gets a confession, it's from a wholly incredible source. To compound his troubles, he has a linguicidal new boss, more bills than a flock of pelicans, and a future ex-wife becoming less ex by the minute. In detection and in life, it seems, there is always more going on than meets the eye . . .

'Slider and his creator are real discoveries'
DAILY MAIL